Joan Hessayon wa[s] born in Lancashire, Essex
but grew up in Mis[souri] and [...] went to Co[llege]
where she met her husband Dr David Hessayon,
the creator of the bestselling *Expert* series of
gardening books. They married in 1951 and share
a love of history, plants and writing. Joan
Hessayon's first novel was published in 1983,
her most recent novels, *Capel Bells* and *The
Helmingham Rose*, are also published by Corgi. She
lives in Hertfordshire and has two daughters and
four grandchildren.

'I thoroughly enjoyed *The Paradise Garden*.
Joan Hessayon's knowledge and interest in the
world of business . . . the registration of old
houses and particularly her vast knowledge of
gardens and gardening, all touch upon real
interests and influences on my life. I hope others
enjoy this book as I did'
Sir John Harvey-Jones

Also by Joan Hessayon

CAPEL BELLS
THE HELMINGHAM ROSE

and published by Corgi Books

The
Paradise Garden

Joan Hessayon

CORGI BOOKS

THE PARADISE GARDEN
A CORGI BOOK : 0 552 14692 7

First publication in Great Britain

PRINTING HISTORY
Corgi edition published 1999

Set in 11/12pt Plantin by
Phoenix Typesetting, Ilkley, West Yorkshire

Corgi Books are published by Transworld Publishers Ltd,
61-63 Uxbridge Road, London W5 5SA,
in Australia by Transworld Publishers,
c/o Random House Australia Pty Ltd,
20 Alfred Street, Milsons Point, NSW 2061
and in New Zealand by Transworld Publishers,
c/o Random House New Zealand,
18 Poland Road, Glenfield, Auckland.

Reproduced, printed and bound in Great Britain by
Cox & Wyman Ltd, Reading, Berks.

This book is for Dave with all my love

Acknowledgements

Gosfield Hall is an actual house, with the history I have described in the story. However, I veered away from the truth after 1958. In fact, it was purchased by a charity in that year, Mutual Households Association, which modernized it. Today, as Country Houses Association Limited, this organization aims to save historic houses of national interest. Gosfield Hall is one of nine similar establishments in Southern England. All of them offer superior accommodation to retired people. Gosfield Hall is open to the public during some summer afternoons.

I am indebted to Country Houses Association Limited and to the administrators, Geoffrey and Greta Jewell, for their help in discovering the delights of the Hall.

Paul Norris took some terrific photos and videos of the Hall for my research.

The reminiscences of Lesley and Peter Stant of Broadfield Nurseries made the life of market traders dealing in plants seem very real and very hard work.

Clare Kershaw advised about the financial details of running a restaurant chain. My thanks, also, to Derek Wood and Andy Withers of Barclays Bank. None of them, of course, had any control over the way I used their information, so can't be responsible for mistakes.

I want to thank my eagle-eyed manuscript readers, Gill Jackson, Angelina Gibbs and Chris Gibbs. And, of course, I could not have managed without the advice, enthusiasm and encouragement of my editor, Diane Pearson.

My research of the eating establishments of East Anglia, London, Boca Raton and Deerfield Beach was very pleasant indeed. With the exception of the Miami Spice chain, they all exist and I can recommend every one.

I discovered that I couldn't run even a fictional business without a great deal of help, and for that I must thank my husband, Dave. As always.

Chapter One

Fran stood in the kitchen, the phone cradled against her neck, trying to remember whose call this was. If her mother had phoned, then in a few weeks' time she would be asking for help in paying her BT bill. If Fran had called – and she couldn't remember having done such a dumb thing – then she would never be able to pay for such a prolonged monologue. The company would surely cut her off.

'But, Mum, you have your pension. Dad left you some money . . . I know it was only ten thousand pounds, but . . . of course I'd spend it if I had ten thousand! I've got debts! No, Mum, don't cry. I'll send you twenty pounds, but really this must be the last time. I've known women of your age who get little part-time jobs. I know Dad never wanted you to work, but . . . No, no, don't cry. Of course I have respect for grey hairs. I've got a few myself. Mum, I'm busy. I'll call you. Got to run. Mum, don't cry . . . don't say that. Please. Bye-bye.' She hung up the phone and wiped away the tears that were beading her lashes.

'You don't love me,' mimicked her son, Trevor, a well-built young man of eighteen who was his mother's main support and biggest worry. 'After all the years I slaved for you. You just wish I was dead. Then you could sell my house and go to raves every night.'

'Don't make fun of your grandmother.' She sat down to drink the remainder of her coffee. 'And count your blessings. We don't live with her any longer.'

'Thank God for small mercies. Oi! Don't wear nail varnish if you want to impress the TV people that you are a serious gardener.' This time his voice was his own, an attractive tenor. Fran supposed every girl at the university was mad for him. He resembled his father, handsome, and, when he felt the urge, capable of charming the birds from the trees.

At eighteen, Fran had fallen for Sean Craig's charm which had proved to be nothing more than a convenient mask for a very selfish personality. She liked to think that Trevor was different, a young man of some substance, intelligent and responsible. Unfortunately, his preferred manner of dress, grunge, except when she was willing to iron a clean shirt for him, spoke of a certain immaturity.

She examined her nails, noticing the torn ends and the mud caked under them. 'I'm wearing nail varnish because I can't get my nails properly clean. I want to look nice. You don't understand about looking nice. You prefer to look like a tramp.'

He grinned at her, showing off his dimples, putting on the charm. 'Of course you are gorgeous however you dress, but you want to look right for the part, don't you? You've spent hours looking at those gardening programmes, yet you still don't know what they want. Look casual. You don't look good in a pony-tail. Let your hair hang loose. Wear a little scarf around your neck. Get horticultural. Anyway, good luck. I've got to run. I'm picking up Angus.'

'That car's not safe.'

He laughed. 'For two hundred and fifty pounds, what do you expect? Don't worry. We're only driving to Freddie's. Then we're going in his car. I've got classes I mustn't miss, so I daren't trust home transport. That reminds me, start for the studio in good time. You don't want to be late on this of all days. It's the first day of the rest of your life. You could be a star!'

Fran got up and put the kettle on. Her stomach felt queasy and she was beginning to wish she had never agreed to audition for a gardening programme. What did she know about the producer, Lester Manners? They had met in a transport café on the A120 just a week ago. She had been returning to her cottage outside Toppesfield in north Essex following a visit to Capel Manor, her old Alma Mater, and he was returning to his TV studio outside Maldon. The place was crowded and he had asked if he could share her table. Then she dropped her Danish on the floor, and he had insisted on buying her another.

Lester told her he was making a series of programmes for satellite television featuring Gypsy Harry, the gardening guru. It was slightly offbeat, which was what he was sure the satellite channels really wanted. She was a garden designer? Well, what a coincidence! He needed an attractive female to act as a foil for Harry. Would she like to make a guest appearance? It could be the start of something big for her.

Fran never refused an opportunity to make

money, although most of her opportunities turned out to be pipedreams, steps to further disillusionment and despair. It was the middle of a particularly cold January, and she had begun to panic. It was now a full year since she and Trevor had moved away from her mother's semi in Enfield.

For twelve whole months the two of them had lived in this unheated two-bedroomed cottage a mile and half from the nearest house. Painted white many years earlier and with a thatched roof in need of replacement, the cottage had seemed the answer to any townie's dream. Four small-paned windows, two up, two down, and roses on an arch around the door gave a romantic look that cancelled out any doubts she might have had. A single-storey extension to one side was built of weatherboard and painted black. So picturesque! she had thought, and with an acre of land. This was the fulfilment of a dream.

The road that ran sixty feet in front of the house was a single-track farm road down which few vehicles ever passed. The wide metal farm gate led onto their property, but there was nothing resembling a driveway or a garage. They simply parked Trevor's Ford and Fran's white van on the grass.

She had seen the extension as a future spacious living-room, but there was nowhere else to store their possessions, so the room soon filled up. Besides, it was just a barn, the roof open to the rafters, the walls simply two by fours and weatherboarding. It was hot in the summer and cold in the winter.

She had not wanted to spend money on a survey, so the breakdown of the sewage system came as a terrible surprise. Mother and son had both been born and brought up in the busy north London town of Enfield, where electricity, gas, mains water and sewage were taken for granted.

It had not occurred to her to ask about mains drainage, so naturally she had not even considered that they might be depending on a septic tank, much less that it would require replacing. Her mistake cost her two thousand pounds, the last money in her savings account, plus a thousand borrowed from a terrifying acquaintance of Sean's whom she had met in an Enfield pub. Meanwhile, ads in local papers had brought her no customers eager to have her design their gardens.

The new shower room had to be put into the extension where the old toilet and washbasin had been. A night-time visit involved trotting down the steep cottage stairs, going through the kitchen, up one step to the annexe, down one step to the cement floor, then up one step into the bathroom.

A coat of paint on the kitchen walls, some rough wood shelving, and a wood-burning stove in the fireplace were all that they could run to. Plans to redecorate the sitting-room on the other side of the front door somehow never came to fruition.

Sometimes, in the dead of night, Fran would lie listening to the mice running about in the thatch and contemplate her gradual descent into direst rural poverty, but mostly she shut away such thoughts and hoped for a miracle.

When she saw an ad in a local paper for the goodwill of a stall for one day a week on Braintree market, she had leapt at the chance to purchase it for six thousand pounds, although she had needed another mortgage on the cottage to get the money. Later, she learned that the council frowned on such

13

deals, that she was not guaranteed a stall simply because she had bought the goodwill, but that she could easily rent one for just one pound seventy per foot of frontage, provided there was a stall available.

The first Thursday on the market had been hell. Afraid of having too little stock to sell, Fran had relied on Trevor to obtain some plants from friends. She had arrived in her diesel van with her metal framework, trestle tables, plastic sheeting and plants at six o'clock in the morning. Then began a struggle to erect the three hundred pounds' worth of staging for which she had paid six thousand.

Once the van was unloaded, she had to move it away, and pay a parking fee. By eight o'clock her stall had been erected and the plants set out as attractively as possible. She was exhausted, long before she served her first customer at half past nine.

Other stallholders were extremely friendly, as were some of the customers. Some customers were not so friendly, and she had to learn to absorb a certain amount of rudeness without retaliating.

Bertram Noakes sold children's clothing. His stall was next to hers, and he began to give her some good advice. Because of Bertie, she learned to pitch, that is, to sing out her bargains. She also shed her inhibitions, learning to chat outrageously with the customers, to listen to their troubles and triumphs, to sell herself as surely as any performer on a stage.

She discovered that she could take almost seventy cuttings from one *Sedum* autumn joy, that *Chlorophytum*, the spider plant, was always popular, that wallflowers had a ready market and that sweet williams were great favourites.

But best of all were bulbs. In September she bought prepared bulbs of daffodils, hyacinths and tulips which had been specially treated to bloom at Christmas. She had learned that it was no use planting these in bowls which would then be sold on her stall. One bulb in the bowl was sure to be ahead of its neighbours and this uneven growth would turn the customers away.

The trick was to plant the bulbs in tomato boxes and this Fran did in September, laying straw over them and then covering them with sand. Then she placed them outdoors where they could get the cold and dark they needed. The covers came off on the first day of December and the bulbs were planted up in pretty pots (seconds from a wholesaler) with a ribbon bow pushed on a wire into the soil. Plants at the same stage of growth were selected for each bowl and she sold them as fast as she could wrap them up and take the money. Within three months she had retrieved her investment and made a modest profit.

In January those that had not been ready for the Christmas market could be potted up. She marked everything up one hundred per cent, but soon learned that this was sometimes too little, for there were several weeks after Christmas when she didn't take enough money to cover the cost of the stall and parking the van.

Those were the bitter days when she had almost as much to load up in the afternoon as she had unloaded in the morning, days when she could not get warm no matter what she wore on her hands and feet. There were days when the rain plummeted down for hours on end, and she had to take a stick and gently relieve the bulge from the plastic above her head. There were many days when she was so tired that when it came time to load up three-quarters of the stock she had unloaded hours before, she couldn't stop her arms from trembling.

And in spite of the tiredness and discomfort, Bertie continually warned her that she could not make a living from working only one market-day a week. She should sign up for other markets – Halstead or Sudbury, or both. Fran knew she hadn't the strength for more days on the market. She also knew that she couldn't grow more stock for the stall without help, and Trevor had soon lost interest in helping her.

She had spent a few hundred on the great metal hoops and strong plastic of a growing tunnel, like the ones that dotted the countryside, only much smaller. Her polytunnel contained a thousand twigs of box hedging, several hundred primulas and the small beginnings of such old favourites as flowering currant and forsythia. Inexperienced as she was, she knew that this meagre stock would not pay the bills, but in any case they weren't mature enough to sell.

On this the last day of January, the sky was overcast and there was a bitter wind from the east which rattled the loose plastic of the tunnel. If it tore, she would not be able to replace it.

So it was with some eagerness that she drove her old van into the yard of what appeared to be a pink farmhouse in need of a coat of paint. Looking about for Lester Manners, she thought that this could surely not be a recording studio. There was a derelict Vauxhall with no wheels sitting on the drive, and the family Labrador seemed too lethargic to protect his master's property.

The farmhouse door opened and her acquaintance from the transport café came outside to greet her. Lester Manners was probably no more than thirty. His skinny shanks were encased in faded jeans and his narrow chest protected from the wind by a sweatshirt which declared *Gardeners Do It In The Potting Shed*. Obviously a man of wit and originality.

'I wasn't sure you'd come!' he called, rubbing his hands together.

'Of course I've come. I promised, didn't I? But where are we going to film today? Not in this garden, surely.'

'At Harry's place, in his greenhouse. Why don't you drive us both and I'll cadge a lift from Harry back here when we've finished recording. I've got my studio here. Stay where you are.' He ran back into the house and quickly re-emerged carrying a heavy video camera and several large bags which he put in the back of her van.

As he let himself into the front seat, she wondered how far away it was. She didn't have much petrol.

'Harry's in Maldon. I'll show you the way. It's just a mile or two. Interesting motor,' he said, patting the dashboard. 'I'm surprised it still runs. Got a bit of a rust problem, Fran. Still, don't despair. We'll soon all be rolling in the lolly. Wait and see.'

If she had been worried on seeing the farmhouse, she panicked at the sight of Harry's place, which was a small scrapyard.

Harry, in the flesh, scared her. Despite the bitter

weather, he was wearing only an undershirt on his upper body which bulged with fat and muscle. His black trousers were so filthy, she thought they could stand up by themselves. Even Trevor never allowed himself to get this dirty. Assorted tattoos completed Harry's villainous look. There were naked ladies and pulsating hearts, as well as the letters NF intwined with a billowing red ribbon on his right arm.

Ignoring her entirely, he spoke to Lester. 'So you made it. I'm never sure with you, although I expect you have some idea how pissed off I'd be if you hadn't showed.' Now he looked at Fran critically. 'I expected somebody younger. Is this the best you could do?'

'Harry!' said Lester, loudly and slowly. 'This is Fran Craig. She is a qualified garden designer. She trained at Capel Manor. She knows what she is talking about, and the people who buy TV series expect that sort of thing. Now say hello to the lady.'

'It's my show,' said Harry.

'Oh, how nice,' replied Fran, at her most reckless when anger outweighed her fear of poverty. 'I can't imagine how anyone could doubt that. I'll bet they want you on *Gardener's World* every week.'

Her sarcasm didn't faze him. 'I wouldn't appear on that crap. Middle-class types talking to the zombies in the suburbs. I'm down-to-earth. I talk to real people, tell it like it is and I don't go wasting money on poncey gimmicks.'

'Like greenhouses.' Fran knew she should not get out of the van. She should turn around and drive straight home, but the faint chance that she could earn some money caused her to follow Harry and Lester down the yard to a greenhouse that Harry must have received as scrap.

'I'll show you my garden first. So's you can see what real garden design is. This way.'

Lester's smile, flashed at her behind Harry's back, held a frantic appeal. Fran had no other plans for the morning, so she shrugged and followed Harry, watching very carefully where she put her feet.

The hard landscaping, the non-flowering part of Harry's garden, consisted entirely of scrap. He had made a winding path of broken concrete, past a garden shed of odd bits of wood and corrugated iron, all painted red, to a terrace of second-hand lumber stained green and with chicken wire nailed over each board. There was nothing on the terrace, not so much as a pot.

Harry scratched his armpit. 'I shall tell the viewers to be careful with decking, because it gets slippery when it's wet. I put the wire over it to keep people from slipping.'

'Isn't the wire netting a bit loose?' asked Fran. 'Women could get their heels caught in it.'

'What women do I know what wear high heels? There's no danger.'

Lester said they had better return to the greenhouse for the filming as he wanted to catch the light.

Fran saw another greenhouse tucked behind some small willow trees. 'Is that where we're going to film?'

'No, that's private,' said Harry, and took her by the arm to turn her round.

She was sure she had seen something growing in the house and now guessed that it must be cannabis. She did not like Harry and saw no possibility of making money from Lester Manners.

'Lester,' she murmured, 'what about payment? We didn't discuss money.'

'You film two segments of two or three minutes each and I'll give you fifty quid. Or, if you would rather, you can wait and get paid when I've sold the series. You'll get a repeat fee that way, every time they show it. And you know how satellite TV shows everything half a dozen times.'

'I'll take the money now, thank you, or I'm not staying.' She eyed Harry, who had gone ahead to open the greenhouse. Even with television's passion for alternative this and that, she didn't think he was about to become a star. Anyway, no-one ever watched daytime satellite. Everybody knew that. Lester would be lucky to get his series shown for nothing.

The greenhouse was warm and damp, causing Lester to complain about his lens misting up. He wanted some windows opened in the house, but Harry refused, saying the cold draught would kill his plants. Though very small, the house was filled to capacity with plants, some of them distinctly unhappy. Fran thought they might have been gifts, or perhaps he had been through the neighbours' household rubbish.

'I bet you think I can't grow nothing,' challenged Harry. 'You think just because them things ain't in the best of order, they ain't worth saving. But that's where your Titchmarshes and your Seabrooks are wrong. Love nature, that's my motto. Save everything. Love 'em. They will recover. Look here, this Cape primrose will bloom if you're just patient.

And what about these cyclamens? Beautiful or what?'

'The cyclamen are beautiful, but I would have thought the house is too warm for them. Are they new? As for the *Streptocarpus*, I've thrown out better plants.'

Harry turned to Lester. 'I warned you, I ain't having no Latin names on my show. My show, Lester. You hear me?'

'Fran,' began Lester earnestly. 'The ethos of our series is that it is for the common man, the biker perhaps, who would not normally watch a programme about gardening. Harry will show that gardening is for everybody.'

'You know the difference between Titchmarsh and Seabrook and me?' asked Harry suddenly.

'I can't imagine.'

'More hair. They got more hair, and the poofters what run TV only hire good-looking guys.'

Half a dozen tart replies came to mind, but Fran wanted her fifty pounds and to get away as soon as possible. Unfortunately, they had to wait for a microphone, and Jack, the sound-man, was twenty minutes late. Jack was little more than a boy. Fran was certain that he couldn't be as old as Trevor, and he seemed to be suffering from a hangover. Nevertheless, of the three employees of Manners Productions, Jack seemed to be the only one who knew his job and was prepared to do it with the minimum of fuss.

For the next two hours, Lester hoisted the camera and filmed sporadically. The session was punctuated by rows about content, camera angles and the sound of road traffic and aeroplanes. Fran, now thoroughly fed up, knew that she was being awkward, but she didn't care. After the first hour, she was anxious not to be on television in Harry's programme. Whatever career she might manage to have would surely be damaged by an early association with Gypsy Harry.

When Lester ran out of film, they went into Harry's shack to watch a screening of the unedited video. Her scenes with Harry were full of bad-tempered exchanges and veiled insults. She thought her own contribution to the simmering row was subtle and witty, but Harry went for the jugular. Lester would be unable, she thought, to put together anything worth viewing.

'I'll edit out the rough parts,' said Lester, giving her the fifty pounds in ten-pound notes. 'You'll see. We've got great material here.'

Fran gave him a wry smile as she stuffed the money into her handbag. Jack said he would see her to her van. 'Listen, Fran,' he said when they were away from the star and his cameraman-producer. 'The camera likes you. I mean it. You look great. You shouldn't have settled for fifty quid. Old Lester can stretch out that material for several programmes. He might sell it all over the English-speaking world.'

'Don't be silly. That stuff he recorded was appalling. He'll not have enough for one programme.'

Jack shook his head. 'You don't understand. There's more air time than there are good programmes. He'll sell it. You're confused because we all look like a load of layabouts to you. But you're the one who's wrong. And you never even signed a contract. If you get another opportunity, don't blow it. Get them to sign on the dotted line. Join the union. Get what you deserve.' He shut the door of her van once she was settled behind the wheel. 'One day you might even be able to afford a decent motor.'

Fran drove immediately to a petrol station and put in a carefully measured two pounds' worth of diesel. Then, because she had been talking almost non-stop for the past two hours without so much as a cup of instant coffee, she parked in a side street and went in search of a café.

Grey net curtains and a fading sign which said Flutterby Café seemed rather unpromising, but Fran entered because she thought it would be cheap. She should have driven home, she should have fixed her own cup of coffee and sandwich, instead of wasting part of her precious fifty pounds on luxuries. But a disappointing day which, nevertheless, netted her so much money, called for a modest celebration. She would have liked to buy a couple of small steaks and a bottle of red wine for herself and Trevor this evening. However, Trevor had other plans involving a fellow student on his Social Studies course. So Fran would fry an egg for herself and watch the telly.

She walked up to the counter and asked the young man what sort of sandwiches he had. Cheese, tuna mayonnaise or prawn, she was told. Since this was to be a celebration, she chose the prawn and a cup of coffee. There were no other customers present.

She was told to sit down and she would be served. Taking her place at the only table with a clean plastic cloth, she watched the young man as he brought her white coffee in a mug, a spoon which he placed on the table, and a prawn sandwich in cling film. The sugar bowl looked as if it needed dusting, but the sandwich was quite good. She didn't like what most people considered to be a decent cup of coffee, so she was not disappointed by the weak liquid she was served.

'May I have the bill, please?'

The young man came to the table and laid down a scrap of paper. 'One coffee, one prawn sandwich on a bap. Six pounds fifty.'

'What? That's ridiculous. You didn't even give me a plate.'

'I know,' he said, making change for a ten-pound note. 'But I just work here. Don't think I get the money. They pay me fifteen quid a session, and sometimes the session lasts for eight hours. Anyway, the old man who used to own Flutterbys has died and the nephew has promised to do something. There's no money been spent for ages. The fridge doesn't even work half the time. I don't know what this nephew thinks he can do, except maybe close us down. I even have to make the sandwiches myself. I'm no chef! But there's a shortage of jobs and what can I do? I tell you what. I'll charge you a fiver. Here. That's only fair.' He put five coins change on the table, watching her carefully.

Fran, knowing what was expected of her, gave a pound to the waiter, and consoled herself with the thought that she had at least been saved the cost of a tip and fifty pence.

She should have asked herself why she was given such a bargain. For the next three days she was ill with food poisoning and had time enough to wish she had chosen the cheese. Trevor seemed very worried about her, but his social life took precedence, so she spent the time sleeping or watching television until her strength returned.

On the fourth day, Doreen telephoned. Fran had no friends in Essex, and there was scarcely time to visit Enfield to maintain her old friendships. Besides, every one of her women friends was married, perhaps not happily, but at least they were part of a pair. Fran, now determinedly on her own, felt like an extra thumb. So she kept in touch only with Doreen, an old schoolmate, who was unattached. But then, Doreen was semi-detached from the real world.

The phone rang just after the postal van had made a large delivery, and she was still knee-deep in boxes containing plant plugs which required immediate attention. She left the boxes and lunged for the phone, grimacing when she heard her friend's voice. Doreen had three children by three different men, and a recurring problem with strong drink.

'How are you, Doreen? I haven't heard from you in three months. Did the children have a nice Christmas? . . . Yes, I know it must have been difficult for you, coping on your own, but . . . Doreen, you did get the money I sent for them, didn't you? . . . I know, dear, I've had a few problems that way myself. The bills do keep coming in. How's Darren? And Kathy? Oh, that's too bad. But at least Serena is well, isn't she?'

Holding the phone away from her ear, she stretched towards the kitchen table, hoping to be able to reach her cup of coffee. Doreen was well launched into a melancholy catalogue of recent misfortunes which didn't require careful listening. Fran knew all too well what was coming.

'Listen, Doreen. I've been a bit strapped for money lately. No, it's wintertime, you know. I'm not selling any plants at this time. Well, I just have to live on my small savings. Look, dear, I must go out to the garden . . . I know it's snowing, but I have this plastic tunnel that . . .'

She had a sudden terrible thought. Doreen might have called with a view to bringing the children for another holiday. Trevor had been forced to move out for two weeks in August so that Doreen could visit with the children. Fran had slept on a camp-bed while the three children, all under five, had made a mess of Trevor's room. Doreen seemed displeased that the weather had not been kinder, the food not more plentiful and the children not more easily entertained. Fran had ended the two weeks exhausted and a hundred and fifty pounds out of pocket. As she later told Trevor, she felt the money was well-spent if it gave her relief from Doreen's problems for a few months.

Trevor, being cruel as only the young can be, always referred to Doreen as 'that cow', while her mother, being unsympathetic as only the old can be, invariably called her 'the parasite'. As frequently as Doreen advised Fran not to give another penny to her mother, so her mother was furious whenever she thought Doreen had wormed a few pounds from her. Fran wanted to be able to help them both: her mother because she was sixty-two and had taken a terrible downward turn in her fortunes following the death of Fran's father, and Doreen because she was completely incapable of seeing the true nature of the three men who had fathered her children.

It was Sean, her ex, whom Fran resented giving

money to. And it was Sean who could worm the largest sums from her. She wondered why she always gave in. She had not seen him since just before Christmas and his silence seemed somewhat ominous. What was he up to this time?

It was not until the middle of February that Sean came to call. A man of medium height with dazzling blue eyes and black wavy hair, he was lean yet well-muscled. His only flaw was a pair of slightly bowed legs, but they looked great in jeans, as she used to tell him quite frequently.

'What are you doing here?' she said when she had opened the door to him.

'I came to see my son. Any objections?'

'He's at college. Why didn't you call before you came out here?'

'Your number is not available,' he said with his usual cheeky grin. 'Don't tell me you haven't paid your bill.'

'I was a little late, that's all. It's supposed to be reconnected today. I have no money, so there's no use asking me for any. Trevor will be home about eight o'clock tonight. Or you might come round at about seven thirty tomorrow morning. It being Saturday, he won't leave the house before nine or ten. Come back then. Goodbye.' She tried to close the door, but Sean's foot was in the way.

'I've come all this way. The least you can do is to make me a cup of coffee.'

She opened the door and he walked into the kitchen, looking around as he pulled off his jacket. 'You're living like pigs, Fran. When are you going to give up and get yourself a proper job?'

'We are not living like pigs. I was about to clean

up. I've been outside working. March is always the beginning of the season, you know. I've got dozens of fuchsias and primroses to sell on the market. I'm doing pretty well now, enough to live on, but it's hard work. Something you wouldn't know anything about.'

He had been reasonably cheerful, but now his mood changed. 'Just because you've failed with your grand ideas, you needn't take it out on me. It's not as if I didn't give you a good start. You took everything I had. The roof over my head.'

'That was instead of your ever paying me maintenance. I supported Trevor, remember? I worked as a gardener, maintaining other people's gardens to support him through school.'

'And pay for your fancy course at the horticultural college.'

'At least I've got a qualification. And I've paid Trevor's expenses at university.'

She slammed the kettle onto the counter and rammed in the plug, hating these quarrels. 'It's half past twelve. Do you want a sandwich or not? I've got cheese or tuna, and I've made some vegetable soup. You might as well have some.'

'Thanks. I'll have tuna.' He picked up the dirty breakfast dishes from the table, put them in the sink and began to wash up. Sean had always been helpful around the house. And handy. He was a skilled cabinet-maker when he chose to work, and had fitted kitchens for many wealthy people, earning good money. 'You're bringing up my son in a slum,' he said.

'He's eighteen and never home these days. He only boards here.'

'Has he got a girl? I'll bet he takes after his old man.'

'He doesn't sleep with every girl he meets, if that's what you mean.'

He fetched some plates from an open shelf. 'He wouldn't tell his mum about it, that's for sure. These pots were a wedding present, weren't they? My God, Fran, I can't bear to see you in this kitchen. You're working yourself to death, and for what? You're never going to make it as a designer. Don't you realize that it doesn't matter what you know, it's who you know? You don't have any contacts. Now, if you could get yourself a job working for a recognized garden designer, you might eventually build up a list of people to enable you to strike out on your own. You always were a fool.'

Fran knew he was right. She had sold the family terraced house three years earlier and put the money in the building society, while she and Trevor moved in with her parents. She had worked hard as a jobbing gardener, getting her meagre qualification in the meantime. Then, in a burst of optimism, she had sought a home in Essex so that Trevor could take up his place at Essex University while still living at home. The property had cost ninety-five thousand pounds. For that money, it was not possible to buy much more than a garage in Enfield, twelve miles from London. She thought she had achieved a near miracle by getting a two-bedroomed home and an acre for so little, just fifty or sixty miles away.

Later, she realized that she was so far out in the wilderness that she could not hope for passing trade for her intended garden centre and nursery. That meant relying on selling her plants to those garden centres which were on main traffic routes. With hindsight, she knew she should have concentrated on one sort of plant, become a specialist to whom garden centres would turn. Instead, she tried to grow all sorts of plants and couldn't meet her competitors for price or reliability. To make matters worse, water rates and heating costs limited her range. Although it took a frightening share of her savings to purchase the licence, the market stall had saved her bacon. Working just one day a week, she usually made enough to keep herself and Trevor in food, and Trevor in clothing and petrol.

She put the sandwiches on a plate, dished up the soup and found half a bottle of red wine. Trevor had been particularly busy during the previous week, and Fran was starved of company, which was why she now smiled at Sean.

'So, how's Maureen?'

He grinned roguishly. 'Maureen and I are no longer together.'

'Well, that didn't last long. Who is it now?'

'I'm fancy free. There never was anyone but you, Fran. You know that.'

'You had a funny way of showing it.'

'Here, have one of your delicious sandwiches. You know, you never gave me credit for anything. When you first moved to this slum and couldn't get going because you didn't have anything to sell on that stall of yours, who got you some plants?'

'Trevor,' she said. Fearing what was to come, she put down her sandwich. 'He brought me some plants he said he had been given. You didn't have anything to do with it, did you?'

'Your son and I risked our freedom and our good name to help you.'

She stood up. 'I don't want to hear this.'

'No?' He stood up, too, wiping his mouth with the back of his hand. 'But you took them, didn't you? You sold them. One dark night, Trevor and me drove up to a roundabout and dug up every blooming plant on it. Fifty shrubs about two years old, if I remember rightly. And don't tell me Trev told you they had been given to him, because our son is not a liar.'

'Just a thief,' she said. 'He said don't ask. I was desperate, so I didn't.'

'Sit down. Come on, luvvy, have some wine. It was a long time ago. Nobody's going to get caught now.'

'I'm so ashamed. I sold stolen goods. It wasn't all that long ago. A year. Oh, God. Why did you take him with you? Like father, like son. You're a bad influence. Stay away from him. I couldn't bear it if—'

'It was his idea! I went along because I didn't want him to get into any trouble. Sometimes life offers us hard choices. I preferred to take the risk with him.'

She drank her wine, and Sean poured the remainder of the bottle into her glass. Fran had suspected but refused to acknowledge that the shrubs were stolen. A very real fear of imminent starvation had undermined her scruples. Now that she was making a living of sorts, her conscience was returning to haunt her. She had potted each shrub in a clean black plastic pot and labelled them all carefully, pricing them at five pounds each. They had all sold in the first three hours. She had not declared the sale in her accounts, because she had no receipt for the purchase of fifty shrubs. She sighed. So it had come to this. Fran Craig was a shoddy little thief, just like her ex-husband.

'You're shaking,' said Sean, and put his hand over hers. 'Listen, darling, I've got a proposition to make. Are you listening? Cheer up, now. Old Sean's going to do you a favour. I can't bear to think of the two of you living in this mess. I'll build a new kitchen for you. I'm sure I can buy some decent cabinets from a house clearance or demolition. Say a hundred pounds from you and the rest, plus the work, from me. How about it?'

Still upset, Fran blinked at him, pathetically grateful for the unexpected offer. It meant having something a little better in the way of a kitchen than she had been enduring. It meant the first step on the way to making a home to which Trevor might one day bring a friend. It meant a little company during the time when Sean was in Essex to install the kitchen.

'That's very kind of you. It really is and I appreciate it. Things haven't gone exactly as I had hoped, I admit. So, let me see. You're going to need some money, aren't you?'

He shrugged. 'If you've got it. I'm a bit broke at the moment, although I've got a big job coming up in a few weeks. I could fill in the time building your kitchen.' He watched as she went to the tea caddy on a low shelf. 'Good God, woman, is that where you keep your money?'

'Banks tend not to want my business,' she said, and kissing the small wad of money, she handed it over, then added carefully, 'but I'll be moving it after you've left.'

As the weather got warmer, Fran was forced to get up ever earlier in order to water the pots in the tunnel and outside it. She had hundreds of bedding plants growing in trays. She would pot some of them up and sell them later on for slightly more than those in trays. There were several hundred small shrubs outside, as well as a thousand fuchsia cuttings in the tunnel. Some of the plants were moved outdoors during the day, but they all had to be returned to the safety of the tunnel at night. This work, alone, was enough to tire her out.

Life was becoming one long chore without a day off, and with little of Trevor's company or help. Her dangerous acquaintance from the Enfield pub was demanding the repayment of his money, reminding her that, out of friendship and pity, he had only charged her ten per cent interest. Reminding her, also, that he was not a nice man when debts were not paid.

So it was with great pleasure and relief that she took a call one day from someone who claimed to be from Radio Essex, asking her if she would like to do a fifteen-minute stint on Ricky Blane's show, talking about chores to be done in the garden in March, which was not far off. She would be paid, they assured her, and Fran wondered what fantastic sum she might be offered.

Chapter Two

Some people insist that travel is broadening. Yet Mark Twain said that a jackass who travels round the world is still a jackass.

Richard Dumas, roused from his jet-lag-induced sleep, blinked in the pale January light of an English morning and felt very much like a jackass. At forty-four, he had never before left America and had only briefly left South Florida. Now, sitting next to his business partner, Jorge Arnez, and directly in front of the languid Englishman, Sebastian Race, he regretted the whole damned project, and was ready to go home. He focused a bleary eye on his watch and calculated that he had been in England for just three hours, most of that spent travelling from the airport.

He twisted against the restraint of the seat-belt, so that he could see Sebastian's long face as they drove in an eight-seater people mover. 'Are we in Essex yet?'

'We have been for some time. We are now in Gosfield. The nearest town of any size is Halstead, two miles away. Braintree, home of the district council, is about six or seven. We're about an hour's drive from the sea and the same from Cambridge, as you requested.'

'I must have slept all the way from Gatwick.'

'Yeah, and snored,' said Jorge, laughing. 'I slept on the plane. More experience of travelling.' The Cuban-American, a full five inches shorter than Richard's six feet one, ran his fingers through his thick black hair and grinned with some affection at Richard. 'Glad you came?' Fortunately, there was no time to answer.

'We're here!' cried Sebastian. 'Turn there, driver. Drive slowly around to the courtyard. Look at those trees! Some of them are hundreds of years old. Protected, of course. Can't chop them down without permission.'

'Permission from whom?' asked Richard suspiciously. But now the building was in view.

'Olé!' cried Jorge. 'Look at that. You sure do get your money's worth in England. All yours, Dickie, for a million dollars. Couldn't get that much building in Boca Raton for a million.'

'That's pounds,' said Sebastian Race with a nervous glance at Richard. 'A million pounds, about one point six million dollars. It would have been much more but, well . . . You see, there used to be about three thousand acres of land. Property like this is supposed to have land. There is the lake which you will be able to see from your apartment. Gosfield Lake. Man-made, but not owned by Gosfield Hall any more. You have just ten acres. You really didn't need much land, I thought. You didn't say anything about having land.'

The Englishman was tall and lanky, dressed in tweeds just as Richard would have expected. He was about the same age as Richard. A full head of brown hair, no hint of a pot belly and eyes that looked as if they would one day pop out of his head, all gave him an insipid look. Yet he was handsome. Definitely good-looking. But then Richard thought most men were handsome in comparison to himself. He spent no time looking in the mirror, being devoid of vanity. Unfortunately, he had to watch himself as he shaved off what remained of his hair, and gave himself a smooth chin each day.

Now he studied the building, Gosfield Hall, his new home and the seat of the business in which he had bought a controlling interest from the Englishman. The place was enormous, three or four floors of old red brick, lots of windows. He thought it looked grim, and shuddered at the thought of living in this building all alone. There must be thirty thousand square feet. What in God's name must it cost to heat? And yet had he not specifically said that he wanted an impressive home? In the depth of his anguish, in his determination to regain what he had lost, Richard had acted with uncharacteristic sloppiness. He couldn't regret coming. Not yet, at least. The stakes were so high. But this? There would come a time when he wished to sell it, and, little as he knew of English real estate, he was certain that such a property would be hard to shift. He didn't know whether to laugh or cry. How different were his expectations from Sebastian Race's reality. They had not come from different countries, they had come from different planets!

Sebastian looked at the building with reverence. 'Gosfield Hall was built in the time of Henry VIII and Queen Elizabeth slept here. It's a quadrangle, four sides round a really wonderful courtyard.

There's a gate on the west side, as you can now see. I'll run ahead and ring for the Stones when the car stops. Husband and wife. Live in. You can drive into the courtyard, driver. Above the gate is the Queen's gallery. Over a hundred feet long. Each frontage of Gosfield Hall is different and each has one large feature. Isn't that amazing?'

'What does it cost to heat?' asked Richard, not interested in who had slept where or for how long. 'Is it fit to live in? Am I going to have to camp out?'

'No, no, I assure you. You said to furnish an apartment for you and I have done that. In keeping. Very comfortable. Some central heating was installed in the late nineteenth century, then when the place was going to be a nursing home, they put in more heating in 1956.'

'Nineteen fifty-six,' repeated Richard.

Sebastian shrugged, rolling his huge eyes. 'There isn't heating everywhere. Not through the whole property. It was a terrific bargain and I did send you a photograph.'

Richard gave the Englishman a hard stare, but was careful not to meet Jorge's eyes. His friend would be laughing, and Richard did not like being laughed at. Worse, Jorge might be in his worried mode, fearful for Richard's sanity, and not without reason. He had bought a property for one and a half million dollars, sight unseen. He had depended on Sebastian Race's good sense and been let down badly. This did not promise much for the chain of six restaurants he had also bought into, also sight unseen. Richard had his reasons for rushing head-long into an English business and an English home, but he was normally a cautious man and he felt like a fool.

Some people might think that money grew on trees. Richard was not one of them. He had worked hard ever since he left school at fifteen to amass a modest fortune. Now a quarter of it was tied up in an ailing business and a pile of old bricks. He had never in the past been quite so foolish, not even when he was sixteen. He had not been thinking clearly ever since Jenny's death and the betrayal that followed. No wonder Jorge refused to let him come to England on his own. Richard had been unwilling to admit that there was anything wrong with his mind, until now.

'Not your usual style of doing business, Dickie,' murmured Jorge, coming up to stand beside him. 'Not exactly as comfortable as your condo and a damned sight too big for the business. However,' he added on a more sympathetic note, 'it is very impressive. I expect there is a certain person in England who will be very impressed.'

Sebastian led them through a pair of huge doors, gabbling on about the beauty of the place as he went. A young man, introduced as Geoff Stone, had taken the bags from the driver. In the entrance hallway which ran across the width of the court-yard, Richard noticed dirty grey stone laid with small black squares, gloom and a dank chill, which made the house colder than it was outdoors. The windows were huge, but he was aware only of gloom. It matched his mood.

Sebastian pointed to some metal rods hanging from the ceiling at regular intervals down the length of the hall. A bar stretched out from the bottom of each rod, each end of which held one electric light bulb shielded by a small shade. 'Original gas-lamp fittings!'

'I'll get some decent lighting in here as soon as possible.'

'Well . . .' murmured Sebastian with a worried look. 'But let me show you the grand salon.'

They turned to the right and followed him in silence, their footfalls echoing in the cold empty space until they entered a vast room with a ceiling not less than twenty feet high which was painted with figures, although Richard could hardly make them out as the painting seemed very old and in poor repair. It reminded him of the famous Renaissance-type house, Vizcaya, outside Miami, which was the only old house Richard had ever seen. And it had been built in 1916.

'Will you look at that fireplace!' cried Jorge, walking over to stand by it. 'It's got gay statues holding up the mantelpiece.'

'That's not . . .' began Sebastian, angrily, but then shrugged.

On either side of the fireplace were carved marble figures of two boys face to face, their lower bodies turned into intertwined fish tails. Richard thought it was hideous, but Sebastian's hand reached out to touch the carvings with reverence. The English probably liked this sort of old stuff. He couldn't see the beauty of it, but made no comment. Jorge was enjoying himself, teasing Richard, but at the same time making light of the disaster.

'I suppose there is somewhere comfortable for me to live?'

'Oh, yes. An apartment, as I said. But let me show you the library. Your flat is directly above, on the first floor. And there's a guest flat for you, Jorge.'

But first they had to see the dreary panelled

library which faced south towards the afternoon sun, before taking the creaking uncarpeted stairs to the ballroom, which Richard quite liked. It had huge mirrors at either end and two hooks on the ceiling where crystal chandeliers should have been. They were sorely missed since when lit they would endlessly reflect in the mirrors. Very large windows along one side let in the thin January light. The walls were panelled and there was some gilded decoration. He could almost imagine himself wanting to sit in this room. If there were furniture and lights and carpets and heating.

After that, they had to see the long gallery, and finally Richard's apartment.

They entered through a newly fitted kitchen area. There was milk in the tiny refrigerator and the cupboards were well stocked with glasses and drinks. Sebastian, who had spent just one week in Florida, had remembered that Richard preferred bourbon with ginger ale, and that he liked percolated coffee with milk and sugar. There was rum, Coca-Cola and pina colada mix for Jorge, too. There were even packets of dry roasted peanuts and potato chips.

Sebastian Race had done it up with period furniture and brocade curtains. The walls had the most amazing plaster mouldings which had been painted cream to contrast with the pale pink wall colour. A vast gilded mirror took up almost all the space above the mantelpiece. Richard thought the intricately carved frame must be eighteen inches wide. There were even pillars leading to the large bay window.

Much of the furniture was gilded, but several of the chairs and the divan looked reasonably comfortable, if a trifle too soft. It was certainly grand. It was also warm, due to a blazing fire.

The bedroom was furnished in matching grand style, but there was a handsome, well-furnished modern bathroom. Another room was left unfurnished as Sebastian said he didn't know whether Richard would use it as a study or as a second bedroom. Richard said he wanted a study, a Compaq Presario with Windows 95, a telephone line for the Internet and an adjustable chair. He wanted it as soon as was feasible.

Jorge's apartment was comfortable and warm, although not so fancy nor so large as Richard's. But then, Jorge would be renting a house as soon as possible and getting it ready for his wife, Maria. He didn't need to have anything too comfortable in Richard's house.

Sebastian said they must both be very tired after the overnight flight from Miami, but he just wanted them to know that Geoff and Harriet Stone lived on the ground floor, could be summoned by the bell next to the fireplace and would prepare meals for them. They could have supper in Richard's rooms at seven that evening. Two cleaners would come in daily and a gardener had been looking after the ten acres of grass and shrubs since God only knew when. Jim Hornby was a law unto himself.

Sebastian said he would like to take the two Americans out to lunch at the Green Man pub in the village of Gosfield, then leave them to catch up on their sleep.

The pub was small, old and cosy and the food was excellent, but Richard wasn't hungry, by now so tired that he couldn't even work up any anger about the predicament in which he found himself.

Jorge was also tired, but not so much so that he couldn't get in a few playful digs about white elephants and Richard never getting his money back.

Sebastian, nervous and unhappy, said very little except that he thought it was a beautiful house, and Richard had, after all, approved the purchase. Richard said that the ham sandwich was excellent.

Within the hour, he was stripped to his underpants, ready to crawl into bed for a few hours' sleep. Having changed his watch to register English time, he could now not calculate the time back home – his first experience of the devastating effect of jet lag. He would be careful to make no binding decisions during the next few days.

He awoke to darkness, found the switch to a table lamp and looked at his watch which said five o'clock. He didn't know if it was five o'clock at night or in the morning. Dressing quickly, he went into the living-room, found the remote control for the television and began browsing through the stations. It was only five o'clock at night. He looked out of the window. Already dark.

He sat down in an upholstered chair and waged his now familiar fight with depression. He had come a long way financially, had made something of himself despite a poor education, but he was in danger of failure three thousand miles from home, and Richard had a terror of failure. If nothing mattered except making money, then to lose serious money was to lose all that was worthwhile. He had never yet walked away from a business enterprise out of pocket.

Yet within hours of arriving in England he faced the prospect of losing quite a lot of money.

Ironically, it was not because of the chain of restaurants he had bought into, the money involved in
six run-down restaurants being chicken feed. He
was in trouble because he had thought it was safe
to empower the Englishman to purchase for him a
large home which could also act as headquarters
for the business. When he had said spend up to a
million, he had been thinking of dollars not
pounds. His first grave error. He must be aware at
all times of the currency in which he was working.
The exchange rate was about a dollar sixty to the
pound.

He shivered. Mistakes involving large sums were
serious. Richard did not make elementary mistakes
over money. Money was his saviour, his god, his
companion, his reason for living. Money could take
a man out of his background and give him a new
one. Money was insurance against unhappiness, or
the means to buy off unhappiness. Money was a
shield, and no man could have enough of it. Yet, in
his recent madness, he had risked one point six
million dollars.

This was not the way he had planned it. He had
thought that he would make a handsome profit on
any house he might buy. He had intended to
upgrade it, turn it into a show place. But houses like
Gosfield were surely only fit to be museums. He
had not got his mind tuned in to this sort of
property. On the other hand, for all he knew,
thousands of Brits lived in places like Gosfield.
He hoped film stars bought such places, or perhaps
Arab sheiks. Did they have a film colony in
England? He was ashamed to admit he didn't
know.

Also, he had not thought to specify a property in

good condition, because he assumed that common sense on Sebastian's part would have ensured as much. Furthermore, did Sebastian Race really suppose that so large a property was required? Good God! They could house an army here!

He closed his eyes and rubbed them with thumb and forefinger. Although Jorge was an executive in the restaurant chain and Sebastian and the two sisters who were Sebastian's cousins were fellow shareholders, Gosfield Hall belonged entirely to Richard. It was true that he had wanted a home grand enough to impress the one woman he thought loved him. That was important. But this? This tumbledown ancient wreck with one decent apartment? The room seemed cold, but now he began to sweat. Nothing in his past experience, in his development as a man, had taught him how to survive humiliation.

Richard Dumas had been born in Illinois, but had moved to Florida with his parents and older sister in 1960, so he had no recollection of the Midwest. The family name was Zumacher, but Orin Zumacher didn't want to be of German extraction, preferring to be French after the Second World War. He had changed his name to Dumas before Richard was born.

When he was eight, his dad, a printer, had left home and was never seen or heard from again. Richard's sister, Kate, ten years older, soon married and went to California. His mother, Elsa, got a job as a waitress at a sleazy joint called the Pink Pelican restaurant on the Intracoastal in Deerfield Beach, moving on to the Barefoot Mailman, McDonald's, Arby's and the Ramada Inn. Waiting on tables was all she knew, but she managed to do quite well on tips.

As soon as he was old enough, Richard worked during the long hot summers as a busboy clearing away dirty dishes from restaurant tables, and was later a waiter in various underpaying establishments.

When he was sixteen, his mother decided that they should relocate to California so that she could be near her three grandchildren whom she had never seen. Richard, who had never got on with his sister, refused to go. So Mom left him on his own and flew off to California, shipping ahead all her possessions and leaving Richard to cope alone in a two-room apartment with cooking facilities. He had seen her only once since that time.

By now he had left school and lost contact with his old schoolmates. He got a job at a garish place on I-95, called the Purple Pickle, selling corn dogs and French fries. Competing directly with the Ramada Inn, Crabby Jack's, a Chinese place and a couple of bars, it really couldn't compare for quality or price with the nationwide fast food chains and did well to avoid going under for so many years.

The owner, Chuck Newman, employed several stratagems for clinging to his business. First of all, he barely met the health requirements of City Hall. Then he took a cavalier attitude to his staff.

Richard, having no close friends or family and no idea how to occupy his free time enjoyably, had worked twelve-hour shifts. However, Chuck Newman had let his manager know that there would be a bonus for keeping overheads down, so the manager altered the clocking-on records to make it appear that the employee had worked fewer hours than had actually been put in. Thus, Chuck stole from the most needy of his employees, and rewarded the manager for this criminal act. It was a common practice, but the young Richard had no-one to advise him when he found out that many of those tiring hours brought him no reward at all. Stealthily, he gathered evidence of the scam and reported the Purple Pickle to the guys at Deerfield Beach police station. For his trouble he was fired. Worse, the investigation came to nothing because none of the other employees would make a complaint.

For three years he worked at two jobs, sometimes putting in twenty-hour days if both employers should happen to want him to do overtime. He never refused the chance to make a few extra dollars. Mostly, he slept in his 1967 Chevy, having given up the apartment, and lived off hamburgers from Burger King and fish and chips from Arthur Treacher's. He also helped himself to some food at the restaurants where he worked until they folded. Catering was a cutthroat business in South Florida. Snow birds (Northerners escaping from colder climates) relocated in search of heat and sunshine, and the first idea they had to support themselves was to sell cooked food. The turnover in failed businesses was tremendous, and he had heard one time that there were sixteen thousand restaurants in Broward County alone.

When he was nineteen, Richard bought one of these no-hopers and painted it himself, upgrading the kitchen and buying booths and tables second-hand. He called it The Grouper (a kind of fish) and kept the lighting bright and the music loud. Too young for a liquor licence, he had to attract teenagers who were themselves too young to drink, and he had to keep them in order. Although keeping The Grouper drug-free was an impossible task, he did pretty well. He advertised wherever he thought it would do some good and had a few promotions. Two fish dinners for the price of one, that sort of thing. And he waited on the customers while employing a good chef, a Chinese who didn't speak much English but understood American tastes in food. Within eighteen months he had sold the place for three times his modest investment. He felt bold.

His next purchase was a failing company that produced components for IBM which had relocated to nearby Palm Beach County. Richard knew nothing about components, but he set about firing the useless management, relocating to a cheaper property and keeping an eye on the costs. He became such a threat to the more established competitors that the main one bought him out within three months. He was twenty years old and had very nearly a million dollars in the bank while living in a modest two-bedroom rented apartment on Fifth Street in Deerfield Beach.

For a year and a half he cherished his money, playing the stock market cautiously but not risking his fortune on anything. He bought a swanky apartment in Boca Raton, which adjoined Deerfield Beach, but was a much more desirable address. He concentrated on trying to look like a millionaire.

Approaching twenty-two and growing bored, he bought a few acres in Boca, which was a favourite destination of wealthy holiday-makers, wealthy retirees and, so it was said, wealthy Mafia men in search of sun and congenial company. He parcelled the land and sold it within the year, offloading all but one large plot on which he planned to build a four-storey condominium. It necessitated borrowing a very large sum of money and taking on an older partner, one whom the banks could trust.

Now he felt both bold and lucky, but he ended up making a pact with the devil. Who better, he thought in his innocence, to help him up the next step on the ladder to fame and fortune than Randolph Muskovy, a property developer of great experience and cunning? Within six months, Richard had not only delivered himself and his business interests into the hands of a control freak, but he had married the Muskovys' only child.

He and Jenny started married life with high hopes, each convinced that no-one else would find them attractive. Jenny had no hobbies, although she watched all the daytime soaps and could recount the plots of each. Florida might be a paradise for lovers of water sports or golf or tennis, but she was interested in none of them. Nor had Richard ever been interested in amateur sport. All that energy, he used to joke, all that aggression and competitiveness, and no money in it!

He preferred to get his exercise by power walking, and he would talk about its healthful benefits. He would put on his shorts and tee shirt, slip out of the house at half past five and begin to walk as fast as he could without breaking into a run. But while other men monitored their blood pressure and their pulse, or measured their muscles, Richard spent his walking time looking for business opportunities. He'd pass a derelict building that was up for sale, note the name of the real estate agent, plan what he would put in it or how he would upgrade it before selling it. Later, he would ring up and buy the property, ahead of the competition, feeling fit, yet not afraid that his hour's solitude had been wasted.

And he needed that solitude. He and Jenny had few friends, and their only shared activity was the television. Jenny chose to spend each day with her mother, while Richard was obliged to spend each day with her father.

Randolph Muskovy was not above cutting corners to make money, but he did not like to think that anyone else was getting rich. He used to turn bright red if he happened to read in the papers that a competitor was doing well. Not surprisingly, he suffered a coronary when he was sixty, forcing Richard to undertake all the work of their enterprises. Yet the older man didn't relinquish the reins. Richard became his daily servant, always in the wrong, never quick enough about whatever he was doing. Nor could Richard relieve his frustration by complaining to Jenny. She was convinced that both her parents were perfect, while she had no such silly ideas about him.

Randolph's great passion was his small plane, and surprisingly for such a timid woman, Mrs Muskovy was happy to travel with him. When Richard and Jenny were thirty, the plane crashed, killing both the Muskovys. It was not long before they discovered that Randolph had left his fortune and control of the business to Jenny, his adored only child.

Henceforth, Richard was never allowed to think of himself as a multimillionaire, although at least half the money invested was his, nor as a successful businessman, although he had been solely responsible for the running of the business for several years.

49

The loss of both parents with such violent suddenness had turned Jenny from a timid, rather plain young woman into a small-minded harridan who delighted in reminding him that Daddy had created his comfortable lifestyle, and she could destroy him if he decided to take too many risks with her money.

She began to chain-smoke which gave her an irritating cough almost immediately. Having no mother to visit, she spent her days flitting from one doctor to another, always with some exotic complaint that she was sure would kill her. At forty, she began to lose weight and it was several months before her weary, increasingly cynical doctor decided that she might really be unwell. Within twelve months she was dead of lung cancer.

There was a knock on the door. 'Jesus, it's cold in that hall!' said Jorge, letting himself in. 'I've been knocking around this mausoleum for the past ten minutes. Couldn't remember which way your apartment was. Kept opening doors and there were more stairs. You don't know what you've got here.'

'A white elephant,' said Richard. He went into the kitchen and began to prepare a rum and Coke for Jorge. 'I have my doubts about Sebastian Race. He doesn't seem to have any common sense. I mean look at this place.'

Jorge obligingly looked around him, taking in the gilded chairs and marble-topped side-tables, the ornate old-fashioned furniture. 'He's charged all this furniture up to you, you know. I haven't asked him, mind you, but I'm getting the measure of the man. Trust me, he's spent your money like water.

Maria will think this is terrific, but I'm not sure it's your taste.'

'It's not.' Richard handed the glass to Jorge, then looked about for a coaster. 'Wait until I find something for you to put that on. I don't want this furniture damaged before I can get it returned.'

'So, given what we think we know about Sebastian, what do you suppose his chain of restaurants is going to be like?'

'My chain of restaurants,' corrected Richard. 'I have control, just. It's worth reminding ourselves of that occasionally. I have no idea what to expect. We've both read the accounts, and I trust the independent assessor.'

'Ah ha!' laughed Jorge, wagging a playful finger. 'I think you're going to lose this bet. When did you last go into a business venture so ill-prepared?'

'Never.'

Not many weeks ago, Richard had invited Jorge out to lunch. They had come together on a successful business venture in the late Eighties, a valet parking company that was so successful they were soon arranging the parking at the best parties in Miami, supplying handsome young men in white jackets to park the Cadillacs and Lincolns of the rich and famous – or infamous. Jorge had some interesting contacts. Jenny had never liked Jorge and Maria, and they had never liked her. So, when Jenny died and there was so much unpleasantness, the Arnezes were among Richard's few sincere supporters.

After lunch, while they were enjoying a brandy, Richard had manoeuvred the conversation onto general business principles, claiming that he knew what made a shop, service business or manufacturer tick. He claimed, with uncharacteristic boastfulness, that he could make a success of any business he chose to buy, in any country.

Jorge, unable to guess what was coming next, simply said he supposed so. Richard then wagered ten thousand dollars that he could do it. Why, he could buy a business in England (for he would need to be able to speak the language) and turn it round, making a sound profit. If Jorge didn't believe it, he and Maria could just come along to England and watch him do it. He reckoned he could do the business in six months.

Jorge had given him a long speculative look, during which Richard was sure he would be turned down. 'Are you sure this is a good idea, Richard? I mean, England? You don't have to do it this way,' Jorge had said.

'It's the only way,' Richard had replied quietly.

Jorge suddenly reached out and patted him on the arm. 'I'll do it,' he said, 'if Maria is willing. Six months? No more, Richard. That's long enough.'

Richard had then pulled from his pocket a small ad he had cut from a British financial paper.

BUSINESS PARTNER WANTED FOR
CHAIN OF SEASIDE RESTAURANTS
6 busy restaurants in East Anglian seaside resorts
average 40 covers
Group Turnover £720,000.

Faxes passed back and forth, and Sebastian Race soon made a flying visit to Boca Raton. The restaurants had been left to two sisters and their cousin who had no idea how to maximize their inheritance. They hadn't expected to snare a wealthy American, but they were eager to get Richard involved.

The restaurants were clearly run-down and doing poor business. Only fifty people actually ate each day in the cafés, on average, but the properties were on long leases. The family valued the cafés at half a million pounds. The independent assessor thought a figure of four hundred thousand was closer to reality.

A limited company was formed with one hundred thousand shares at four pounds each. Richard had fifty-two thousand, while each of the three members of the Race family had sixteen thousand. Shares had to be offered back to the shareholders at par. Richard was appointed Chairman, but no contracts of employment were offered.

'But as far as the business is concerned, what have I risked?' said Richard now. 'I could buy out Sebastian and his two cousins from the petty cash. No, it's an interesting challenge with virtually no risk.'

'Agreed.'

'Gosfield Hall is my problem. When have you ever known me to make a mistake like confusing pounds for dollars?'

'Never,' said Jorge. 'In fact, I'm not sure how you came to own this place. Didn't McCarthy warn you?'

Richard took a turn around the floor. 'He's a good accountant and a loyal friend. He came into my office. "Do you really want me to send a cheque off for this place?" he said. I can hear him now, see him frowning at me with his glasses shoved up on his forehead. But he was acting as if I was some kind of nut, and that annoyed me. I said I did want to buy it, and why hadn't the money been transferred? Something like that. He gave me a funny look and walked out. Sebastian sent me a photo of one of the sides of the place. I thought it must be about twenty or thirty feet deep, a splendid house, just what I was looking for.'

'Weren't there any details from the real estate guy?'

'He said there weren't.'

Jorge sighed, then took a long pull on his rum and Coke. 'You see why Maria and I thought it would be a good idea to come over with you. You've not been yourself, fella. We're worried about you.'

'I'm OK now. Got my head sorted out. Listen, I'm firing on all cylinders. This is a real challenge and that's just what I need. But about this house. I must spend money on it in order to offload it. And it might take years to sell. And do you suppose the Brits buy houses of thirty thousand square feet? This thing is the size of a hotel.'

'Sell it to a hotel chain.'

'Maybe. That would be a logical move.'

'Well, so you've been careful to keep me in the dark,' said Jorge, rising to refresh his own drink. 'What are your plans for the chain?'

'A youthful visual and food image. Modern, perhaps with a strong American feel. I understand Bruce Willis and company have done well with Planet Hollywood. American food clearly goes down well. Not hamburgers, though. That's played out.'

'Got to find something the Brits will eat,' said Jorge coming back into the living-room. 'We don't know what their tastes are.'

'Food's food, so long as it's fresh and well-cooked,' said Richard. 'It doesn't matter what type of food we serve provided the atmosphere is right and the prices are competitive. I propose to go for the young market, those who are adventurous enough to try something a little different. They won't want a restaurant that their parents frequent. All of the Flutterby cafés are in towns by the sea, or so we've been told. Now you and I know about vacation trade. We'll go for the young beach-volleyball and lifeguard market.'

'What about Cuban? Maria could advise on the dishes. We could have a real Cuban feel to the places, play salsa music.'

Richard didn't like Cuban food, a fact he had kept carefully hidden from Maria and Jorge. He had eaten his way through many meals of refried beans and guacamole, cooked bananas and exotic drinks at the Arnez home and in restaurants owned by their friends. He had noticed, however, that these restaurants were very popular, and not only with exiled Cubans. Yes, the idea had merit. The restaurant designer would have a theme to work around. Brits might not be acquainted with Cuban food, but they would eat it, provided the whole package was presented to them confidently and with style.

Shortly before seven o'clock they heard Geoff and Harriet Stone entering the kitchen with their trolleys of food. The couple, in their mid-thirties, were pleasant to look at, both dark-haired and short. They were both nearly paralysed with fear, however. Richard made a mental note to speak to them alone the next day and try to put them at their ease. Presently Jorge and Richard were served with tomato soup, lamb chops, Brussels sprouts and roast potatoes followed by treacle sponge and custard.

They also received glasses of both white and red wine and were offered port and highly aromatic Stilton cheese, followed by strong coffee.

When the serious young couple had left, Jorge burst out laughing. 'As you said, food's food. If this is what Brits like, how can they possibly enjoy good old Cuban American food?'

'I was wondering the same thing myself. So perhaps this is just the Stones' idea of a great meal. I must try to impress on them that we will want a salad with our meals, and no dessert or cheese.'

They chatted for several hours, discussing ideas, talking figures. At about ten o'clock it occurred to Richard that Jorge was not making his usual spiky comments, and he looked over to see his friend sound asleep. Shaken awake, Jorge retired to his rooms and Richard was soon in bed and sleeping fitfully.

The next day he felt more alert and, consequently, more confident. He and Jorge tossed a coin for the keys to the Mercedes which Seb had bought on instructions, the loser having to make do with a gleaming BMW.

There followed a day-long trip to view each of the Flutterby cafés. None had more than thirty-five covers, while the café in Woodbridge had only twenty-four. All were on side streets of seaside towns that presented a dismal scene in late January, with the exception of Woodbridge which wasn't by the sea at all.

The sullen sea mocked them, and the wind tore at their faces and numbed their fingers. Just when they thought the weather could not be more miserable, the rain came, soaking Richard's camel-hair coat, and penetrating Jorge's raincoat, which turned out to be merely showerproof. Seb pulled his flat cap tighter and turned up the collar of what Richard understood was a coat called a 'barber'. This 'barber' was certainly waterproof, and he decided to buy one at the earliest opportunity.

Few people were out and about, all huddled against the weather, none interested in spending money in the six small diners (Richard and Jorge refused to dignify them by calling them restaurants) with plastic tablecloths and net-curtained windows dripping with condensation. Felixstowe, Maldon, Clacton, Walton-on-the-Naze, Woodbridge and Aldeburgh combined to silence them all.

As darkness fell, Jorge roused himself to say firmly that he had seen enough and now wanted a proper dinner. Sebastian drove them back to Woodbridge where they dined at Seckford Hall, which was a hotel with a reputation for fine food. The Americans begged for a simple salad followed by plain steaks and French fries, while Sebastian had a vegetable terrine, followed by duck cooked until it was just pink. The desserts were so elaborately presented that Jorge said it was a shame to eat them. Sebastian persuaded them to have the selection of cheeses, and this time Richard liked them better, although he still preferred Velveeta. Jorge raised his eyebrows at Richard, a gesture that said, so this is what Brits like to eat!

'Let me go over a few points, Seb,' Richard said as they drank their coffee. 'You and your two cousins inherited these restaurants from your uncle. The whole kit and caboodle is not worth much, so you advertised for partners to put in some cash and new ideas. You got me. Correct me if I am wrong, but you know nothing at all about catering.'

'Well, that is not entirely true. I worked in the restaurants every summer when I was at university. My uncle discussed the business with me occasionally. He had some grand ideas, but he was ill for years and never made an effort. I took a course in accountancy, although I never qualified and worked for nearly twenty years for a builder's merchant. The company defied the national trend and collapsed eighteen months ago. I'm pretty broke, behind with my rent. I had to give the house to my ex-wife. I need a job and I don't see why I couldn't be a very good operations manager. I know the country. I am familiar with the properties.'

'Yet you didn't seem to notice that they do no damned business,' said Jorge.

Richard finished his coffee and set the cup down carefully. 'You, your two cousins, Jorge and I cannot possibly make a living out of those six restaurants, Seb. We must do something fairly quickly. We will need a loan from a bank for running costs and we will need some more restaurants. Twelve might do it. Even eight. But we must open some large restaurants in busy cities.'

'That's a terrible risk!'

'Business is a risk,' said Jorge harshly. 'We've got to do something. You bought that damned house for Richard, tying up a sizeable chunk of his capital, on the crazy notion that all that space would be needed for offices! I think you're nuts. We can't afford to pay what staff there is.'

Two flags of colour flew in Sebastian's cheeks,

and he became more animated than Richard had ever seen him, waving his arms and knocking over the salt. 'All those restaurants are in prime positions to take advantage of the holiday trade. You're seeing them at the very worst time. They are holiday restaurants.' He swivelled in his seat. 'May I have the bill, please?'

'Well, old buddy, what's the game plan?' Jorge stood up, looked around the pleasant room and counted the covers. Most of the tables were occupied, and the guests were well-dressed and obviously moneyed. So different from the few lone diners they had seen in their seaside cafés.

Richard stood up too. 'There is no game plan yet. I have to think, find out more, get used to the country. You promised me a computer set up in the spare room of my apartment, Seb. Tomorrow, you said? Not a moment too soon. Don't expect to see much of me, as I'll be travelling around. I prefer to drive myself. There is a lot to learn. I will come up with a formal plan and present it to the shareholders in two weeks.'

'I suppose you bitterly regret coming here,' said Seb.

For the first time in many hours, Richard smiled broadly. 'Not at all. This is what I do. I am a business fixer. This collection of run-down properties offers a great challenge. Wait and see.'

The following day he wrote a few letters, then set off for a journey of discovery, stopping in a dozen places for a coffee or a meal, copying the menu unobtrusively into his notebook. For the next three days he followed the same plan, arriving at Gosfield Hall each evening tired and with no appetite for the meals so carefully served by the Stones.

During the evenings he and Jorge quickly learned that they had not much in common except business, so Richard was glad when Maria arrived to take her husband away to the nearby furnished house Jorge had found. Even Maria's loud complaints about the cold weather, the lack of her sort of food and the complete absence of shopping malls provided an evening of welcome change.

During the second week he employed a surveyor to assess Gosfield Hall – something Seb seemed to have forgotten to do. It snowed, a thin sprinkling on the ground that made the paths dangerous and further dampened Richard's mood. He was lonely and he had to admit that he missed Florida, especially the guarantee of sunny days.

The television was now his only evening companion, not such a dire prospect as he had feared. There were many American programmes on the satellite channels, and he discovered that he could watch Dan Rather on CBS News if he stayed up late enough. But always he kept the telephone nearby, willing it to ring.

When it did finally fill the air with its insistent ring-ring, different from the American single buzz, he leapt to his feet and fell over a chair in his eagerness. As he had hoped, the voice was a woman's, the sound of which was the real reason why he had come to a foreign land from the warmth, certainty and comfort of south Florida.

'Zoe? Is that you, darling? How are you? What?'

'I'm calling,' began a singsong, oh-so-cheerful voice, 'to enquire if you would be interested in replacement windows. We have a special offer . . .'

'You're selling?' he bellowed, enraged and disappointed. 'You're selling god-damned windows?

Get off the line and don't ring this number again.' He slammed down the phone and slumped into a chair, on the point of tears. It wasn't going to work out. He could see that now. He had staked so much on moving to England. 'My God, Zoe,' he cried. 'Why did you do it?'

The following day he couldn't concentrate. His plan was nearly completed. Filled with facts and figures, laced with optimism and confidence, it was one of the best such reports he had ever done. Yet he couldn't find the patience to finish it.

Going into the living-room, he sat down in one of the gilded chairs and turned on the television to graze the satellite channels, stopping on what appeared to be a gardening programme. '*Gypsy Harry's Gardening Tips*, with guest Fran Craig.'

Gypsy Harry looked like a retired wrestler. Largely bald, he had drawn what was left of his white hair back into a pony-tail. It seemed that his special gimmick was the recycling of odd objects among his plants. Today he was in a greenhouse, showing viewers what containers they could use for seed sowing.

A woman walked into the camera's range, appearing relaxed in the eye of the camera while looking stylish and neat in a black trouser suit and white sweater, in strong contrast to the slovenly Harry. She had glorious dark red hair down to her shoulders, parted on one side and constantly threatening to fall over her eyes. Her blue eyes held a mischievous expression. From her straight nose to her over-generous mouth, she was a delight. Her lightly tanned skin was smooth as cream and her voice was the cutest little rasp he had heard in many years. But this was no sexy twenty-something. Fran Craig was pushing forty. A woman he might relate to.

Harry gave a distrustful look at her as she approached the bench where he had just informed the viewers that they could plant seeds in margarine tubs, plastic ice-cream containers or anything else in which they could pierce holes.

'And here is my guest, Fran Craig. Hello, Fran.' The camera swung round to take in Fran's smile. 'You look all dressed up like a dog's dinner. Do you always put on your best bib and tucker to go into the greenhouse?'

'I'm a neat worker, Harry. Many of us live busy lives and may have only a few moments to dash out to the greenhouse before going off somewhere else. My busy life means that I can't take chances when planting seeds. That's why I prefer to use a heated propagator. That way the chances of success are greatly increased.'

'All right for those with plenty of dosh. But now you're going to show the viewers how you pot up your seedlings.'

'Up *yours*,' she replied sweetly. 'I'm going to show the viewers how I pot up *your* seedlings. Aren't they crowded! These must be potted on quickly, as they are already looking a little leggy.'

'Can't see if you're a bit leggy in them trousers,' said Harry.

Fran's mouth opened as her cheeks reddened, but an editing cut clumsily removed her response, so that the next thing the viewer saw was Fran smiling broadly as she displayed a tray of seedlings spread in some sort of container that looked like a crate for extremely small eggs. Harry's scowl made Richard laugh out loud.

He ran a hand over his shaven scalp, suddenly reminded that his wife had been dead for well over a year, and he was fairly desperate for female company. Even as he drank in Fran's beauty and delighted in her barbed confrontation with Gypsy Harry, he felt profoundly depressed. He had fallen in love with a shadow on the screen.

'Have I sunk so low that I can be aroused by a picture?' he asked himself. But the delectable Fran continued to hold his interest. Women had a way of betraying him, of leaving him feeling unworthy and stupid. This perky woman with her bright advice on seed planting seemed to have the answer to a need he couldn't quite define. More than sex, it was something to do with companionship and being loved.

Chapter Three

Five o'clock on Thursday morning. Fran had crawled out of bed and pulled on jeans and a tee shirt, over which she put a green jumper which the moths had attacked a few years earlier. This was in turn covered by a puce cardigan that had lost half its buttons. The sheepskin coat she had bought at a charity shop would cover it all, and she could begin to unwrap as it got warmer, assuming that the day did improve. She glanced at the sky, but it was too early to tell. A few stars were still visible, and the lights of several planes heading for Stansted airport. She trotted down the stairs in her thick socks, anxious not to wake Trevor, and began frying bacon, a couple of eggs and two slices of bread. She had yet to load up her transit van and would need all the energy the food gave her.

She should have loaded up the night before, but, as happened so often, she had fallen asleep in front of the television and been too lazy to go outside at midnight.

She would eat her breakfast with three cups of coffee to get her going, then prepare a couple of cheese sandwiches and a flask, before sticking her nose out into the cold. There was probably still a frost on the ground which would make loading up just that bit more difficult.

Trevor had knocked up some shelving in the van, making it possible for her to load up just once with enough plants to keep her going all day. Her predecessors, she had been told, used to go off for a second load. A stallholder on her own was unable to go off in the middle of the day to get fresh supplies, but it didn't matter because there was seldom a day when she sold everything she had brought.

January and February were the poorest times of the year, but as March approached she could expect business to improve. The ground was now too hard to plant out. Bedding plants could not yet be sold. She must wait until the danger of frost was over. She didn't sell trees because she had to grow them on for too long before making any money on them. Bowls of ordinary spring bulbs, which were cheaper than the prepared ones she had sold at Christmas, were her standby. People like having a bit of colour indoors in March. She had also planted up three dozen bowls of house plants and a few glass terrariums because she had been able to get them cheaply. She was offering them for seven pounds fifty whereas the garden centres sold them for thirteen pounds. She also had another three dozen house plants, larger specimens which she had been bringing on for a year, bravely priced at two pounds. She thought she could make a hundred and fifty pounds if she sold every single item. But the weather had to be kind so that the customers came round. Rain and a strong wind would see her bringing home all her stock.

Money was getting very tight. Her van cost her

twenty pounds a week to run, and she simply had to pay her electricity and water rates, for without power and water she would be out of business. The market inspector wanted thirty-four pounds every week for rent. And then there was her loan . . .

She and Trevor had enough wood to keep from freezing, at least in the kitchen. The rest of the house was bitterly cold. They had to eat; their diet included no luxuries. Fran had begun to cut back where she could. The plants were wrapped in newspapers saved for her by the newsagent in Bocking. She made signs advertising her wares by writing on waste cardboard from the supermarket with a magic marker. Individual plant labels were a luxury she didn't bother with these days.

That left polythene bags, an absolute necessity. She bought them from the cash and carry in Sudbury, but when a person is counting every penny, the few pence spent on bags were bitterly regretted. She had not found a way of getting bags free.

As luck would have it, the sun shone brightly all day, and by half past nine the market was fairly full. Fran sang songs, chatted to babies, called out her wares and generally put on a performance for those who wandered past her stall. Bertie teased her about overdoing it, but she knew she had to make this day pay. And she was rewarded by selling out at half past three.

She could go home! But first, a quick circuit of the market for some fillets of plaice, a few potatoes, a pound of sprouts and a cake from the cake stall.

The first meeting of the shareholders in early February was supposed to be informal yet businesslike. Richard would read his plan which he thought would stun and delight his fellow shareholders, then they would discuss it in detail and finally vote on it. Richard believed himself to be clumsy, unattractive and slightly overweight. However, he had no such modest ideas about his talent for business. He could read a set of accounts in the time it took others to get out their glasses. He could spot a fault in a report which had previously passed through half a dozen readings. His own reports were models of clarity and, when he chose to turn on the passion, he could motivate two people or two thousand to work together and give more of themselves than they knew they had to give.

His views were clearly set down in the report on the old Flutterby cafés. He had a watertight plan, had already discovered that Bloom Interiors were the finest designers of commercial properties, knew where he was going with the chain and the time scale towards profitability. This was an ambitious five-year plan. He proposed to motivate two of his little band of shareholders, not to work hard, but to leave himself, Jorge and Sebastian alone. He and Jorge, who was a director but not a shareholder, would run this chain with some help from Sebastian, and there was no place for a couple of interfering spinsters.

As there were only four shareholders, Richard invited them to his flat where they could all sit round his dining-table in relative comfort. His first surprise was the sisters. Instead of being a pair of spinsters in their sixties or seventies, as he had expected, they were two unmarried, rather attractive women in their early to mid-thirties. Unfortunately, they behaved like a pair of comic

actresses in a sitcom, their comments unintention-
ally funny, their facial tics and grimaces worthy of
Ellen DeGeneres.

At first glance they could be taken for twins:
brown hair waving to their shoulders, brown eyes
behind identical pairs of very modern black-
rimmed glasses on pert little noses. They wore neat
suits – one black, one grey – and white businesslike
blouses. There the similarity ended, for Karen, the
elder, was bossy, convinced of her business acumen
and eager to inform Richard, in a rather prissy
voice, that she hoped he would take her advice on
certain matters, because she knew a thing or two,
and after all, she was British.

Helena was sweeter, intent on impressing him
with her willingness to oblige. She made a great
show of taking up a pencil the minute he began to
speak, following the text with its point, nodding
vigorously when she understood what he was
saying. So animated was she with her little titters,
sucking of teeth or vigorous shaking of her head,
that he found it surprisingly difficult to concentrate.

'Let us remind ourselves where we stand. We
have six cafés in seaside towns, not prime sites
but having very nearly forty covers and fifty
customers a day with an average spend of eight
pounds per person. Say one hundred and twenty
thousand pounds a year. We have formed a limited
company. I have fifty-two thousand shares. Each of
you has sixteen thousand. I have been appointed
chairman. All shares must be offered back to the
company at the original price of four pounds if any
of us wishes to disinvest. Understood? No service
contracts have been issued.

'My proposal is to turn all the cafés into Cuban

cantinas,' Richard went on. 'We must choose a new name for the chain, something catchy. But we can discuss that later. At the moment—'

'Miami Spice,' said Karen.

'We'll discuss that later,' said Richard.

'Unfortunately,' murmured Helena, 'we have this pop group, the Spice Girls, and they might—'

'I like it,' said Seb.

'Later,' said Richard with a slight edge to his voice. He struggled to refocus his mind and find his place in the report. 'The first thing we must understand is that the present state of affairs cannot continue. We must move forward. We need two one-hundred-cover units in the main shopping areas of Colchester and Chelmsford. They will be shells and will need to be completely fitted out with kitchens, etc. Of course, the six cafés we already have must be refurbished, have new menus and prices that will give us ten pounds per customer on average.

'Let me summarize. We will need three hundred thousand pounds capital for the new restaurants. We will need four hundred thousand pounds for fitting and refitting of the new and existing restaurants. Running costs will be about six hundred thousand. That's a total of one million three hundred thousand. Well, there is my two hundred and eight thousand that I paid for my shares. Say a borrowing requirement of one million one hundred thousand.'

'Oh no!' cried Karen. 'I couldn't possibly be associated with that much money.'

'Who's going to supply this money?' asked Seb. 'You, Richard? Are you going to stump up one point one million?'

'Certainly not. Banks, venture capitalists, those sort of people. I cannot tie up any more of my money. I have businesses in America to run.'

Karen couldn't keep the panic from her voice. 'But they're only little seaside cafés. Why would anyone lend us money?'

Helena was biting the end of her pencil, but she added nothing to the debate.

Richard leaned across the table, wishing he had stood up to give his report. Standing would have given his words extra weight. 'Try not to be frightened by the sums involved. This is the way business is done. Look at it from the other side. We need only slightly more business in the seaside cafés, say eighty customers a day instead of fifty, with an average spend of ten pounds. Say eight hundred pounds a day and calculate just three hundred days a year, as we'll be closed sometimes. That's double the turnover.

'In our bigger restaurants in large towns, we should be able to attract two hundred and fifty to seven hundred customers a day at fifteen pounds per customer. By the same calculation, that's a turnover of at least a million pounds a year on each of the big new restaurants, as well as an average quarter of a million on each of the seaside cafés. It soon adds up.'

'Yes, it sounds like a lot of money, but there are always expenses,' warned Seb.

Richard ignored the insulting suggestion that he was too stupid to calculate costs, and said with a smile. 'I have calculated costs, believe me. Staff, twenty-five per cent. Food, thirty per cent. Light, napkins, rates, depreciation, furniture, etc., twenty per cent. Other costs, like advertising and so on, ten per cent. Now, the important thing is, that leaves fifteen per cent for profit. Do you want me to spell out the pre-tax profit on a turnover of three and a half million?'

There was a devout silence as they contemplated such magnificent sums. Richard knew he had them and waited a moment before continuing.

'We are gathered together to make money. That is right, isn't it? You'll not be satisfied with getting just two and a half per cent of the profits each, will you? We want big money.'

They nodded, scribbling on their notepads, no longer capable of making objections, their minds on dreams of wealth, sudden and unearned. 'Our objective is five years away. We will build up the chain over five years, then either launch it on the stock market or sell the entire chain to a rival trade buyer, a company that already has a nation-wide chain, perhaps. Then our shares will make big money.'

'Oh, no,' said Karen in some agitation. 'It's still a terrible risk. I couldn't possibly agree to such an undertaking. We could all end up being bankrupt.'

'Bankruptcy is a much more serious business in this country than it is in America,' said Sebastian sternly. 'We must be protected.'

Richard drew in his breath, striving for control. Jorge had now withdrawn himself from the discussion, sitting outside the argument, as it were, and simply enjoying Richard's frustration. 'No-one is going bankrupt. We are all going to make a great deal of money. Anyway, this is a limited company. The company might conceivably fold, but we will not personally be bankrupt. We will not have our homes taken away from us.'

'Well,' said Karen doubtfully.

'I put my trust entirely in you, Richard,' said Helena, gazing up at him. 'You will lead us. I personally would like to make a lot of money.'

'When I have the shareholders' approval, I can approach a bank with a detailed plan of what we propose to do and ask for the money. May I take it that you, Helena, and Karen feel you can trust Seb, Jorge and myself to be the board of directors and carry out this business properly?'

'You have my vote, I guess,' said Karen glumly, still not totally convinced of the wisdom of the move.

'Then—'

'Does that mean that we can't come to board meetings?' asked Helena.

'Well, you would only be bored. No pun intended.'

Karen bristled. 'I wouldn't. I could just listen quietly.'

'Karen,' said Sebastian. 'We will not meet all that often, and I will keep you informed. If you are not a board member, you can't just sit in.'

Karen directed an arch look at Jorge. 'George is not a shareholder, yet he's sitting in on this meeting.'

'My name is pronounced *Hor-kay*!' cried Jorge.

'Jorge—' began Richard loudly, then took a deep breath and strove for a quieter tone. 'Jorge is a director, also the company secretary and is taking the minutes of the meeting. That is his job.'

Jorge, of course, was doing no such thing. He had thrown down his pen and was now convulsed, holding his sides and laughing loudly. Richard did wish that Jorge didn't find life one big joke.

'For God's sake, Karen,' said Sebastian. 'Let's get on with it.'

There was a knock on the door. Richard's new secretary, Liz, a no-nonsense married woman of forty-eight with considerable business experience, came in with a message for him on a piece of paper. Sebastian had interviewed a number of women before recommending Liz. Richard had to concede that Sebastian seemed to have done well, judging his own personality and Liz's ability perfectly. He got on with Liz as if they had worked together for years, although he had already discovered that she was rather careless. He gave her a lot of latitude, because she was English and therefore able to prevent a few minor embarrassments.

The paper she placed before him read: 'The environment officer from Braintree Council wishes to see you.'

He turned to Sebastian. 'An environment officer from Braintree. Who would that be and why does he wish to see me?'

'This is a Grade I listed building. The environment officer must give permission for any permanent changes. There are lots of rules, but I don't know them.'

Richard smiled at Liz. 'Tell him to make an appointment. I'm in the middle of a meeting.'

She grimaced. 'I'm afraid he did ring for an appointment. He's a little early, but I told him you would see him this morning. It really is important.'

Richard looked at Jorge, who shrugged. 'Custom of the country, I guess. Anyway, we're finished here. We needn't bore Karen and Helena with any more of this business. I'm sure they trust us.' He smiled engagingly at the sisters, intent on charming them out of further involvement with the detailed planning.

An hour and fifteen minutes later, Richard rejoined the shareholders and Jorge. Jorge stood up immediately and came forward to ask in a whisper if Richard was all right. 'God knows, you look terrible,' he said. 'Is there something wrong?'

'You won't believe it when I tell you,' replied Richard, 'but we'll talk about it later.'

It was one o'clock, and Helena pronounced herself famished. Sebastian suggested that they try the White Hart pub at Great Yeldham, and they all went off to lunch in good spirits. Sebastian was particularly chirpy. He sat back in his chair, saying that he wished he had a Cuban cigar and permission to smoke it, and added that he could sense a real feeling of working together among the shareholders, a coming together for future wealth, a great business being born. One day they would all be as rich as Richard was. His voice grew louder as he spoke, but suddenly he had another thought, and asked Karen who her father was and what relation he had been to Uncle Edgar.

'Aren't you first cousins?' asked Richard.

'Oh, no,' replied Karen, 'our fathers were, I believe, second cousins. I'm not sure. We met once when I was ten and Helena was eight. Do you remember, Seb?'

'At Uncle's home,' said Sebastian. 'He said we three were the younger generation and that we should get to know one another. However, I was seventeen and didn't want to get to know a couple of kids. You see, Richard, we are the last of the line. Uncle Edgar was actually a great-uncle, and there are, alack and alas, no more Races but we three survivors, not counting my daughters who don't want anything to do with the Race family. We're the last remnants of a great line.'

'Listen to him,' giggled Helena. 'And he hasn't even had a drink yet.'

Sebastian grinned at her. 'Uncle Edgar was a hundred when he died, and everybody else went before him. Karen and Helena and I met for the first time in twenty-seven years – may I say that, Karen? – at the solicitor's office. He left bequests to some servants and the cafés to us. We sold the house and contents and got—'

'Fifty thousand pounds each,' murmured Karen. 'Uncle lived extremely simply. He didn't even have electric light or central heating. Mind you, that's probably why he lived so long. But he was a boring old soul. However, enough of that. Let's talk about you two. I've always liked Americans. You men are so much more relaxed, so much more manly. Are both of you married?'

'I am a happily married man with five children,' said Jorge. 'But my friend, Richard, is fancy free. A widower. What about you, Seb?'

'Divorced these last five years, thank God. My wife could take on the witches of Salem and come out on top. I've got twin daughters of twenty, both of them married out of the schoolroom, as they say. I'm single again and intend to stay that way.'

It was not until they were drinking their coffee that Jorge told Richard what decisions had been made in his absence.

'The chain is to be called Miami Spice as the majority of you want it. We will not have tablecloths on the tables, but you and I have been outvoted on the matter of cutlery. The Brits like lots of knives and forks, which will add to costs, but can't be helped. No-one sees the need for large ice-making facilities, because apparently the Brits don't like ice in their drinks, or at least not more than one or two cubes. So that will save money. Oh,' Jorge laughed. 'It seems the Brits do have sales tax after all, but they call it Value Added Tax, and they include it in the prices on the menu by law. And, wait for this, Richard. It's seventeen and a half per cent!'

'Which is perhaps why food is so expensive here.' Richard picked up his wine glass, but found it empty. Coffee was not going to soothe away the irritations of this day. A man accustomed to controlling every facet of his businesses could not be happy that he had been left out of the name-choosing process.

He was operating in a foreign country, in a field that he was unfamiliar with, while being preoccupied with the maintenance and expense of his new home. This was no way to run any business, and he vowed to himself to pay closer attention to the job in future. Jenny's death and his later betrayal could not be allowed to destroy his money-making skills. He would put the past behind him. Nevertheless, his first action on returning to Liz and his office was to ask if there had been any phone calls from Cambridge.

That night when Jorge came over to have a pre-dinner drink, Richard explained to him what the environment officer had said.

'This guy turns up,' said Richard indignantly, 'to tell me that there is a system of listing of old buildings. Now, Gosfield Hall is one of only four per cent of buildings that are Grade I. English Heritage, whoever they are, decide which buildings are Grade I. This building is a national treasure because it dates from 1560 at least. I can't change anything without permission, and getting permission is like pulling hens' teeth. The outside brickwork needs pointing – well, it would, considering that no-one has really taken care of this place since 1958! But, you won't believe this, I can't just get in a bricklayer to point the bricks. I've got to use lime mortar like they did in the old days. It seems the bricks break up if you use the wrong stuff. You know how we've seen all these old houses that look like they're going to fall down? Well, they don't because lime mortar was used. It gives. It bends, but it doesn't crack. Of course, it's more expensive than modern materials and trickier to use. Also, of course, a bit more dangerous for the builder to use. Also, did you know that wet oak leaves make tannic acid, and that tannic acid dissolves lead? Well, we've got dissolving lead on the roof and it needs to be replaced, but with Code 5 lead, whatever that is.'

'This is your house, Richard! You paid for it. Put your foot down.'

Richard laughed. 'I said to Toombs, duck-egg blue is a damned stupid colour for the outside doors on this house. How about glossy black? That always looks smart. And he said, "How about dark green? That is the proper colour." It will take me some time even to get permission to paint the damned doors the colour of *his* choice.'

Jorge was incensed. 'Hey, we got to get ourselves a good firm of lawyers. Fight this. You know what bureaucrats are like.'

'No, I'm not going to fight city hall. This is a very important house. You don't understand. It's so old!

And do you know what? Down in the cellar, there's evidence of an even older house. I've told Frank Toombs that I'll do whatever he says. I want to do it right.'

'How much?' asked Jorge quietly.

'A million maybe. Don't worry. I'll make a profit. You know,' Richard stretched out in his chair and sipped his drink for a moment, the picture of contentment. 'I've been associated with a hell of a lot of properties in south Florida. I know about the construction trade. I know how buildings are put up. But this is different. Something new. It's a kind of hobby. And just think. Karen Race may think she can stick her oar in where the cafés are concerned, but she can't do a damned thing about Gosfield Hall, because she doesn't own so much as one brick.'

'Amen,' said Jorge. 'I'll drink to that.'

Over the next few days Richard devoted himself to his work, hardly noticing the nightly ground frost, the strong winds or the occasional driving rain. Borrowing money was his priority, and, for such a large credit facility, he had to have a copper-bottomed plan.

Three weeks after arriving in England, Richard took his fellow directors into Halstead to visit the manager of Anglia bank. Halstead was an ancient town of ten thousand people, once the centre of Courtauld's silk-weaving business, later the home of parachute nylon. But all that was in the past, as was much of the industry that had relied on the railway. In the Sixties the railway had closed down, changing the nature of the town for ever. It boasted, Richard had been told, a dozen pubs, very few chain stores and a lively sense of community. It also had a football team. Richard, never too interested in history, and knowing nothing about football, nevertheless sensed the community spirit of the town. He liked to joke about coming to the big city when he left the much smaller Gosfield for the delights of its neighbour.

The bank was housed in a very old building that didn't look like a bank at all and had no parking space of its own. One parked on the steep High Street if one was lucky, or miles away and walked. Richard and Jorge were amazed by this arrangement, but a few weeks in England taught them that car parks were afterthoughts, not prime concerns, for businesses of all sorts. Richard had actually suggested that tearing down a few of the old buildings and putting in car parks would do wonders for the town. The stunned reaction to his words from all his listeners in the Bird in Hand one evening taught him that though the two countries might speak the same language, they viewed everything in totally different ways.

The manager of Anglia bank was quite young, very presentable and suitably serious. Clarence Parks seated them all before telling them that the bank had dealt with Flutterby cafés for forty years and wished to continue to have some input. He invited Richard to tell him about the new company's plans.

Richard, speaking for the other two, laid out his proposal.

Clarence Parks didn't reply for a moment, and when he did it was in measured tones. Despite the bank's long association with Flutterby cafés, they could not lend such a large amount. They would give Richard a borrowing facility of three hundred thousand towards running costs, but would need some collateral. Interest would be two per cent over bank rate, making it nine and a quarter per cent.

Parks recommended that the two large sites be purchased on a straightforward mortgage, and that Richard should go to the City and find a merchant banker for the vast sum necessary to do business on such a large scale. 'For you will need an expert to take you into the stock market. You'll need one of those men to guide you.'

Richard then offered the deeds on a small shop unit of his in Deerfield Beach to be collateral for the borrowing facility. Parks said that would be acceptable to the bank.

Meanwhile, Jorge and Maria flew back to Florida and returned within the week accompanied by a distant relation of Maria's who was an executive chef in Miami. For a staggering sum he was willing to develop the menu, organize the suppliers and train the permanent head chef and the staff. There would be little change from twenty thousand dollars for Ramone's six weeks' work, but it was a highly skilled job and essential if the chain was to succeed. Sebastian was put out because the directors had agreed that he should be paid a salary of only twenty-five thousand a year. He thought paying so much to Ramone for just six weeks was unfair. It was pointed out to him that Richard and Jorge were to receive no salary for a year until the chain was viable, and he calmed down.

However, Sebastian Race quickly proved his worth to the organization by finding two large properties within the week, for which the mortgage company was happy to do business. Both were central sites, one in Chelmsford, one in Colchester, and both were being pursued by a brewery chain, Better Brewers, on the lookout for non-pub outlets. Seb outmanoeuvred the opposition rather neatly, and the deal was completed before Better Brewers knew what was happening.

Alan Pledger, the brewery's representative, complained vigorously, but Richard checked the deal and found it perfectly above board. Mr Pledger was left gnashing his teeth as he looked for other prime sites.

The merchant bankers proved disappointing. They were not interested in very small restaurant chains. This left the company eight hundred thousand pounds short of their goal. Then Richard had a happy thought. He remembered having done a little business with a funny Englishman named Nigel Falkland. Nigel was pedantic, rude, humourless and pompous, but he was extremely shrewd and he often took on little ventures like the Miami Spice chain. Richard telephoned him and, fifteen minutes later, faxed all the information about the chain.

Two days later Nigel Falkland arrived at Braintree station, having insisted that a taxi be on hand to ferry him to Gosfield Hall. However, Sebastian was waiting with a piece of cardboard saying 'Nigel Falkland.'

Richard referred to him as their business angel, but Seb saw nothing of the angel about this man from the City. He knew the type. In another incarnation, Mr Falkland would be wearing a bowler hat. Even in these modern times, he wore a blue

81

pinstriped suit, a blue shirt with a stiff white collar, and a tie with muddy diagonal stripes. A bright red carnation was stuck through his lapel buttonhole, and he raised it to his nose as he looked about for his chauffeur. Seb introduced himself as they got into the Rover.

'I knew a Race many years ago. Insurance. Matthew Race,' said Falkland. A small man, he was almost lost in the leather passenger seat. 'Very shrewd.'

'My father!'

'I haven't seen him around for years.'

'The old boy died last year, I'm afraid. Heart.'

'He was a decent man,' said Falkland carefully, then changed the subject to one of restaurants in general and the two Americans in particular. He had, he said solemnly, a great respect for Richard Dumas. Americans could be very dynamic, not to say aggressive, but not always sound. He did think Dumas was sound. Had not Seb found this to be so? Seb nodded dumbly. He found Falkland absolutely terrifying and wondered what Richard made of him.

When they reached Gosfield Hall, no time was wasted on chit-chat. Falkland confessed to a deep desire for a cup of coffee, and this was the only emotion he showed during the entire morning. They trooped upstairs to Richard's apartment, where Falkland took his time examining the furniture, finally saying that it was excellent. Seb was given the credit and received a word of praise.

'Now then, down to business,' said Falkland. He sat down at the large table with his back to the window and began to remove the contents of his black briefcase. He placed a notepad in front of

82

him, lining up the lower edge with the edge of the table. He removed six pencils and two felt-tip pens from the depths of the case, and these he lined up in a row very neatly just above and to the right of the pad. Finally, he withdrew a clear plastic folder which contained the faxes he had received from Gosfield. These were removed from the folder and stacked on the pad. Falkland then took a fountain pen from his inside jacket pocket and cleared his throat.

'These are my terms. I am not interested in a large shareholding, nor am I interested in the long-term future of the business. I am willing to lend the company eight hundred thousand pounds for five years at fifteen per cent per annum. Repayable in five years' time. I must be non-executive chairman and I wish to have a nominal holding. If each of the four shareholders sells me three thousand shares at the present price, that is, four pounds a share, I will make the money available immediately. Of course you will need me and my skills in five years' time when you go public.'

'Fifteen per cent is damned steep, Nigel,' said Richard quietly.

'You could go elsewhere,' murmured Falkland, picking up all the pens and pencils and laying them once more on the table.

Richard didn't answer immediately, then said, 'I think the shareholders will agree. I must put it to them formally of course.'

Falkland looked at Richard and smiled slightly, a terrifying sight. 'I almost forgot. I will need collateral for the loan.'

Now Richard breathed deeply, frown lines going all the way up his bald head. 'You could hold the deeds to this place. To Gosfield Hall.'

Falkland looked around carefully, as if actually assessing the value of the building. 'That will do.'

Jorge apologized for not being able to go to lunch, but Richard and Seb spirited Nigel to Coggeshall, twenty minutes away, where they ate a simple meal at another White Hart, this time a hotel of that name.

As they were coming out of the restaurant, Falkland spied an antique shop across the road. Fortunately, there was very little traffic, for Falkland crossed the road without looking either left or right, leaving Richard and Seb to trot after him. Striding into the small shop without a word to them about his intentions, he immediately went to a suite of furniture that Seb thought looked to be in extremely poor condition. After a brief skirmish with the owner about the price, he bought the three-piece suite, two thousand pounds' worth of Edwardian furniture in a state of complete collapse. Within minutes he had written out a cheque, arranged for delivery in London and returned to the grey winter chill. Sebastian thought he was the most terrifyingly bloodless man he had ever met.

However, at the shareholders' meeting the following day, he kept these thoughts to himself. Karen and Helena each agreed to sell three thousand shares. Richard made Falkland sound like a genuine angel, and the meeting was over in minutes. Later, Karen confided to Seb that she was amused Richard had lost his position as chairman. Being merely a managing director sounded more suitable for the American.

*　　*　　*

Activity was frantic thereafter. The three men worked furiously, arguing with the designers, the builders, the suppliers and Ramone. Nothing was heard from Helena, but Karen wrote to say she thought it would be charming to have the waiters dressed in those dinky little silk shirts with ruffles on the sleeves. Wouldn't it be a hoot? And what about having little dance floors in the bigger restaurants so that customers could rumba or samba, or whatever it was that Cubans did? And how about pictures of Castro and Che Guevara on the walls?

Jorge said that for the sake of peace at home, he would not tell Maria about the last suggestion, since his wife devoted much of her spare time to organizations that fought Castro. The mention of his name was apt to send her into a frenzy of Cuban Spanish.

Richard preferred to spend his time with the builders who were working on Gosfield Hall. They were a large company of specialists who charged, it had been suggested to him, twice as much as any ordinary independent builder would, but Richard did not want a botched job. The house, he was beginning to appreciate, was exceptionally beautiful in its way and very important to the history of Essex. It was Mr Lomax of the building firm who had put him on to Essex Restorers, the very people to restore his painted ceiling. However, it had not occurred to him that the restoration would cost five thousand pounds. Returning the room to its former beauty was going to be more than ten thousand pounds, even before it was furnished.

He had already been told that two miles of piping would be required to heat Gosfield Hall adequately. And it would cost approximately one thousand three hundred pounds a quarter to heat! Resigned to the expense (for he now had an idea how he could make a profit from the house) he intended to finish it to the highest possible standard. However, doing so required a steady nerve.

He turned his thoughts to the promotion of the chain which was to open in March. There would be ads in the magazines *Essex Countryside* and *Suffolk Countryside*, and in the *East Anglian Daily Times*. Promotional space would be forthcoming. There was genuine interest in some quarters in the chain and its exotic food. He felt in his bones that the Miami Spice restaurants were going to take East Anglia by storm. When it came time to offer the shares publicly, they would all make a handsome profit, despite the fact that Falkland was taking such a hefty cut.

His advertisements were punchy and to the point, but the free publicity did not proceed in the way he wished. At nine o'clock on the morning of the agreed day, a photographer from the newspaper had called to take a photo of him. He had tried to tell the journalist that this was not solely his business enterprise, that Jorge was the Cuban whose wife had helped with the menu. He had mentioned that the new Miami cafés were rising from the ashes of the old Flutterbys. To no avail. The paper wanted a photograph of the owner of Gosfield Hall. What was more, they wanted it taken of him standing on the west front by the gate, playing the part of an American country gentleman.

Country Life magazine had also telephoned to discuss running a feature of several pages once the house was properly restored. There was considerably less interest in the cafés, the food they would be serving and the jobs they would create, at least as far as the editors of national newspapers were concerned.

Jorge, who had recently been forced to spend a great deal of time with the homesick Maria, told him to make the most of any publicity opportunities that came along. He offered nothing further in the way of advice as he was this day planning to take his wife to London so that she could satisfy her craving for shops by visiting Harrods and Selfridges.

Sebastian, however, had been at Gosfield all morning. Richard had a sandwich and a Budweiser at his desk, but when he had suggested that Liz find Seb to share lunch with him, he learned that Seb had gone off to entertain someone for lunch elsewhere.

'A word with you, Richard,' he said, putting his head round the door at half past three.

'Come in. I hear you were doing some entertaining.'

'Does that mean you think I'm drunk?'

'I never said so,' said Richard, grinning. 'Sit down, for God's sake, and stop swaying in front of me. You're making me seasick.'

Sebastian flopped into a chair. 'You think I'm worthless to the company, don't you.'

'Come off it, Seb. I think nothing of the sort. On the other hand, you do strike me as the sort of man who can't speak his mind unless he's had a few. So, suppose you get whatever it is off your chest.'

'I saw you having your photo taken this morning, and weren't you just lapping it up. All tweeds and second-rate country gentleman.'

Richard raised his eyebrows at the vicious tone, but sat back in his chair coolly as he tossed his pen onto the desk. 'Bothers you, does it? You'll hate me when I tell you they're going to write about Gosfield Hall in *Country Life*. That's your bible, isn't it?'

Sebastian winced. 'It might be.'

Richard wondered how this scene would play in Seb's head tomorrow when he was sober. He was beginning to feel a little sorry for the Englishman. 'Seriously, I'm sorry about the photo. I promise you, I've tried to get publicity for the cafés, to concentrate minds on what we have to sell. But there seems to be more interest in Gosfield and the novelty of an American owning such an ancient British house.'

'Ah ha! That's just it, isn't it? You tell everybody that old Seb bought this house without your knowledge, that you would never have bought it if you had known what he was up to, yet you love being here. Well, let me tell you—'

'Please do. I've been curious.'

'There you were in Boca Raton in your million-dollar penthouse telling little old me to find you something impressive in England. It had to be an hour from Cambridge, yet no more than an hour from the sea, not too big, not too small, and could be used for offices as well.'

'That is what I told you.'

Sebastian sighed, some of his bombast spent. 'You will know by now that it isn't too easy finding just the right house in this part of the world. I understand there are even waiting-lists in London of millionaires looking for suitable houses in the country. I found Gosfield which was too big for most people and far too run-down and I thought, here's a man who could stop a beautiful old house from dropping to bits. Here's a rich American who could save something precious and British for posterity. I thought, he's so rich and so arrogant, he even gets a business partner to buy a house for him. I thought, here's a man who deserves to have his money spent.'

'It was stupid of me. You will be happy to know that I'm feeling better now. But I understand. I really do. When I first came here, I thought you were a first-class horse's ass to have invested my money in a wreck, but the place is growing on me. I'm beginning to love it. It really is a challenge. So I understand that what you did was no more than I deserve. I think I owe you an apology.'

'Well.' Seb struggled to stand up gracefully. Now totally deflated, he didn't have an exit line ready. 'Well, I just want you to know that I took Carl Bloom out to lunch and told him he was over-charging us for his designs. They agreed a cut of five per cent. Not much by your standards, but—'

'That's terrific! Well done. Jorge will be impressed. He's been griping about their charges for the last two weeks. By the way, he and I are to be on Radio Essex tomorrow. I promise we will keep the interviewer to the subject of Cuban restaurants.'

'That's fine. No, no, not to worry.' Seb began backing towards the door, disarmed, as Richard had intended, by the handsome apology and the ready praise.

When he was gone, Richard shook his head. He had deserved to have Gosfield unloaded on him. It was ironic that he had met dozens of people in the course of attempting to restore it, that his local prestige and possibly the success of the cafés was due, in some measure, to Seb's act of spite. Furthermore, despite the jokes he and Jorge made about the possibility of madness in the Race family, Richard now knew that Seb was a smooth operator. He simply lacked confidence. If the cafés did succeed, it would be in large measure down to this wild-eyed Brit, for Richard had several other things on his mind these days, and Jorge was preoccupied by Maria's loud and disruptive homesickness.

Liz came into his office looking agitated. 'One of the restorers has fallen off his ladder!'

'What was he doing? We haven't had listed building consent to begin. Oh, Lord, that's nearly twenty feet. Is he hurt?'

'I don't know. I've called an ambulance, and his mate is with him.'

Richard rubbed a hand over his head. 'Then call the insurers. We're covered. We're bound to be, but I had better just go out and see how the man is.'

'I'll phone them . . .' Liz said in a small voice.

He turned to stare at her. 'We are covered, aren't we? You sent off the cheque.'

'I've been rather busy. I can't remember. I'm pretty sure that I did.'

He sighed loudly. 'If you need an assistant, please employ one. I must leave that sort of thing to you, Liz.' He shut the door, wondering what the British attitude to suing for compensation might be. He knew he would be in deep trouble if it happened in America. He was halfway down the east corridor when Liz called after him to say she had found the policy.

★   ★   ★

The interview with Ricky Blane went quite well. 'I couldn't get the Cuban music you asked for, Jorge, so I'm going to play a piece by Gloria Estefan.' Ricky switched to the music then told them, off air, that they were terrific and that he thought the interview was going well.

'Let's stick to talking about Cuban food,' said Richard, 'and nothing more about Gosfield Hall. When the music stops, you can ask Jorge about fried milk.'

Afterwards Jorge was a little disappointed that he hadn't had a chance to explain the struggle to oust Castro to Essex listeners, but he was a shrewd businessman and knew that the important thing was to get across that eight new Cuban cafés would be opening in a few weeks.

And then Richard met Fran Craig and the day had to be counted a great success.

Fran arrived at the studio in Chelmsford a full fifteen minutes too early, and sat in the waiting-room listening to the guest before herself. He turned out to be an American who owned a chain of Cuban restaurants in East Anglia that was due to open shortly. No, he said, in a compellingly deep voice, he was not Cuban, but he had come from Florida where Cuban food was extremely popular. He issued an open invitation to listeners to visit one of the cantinas during the first week that they were open. They should watch their local papers for the date. If they mentioned having heard about them on Radio Essex, ten per cent would be taken off the bill.

There was no opportunity to hear the name of these restaurants or their locations, as an assistant came to usher her into the presence of Ricky Blane while the guests' musical choice, a salsa piece by Gloria Estefan, was being played.

She did catch a glimpse of the American as she was introduced to Ricky. His appearance was quite as compelling as his voice. She nodded, smiling as they passed in the corridor. To her surprise, he turned right round and smiled as if he thought she was a celebrity. It was the perfect tonic before going on the air to spend fifteen trying minutes answering questions. She had made some notes, but Ricky told her that reading from them would sound too formal. He reached across his desk and crumpled them up, telling her to rely on her memory. He would ask leading questions, and that way spontaneity would be maintained. It seemed to go well, but she had to concentrate hard. There was none of the free and easy air of the Gypsy Harry filming. But then, lots of people listened to Radio Essex. It had to be good.

When she returned to the waiting-room, feeling like a limp rag, and clutching a cheque for fifty pounds, the American was still there.

'Miss Craig, I recognized you from the television. I just had to wait to meet you. I thought you were wonderful on the Gypsy Harry show. You certainly put him in his place. But you weren't on the last show. Are you not a regular?'

'You saw me? You actually saw me? That's wonderful. You know, I had no idea they would broadcast my contribution. Harry and I didn't exactly hit it off. Amazingly, Ricky Blane says it was the TV show that caused them to call me and invite me here, but really, I don't think Harry knows anything at all about gardening.'

'He looks like a villain. But it was very entertaining television. I don't suppose you get many viewers at ten o'clock in the morning.'

'I've no idea.'

They stood smiling at one another rather awkwardly. He was totally bald, like Kojak or Yul Brynner, but paler. She guessed that, like Kojak and Brynner, he had lost all his hair on top and decided to shave off the rest. It suited him. He had a magnificently shaped head, and with his sunglasses on looked like the richest and most glamorous man on earth. His teeth were perfect and he was about six feet tall, with broad shoulders and narrow hips. She thought his suit must have cost a thousand pounds.

'Did I hear Ricky Blane say you are a garden designer?' He reached inside his jacket and pulled out a visiting-card. 'Will you give me a ring? I would like to have you look over my garden.'

'Of course, I would be delighted.'

A short, heavily tanned man came to join them. 'Miss Craig, I enjoyed your radio broadcast, but I'm afraid I didn't see you on television. However, I have listened many times to my friend's description of your amusing show. I wish I had seen it. My name is Jorge Arnez, a director of the Miami Spice restaurants. Here, let me give you one of our leaflets. You must visit our cantinas. We are opening big restaurants in the High Streets of Colchester and Chelmsford. Do you live close to Chelmsford?'

'No, I'm closer to Colchester.'

The bald American was still looking at her as if he wanted to eat her up. It was terribly flattering and just what she needed to bolster her morale.

'I hope you will excuse us,' said the American. 'We're off to London to join some friends. But do please call me.'

'Oh, I will,' she said heartily. She had managed to read the visiting-card. 'Richard Dumas, Gosfield Hall.' He must be rich, and this was her great opportunity.

She hung back on the pretence of wanting to speak to the receptionist, then hurried to her van when she was sure they had left for London. She knew vaguely where Gosfield was, quite close to Halstead. This would be the perfect time to suss out Gosfield Hall and perhaps come up with some ideas about what to do with Mr Dumas's garden.

It was fully forty-five minutes before she finally found the Hall. Driving slowly down Hall Drive with its deep pits and its traffic bumps, she crowed with delight when the house came into view. It was huge! She parked her van and got out to wander around its magnificent walls in the warm March sunlight, coming eventually to the arch that led to the courtyard. The grounds, though simple and informal, were perfect as they were. What could she possibly suggest that would preserve the ancient trees, the old statuary, the magnificent views of farmland and the ancient church?

Gazing at so much beauty and guessing that it housed an incredibly wealthy man, she felt tears of relief falling down her cheeks and made no effort to wipe them away. 'I'm saved,' she said. 'This is the beginning of the beginning. And he likes me!'

Chapter Four

Colchester, England's oldest recorded town, was always busy. On this March day it was drizzling, and a chill wind was blowing up the High Street. Even so, the pavements were crowded with university students, mums with pushchairs and the elderly.

Helena Race found the shop that was to be the Colchester branch of Miami Spice, noted that its position was opposite the town hall, and frowned at the brown paper stuck to the plate-glass windows to deter the curious. Fortunately, the front door was open, so she went in and quickly found herself surrounded by workmen wearing breathing masks as they sawed and drilled, turning the air into a choking cloud.

'Sebastian!' she called, above the noise. 'Are you there?' A figure emerged through the haze.

'Hello, Helena. How nice to see you.' Sebastian was very happy to see his distant cousin who was looking stunning in a purple suit with a mock leopard fur collar and matching hat. Her clumpy-heeled black shoes and good leather handbag matched her umbrella, giving an impression of quite a lot of money well-spent. 'I'm going to lunch in a few minutes. Will you join me?'

'That's why I came, actually. I want to talk to you. Is Karen the only one who thinks there's something funny going on?'

'She only thinks that because the Yanks didn't appreciate her remarks when she saw the designs for the restaurants.'

Helena giggled. 'She simply said that all we needed was for Carmen to come in with a rose in her teeth.'

'She's got to stop being so sarcastic. Don't you know Americans have no sense of humour? Anyway, they probably think Carmen is a member of the Mafia. Tell her she's got to be polite when we're all together.'

'Karen always makes these little comments when she doesn't feel comfortable. But it is a strange situation, don't you think? Our little English cafés being run by Americans. Karen is also very rude to me, you know. She wants to know why I seem like a fool.'

'She's a brute. That's unforgivable. You are not a fool. You are a pretty, pleasant, polite young woman.'

She picked her way around the large room where the first elements of the design were taking shape. 'A lot of money is being spent to create a hacienda effect on just one wall. The design is terribly kitsch, or at least Karen thinks so.'

'But the rest of us know what we are doing. Think your own thoughts, Helena. Form your own opinions.'

She sighed. The sisters had been sharing Karen's house for just three months, and Helena knew she was going to have to move out soon, before they did each other some permanent harm. She felt that she and Karen were not at all alike, so it annoyed her whenever some well-wisher assured her that the two were almost like twins.

Sebastian picked up his raincoat from the dusty floor and shook it. 'I'll take you to the Café Rouge down the road. Then you can see how our own chain should be designed.'

It was a walk of just two minutes to reach the French-themed Café Rouge, and they were silent on the way. However, once seated on the simple wooden chairs, they looked about them and murmured approval.

'You see?' Seb waved a hand. 'A few simple touches to suggest – suggest mind you – a French café, and that's all that's necessary. Do you remember what it's costing to refurbish all our cafés and build the two new ones?'

'Over half a million. My God, Seb, that is a hell of a lot of money. But nobody is paying any attention to the food.'

He snorted. 'You haven't heard Richard's profound philosophy. "Food's food." He thinks décor and hype are the most important things. Oh, and location. But in fact I have to admit that a lot of thought has gone into the food, its quality, its style, the size of the portions and, above all, its price. Everything down to the last penny. Seriously, Richard's point is, you can have the finest food in the world, but if nobody knows you're open or where you are, or if you charge too much for what you are offering, you will fail. He does think that it doesn't matter whether we offer Cuban or Welsh. You just have to identify your market.'

'And he thinks you should do all the work,' she said quietly, putting her elbows on the table and tucking her hands under her chin.

He smiled at her, but the waitress arrived just then, so he ordered a crisp dry white wine. Being a trifle pompous, he couldn't resist telling the waitress he hoped the carafe would be nice and cold, before suggesting to Helena that they have steak and chips, which were so much nicer when cooked by the French. 'I've something to tell you, but we must wait until we've had some wine. You're going to love this.'

Laughing, she picked up her glass as soon as the waitress had filled it and drank deeply. 'All right, cousin. I have imbibed, so I'm ready for any shocks. Let's hear your news.'

He leaned forward across the little table. 'First off, I must tell you that Karen's joke about having the waiters wear satin shirts with frilly sleeves went down like a lead balloon. And as for having pictures of Che Guevara and Castro on the walls, Jorge was so shocked he didn't even dare to tell his wife!'

'But can't you just picture it? Irony. They don't understand irony.'

'Richard's got it in for me. I bought Gosfield Hall, you know. Chose it, assured him it would suit him perfectly, spent one and a half million dollars of his money.'

'It's a white elephant. Did you mean to screw him that way?'

He thought a moment. 'No, that was not what was in my mind. Buying property for someone else is an impossible task, and a thankless one. He kept going on about how he wanted an impressive house. Well, when the agent showed me Gosfield, not seriously but because he said it had been a commercial property on and off since the war, I suddenly thought – that's it. Richard has so much money that he won't notice having a few millions siphoned off for a good cause, and it's my opportunity to do something for Essex. Don't laugh.'

'Oh, what a hoot,' she cried. 'You wanted that fine old building to be saved for the nation.'

He smiled and reached across the table to squeeze her wrist, spilling some of her wine in the process. 'I knew he wouldn't be able to resist restoring it. And I knew also that he wouldn't be allowed to vulgarize it. Old Toombs is there almost every day. Richard spends all his time trying to justify what he wants done. I think I deserve a medal.'

'So do I, dear.' She bit into her steak, giving him, at the same time, a most sympathetic look. He poured two more glasses of wine, then signalled for another carafe. 'Shall I tell you a trade secret? You know how they put up blackboards in restaurants on which they write the menu? Well, first they wipe it over with something like Coca-Cola. Then they let it dry and the writing looks brighter and doesn't smear so much.'

'And how do you get along with Richard? Is he difficult?'

'Nothing I can't handle. I just marched into his office the other day and I said I knew he blamed me for saddling him with Gosfield and I told him why I had done it. I said I thought here's a man who is begging to have his money spent. He agreed that he deserved what he got. He even apologized for niggling about it behind my back. He appreciates

99

my work. You can bet on that. How's your lunch?'

'Delicious, thank you. The French are such good cooks. I don't know that I fancy Cuban food.'

'I don't know that Café Rouge is actually French, but . . .' He studied her face, saying nothing for so long that she blushed. 'How come you've never married? And don't look so shocked that I've asked. We're cousins of a sort. I have a right to know.'

She put down her knife and fork and reached for a hankie as tears filled her eyes. 'The reason I moved in with Karen is because my life has fallen apart. I was in a long-term relationship. Ten years, would you believe. Oh, I foolishly settled for so little. But I didn't want to be a dried-up virgin like my sister. He's married and so we could really only be together at weekends. He bought me a little cottage in Bocking, and I worked for his firm. Secretarial. I really am very good. Anyway, one day he said his wife had given him an ultimatum. I thought he was going to say that he was getting a divorce, but he chose her because of the children. So I lost my lover and my job. He let me keep the cottage – it's a terrace, actually. I sold it and I'm living off the interest and some temping jobs. Karen's house was our parents'. Mum said she should have it as she was unlikely to marry. Karen's such a dry old stick, always was, even as a child. But I think she's happy. She's sort of a career woman. Works for BT. I'm not exactly sure what she does. Anyway, she couldn't refuse to take me in, but we're getting on each other's nerves.'

'You poor dear. When you're feeling stronger, you can get a really challenging job and rebuild your life.'

'My biological clock is running out! I want

babies. It's all I ever wanted. Why is it I never choose suitable men?'

He watched as she tearfully finished her lunch. She was a pretty little thing. He was proud to call her cousin. Seb was no psychologist, but he believed that women who chose unsuitable men had low self-esteem. Yet how could she not know how attractive she was? He shrugged. His biological clock had a long time to run, and he had no intention of getting involved with any woman who wanted babies.

'Your turn,' she said. 'Tell me about your life.'

'Nothing much to say, really. My father used to tell me that I had no stickability, that I'd come to a bad end. Falkland knew him, by the way.' He looked into the distance, forgetting momentarily that Helena was watching him. What was there to say about a life he considered miserable and without achievement of any sort? 'I lost my wife, my home, the affection of my daughters and my job, in that order. If ever a man made a hash of things, it's I.'

'Did she leave you?'

'She preferred a chap she met at church! I couldn't believe it. He's short and fat, but he does have a good job in Chelmsford. Estate agent, you know the type.'

'Poor you. I suppose she got the house?'

'Yes, and I lost the battle for the love of the girls. It got so nasty, I didn't go to see them for a whole year. I did write and send presents, but I couldn't face the rows and the name-calling. After that, they didn't want to know me. I only found out they were married weeks after the double wedding. Somebody at work told me. Then the company went bust and I haven't worked since.'

'You're working now. You are an important part of the whole operation. Buck up, Seb. You're an executive and company director.'

He smiled wanly. His pretty cousin could say what she liked. His parents had always told him what a fool he was, and his mother had blamed him to her dying day for the fact that her grand-daughters would no longer speak to her. As for his directorship, he didn't know if he wanted the restaurants to succeed because he needed the money and the work, or to fail because that would bring Richard Dumas down a peg. He hated the American, sensing the man's contempt for him. He might laugh with Helena about having stuck Richard with Gosfield Hall, but he would love to own such a magnificent property. Every time a member of the press turned up to photograph Richard posing before the huge house, Sebastian felt physically sick. He patted his jacket in search of a cigarette, before remembering that he no longer smoked, and grinned with effort at Helena. 'Come on, old girl. I've got to get back to work. God knows what those idiots will do if I don't keep an eye on them.'

Fran, in knickers and bra, rummaged through the dirty-clothes basket in search of her favourite blouse. She had already looked in vain in the cupboard. 'On the clothes rack,' she muttered, and ran down the steep narrow stairs to the kitchen. There, draped over the rack, was the much-washed white cotton blouse with the stand-up collar, looking very wrinkled. She made a little leap, retrieved it and took it over to the ironing-board which was still standing following its brief use two days before.

It was ten o'clock, and she had an appointment at Gosfield Hall at half past. In her haste, she knocked the iron off the board onto the brick floor. Then she discovered it would no longer heat up. 'Damn,' she said. 'Damn, damn, damn. What am I going to do?'

Racing back upstairs with the unpressed blouse, she quickly put it on and buttoned up the cuffs and front. Her trousers were black, her best pair. The matching jacket would cover most of the blouse, but what if she were invited indoors for a coffee or something? Her new client would think she was a scruff as soon as she took off her jacket. Taking up the dirty-clothes basket, she turned it upside down, emptying the contents on the floor. Her good turquoise boat-necked jumper gleamed among the muddy jeans and sweatshirts. She sniffed the armpits, decided it would do and pulled it over her head.

There was no time to put her hair up. She examined the parting in the mirror to check for regrowth, gave it a vigorous brushing and allowed it to frame her face. It needed to be professionally cut and coloured. Red was her natural colour, but the white hairs tormented her. She was not ready to let them remain unchallenged. On the other hand, her home efforts had not been at all successful, giving her a harsh red that dimmed her natural colour.

Some foundation, a little lipstick and a lot of mascara completed her preparations. She had been up since five, had worked furiously in the poly-tunnel and out of doors, watering and checking for disease, and she was very tired. There never seemed to be enough hours in the day, and Trevor spent less and less time at home, unwilling to lend a hand even when he was with her. She figured he had a special girlfriend, but he would not discuss the subject. In any case, she was usually asleep by the time he got in at night.

For once there was enough petrol in the tank to get her to her destination and back. She drove like a lunatic, praying she wouldn't be stopped for speeding, and arrived at Gosfield Hall only five minutes late. Her old van looked ludicrous parked next to a BMW and a Mercedes, but she assured herself that it was out of sight of the residents, and went in search of what could be called a front door.

The courtyard seemed to be the right way in. She pulled the bell knob, noting with surprise that the great old doors were painted in duck-egg blue. One of them opened and Richard Dumas stood before her, smiling, wearing a camel-hair jacket, silk cravat, cream shirt and brown trousers with a crease you could slice bread on. She figured he had spent more money on his clothes than she made in a month.

Richard beamed at her, feeling slightly foolish. Could she detect how he felt? For she was even more attractive in the flesh than she had been on television. Her hair was glorious. Genuine red? He didn't care. She began apologizing for being late while trying to control a sheaf of papers and lamenting the fact that she had left her tape-measure behind.

He took the papers from her hands, called up a spare tape-measure from the workmen, and they went outside to assess the grounds, meeting the gardener as they walked.

Jim Hornby had been keeping the grounds under control for the last ten years. He had been in the habit of mowing the lawns once a week, weeding one day a week and making the odd small repair on the outbuildings as he saw the need. Although he had been employed by the previous owners he had been his own boss, doing what he wanted at any time that suited him. The owners had seldom visited Gosfield and never mentioned his work. Being an independent soul of sixty, he had liked it that way.

On the other hand, the new American owner now required him to work five days a week. He had told Richard that there wasn't enough work for a full-time gardener, although he was secretly delighted by his greatly increased wage packet. Ominously, Richard had assured him that a garden designer would soon provide him with additional work.

Richard and Fran walked the grounds so that Fran could chart the position of the huge conifer and deciduous trees which must not be touched. The grounds covered ten acres and were mostly flat. On one side there was a lawn bearing a random planting of rhododendrons which would look magnificent in another couple of months. There was the inevitable collection of outbuildings, some with corrugated roofs, a brick-walled area that she thought she could do nothing with. The covered round structure, open on the sides, next to a conical roof set low to the ground turned out to be a mechanism for a donkey to be harnessed up and led round and round to bring water up from the neighbouring well. A huge tank, partially hidden, was a water reservoir in case of fire.

Fran looked at Richard with trepidation. 'I really

think there is nothing much I can do with this area of the garden. It's the working part of the grounds.'

'Never mind. This isn't really what I wanted to show you. Let's walk on.'

The part of the drive that led to the courtyard on the west side wound its way through some magnificent trees and shrubs, although the impression was one of informality which Fran said was appropriate for a house so old and so large.

When they reached the south front, he hoped to impress her with his new knowledge. 'This is my favourite part of the house. Earl Nugent re-modelled this side, extending it in the centre sometime between 1736 and 1748. On the ground floor is the library, and above is the rococo suite which is where King Louis XVIII lived for two years. It is now my apartment. The house was originally built as a fortified square around a ten-thousand-square-foot courtyard, and the rooms were twelve feet wide, but it has been so altered over the years that no two sides are the same.'

While two sides of the house were brick, the south side was plastered. There were two floors of huge windows, with single and double dormer windows let into the red roof. In the eighteenth century a man of taste had altered this side by building a central ten-by-thirty-foot bay extension, topped by a pediment. On the ground-floor part of the bay were vast arched windows, three across the extension and one on each side of it. The remainder of the windows on this side were rectangular sashes. This style, grafted onto what had been a Tudor structure, was bizarre, yet worked very well.

'I like this side,' said Fran. 'When was the house built?'

'Henry VIII, and later Queen Elizabeth slept here.'

'And you live here alone?'

'I do. I'll show you around inside later. Now this is the view I have from my windows, and I would like to look out on something pretty. Have you any ideas?'

'Yes, I do. I thought we could turn this garden into a broderie parterre. An enclosed garden, very formal with clipped box hedges about a foot high planted in scrolls. Inside the scrolls would be seasonal bedding and outside there would be gravel.'

'*Gravel!*'

She jumped at the ferocity of his reply. 'Well, well, that is . . . I'd better take some measurements. Jim, will you lend me a hand?'

'Huh!' said Jim Hornby with great scorn. He had been following them uninvited as they walked the grounds. He moved quickly to take up the other end of the tape-measure, but he was unconvinced of the wisdom of employing this woman. 'What the rabbits don't eat, the deer will. Of course, if you're going to have gravel, you might manage well enough.'

To her dismay, Fran eventually discovered that the area of grass outside the south front was one hundred and seventy feet by forty-five, with a pond twenty feet across. This small portion of the grounds was larger than anything she had ever worked on, and awkwardly shaped as well.

'I said the garden here would be enclosed.' Fran frowned at the gardener. The man had decided she was the enemy. She would have to see what she could do to bring him round. And what would it cost to enclose over seven and a half thousand square feet? She bit her lower lip, then suddenly smiled. 'Do you see how the ground slopes down slightly? Well, I would make a broderie parterre just of that comparatively small part. Here, I have a picture.' She pulled a much-folded illustration out of her pocket. It had been torn from a magazine and was terribly creased.

Richard studied it carefully. 'It's very symmetrical and stiff.'

'Well, yes.'

'And lots of clipping to do,' added Jim, looking over Richard's shoulder.

'What about the pond?' asked Richard. 'I see that in the picture, the pond is in the centre of the design. But our pond is set off to one side.'

It was a cold day, but Fran could feel the sweat trickling down her sides. The pond was off-centre and it would need clever treatment. A designer with more experience than she had might know instantly how to incorporate a twenty-foot raised pond which extended out from the rectangle of lawn. At the moment, her mind was a complete blank. Why had she thought that her new client would like whatever she proposed? And why hadn't she remembered that the pond was not central to the lawn after her visit the previous day?

'We'll work out something,' said Richard smoothly. 'Thank you for pointing out the difficulties, Jim. We must all co-operate on this for the good of Gosfield Hall. I am the caretaker of a precious building and must consider everything carefully. Anyway, Frank Toombs will tell us what we can and can't do. We won't keep you from your work any longer.'

'When we get indoors, I'll show you some draw-ings,' said Fran when Jim had reluctantly departed. 'I want to have this parterre planted with tulips for a spring show. I'm sure we can get around the problem of them being eaten. There is a particular reason why I want you to have tulips.'

'I can't wait to hear it. Let's go in through the door on the east side. It leads directly into the grand salon and I've managed to get going on this room in a very short space of time.' They didn't speak at all as they walked a hundred yards to the middle of the east side. He opened one of the huge doors and ushered her into the room that had struck him as cold, ugly and in terrible condition when he first saw it. Today it hummed with life as the restorer was perched on scaffolding between two tall ladders carefully painting the central panel of *Minerva Presiding Over the Arts*, while decorators were painting the walls. The fresh colours glowed, and Richard could now imagine what the finished room would be like. Fran gasped with delight and hurried over to the marble fireplace to caress the four fishtailed boys which appeared to hold up the mantelpiece. 'Italian work,' said Richard with pride. 'Frank Toombs told me. Probably late eighteenth century. And the ceiling was painted by Sir James Thornhill who worked on the Painted Hall at Greenwich Naval College.'

'It's so beautiful, it makes me want to cry,' she said passionately. 'How wonderful to own such treasures. Did you know how important the house was when you bought it?'

'I'm afraid not. However, I am beginning to love every brick. It's just that this house is hardly suit-able for one widower. Do you have a large family?'

'I'm divorced. Just one son, at college. But we must leave the restorer in peace. Where can I show you my plans?'

'We'll go upstairs to my apartment. But first, will you take a look at the hallway? I wondered if you had any ideas on how to make it less gloomy. The floor has been cleaned up and polished, but I can't like those damned light fittings.'

The long hall was at least six feet wide, its white stone flooring set in a diamond pattern with small black intersecting diamonds. The very large small-paned windows admitted the grey March light, but the impression was gloomy and institutional. Fran heaved a sigh of relief. Basically, the hall was very beautiful. It needed to be furnished, but that could easily be done.

'What do you think?'

'I could do something here. Shall I?'

'Please. Now come upstairs and see how I'm roughing it here.'

She was plainly overawed when he opened the door to his apartment. He was pleased with her reaction, although, personally, he preferred simpler furniture and a homelier, pared-down style.

Fran spread out her plans on the round mahogany table, really just a few rough sketches and some colour photocopies of knot gardens and other sorts of parterres. 'Now, you see here that I've drawn a geometric design for the beds which would be edged in box hedging. Between the beds there are gravel paths, and the central feature is the pond and fountain. I forgot that the pond isn't in the middle, but I can adapt this plan. Isn't it pretty?'

'I'm not at all sure. This is so different from anything I've ever seen. Are you sure this is what I should have? I think I should ask the man from English Heritage next time he visits us.'

'You might want a raised mount on one side where you can sit and look at the garden. Or over here somewhere I could build a small maze. Now, as for the clipped greenery, we could take some design from the house, some carving perhaps and reproduce that in box and lavender or . . .'

Richard made some noncommittal noise in his throat, neither yea nor nay, and suddenly Fran saw her plans as over-zealous and inappropriate.

She looked out of the window. A couple of magnificent stone deer on each side of this south range would have to be incorporated in the design. 'The yews would stay, of course. But they could be trimmed and other yews planted.'

He frowned. 'Yes. Yes, of course. Very unusual. It's rather formal, isn't it?'

'You don't have to have it. I mean, I could design something much more informal.'

'Not so fast. It's just that I haven't seen anything quite like . . . I was expecting something more . . . Isn't this type of garden a lot of work?'

'I'm afraid it is.' She began nervously shuffling her papers across the table. 'I could do anything you like, you know. It's just that this would sort of fit in with the house. And think how lovely it would look from your windows.'

'That's true. I wonder what Frank Toombs will have to say about it. He's the man who tells me what I can and can't have. In the meantime, you might make a few other drawings. Of something totally different.'

'Yes,' said Fran doubtfully. 'I could do that.'

'And what about the tulips? Where do they fit in?'

'They would be planted in the beds to bloom in the spring in the spaces of the design. Then in the summer they would be taken out and bedding plants put in. But, as you say, that's a lot of work.'

'Why, in particular, did you want me to have tulips?'

'Oh.' With hands that shook very slightly, she gathered up all her papers and replaced them in the folder. 'It's just that I looked up the history of tulips after I met you and I thought it would be appropriate.'

'I don't believe I've ever seen a tulip growing. Are they in bloom all the time?'

'Good God. I don't suppose they do grow in Florida. They bloom in April and May, and some in June, depending on the type. They were discovered in mountain ranges near the Russian–Chinese border. They are found naturally very high up in mountains, which is why none of them grow in Florida, I guess. They were introduced to Holland in 1593.'

'Sort of the right period.'

'Yes, but that's not the only reason I wanted to see them here at Gosfield. In 1600 the very first tulips were planted in England, but people didn't go quite so mad for them as they did in Holland. For the next thirty odd years, the tulip grew in importance. No Dutchman who considered that he had taste was without a collection. Then the middle classes went crazy for them, and shop-keepers. One man in Holland paid half his fortune just for one bulb to keep in his conservatory to impress his friends.'

'Interesting, but I don't see—'

'Now tulips in those days were subject to a

disease which made them weak, but also caused them to have the most beautiful streaked, feathered and flamed colours. And people who grew them never knew until the bulb bloomed what it was going to be. The demand for rare species was so great by 1636 that regular markets were established on the Stock Exchange in Amsterdam and other towns. They started buying and selling tulips that were still in the ground.'

'Futures!' cried Richard, now understanding why Fran thought tulips would amuse him.

'Then some people began to say that it couldn't last. When the bulbs were ready for sale, people wouldn't or couldn't pay the price they had promised.'

'Hey, that's really fascinating. I like the idea of owning tulips. Are you going to show me some?'

He was smiling at her, but the intensity of his gaze made her nervous. There was definitely something sexual in his manner, which disconcerted Fran. She had had her share of men making passes at her since her divorce, but none of them had seemed interested in her the way Richard Dumas did. 'I'm going to show you lots of things you've never seen,' she said, then decided that this sounded like a come-on. 'Horticulturally, that is. You could fly over to Holland in the spring and see the magnificent displays.'

'Not without you.'

'I'd be happy to accompany you, Mr Dumas, but about this garden . . .'

'Look, you're going to have to come up with some more designs. This is just not what I'm looking for. Suppose I give you a cheque. You keep an account, and when you have spent it all, I'll write another cheque. That way, you won't have to come to me every time you want to purchase something.'

'But we haven't decided whether you want something formal like my plan.'

'No, because I'm not sure,' he said, getting up from the table and heading towards his office. 'But you're going to do something for my hallway. Remember? And what about your time? I must pay you for your time.'

Fran got up from the table and walked around the room, ostensibly to admire the marble columns that marked the beginning of the extended front, but in reality to test the strength of her legs. It had been a heady morning, both good and bad.

She guessed that the main room was about fifty feet long by twenty wide, and that was before taking the extension into account. There were other rooms, too, reached through handsome mahogany doors with heavy broken-pedimented overdoors. She couldn't believe she was actually standing in such a glorious room, nor that she was about to receive a cheque for her designing work.

Unfortunately, her knees were unwilling to support her, her mouth was dry and her mind a virtual blank. For some reason, it had not occurred to her that her first design might not meet with approval. She had no idea what to try next. As he was clearly a man who had never in his life given a thought to gardens, she couldn't figure out what might please. Fortunately, she did have some ideas of what to do in the long hallway. She would busy herself with house plants and containers, plinths and statues for a while. With luck, something would occur to her that would be suitable for a garden on the south front.

'Here you are. You'll want to put this into a separate account at your bank.' Richard handed her the cheque, and she glanced at it briefly.

'A thousand pounds. I think I can do—'

'Ten thousand,' he said firmly. 'Always look at figures carefully. There have been some terrible disasters caused by people being careless with figures.'

'Ten thousand? I couldn't take this, Mr Dumas. Oh, it's too much.'

'Put it away,' he said. 'Excuse me while I get my coat. Haven't you got a coat? Aren't you cold? It's freezing outside. I'll take you to the White Hart at Great Yeldham. Have you been there? It's any American's idea of what an old English pub should look like.'

'No, I've never been.' She was sure it was too expensive for her. She had passed it many times and wondered what it might be like to eat there. It seemed that this man was intent on spoiling her. It was rather a strange feeling to know that a rich and powerful man was taken with her. She wouldn't put it higher than that. She couldn't say that he was in love or lusting for her. But he was definitely interested. A cheque for ten thousand pounds now rested in her handbag as proof of that fact. What an extraordinary thing for a clever business man to do! She was willing to bet he wasn't so free with his money as a general rule.

They sat in the bar of the White Hart, in easy chairs before the fire. Fran had asked for a glass of white wine, being unable to think of anything more interesting. Richard had Jack Daniels, ice and ginger ale, and they both studied the large menu. The prices frightened her, the food seemed exotic and elaborate, and she had no idea what the chef was talking about when he described half the dishes.

'Oh, this looks good. I think I'll have the sausages and mashed potatoes.' Congratulating herself on having found a dish she understood, she thought gleefully that she could fill up at lunch and not need to have more than a couple of slices of bread in the evening. She remembered, as the wine hit her empty stomach, that she had not eaten breakfast.

'Would you like a first course?'

'No, but perhaps they have some interesting puddings.' She gave him her warmest smile. 'I know nothing about you. How did you happen to come to England to open a chain of Cuban restaurants? I mean, you're not Cuban yourself, although I know your friend is.'

'My business is Business with a capital B. I like to take a company that has fallen on hard times, or perhaps never got off the ground. I read the balance sheets very carefully indeed, see where they're going wrong, buy it or get a controlling interest and set about fixing the problem. After the company is up and running, I sell it on to people who are able to run it properly.'

'Are you what's called a corporate raider?'

He looked slightly annoyed. 'I've been accused of it. My definition of a corporate raider is of someone who is seriously rich. Either personally or through a company he owns, he begins to buy shares in the target business. The directors, to protect the status quo, try to enhance the value of the shares. Then the corporate raider sells his shares at a profit. But you're probably thinking of an asset-stripper. He's a real villain. He'll look for a company with huge reserves hidden in under-valued properties which were not being run beneficially, that is beneficial to the shareholders. The guy will buy a controlling interest or take over the company. Then he revalues the properties. He'll sell these properties for cash, most of which will come to him. Then he will sell the company for a profit, or he will offload his shareholding. Whatever. And make a second killing. I'm not an asset-stripper, either. I believe our table is ready.'

She stood up, gulping the last of her wine. 'I didn't mean to be offensive. I never thought about it. The words just came out of my mouth. Do forgive me.'

'Don't worry, I'm not offended. Most people have no idea about business. The perception is that all businessmen are thieves, lining their own pockets. But incorporated or limited companies have to be run properly or there are terrible penalties. I pride myself on being honest. I play it by the book. I pay my taxes.'

Fran, who paid cash whenever possible to avoid VAT, who had started her business with stolen plants, concentrated on the huge dish of buttery mashed potatoes and exquisite sausages that had been set before her.

'Now, about firing people—' he said.

'I'm sure you don't do that.'

'Well, look at it this way. The ship is sinking and there's one lifeboat which will hold twenty people. There are forty in the water. If they all try to get into the lifeboat, they will all drown. However, twenty can be saved.'

'Difficult to know who should be saved, I guess.'

'Those who can pull their weight. That's who. A

lot of managers can't help empire-building. They take on people in their department, even though they don't really need them, and the company is going down because of this overload of staff. Or, more likely, the managers, especially the chief executive, aren't up to the job of running the company. Running a business is all about figures. You've got to know money. And you've got to keep your eye on the ball. Some men rise to the top of their companies, or their own business is doing really well, and they begin to take it easy. They develop a passion for boats, say, and they're always out on the water, when they should be minding the shop. Or, they meet a bimbo who screws them brainless. Or, the State Governor or maybe even the President wants their time as advisers and they're flattered out of their tiny minds. Maybe they get the society bug, buy a big house, the wife tries to launch herself into high society. I've seen it all. What it amounts to is taking your eye off the ball. And it's not fair to the workers. They deserve to have their company well run.'

'So, the chain of restaurants . . . ?'

'A little different. Sebastian Race and two cousins inherited the chain from an old uncle who had let them run down. Seb wanted to maximize the inheritance, so he advertised in the *Financial Times* for someone to buy in. I saw the ad and wanted to try my hand at running something in England. I put in some money, brought in Jorge Arnez, came up with a business plan that the bank liked and we borrowed enough from the bank and other interested parties to really do something on a larger scale.'

'And when it's a success, you'll sell your share.'

He smiled. 'Probably. I'm a self-made man and that's how I've done it.'

On the way back to Gosfield Hall Richard told her about businesses he had saved in Florida. Unfortunately, Fran fell asleep in the car, and heard very little until the words, 'I'm sorry to bore on like this,' penetrated to her subconscious and sounded a warning. One simply didn't fall asleep on a man who had just given one a cheque for ten thousand pounds.

'I've been up since five o'clock this morning. Do forgive me. I run a small nursery, as well as other things and I'm awfully tired.'

'Too tired to drive? I could take you home, and you could come in by taxi tomorrow. You've had a few glasses—'

Fully awake now, she recognized her danger and vehemently refused a lift. How could she possibly let him see where she lived? He'd never trust her again!

They parted standing by her dusty van. She promised to provide just the right touch for his hallway which looked out over the courtyard. He invited her to dinner the following evening. He had heard that a place called Le Talbooth was pretty good. Pretty fancy. She might want to dress up. She agreed that she would be all dressed up for the occasion (wondering the while what she could possibly wear) and shook his hand gratefully.

Driving carefully to the bank in Halstead, she wrestled with her conscience all the way. Once at the cashier's window, she hesitated only a few seconds before putting the cheque into her own account, thus wiping out a worrying overdraft. She had a frightening debt to a man in Enfield, as well as some pressing bills to pay, and what could be the harm of taking a few thousand pounds from ten thousand? She would do more than enough to earn her fee. And she would make sure she concealed her new wealth from Trevor. She loved him deeply, but she knew she could not resist his entreaties if he discovered she actually had money to spare.

Chapter Five

Richard walked slowly back to his office on what he had learned to call the ground floor and greeted Liz.

'Good afternoon,' she said, glancing up from her computer. 'Everything settled with the designer? Because I've had half a dozen calls for you all requiring attention.'

'I'll take them in a minute. Look, Liz, I have made a rather unusual arrangement with Fran Craig, one that I would prefer to keep quiet about. She's clearly on her uppers and so I gave her a cheque in advance from my personal account. Now, it might look foolish, but I've based my career on knowing when to trust people and when not to. So, I think it will be all right. I've given her ten thousand pounds to be getting on with. She should have something to show for it very soon. I'm expecting her to try her hand at making the hallway look a bit more inviting.'

'You could hire an interior designer.'

'Maybe I will later on. I wanted to see what she could do with the hallway. I'm not quite satisfied with her design for the garden on the south side. She's going to have another go.'

'I certainly never talk about what goes on in this office, Richard.'

'Of course not,' he said, picking up a letter that had arrived in the morning post. 'It's just that I've seen Seb Race in here quite often.'

'There's nothing to worry about in that,' she said, rather too vehemently. 'We occasionally go to the pub for a drink after work. That's not personal, just socializing before going home. I'm a married woman, for heaven's sake! If I thought . . . but no-one, I'm sure would imagine that we—'

'It's OK, Liz. Your life is your own. Just don't tell Seb anything about my personal affairs. My life is my own, too.'

He put down the letter and left the office without asking about his phone calls. Liz gave a silent whistle. She knew she shouldn't encourage Sebastian, but he was so pleasant, and her husband was being such a pain at the moment. It was nice to have a glass of wine and talk to someone interesting for half an hour.

As for Richard Dumas, she thought her new boss was being given the run-around by the bottled redhead. She assumed he had only been willing to give Fran Craig such a large cheque because she demanded it. Surely a shrewd businessman would not hand over so much money otherwise.

Richard returned. 'I'm sorry. What were the phone calls?'

'The cabinet-maker can't start work tomorrow. He hasn't finished his present commission. He thinks he might be able to start in ten days' time. Geoff Stone telephoned from his apartment. He wanted to call a plumber, as the toilet in their flat is not working. I told him to go ahead.'

'You're very good at handling all of these calls, I'm sure.'

'*The Times* wants to do a piece on you for their business section. I forgot to tell you yesterday. Can you be interviewed on Thursday? The photographer will take a little longer. He wants some photos of you here and also in Colchester or Chelmsford. The phone call that absolutely must have your attention is the one from Seb. He says the shop fitting has gone all wrong at the Harwich site. The carpenters got the measurements wrong, would you believe? The café will not be ready to open on time. What do you want to do about it?'

'We're already a week late from our most recently announced date, and three weeks behind my original schedule. We'll open as planned. It really is too late to recall all the invitations. Ring Seb and tell him. Why didn't you pass this message on to Jorge?'

'He's taken his wife to Lakeside.'

'What is it?'

'A shopping mall about fifty or sixty miles from here on the M25. It's huge, although I'm sure there are bigger ones in Florida. It's my fault, I'm afraid. He said his wife is driving him crazy because there are no malls around here, so I told him about Lakeside. Oh, and Mrs Arnez telephoned first thing this morning to say that she will expect you to have dinner with them this evening. Half past six.'

'Oh, happy day,' he said dryly, 'dinner with Maria is just what I wanted,' and went out again.

After leaving the bank, Fran planned to visit a garden-ornament supplier to buy some plinths, a few stone tubs and some statuary. Thoughts of dinner the following night diverted her, however. As soon as she got behind the wheel of the van, she drove into Colchester. First, she bought a packet of envelopes and stamps, and made out four cheques, paying off the bills she had been carrying in her handbag for a month. There was a pressing need to do so quickly, as she owed money on her Barclaycard, and wanted to make some immediate purchases on it.

Her conifer supplier had refused to send her anything more until she settled his account, which was another hundred pounds. Several smaller bills were also settled, leaving Richard's ten thousand pounds with a thousand-pound hole in it.

She was stealing his money, and the knowledge left her sick with guilt. Yet, what else could she do? A surge of panic and anger brought the blood to her pale cheeks. He shouldn't have given her the money. It was his fault. Didn't he realize that the temptation to set her affairs straight would be overwhelming? However, she told herself desperately, she would keep all receipts so that she could eventually account for all the money. This commission was sure to bring others, and then everything would be all right. Meanwhile, she would make sure she gave him value for money. And she would see about his naked hallway just as soon as she'd bought herself something to wear to dinner the following night. He wouldn't want her to shame him at a posh place like Le Talbooth, would he?

Debenhams yielded a devoré velvet scoop-necked dress in rich green which was not only flattering but cheap. She had a decent black coat, but needed a pair of black suede shoes, because the pair she had were nearly bald. Courts were a sensible choice, she thought, or they would be if these new ones were not quite so high. She mentally shrugged as she strove to walk around the shop gracefully. She had to have them. They looked good on her legs and, besides, Richard was a very tall man. Less exciting but more important, she had to buy a new iron and a bra.

It was now too late to buy anything for Gosfield Hall, so she went home. A huge wash-load of her own clothes, followed by another of Trevor's, left puddles from the leaking washing-machine on the kitchen floor. Briefly, she flirted with the idea of buying a new one with Richard's money, but managed to put the wicked thought behind her.

She dried everything that didn't need ironing on a rack before the fire, and ironed dry everything she thought was urgent, while a lasagne for Trevor bubbled away in the oven.

At seven, she gave up waiting for Trevor and ate dinner alone. At nine, she put the lasagne in the fridge. At half past nine, she went to bed, vowing to rise at five.

In the event, she didn't wake up until half past seven. Trevor had already eaten his breakfast of toast and cold lasagne, and was on the point of leaving the house.

'What are you doing today, Mum?'

'I've some things to pick up for Gosfield Hall. I've got the account, darling! This is my first real break. Mr Dumas is taking me out tonight to discuss the projects, so don't expect me to get your dinner.'

'Great. Give us a tenner.'

She went over to her handbag. She had left

125

twenty pounds in her purse for just such a request. However, there was only a ten-pound note left. 'You've already had ten pounds, you little brat. Get out.'

'It must have been burglars. Come on, Mummy dearest.' He grinned at her in his cheeky way, and so, as he knew she would, she gave him the other ten. He blew her a kiss and left the house.

Although it was late, Fran thought she could do everything that was necessary in good time. She ran out to the polytunnel and began gathering house plants, including those which she had planned to sell on the market. Four spider plants, three Boston ferns, two arcca palms, and every philodendron, *Scindapsus*, rex begonia and asparagus fern she possessed. While some of the plants were large, others were quite small. However, she didn't want to buy any plants, as she planned to charge Richard full price for tiddlers in order to write off some of the money she had already spent on other things.

A dangerously speedy journey to the stoneware supplier enabled her to buy six decorative stone containers and as many plinths, five urns, and one statue of Venus trying to hide her nudity with a piece of cloth, and still arrive at Gosfield Hall by noon. The van's suspension was just about up to the load, and she drove off carefully with very nearly a thousand pounds' worth of brand-new garden ornaments. At Gosfield she drove into the courtyard, with the gardener in hot pursuit. When he got up to the van, she told him firmly that he must help her unload and get all the stoneware into the hallway. Richard's secretary strode up to her with a very fierce look on her face to say that he and his colleagues had gone to lunch in Colchester.

'That's great,' she told Liz, 'I will be able to set this all up before Mr Dumas gets back. I do hope he likes the effect.'

'I'm sure he will,' said Liz with heavy sarcasm. 'But all these stoneware pieces are new and not particularly well-made! They must have come from a garden centre.'

'Yes, but they give a perfectly adequate effect.'

'For Gosfield Hall?' asked the secretary pointedly. 'I don't know if Mr Dumas wants his ancient and important house filled with moulded concrete, or whatever these things are made of.'

Fran, who had just directed the gardener and two other workmen to set Venus on a plinth, now looked at her purchase through other eyes. The mouldings were crude. The pieces had been aged by artificially darkening all the intricate creases. In an ordinary garden, covered in moss, viewed from a distance through trees and shrubbery, they might look quite acceptable. But here? Fran was riven with doubts.

'Mr Dumas gave me some money to do something for this hall. He gave me nowhere near enough to buy genuine marble statues, so this is what he must have intended.'

The secretary said nothing for a moment, looking with distaste at the containers that Fran had ordered to be set on low plinths before each window. 'You may be right,' she said at last.

One of the bowls held the handsome *Asparagus plumosus*. In another was her old friend the spider plant from which Fran had taken dozens of cuttings. 'Later, I'll put in some flowering plants,' she told Liz and Jim Hornby. Neither replied. 'Now, Jim, I want one plinth against the far wall directly opposite each window, all the way down. Oh, I'm sorry. I'm spilling the compost. I should have brought some plastic sheeting.'

'You're making a right mess,' said Jim, kindly. 'Mrs Morgan, you'd better send for Harriet Stone. She will be pleased!'

Fran worked on, planting up the troughs and urns, placing the plinths and statues to her satisfaction. When she had finished she walked to the far end of the hall, close to Liz's office, and looked back to see what the effect was.

Liz had joined her and now stood by her side. 'Rather pretty. It certainly gives some warmth to this hallway. Mr Dumas was unhappy with it, said it looked like a hospital corridor.' Her tone suggested that she was rather surprised, but she offered Fran a more friendly smile than she had earlier, before saying, 'He will want an account of what you have spent here. You know, to keep a record of where the money is going.'

Fran nodded vaguely, busy fussing with a spider plant that didn't need any attention. 'Yes, of course. I'll bring one this evening. Mr Dumas and I are going out to dinner.'

Liz lifted her eyebrows, but said nothing.

The phone was ringing when Fran opened her own front door. It was Sean.

'Hey, Fran, this kitchen is going to cost a bit more than I expected. I'll need another couple of hundred. Have you got it?'

'Yes, but when are you coming?'

'No, sweat, sweetheart. I'll be there a week on Saturday. Put a cheque in the post tonight. Promise? I need the dosh. Trevor is coming down on the Thursday if he can get out of a few classes, otherwise on Friday afternoon. I'll bring him back with me and we can get your kitchen looking halfway decent.'

Fran sighed with pleasure. 'Oh, Sean, I'm so pleased. Thank you for doing this for me, darling. I'll go and write the cheque right this minute. Don't worry. I'm going out to dinner and I'll pop it into the first postbox I pass. Bye.'

At seven o'clock exactly, she rang the doorbell of Gosfield Hall. Richard came from the direction of his office to let her in, but he arrived so quickly she thought he must have been hovering just out of sight in the hall.

'Come in, come in! You look terrific. Let me take your coat, although we'll be going in a moment. I understand it will take us half an hour to reach Le Talbooth. It's in Suffolk.'

'I know,' she said quietly, slipping out of her coat and giving him a chance to admire the green dress which fitted her rather snugly. 'What do you think of your hallway now?'

'Brilliant. Really. I mean it. It's wonderful. Just needs a few pictures on the wall. I'll have to ask for your help in several other places.'

'Your secretary thought I should have bought genuine old statuary, instead of this modern moulded stuff. But you didn't give me . . . that is, you'd have to buy it at auction or an architectural salvage place and some of those pieces cost more than you gave me altogether.'

'Liz told you that? How helpful of her. It is all exactly as I want it. Don't pay any attention to her. Do as I wish, not as my secretary wishes.'

As they passed through Halstead, he pointed to

the Bird in Hand. 'I eat there quite often. Everybody talks to me.'

'Why shouldn't they?'

He shrugged. 'I don't know. It's just that people tend not to talk to me in Boca Raton. Perhaps the guys at the Bird think I'm lonely and in need of company.'

'And are you?'

'Not now.' He turned his head to smile at her, and she felt a slight nervous pressure in her chest. His admiration confused her, making her even less sure of how to behave in his company. He drove with casual expertise, seemingly at home even on obscure little lanes while driving on what to him was the wrong side of the road. She tried to make conversation, but to her own ears, it sounded forced.

She was awestruck when they reached Le Talbooth. The old building had been sensitively modernized and lay in an idyllic position next to the river Stour. The menu was comprehensive and, to her mind, rather exotic. She floundered, hesitated, then told Richard frankly that she didn't know what to have. He ordered for her, and she began to relax. She didn't care what she ate, so long as she didn't do anything gauche.

The meal lasted for two hours, about an hour and fifty minutes more than Fran was accustomed to spending on dinner. And even after two hours the evening wasn't over, for they had coffee in the lounge. By the time they got into the car for the journey home, Fran was pleasantly tired and in a mellow mood. Richard didn't speak on the way back to Gosfield, allowing her to sleep.

'Fran, wake up. We're at Gosfield. You've slept for half an hour.'

She jerked awake, incoherently mouthing excuses and apologies. 'Up early. Terribly sorry, really I am. What must you think?'

'I think you work too hard. You need more rest. Don't think you have to kill yourself working for me. You had better come in for a cup of coffee. You'll never stay awake to drive home. You did come over in that rust bucket of yours, didn't you?' he teased.

'Yes, but I'm all right. I'm sober, I promise you.'

'I should have picked you up at your home this evening. What kind of gentleman am I?'

'No, no. Much better this way,' she said. She didn't add that Toppesfield could have been easily reached off the Sudbury road they had taken to the restaurant. She hoped he would never find out where she lived, but he was a curious man and couldn't be trusted never to turn up on her doorstep.

Once in his apartment, Richard struck a match to the carefully laid fire in the grate, and made the coffee himself, very strong and very black. Nevertheless, Fran could barely stay awake and soon stood up to walk around. She must not fall asleep here.

Dance music began to play, coming from the next room. She turned and found Richard so close that it was only natural to slip into his arms as he led her in a slow, rather inexpert two-step. In spite of his height, they fitted together very well. He wasn't a good dancer, but just to be held and danced with was such a novelty for her that she almost purred with pleasure.

He was a very nice man and, incredibly, he found her attractive. It did a great deal for her fragile ego

131

to know that a rich and successful man should want to spend time with her. Almost without thinking about it, she reached up and patted his cheek tenderly. He clasped her hand and held it tightly, kissing the palm.

'Mmm, nice,' he said, 'but I'd rather you touched a more intimate part of me.' Her eyes flew open, but he simply brought her hand up to touch the slight, invisible fuzz that circled his bald head where he hadn't shaved closely enough. She burst out laughing, and she was still laughing when he kissed her. She didn't resist, didn't attempt to draw away, just gave way to the feeling of joy, the illusion of being loved and desired. Bliss.

There was no time to wonder what and where the kiss might lead to, because the phone rang. Richard, who had seemed so intent on pressing his mouth to hers, broke away abruptly, a preoccupied look on his face.

'Answer it.'

'Let it ring,' he said.

'It's somebody important. Answer it.'

He kissed her quickly on the nose, before hurling himself at the phone.

'Hello? Hello? Is that you, Zoe?'

He held the phone out from his ear. She could hear the faint buzz of a disconnected line.

Crossing the room, she took the receiver from his hand. 'Look. One, four, seven, one. Wait. Ah, a Cambridge number. Where's a pencil?' She snatched it from him and scribbled a number on his Yellow Pages. 'There you are! Your mystery caller. Do you know the number?'

He reached into an inside jacket pocket and retrieved a scrap of paper. 'My daughter. She's married an Englishman and lives in Cambridge. He's some sort of scientist.'

Fran smiled at him affectionately. 'Have you had a terrible row with her?'

'Nothing so emotional. You might say we are estranged. I've been hoping for weeks that she would call.'

'Then you must ring her back immediately.'

He was torn, rubbing his head and pacing in a small circle. 'I'll call her tomorrow.'

'No,' she said, going in search of her coat. They had come so close to something disastrous. Here was her chance to escape. She smiled at him warmly, her hand on the doorknob. 'Ring her tonight. Strike while the iron is hot. I'm going home.'

'Wait! Will I see you tomorrow?'

'No, I'm busy.'

'We're having a cocktail party a week on Friday at six at the Colchester Miami. The chain opens on the Saturday. Everyone will be there. You'd enjoy it.'

'I can't. I'm tied up that weekend. I'm sorry, but you really should ring your daughter. I've got a good idea. You can invite her and her husband to the cocktail party. Please, Richard, ring her or you'll never forgive yourself. Bye.'

It took Fran ten minutes to find her way out of the house. Every door seemed to lead to another stairway or another cluster of icy empty rooms, but the delay cleared her head of all that romantic nonsense that had so nearly been her undoing. Emotional entanglements were not what she needed at this desperate stage of her life.

Nevertheless, it had been a glorious evening, her

first proper date since she married Sean. After her divorce, she had occasionally met male friends at the pub to have a few beers. She had never been tempted to invite those rough men home, and once she and Trevor moved in with her parents, there was no opportunity to develop any friendships. Sometimes she felt lonely. Mostly, she was grateful for a life on an even keel, after years on an emotional roller-coaster with Sean.

She had not planned to encourage Richard's romantic tendencies, not wanting to change the nature of a very satisfactory arrangement. She hoped he wouldn't expect too much intimacy from her the next time they met.

There was a very good plant wholesaler in Colchester, but by the time Fran arrived the next morning the best plants had been sold, although there was still plenty to choose from. Having the money to do so, she bought fifty pounds' worth of house plants, planning to sell them for a hundred. She loaded up the van and started for Braintree.

There followed the tedious business of setting up the metal framework of her stall in Market Place, putting up the tables at the front, and draping the plastic sheeting overhead. On good days, she left it off. But today looked very ominous. Fran pulled the pots from the van and arranged them as quickly as possible. There were quite a few people about, very encouraging for so early on a Thursday morning, and she hoped to make some lucrative sales.

Within the hour it began to rain, not hard at first, but hard enough to send shoppers hurrying into shops with their heads bent against the downpour.

Very soon a strong wind arose from the south-west and began tearing at the plastic sheeting. Fran's pots fell over faster than she could right them. Soil leapt from the pots to litter the counter top and expose plant roots. She tried to steady them all, but quickly decided that her best policy would be to put them under the counter until the storm blew over.

It lasted for an hour and a half. At half past eleven she agreed to look after her neighbour's fruit and vegetable stall while he slipped into the pub for a sandwich and a pint. During that half-hour she made twenty pounds for him and nothing at all for herself. When her turn came she bought a sandwich and returned to the stall to eat it, lest she miss even one small sale.

By two o'clock she was defeated, drenched by the relentless drizzle that had replaced the storm, cold, tired and disheartened. She had taken fifteen pounds and paid the market inspector thirty-four.

The van had to be unloaded and the plants taken to the polytunnel. Those plants that had spent the day under the plastic had to be watered, which was very galling. Had there been time, she would have set them all outside for the day.

Eventually she went indoors where a note was waiting for her from Trevor. He had gone to Enfield to stay with his dad, having decided that attending classes was a bore. He would see her in a few days' time on the Saturday, when Sean would be fitting the new kitchen.

Fran read the note twice, then smiled. Sean would see that Trevor did his share of the work in the kitchen. And Sean was coming a week on Saturday. He had said so.

She sat down at the Formica-topped tubular

metal kitchen table and looked around her. The room was a decent size – about ten by fifteen feet – but it had not been touched since the Fifties. A deep butler sink skulked in a dark corner, flanked by wooden draining-boards that had mould growing in the corners. There were no cupboards, just boards that had been Rawlplugged to the old walls by Trevor and herself. The fireplace was small and made of beige tiles. Ideally, it should be replaced with a larger opening, a basket grate and a mantelpiece appropriate to the age of the house. Instead there was a wood-burning stove that kept them cosy in the kitchen. The brick floor should be dug up and a concrete underfloor laid. At present the bricks were laid directly on the soil; they were permanently damp, uneven and very hard on the feet. There was no damp course, which caused innumerable problems. The builder told her that was the reason for the house being sold for so little. The whitewashed walls were green in places, and spending too long in the kitchen made her chest ache.

Her desk was simply three white melamine boards, the corner of one side propped up by folded cardboard to provide a reasonably level working surface. The fridge and washing-machine were more or less level by the same method.

As she looked around, her mind raced ten days ahead. Perhaps she should buy some new pans. And a table! Why not? She could afford it, or Richard Dumas could. Surely Sean had decided on plain pine, really suitable for this kitchen. And surely he would bring a new sink! She craved a sink unit. In fact, she craved something approaching the civilized little kitchen where she had spent so many hours at their home in Enfield.

It seemed that in the last five years she had gone backwards. As her sisters-in-law bought yet more luxuries for their homes, exchanging the carpets of the last decade for newer versions, adding video recorders, second and third televisions and coloured bathroom suites, so Fran had exchanged her modest terraced house, first for two rooms in her parents' home, then for a cottage that should have been demolished.

It was true that she had received the bulk of the money the house sale made, but though they had made their mortgage repayments regularly for thirteen years, virtually none of the principal had been paid off. What Fran received was the difference between the buying price and the selling price. What was left had scarcely paid for a small mortgage on her present home and Trevor's university expenses.

She wondered how she could have slipped so far down the economic scale, as she had worked hard since leaving school. Her father had made sure she understood that she had no intelligence, unlike her younger brothers, and that he didn't intend to waste money educating her 'beyond her brains'. Having no confidence, she had stuck to odd-job gardening for years until, long after she and Sean had broken up, she found the desperate courage to apply to Capel Manor to study garden design. She smiled now at the memory of herself, legs trembling, mouth extremely dry, as she entered the fine old ballroom of the mansion where tables had been set up to register students.

Later she discovered that she was not the only potential student who was frightened. Many of those who came to Capel to better themselves were mature people who had missed out on a proper education the first time round. And the school appreciated the effort they were making. At the end of the year, Fran received her certificate from Dr Dowbiggen, the Chief Executive, as well as the prize awarded to the student who had made the most progress during their stay at Capel. For the first time in her life, she realized that she had some talent. The course stimulated her so much that she could scarcely sleep at night. She found the time to read as she had never done before, to put her ideas down on paper without fear of being laughed at. She discovered an ability to draw, at least well enough to sketch out several plans for a garden.

The graduation ceremony was the first and only occasion when her parents and Trevor had put themselves out to discover what she was doing. Dad took them all out to dinner at the Plough on Crews Hill, and she basked in his sudden approval. During the entire evening, he made no mention of his sons. It was some sort of record, but it was not destined to be repeated. He died the following month.

Never having found the key to a happy relationship with her mother, she knew that she had to move out of the family home. And, in so doing, had incurred the wrath of her mother and both younger brothers. Her sisters-in-law, having their own problems with Mum, had been more sympathetic.

She stood up resolutely and smiled. A few days from now, this room would be transformed. She had a wonderful commission, money in the bank and the possibility of being taken out to dinner from time to time. She must not brood. The thing to do was get some rest. Tomorrow she would do some shopping, make a few dishes that Sean and Trevor liked, then begin dismantling the kitchen. The supplies could all go into the front room. She would take down the shelves, manhandle the table and chairs out of the room and wipe down the wood-work, ready for Sean to work his magic. He really was an excellent cabinet-maker. At one time he earned good money, but drink and women had always diverted him.

She straightened her shoulders. She would make up the single bed in the boxroom and sleep there on Saturday night. He needn't think she was going to fall for his blarney again, and let him into her bed. Only once had she given in since their divorce, and she had regretted it for months.

The following days went by in a dream. She had bought a pair of ready-made curtains in pale blue and yellow, and some yellow tiles which she hoped to be able to apply to the walls around the sink.

By ten o'clock on the Saturday morning she was beginning to be a trifle anxious. The kitchen was as empty as she could make it, ready for the work to begin. She had expected the men to have arrived by now.

At eleven she was seething, had tried Sean's number ten times, had slammed the phone down so hard she was momentarily afraid she had broken it.

At one o'clock she dashed the tears from her cheeks as she stumbled to the ringing phone.

'Hi, sweetie,' said Sean's slurred voice. 'Congratulate me.'

'What for? Being late? Letting me down as usual?'

'Now, now, don't be the old Fran. I'm married. Sophie. Say hello, Sophie.'

'Hi, Fran,' said a very young female voice. 'Here's Sean again.' There were girlish giggles and Sean said hello once more.

'Sean, you bastard! You're supposed to be here putting in a new kitchen for me.'

'I'm married,' he said, drunk and cheerful. 'Congratulate me, Fran. I'm a happy man.'

'Is she old enough to drive?'

'She's twenty-two. Don't be such a bitch. Congratulate me.'

'Send my three hundred pounds back to me by Trevor. Do you hear me?'

'Wedding present,' murmured Sean. 'It's my wedding present. You took everything I had. Bitch. I'm keeping the money.'

She heard a confusion of voices, then: 'Hi, Mum. Dad's got married.'

'So I gather. Bring my three hundred pounds back with you. Do you hear me, Trevor? I need that money.'

'I'll see you Sunday night.' He hung up. Fran held the purring phone for several seconds, unwilling to admit that she had no power to command Sean's sensible attention.

Not one to give in to self-pity, she spent the rest of the day and a good part of Sunday putting the kitchen back the way it had been. It was not until Trevor put his muddy feet on the clean floor that evening that she realized it had been raining all day.

'Did you get the money?' she asked, by way of greeting.

'Of course I didn't get the money. You know what Dad's like. Anyway, he's just got married. They've gone to Brighton.'

'How nice. If I can't have the kitchen he promised me, I want my money.'

'You had no right to expect him to build a kitchen for you. You're not married to him any more.'

She threw her tea towel at a chair back. 'It was his idea! He said give him a hundred and he'd fix up the kitchen for me. Only last week, he asked for two hundred more and I sent it to him. No hint of getting married then. Instead, he's having a honeymoon with his bimbo on my money.'

Trevor put his hands in his pockets and leaned against the wall. She knew that mulish expression. 'If you're so jealous, you shouldn't have left him.'

'I'm not jealous! And damn it, he kept going off with other women when we were married. That's why I kicked him out. Drunken bastard.'

'Don't talk like that. He's my dad.'

'Poor you.' She went over to the oven where a stew was cooking. 'Are you hungry?'

'No. I think you're being pathetic. You deprived me of a father all these years, just because he's not perfect. And now, when he's found happiness with someone else, you're jealous.'

'I am not jealous!' she screamed. 'I don't miss him at all. I want my kitchen. Can't you understand?'

'No. You put more value on a stupid kitchen

than you do on human relationships. You've turned into a dried-up old woman. At least Dad's still alive and capable of love.'

She wiped her nose on the back of her hand, feeling sick, feeling afraid. She was losing the battle for her son's love and didn't know how to fight any more. 'Well, you'll sneer on the other side of your face when I marry Richard Dumas. He's rich and he fancies me and I'm going to have him. I'm sick of scraping a living. I'm tired. I want some of the good things in life.'

'Like a kitchen,' he sneered. 'You disgust me. If you loved this man, I'd be all for it. In a few years' time you won't be able to work so hard, and you'll need someone to take care of you. I certainly don't want to have to think of you as a burden when I'm older. I want you to get married. But you're just a gold-digger. How do you think a chap feels to have a gold-digging mother? Can't you find somebody to love? Aren't you capable of love?'

She sat down at the table, utterly defeated. Putting her hands over her face, she rocked to and fro, feeling as if she were bleeding to death. Trevor was silent. 'No, I'm not capable of love. Everyone I have ever loved has used me. You included. I'm through with exposing my heart. From now on, I'm going to be guided by my head. It's taken me forty years to learn, but I'm wise at last. I'm going to the highest bidder. And when I'm rich you won't get a penny, so there.'

'I couldn't care less. I'm leaving.'

'What?' She lifted her head, startled out of her misery. 'Leaving this house? Moving away?'

'I'm moving in with Charlotte. I'll leave you her number, in case you get into trouble. I'm not abandoning you like you did Gran. I'm just going to live with my girlfriend. She's got feelings, and she loves me for myself, not my money.'

'Oh, Trevor, you haven't got any money!'

He didn't look back as he left the room. She heard him clump up each uncarpeted stair, heard him moving about in his room. It was too much to bear. She couldn't cope. What would happen to her? He left fifteen minutes later, and they didn't even say a proper goodbye.

Alone, she summoned all her strength to fight off the threatening panic while she tried to examine her feelings for Sean with total honesty. Was she jealous? She thought about the first time she had met him, how handsome he was, how knowing. She remembered the day Trevor was born. Sean turned up at the hospital six hours after she called to tell him about the new baby. He had been very drunk, but in his arms was a fortune in flowers, a huge soft toy, and on his lips a thousand amusing excuses. Only later did she discover that the money for all these presents had come from someone's purse. Sean had a way of helping himself. He did it smoothly, expertly and without a hesitation due to conscience. It shamed her still to realize that she had been married to a petty thief. Why had she not valued herself enough to wait for a better man?

She remembered the first time she realized he had been unfaithful to her, the hurt, the bewilderment. No, she could honestly say that she didn't feel anything for him at all. She was not jealous.

But she had to think seriously about Trevor, had to sort out what to do next. Yet there was too much pain. She couldn't think about him at the moment, couldn't acknowledge that he had always blamed her for the marriage break-up. He was Sean's son. He looked like Sean and thought like him. She had failed to give him a proper sense of responsibility. She had spoiled him and given in to his taking ways, so this was her punishment for being a poor mother. It seemed so recent that he was just a little boy, looking up to her, doing whatever she asked in return for a smile, a cuddle, a word of praise. To the baby Trevor she was perfect, could do no wrong.

Now she was on the receiving end of his contempt, not good enough, failing to live up to his expectations and desperate for a word of praise and a smile of approval from her grown-up son.

It was getting dark and the kitchen was cold. It was too scary to think about it all in a dark, cold room when she was all alone. She had to find some way of carrying on, and eventually it occurred to her. She would plan out her assault on Richard. She would make a list of all her clothes, decide which were the most seductive. She would touch up her hair and start wearing make-up. He would soon find her irresistible. She'd hold out for marriage, however. She wanted that ring on her finger, and a diamond engagement ring as well.

For a few moments she allowed herself to be carried away with dreams of a proper wedding, not fifteen minutes in a registry office. What did mature women wear when remarrying? She probably couldn't get married in church anyway. But the law had changed . . .

Realizing she was hungry, she took the stew from the oven, fetched the bottle of red plonk she had bought for the men, and sat down to eat alone, to drink alone, and eventually to go alone to bed. It was not long before she admitted to herself that she

144

had not drunk nearly enough to blot out the empti-
ness, nor the sinister sounds from outside on a
moonless night. She thought the dawn would never
come, but when it did, would she still plot to marry
Richard Dumas for his money?

Chapter Six

Two of them wore suits, dark blue with matching shirts, and the bright blue ties Richard had ordered that had 'Miami Spice' embroidered in red. The other six wore their best jackets and trousers, and the ties, of course. They looked uncomfortable, these eight young restaurant managers. Sebastian thought that was as it should be, since they had no business to be at the Hall. He had not seen Richard's point in bringing them to Gosfield for coffee and a pep talk on the morning before the cafés opened. They had been invited to the cocktail party, after all. Surely that was enough.

On instructions, he had assembled them in Richard's apartment. They studied the walls or looked out of the window, they touched the gilded furniture or gazed at their shoes. They would not sit down, being too nervous to settle anywhere. Was this what Richard wanted? Was he playing some sort of mind game?

The bedroom door opened and Richard came into the room, smiling warmly. He walked right up to Corin, the Colchester manager, and shook him by the hand, addressing him by name. Then it was Alan's turn, the Chelmsford manager. These two were senior to the others, a fact which had just been efficiently acknowledged.

Richard went round the room, shaking each man's hand, calling each by his first name. The manager in Woodbridge was a plump young woman with crooked teeth, named Gillian. Wisely, he didn't make a point of addressing her first, but spoke to her when he reached her part of the room. Richard was plainly an expert in political correctness. Sebastian saw the look of awe and respect on the faces of the managers, and began to appreciate Richard's skill.

'Do sit down, all of you. Make yourselves comfortable. Mrs Stone will be here in a minute with coffee and some of her delicious shortbread. In the meantime, I want to have a word with you. I want to wish you well in your new careers, your exciting careers. You actually have two jobs, firstly to make the customers happy, to make them feel they've never had such a good time. They've come to the Miami to eat Cuban food and revel in the atmosphere. We want them to come back often. They've got to be made to feel that Miami is fun.

'Your other job is to keep an eye on the business, to order when necessary, to keep your till receipts impeccably, to make sure that the food served in your Miami is fresh and safe, and, most trying of all, to keep order tactfully.'

Richard spoke for about five minutes, going over some points which had been emphasized at previous sessions. He quizzed them light-heartedly, praised them for knowing the answers, then finished: 'Sebastian, I'm sure, has trained you well for every eventuality. You'll do, you beautiful lot. You look absolutely splendid.'

Sebastian, seated at the far end of the room, took mental note of every word, every inflection. Richard had the finest speaking voice he had ever heard issuing from the throat of an American male. He should have been an actor, or a stage hypnotist. He could mesmerize a person with a few words, and these managers were well and truly hypnotized. They would die for him.

At that moment, as if the whole thing had been exquisitely timed, Mrs Stone entered with a trolley of coffee and biscuits. A thousand years of conditioning caused Gillian, the only other woman in the room, to rise to help serve.

'Sit down, my dear,' said Richard. 'You're a guest this morning. Sebastian and I will do our best to prove that we aren't good enough to serve in our own restaurants.'

Sebastian came over to the trolley as Mrs Stone departed. He and Richard made a great play of serving the coffees, and just when everyone was settling down to drink and the room was descending into silence once more, the door opened again and Jorge came in with his wife. All of the managers had met them before, and all knew Maria in abrasive mode. She seemed totally different today. Was this also carefully choreographed?

'Hi, guys!' called Jorge, and he too went around the room, addressing everyone by name, passing a remark here, a joke there.

Maria went to the music centre, a disc in her hand. 'I'm going to play some salsa music for you all!' she cried. 'You have to learn to be Cubans. Your customers will want to see a little Cuban spirit and rhythm. Drink up your coffees. Get ready to show how sexy you can be. Let's see who can dance. Listen now, this is big band music, you know? Got popular in the Seventies. It's fast with lots of brass and guitars and percussion. Hear it?'

Everybody heard it. She had the volume turned right up. Her body began to undulate, a startling sight, really. She was short and overweight, with hips out of proportion to the rest of her. Yet she was staggeringly graceful. Suddenly, Jorge grabbed her hand and led her into the centre of the room. Sebastian thought there was hardly room to dance, and rushed forward to move a few chairs back.

'Don't bother,' said Jorge over his shoulder. 'We're going to rumba for you, and we won't need much room. Used to be called the *son*; they turned it into a ballroom dance in the Thirties. See, you dance in one spot, no moving all over the floor. Feet flat on the floor, making a little square while your hips do the work.'

Jorge and Maria stopped talking, seemingly lost in the joys of the dance. Sebastian marvelled at their grace and energy, their concentration as they matched their steps to a complex rhythm. He glanced at Richard to see if he was annoyed at having the meeting taken out of his hands, and learned another valuable lesson. This was part of the show. Richard's benign expression said it all.

Maria and Jorge broke apart, Jorge to draw Gillian into the dance, Maria to pull a willing Alan to his feet. They danced with their new partners for a minute or two, offering advice and teasing criticism. Then Jorge urged Gillian to find a new partner, as Maria released Alan for Corin. Sebastian glanced at his watch. Within twenty minutes, eight embarrassed young people had been brought out of themselves to join in what would probably strike them as the finest party they had ever attended. Every one of them was on his feet now, and the music was almost drowned by the sound of their laughter. Richard sat at the dining-table wearing a satisfied smile. Sebastian walked over and sat next to him.

'Brilliant,' he said in Richard's ear, and Richard nodded his acknowledgement of the praise. 'You're the great man who deigns to laugh with them. Jorge and Maria are the happy clowns, teaching them to be honorary Cubans. I'm the swine who keeps them in order.'

Richard turned his head. 'Name of the game, pal. You're a natural. You actually run the chain, and one day you will be a very rich man. Do you expect to be loved as well?'

Richard was far from relaxed a few hours later as he waited for Zoe and Cosmo to arrive. He and Zoe had held a stilted conversation on the phone in which Zoe had said that they would be happy to come to Gosfield Hall before going with Richard to the opening of his Colchester restaurant.

No apologies were rendered, no mention made of the incident that had torn them apart. They exchanged pleasantries and information. Yes, said Zoe, they had a nice house in Cambridge, built in 1910. Richard must come for lunch on Sunday. Yes, Gosfield Hall was extremely large, too big for one man, but Richard said he was enjoying the challenge of restoring it.

Cosmo was looking forward to seeing it on Friday night. Cosmo knew everything there was to know about old houses, and Cosmo was teaching

Zoe. Cosmo had grown up in a fourteenth-century house in Kent.

Richard said he was looking forward to getting better acquainted with Cosmo, but he said it between clenched teeth.

Anyone eavesdropping on the conversation would have thought that they were casual acquaintances, struggling to find common ground, rather than father and daughter who had parted over a year ago, each claiming never to want to see the other again.

Now, as Richard waited to greet his daughter and son-in-law, he paced the hall, just out of sight of the windows either side of the front door, wishing fervently that he had never thought of coming to England.

When the bell finally rang, he paused to straighten his tie, to pull out his shirt cuffs, to clear his throat. 'Zoe!' He held out his arms, allowing her to decide if it would be handshake or a hug.

'Hello, Dad. Aren't you grand?' She walked into his arms, kissed him lightly on the cheek, then stood back to allow him to shake Cosmo's hand. She was nineteen, and since her thirteenth birthday Richard and Jenny had been enraptured by her grace and poise. Two insecure, less than beautiful people had brought a goddess into the world, and they never ceased to marvel at her beauty. Zoe's expensively straightened teeth added to that beauty, but her looks depended on something within her. Confidence, perhaps. She was very intelligent, had sailed through school. Her mother's death had, he thought, destroyed her academic career, for she had run off to marry her Englishman within six days of their quarrel. Looking at her now, he could not believe that she was in any way unhappy, but it was hard to greet Cosmo civilly. Why had the man snatched such a young girl away from her father and her country?

'Cosmo, good to see you.'

Dr Cosmo Bateman shook his head as he clasped Richard's hand. 'You must hate my guts, but I'm happy to bring Zoe here so that you can see I haven't mistreated her.'

Bateman was twelve years older than Zoe, tall and craggily handsome with thick brown hair. Richard always noticed the hair of other men; Bateman was particularly well-endowed. Shoving such thoughts aside, he turned to study his daughter, who was wearing a muted pink suit that complimented her blond hair. It had a very short skirt that showed off her long legs.

'You both look absolutely marvellous.'

Zoe made a face, the one he knew so well. 'Going to one of Dad's business events. Must look good.'

'I thought you might be interested in what brought me to England—'

'Not your daughter, that's for sure.'

'Zoe!' said Cosmo.

'Let me show you round my little cottage.' Richard found it rather difficult to breathe normally. Much as Zoe's childish jibes annoyed him, he didn't want to hear Cosmo correct her. 'You know, I can't get used to the fact that this was already an Anglo-Saxon estate when William the Conqueror snatched it.'

'When was this house built?' asked Cosmo.

'Sometime between 1545 and 1560.'

'Late Henry VIII.' Cosmo looked at the ceiling,

at the floor, at the huge cast-iron grilles that boxed in the small radiator. 'Sort of place Queen Elizabeth would have visited on her travels.'

'I was just going to tell you that.'

'It's going to cost you a fortune, Dad,' said Zoe. 'What will you do with it?'

'Haven't decided yet. First, I'm going to enjoy living here for a while.'

'I'd give my right arm for a place like this,' murmured Cosmo, and Richard silently thanked Seb for having bought it.

'You must see the grand salon. It's got a painted ceiling by Sir James Thornhill.'

'Oh,' said Cosmo. 'How interesting! He painted the ceiling of the Painted Hall at Greenwich Naval College.'

'Yes,' said Richard grimly. 'I was about to tell you that. Shall we move on?'

He gave them a full tour, finding that there was very little he could tell his know-all son-in-law about the history of the house. However, Cosmo was so appreciative of everything he was shown that Richard was able to keep his temper. They finished the tour at the door of his apartment, and both Zoe and Cosmo were loud in their praises of the rooms and their furnishings.

The pain in Richard's chest began to ease. 'Now then, Zoe, what will you have to drink?'

'I'll have a glass of dry white wine, thank you, Dad.'

'You're not old enough to drink.'

She laughed. 'I am old enough in this country, and I'll have a glass of dry white wine.'

Richard hesitated for a split second, tempted to refuse. But she was no longer his daughter. She was Cosmo's wife. 'And you, Cosmo?'

'The same, thank you.'

Richard went into his small kitchen and quickly poured three glasses of Frascati, bringing them back into the living-room on a tray. Cosmo and Zoe had been in serious conversation. They took their wine and raised their glasses in a silent toast.

'Zoe would like to say something,' said Cosmo.

Richard held his breath. That tone of voice belonged to a father and he had used it often. *Now, Zoe, say thank you for having me. Zoe wishes to say she's sorry, Mommy*. It was not a proper way for a husband to speak to his adult wife. Yet Zoe looked to Cosmo with gratitude.

'I want to say I'm sorry, Dad, and hope never to have to refer to it again. Deal?'

'Deal,' he said with relief. 'We're going to have to leave soon. It's fifteen or sixteen miles to Colchester and parking is awkward, so I've ordered a cab. It should be here.'

Helena was wearing an emerald green wool jacket with a navy skirt, which she had thought was just right and very smart, but a glance at the other women told her she should have worn something rather more dressy. Karen's brown tweed suit left her looking distinctly dowdy, for which Helena could only think, 'Hallelujah.'

'How nice to see you,' said Richard, greeting the sisters at the door. 'Shall I introduce you to a few people?'

'No thanks,' said Karen, 'I'll just mingle. Make a few contacts. You never know when they'll come in handy.'

Helena looked up at her host. Richard's attention

was already elsewhere. 'I'm awfully sorry, Richard, but have they by chance anything non-alcoholic?'

He looked down at her, forced to think about her for a moment or two. 'I'll go see.'

Karen had found Sebastian, but Helena hovered by the door, too shy to speak to strangers, and determined to make Richard talk to her. He returned with a tall glass of ice and some brilliant pink concoction.

'What am I supposed to do with this? Drink it or gargle with it?'

He smiled. 'It's cranberry juice. Very popular in the States.'

She felt a small spurt of panic. How could she keep him near her? What could she possibly find to say next? And Karen, inexplicably, was bearing down on them.

'Did you invite the adulterer?' she hissed at her sister.

'Don't be a fool! Of course I didn't.' Helena sensed Richard's amusement, but dared not look up at him.

'Who's the adulterer?'

'The bearded oaf in the ill-fitting tweed suit.' Karen indicated a couple talking to each other in a bored fashion.

'And who did he misbehave with?'

'Me,' croaked Helena.

At last she had succeeded in making Richard laugh, although he quickly controlled himself. 'I believe he's a supplier. Sebastian put him on the list. Is that his wife?'

'I suppose so,' said Helena. Karen harrumphed like one of Bertie Wooster's aunts and moved away.

'How embarrassing for you,' said Richard kindly.

'Especially as your sister is enjoying it so much. You'll just have to ignore them. Come, meet my daughter and her husband.'

He took her by the elbow and guided her to a statuesque blonde who was nearly six inches taller than Helena. She had thought this Venus was a model, hired for the evening, but should have known she was related to Richard. They shared a look of patrician poise. Yet neither seemed to be aware of their stunning looks. Richard really was a genuinely modest man. It completed her miserable evening to find that the glamorous American had such a daughter. How soon could she leave?

'And this is my new son-in-law, Dr Cosmo Bateman. They've come over from Cambridge to help us celebrate.'

Helena craned her neck to look at the two beautiful people. 'Are you a GP in Cambridge, Dr Bateman?'

'No, I'm a geneticist.'

'Oh. What do you think about Dolly the sheep?'

His suppressed sigh told her he had been asked this question a thousand times. 'Very clever work. Too soon to assess its value. Actually, I'm a plant geneticist. You know, genetically altered food?'

She giggled foolishly. 'Don't worry, I'm not going to get into that. I know nothing about it. But tell me, do you live in England now?'

'Yes, we do,' said Zoe in a pleasant voice. 'I love England, and I think Dad is beginning to feel the same way. This is a very amusing venture. Did I hear him say you're a shareholder?'

'Yes, my great-uncle left the cafés to my sister and me and to our distant cousin, Sebastian.' There was nothing more she could think of to say, and Dr Bateman was looking bored. 'Will you excuse me? I really must speak to him.'

She turned and pushed her way through the small crowd. The tables had been moved to make it easier for the guests, and for the waiters who were serving Cuban canapés of pickled fish, chorizo, olives and fried almonds. The café looked very Disney-ish, the canapés were not to her taste, and she wished to get out of this room which was far too small to contain herself and 'the adulterer.'

It seemed incredible that anything worse could happen to her in the space of one short cocktail party, but finding her hair entangled with the mayor's chain of office as she squeezed past him was really the last straw.

The mayor was extremely tall, and the medallion of his chain was just about on a level with her ear. The tug on her hair drew her up short with a squeal.

'Hold on,' said the mayor, 'or you'll be snatched bald—' He looked over at his host who was out of earshot and made a comical face. 'Better watch my words, eh?'

'Excuse me. I'm so sorry . . .' Helena said as she clutched the offending hair and attempted to remove it gently.

'Stop making a fool of yourself,' hissed Karen, who had come from nowhere to yank her hair free.

There was a short, nerve-racking moment as the mayor checked to see if anything untoward had happened to the town's very expensive chain, then Sebastian appeared by her side and ushered her away to a relatively quiet corner.

'You look wretched. What's the matter, cousin?'

'You see that man over there? In the tweed

suit? That's the man I was in love with, the man who—'

'What? Carlton Forbes? Good God, Helena. You can do better than Carlton. He's a halfwit.'

'Why does everybody think it's so funny? I was the halfwit, but he's here at your invitation, apparently, and he's brought his wife. Oh, Seb, I'm so miserable, and Richard has invited us all to dinner across the road at the George, and I don't think I could spend an entire evening with so many Americans.'

'I told him two days ago that I would not be staying. I gathered the daughter and son-in-law would be coming and I didn't want to play gooseberry. I have an idea. Let's the two of us sneak off and have some dinner elsewhere.'

'I'd love that. Must we bring Karen?'

He shook his head. 'She's going to have dinner at the George; I've just spoken to her. Come on, we'll make our excuses and leave.'

They drove to the Bull at Blackmore End which was close to Helena's new home. Afterwards, Seb had to admire Honeysuckle Cottage. He found much to praise, as Helena had treated herself to a newly thatched cottage of palest pink with tumbling honeysuckle round the door. Inside, she had put sisal carpets over the rich dark floorboards and decorated with chintz curtains that had huge cabbage roses on a white background, very striking against the deep earthy red of the walls.

The kitchen was particularly attractive with a small cream Aga tucked into the fireplace, a pine dresser and a small round table with two chairs.

'You've missed your calling,' said Seb when they had returned to the two comfortable chairs by the sitting-room fireplace. 'You should have been an interior decorator.'

Helena lit a match and started the fire which had been carefully laid earlier. 'Thank you, dear. I've pushed the boat out a little, but I have faith in you men. You are going to make a lot of money for us, aren't you?'

'We promise to make you rich. May I have another cup of your delicious coffee?'

'The pot's on the side-table. Help yourself,' she said. 'I want you to feel really at home here.'

On Sunday Richard drove himself to Cambridge and was taken on a tour of Zoe and Cosmo's attractive red brick Edwardian home, had each original fireplace pointed out to him, praised Zoe's taste in decorating each of the six bedrooms, admired the sensitively modernized kitchen, and strove to speak knowledgeably about the furniture and décor in the way the young people had been able to do at Gosfield Hall. He was new at the game, however, and was sometimes surprised by the features he was invited to admire. Like the toilet with a wooden seat and a chain flush.

He had an enquiring mind and many long evenings in which to study. However, he had concentrated on trying to make sense of Gosfield Hall, which had no additions dating from 1910 that he had yet discovered. Later styles, including the style everyone spoke of as Edwardian, were a mystery to him.

Zoe had inherited half a million dollars from her mother, which Richard presumed had more than paid for this charming house with its neglected half-acre garden. It had troubled him to know what he might give the couple as a belated wedding present. Finally he had hit on silverware and had bought them what the English called a canteen of cutlery – eight-piece place settings in solid Georgian silver for eighteen people. It was well-received.

He was actually beginning to like his son-in-law. Cosmo gave the impression of being steady and intelligent, although unlikely to earn the sort of money that Richard found essential for a comfortable life. He decided to give them the profits from the cafés when they were eventually sold. It wouldn't be much, of course. He would throw in the ten thousand he would surely win from Jorge. Happy with these thoughts, he enjoyed his visit and only mentioned as he was leaving that he knew a good garden designer if they happened to be interested.

Trevor had been gone just two days before Fran's mother called to berate her. Poor Trevor had telephoned to say his mother had thrown him out. How could Fran be so cruel? What kind of mother was she?

The kind who told the truth, said Fran. The truth was Trevor had left of his own accord and was living with his girlfriend. It had not been Fran's fault. She had wanted him to stay at home.

Her mother rambled on about morals and young people, about Sean having married a woman young enough to be his daughter, all because his wife had not been able to hold onto him. She then made her usual request for money.

Fran felt a sudden constriction in her chest that prevented her from replying immediately. Bitterness made her harsh. 'I'm terribly sorry,

Mum, but I have turned over a new leaf. No more money. You have two sons who are both younger and wealthier than I am, and they don't give you a penny. You never approve of anything I do, so I needn't try to please you. Kindly do not ask me for money again. Goodbye.' She hung up as her mother spluttered accusations down the line.

A grown-up daughter should have been able to refuse her mother calmly but forcefully, should have been able to say whatever needed to be said with quiet dignity. But Fran was too angry, too determined to change her entire life to bother with dignity. She was finished with loving and she might as well exclude her mother as well as all the other people from whom she had craved approval. In future she would not care about anyone but herself. In the meantime, however, she would look out Trevor's socks. A curt note in the post had asked if he had any more as he was running out.

On Tuesday afternoon she went to Gosfield Hall with a tray of dwarf tulips in full bud, and had planted most of them in containers in the hall before Richard knew she was in the building.

When she saw him coming towards her she felt panic rising in her throat, so that she was scarcely able to greet him in a normal voice. Wondering what on earth a money-grubbing woman should say to her target male, she grinned foolishly and asked him how the cocktail party had gone. This seemed to be the right approach, for he smiled broadly and began an animated account.

Squatting down beside her as she planted the last three bulbs, he murmured, 'I wish you had been there. I have a feeling my secretary is being seduced by Sebastian Race. This is bad news. She's absent-minded at the best of times. You've not met him yet, but just watch the body language when we see them together. I would like your opinion.'

Fran drew in her breath with pleasure. He trusted her judgement! She was about to remind him that women could be seducers, too, but, by the most unexpected stroke of luck, the secretary left her office and was walking towards them just as Sebastian Race came down the staircase at the other end of the house. Richard squeezed her arm conspiratorially.

Liz wore a full skirt to her ankles and a long cardigan over a cream blouse, trying to hide a bulky figure, Fran supposed. She handed Richard a leather book. 'May I have your signature on these letters? I want them to go off soon.' He picked himself up off the floor and sat in the small oak hall chair he had recently bought to help furnish the hall. Fran saw that the book contained sheets of blotting-paper with letters interspersed and thought what a good idea such a book was. No danger of papers being missed, no danger of smeared signatures.

'Richard,' said Sebastian, with a nod to Fran. 'I'm going to Maldon. They're not doing any business at all.'

'Too cold, wrong location,' said Richard. 'Will I see you Thursday morning?'

'Yes, of course. I'm a director and I don't intend to miss a board meeting.'

'May I introduce Fran Craig? She's going to do some garden designs.'

Sebastian shook her grubby hand. 'You fixed up this hall? Very nice. You know, Richard,' he turned away. 'Helena has a real gift for interior decorating. Should you need any help—'

'Thank you. I'll call on her if necessary.'

Liz took the book of signed letters from Richard; Sebastian walked out of the door to the courtyard.

'Well?' said Richard.

'They're definitely thinking about it. There was a lot of sexual tension between them. Did you notice how they didn't even look at each other? And not by accident, either.'

He frowned. 'Hmm. Office romance. Never a good idea. And Liz is, or was, happily married.'

Fran put her trowel into her holdall and began sweeping up her mess with a brush and pan she had brought with her. 'It's awkward if your secretary is sleeping with a man who dislikes you. Could she give him any of your secrets?'

'Who, Sebastian? How astute of you to notice that he doesn't like me! No, he's too lazy and stupid to do me harm. Nevertheless, I'm not happy. What are those things you're planting? Tulips?'

'Yes, it was to be a surprise. *Tulipa greigii*. They're short, only about a foot tall, and they bloom early. These will come into bloom quite soon. Bright red with striped foliage. They're not the sort that were prized during tulipomania. I plant them in tomato boxes in November, then plant them up in pots when they're far enough along. You'd want much bigger tulips out of doors, and I've none of those, I'm afraid.'

'I can't wait to see them bloom. Are you coming out to dinner with me tonight?'

'I'd love to, but I must go home early. I'm rather tired.'

He took her face in both hands and stared into her eyes. 'Do you never get enough sleep? What time do you get up in the morning?'

'Five if I can manage it. I'm a businesswoman, after all. I've things to do.'

They ate lunch at the ancient Bull Inn in Halstead, and Fran was able to get away early, due to having established that she was too tired to return to his flat. She intended to marry him, but was not yet prepared to sleep with him. The idea of it filled her with dread and embarrassment. However, she excused her reluctance on the grounds that she was new to gold-digging.

It worried her, too, that Sebastian might guess that Richard was attracted to her. It wouldn't be difficult, because the dear man made no secret of his interest. Sebastian might be too stupid and lazy to harm Richard, but he could certainly cause Fran serious problems. She must avoid him whenever possible.

She had bought over fifty pounds' worth of house plants from her wholesaler, not first-class specimens, but cheap. After arriving home from lunch with Richard, she loaded up the van ready for the morning. As she still didn't have enough plants to sell, she loaded fifty zonal pelargoniums and as many fuchsias suitable for hanging baskets, as well as seventeen boxes of violas in assorted shades, and ten boxes of brightly coloured primulas. The plants were severely squeezed in the van, but she hoped they would be all right until the morning. At least there was no frost forecast for the night.

Bertie helped her erect her stall. As usual, he was on at her about going on the market in other towns on other days. She couldn't make a living off one day a week, he told her for the thousandth time. Furthermore, she was going to miss out on the Mother's Day trade because she wasn't on the market on Saturday. Fran knew that what he said was true, but now thought that effort put into catching Richard was preferable to slogging away on the market on Saturdays.

The sun was out, the weather not as cold as recently, and sales were brisk. Mrs Parkson approached just as Fran was thinking about eating the bacon sandwich she had brought with her. 'Morning, Mrs Parkson. How are you, dear?'

The old lady had to be in her eighties, but seemed in her usual good health. A woolly hat kept her head warm, an ancient sheepskin coat reached her knees, and the woolly beige stockings protected her legs all the way down to her fur-lined boots.

'I had a bad night, dear. Trouble down below.' She leaned forward and hissed, 'Cystitis!'

'Nasty.'

'Yes, but I don't complain. My daughter came to see me on Sunday. First time in six weeks. We went out to lunch. Very nice. She's got trouble with her ex. I thought you might be able to give her some advice, you being divorced and everything.'

'My ex just got married, and my son has turned against me and moved out. Do you really think I'm the one to give advice?'

Mrs Parkson was at once filled with sympathy. 'Oh, you poor thing. Well, come round to me after you close down here and have a cup of tea. You haven't been over for ages and . . . but you've got a customer. I'll wait.'

Nigel Falkland lived in Islington and worked in the City. Liverpool Street station was within walking distance of the office, and the Braintree train left for Essex at regular intervals. Unfortunately, Braintree was six or seven miles from Gosfield, necessitating a taxi ride or a lift from Sebastian Race. Falkland telephoned ahead and warned his fellow directors that he would be half an hour late as he had business in Braintree. No, no, he hastily assured Sebastian, he didn't want to be met. A taxi, already arranged, would see to his needs.

He had already discovered that Braintree held its market on Thursdays and Saturdays, but he would not be able to visit it on Saturday, the day before Mother's Day. His shopping would have to be completed on this Thursday. He had a plan that would amaze and amuse his mother who was returning from Barbados on the Saturday. He could hardly wait to put it into practice.

He would buy masses of plants, tender things that could not survive out of doors at this time of year, and he would plant up his mother's conservatory before she returned home. How pleased she would be! How surprised! Nigel Falkland loved doing little things for his mother. This was only fair, he thought, since his wife doted on her mother. He sometimes thought they were locked into a mummy-loving contest. But this amusing thought was never expressed. Honoria had no sense of humour.

In the event, his temper was severely tried. It was not possible to get close to Market Place with the taxi. He would have to carry his purchases in several loads over to the waiting vehicle and tip the driver to keep them in the boot until Falkland was ready to return to the station. But that was just the beginning of his irritations.

Fran looked at the well-dressed man with relief. She didn't want to go to Mrs Parkson's flat which was filled with rubbish and smelled a bit. In any case, she had to visit her accountant, being in need of some good advice.

'Yes, sir. How can I help you? A present, is it? Something for your own home? I've got some very nice *Scindapsus*.'

He was wearing a dark blue suit and sober tie under a fitted navy overcoat. His hair was brushed back severely which made him look sleek and old-fashioned, although he couldn't be much more than forty-five.

'Give me one of those boxes of geraniums and one of the fuchsias.'

'Call it five pounds and—'

'Those impatiens and a box of petunias. What do you want for that house plant?' He pointed to a Swiss cheese plant whose yellow leaves Fran had previously pulled off, leaving it looking rather bare but healthy.

'A fiver for you, sir, as you're having the other plants.'

He handed her three notes. 'I'll just wrap up the *Monstera* . . .' She turned to look for a bag large enough.

'I've got to be going, dear,' called Mrs Parkson. 'See you later.'

'No,' called Fran. 'I've got to see my accountant. Another time, Mrs Parkson.'

Fran handed over the fuchsias and geraniums to

her customer who said he would be back in a moment, as he had to put these in the car. He returned quickly, but had to make another journey with more plants. Finally he came back for the Swiss cheese plant, looking disapprovingly at the way it had been wrapped.

'Don't plant the tender things in the garden just yet, sir. Wait until the beginning of June.'

'I'll do what I please with them.' He held out his hand towards Fran. 'My change, please.'

'You gave me two tens and five, sir.'

'I gave you three tens.'

Fran looked down. Distracted by Mrs Parkson, she had pushed the money straight into her pouch. She pulled out a fistful of notes and rifled through them. 'I've only taken two tenners all day.'

He leaned forward, his smooth skin flushing nastily. 'Don't you bloody well play your market tricks on me! I'll not be cheated out of my change. Now give me my fiver.'

Bertie, who had been hovering on the nearside of his stall, now turned and looked at the customer directly. 'There's no need for that.'

'And there's no need for you to interfere. You types all stick together. Now, give me that bloody five-pound note before I call the police. I am a banker.'

Fran, unable to prove herself in the right, found a five-pound note and handed it over.

He snatched the money and stuffed it into his breast pocket. 'If I ever hear of you trying to cheat anyone else, I'll report you to the market inspector. Do you understand what I'm saying?'

'A banker, are you? I think you're a thieving little bastard,' said Fran. 'Don't you ever come to my stall again. I've got a good reputation here and I don't have to be spoken to like I'm scum by anybody, but especially not a banker. Now go away.'

Falkland huffed and grumbled, but he walked away without further exchange of insults.

Mrs Parkson had not left, after all. 'That's telling him. An out-of-towner. Disgraceful. But don't let him bother you.'

'He cheated me out of five pounds and I can't prove it. I know what you taught me, Bertie, always keep the money the customer gives you in your hand until he's had his change. I was distracted.'

Bertie shook his head sadly. 'You should have stood your ground. But don't let it get you down. You're having a good day. Keep pitching.'

As Falkland was walking back to the taxi with his Swiss cheese plant, the obvious suddenly occurred to him. He could not possibly take all these plants back to London on the train, nor walk to his office with them. Fury at his own stupidity didn't last for long. Instead he concentrated his anger on the bitch who had sold him the plants. She had a very sexy quality, and he was rather annoyed that he had noticed it. What was the matter with him? He didn't like the rougher kind of woman, except for that one time in Florida. Yet he found this market trader disturbingly attractive.

'Driver,' he said, jovial and matey, 'it occurs to me that I'm going to have to get you to drive me home to Islington.'

'Oh, I don't know, sir . . .'

'I'll make it worth your while. I shall be going out to lunch and returning to London at about half past two. You can take a few customers in the mean-time, can't you?'

Despite the confrontation, Fran had a very good day indeed. When she had sold everything she had on the stall there were four hundred pounds in her money pouch, which gave her a warm feeling. At four o'clock she folded up her stand and the plastic sheeting, bunged it into the van and drove off to her accountant, John 'Linus' Wilkins, nicknamed after the cartoon character in *Peanuts*. He had a small office on Head Street in Halstead.

Head Street was an extension of the High Street, but being narrower and possibly the oldest part of the town, it suffered from the lack of passing trade. There were always two or three empty shops, testimony to broken dreams. And, of course, there was nowhere to park on the road.

Linus had a spare space behind his office, but getting into it was difficult, as Fran knew from previous experiences. There was an extremely narrow carriageway between his building and the one next door. The van fitted with inches to spare, but she had to pull out into traffic in order to make the left turn. Some of the van's white paint clung to the right side of the driveway from a previous visit, while three bricks had been damaged on the left, a souvenir from her very first attempt. Despite this pattern of failure, she attempted the manoeuvre once more because she was too tired to park lower down the hill and walk up.

Linus opened his back door when he heard the clash of gears and shouted a welcome. Her accountant was short and plump, just twenty-nine years old. He had very few clients and had been introduced to Fran by Trevor who had met him at a football match in the town. 'I've put the kettle on. Did you have a good day?'

'Smashing. Four hundred pounds. Sold out early. But I'm whacked. I could really do with one of your muddy coffees. Oh, Linus, I need help.'

'You usually do. Here's your coffee. I've put the sugar in. Why don't you try going to bed earlier? You never look as if you've had enough sleep.'

'Do I look like a hag? Oh, Linus, I must look my best in future. I must look glamorous and sexy. Maybe I will go to bed early tonight, but there's so much to do. I'm going to tell you all about it from the beginning.'

'You'll start in the middle as you always do, and I'll try to sort it out, as I always do. Nothing illegal, I hope.' He handed her the coffee-mug and led the way through the kitchen to his office.

'Well . . .'

He sighed as he took the bank book she held out to him, opened it and read aloud. 'A deposit of ten thousand pounds. Fran, market traders don't make this sort of money, even on a good day, so who did you mug?'

'Richard Dumas. He's bought Gosfield Hall and he owns a chain of Cuban restaurants. You must have read about him.'

'And he gave you ten thousand pounds to put into your personal account? He must be mad or besotted.'

She grinned. 'He fancies me.'

'Don't we all, dear, but I can't believe he's that silly. I was a guest recently at the East Anglia Institute of Directors. I actually spent a moment or two talking to him. He's extremely shrewd and very impressive.'

She took a deep draught of the hot coffee and made a face. 'I'm to redesign the gardens of Gosfield Hall. He gave me the cheque, suggested I put it into a separate account and keep a record of my time and expenditures.'

'Let me guess. You immediately put it into your personal account and wrote some cheques.'

'I had pressing bills. Anyway, I have done some work for him. I tarted up the hallway at the Hall. Plinths, statues, stone containers, plants. I think I spent a thousand pounds altogether. But I don't know how much to charge for my time.'

'Ten pounds an hour sound like a nice round figure. Reckon up your hours and give me the receipts. I'll make some calculations and we'll see if we can get this thing on a proper footing.'

'Dear Linus, there is one small problem.'

'How did I know there would be?'

'You see, my method of bookkeeping is to have two carrier bags hanging on pegs in front of my desk. In one, I put all receipts. In the other, all bills. The other day I was cleaning up the kitchen at about half past two in the morning. I wasn't thinking, you see, and threw both carrier bags away.'

Linus was no longer laughing. 'Probably a subliminal urge. The bills will come again, if you don't get your electricity or phone cut off in the meantime.'

'I had already paid those bills, and my credit-card bill.'

'By cheque?' he asked, and she nodded. 'We'll transfer the remainder of the ten thousand to a separate account, calculate your hours generously. Did you supply the plants?'

'Yes, I did.'

'We can charge the limit for them, but that won't begin to cover what you paid out for electricity, telephone and credit card. Didn't you owe nearly a thousand pounds on your Barclaycard? Soon those cheques will be cleared. Then you owe that character in Enfield. Oh, God, Fran. This is serious.'

'I have a plan.'

'I'm so glad, because I have to confess I have no idea how you're going to get out of this.'

'I'm going to marry him.'

He leaned back in his chair, and studied her sadly. 'Do you think that's what he has in mind?'

'No, but I'll charm him. In the meantime, he doesn't like the design I drew up for the garden on the south front. He wants me to come up with another suggestion, and I can't think of anything else. I've sat up till all hours and nothing comes.'

'Go to the Record Office in Chelmsford. Look up Gosfield Hall and see what the gardens were like in previous centuries. It's a listed building and is bound to have had some formal gardens. Simply do a design based on what was there. That should impress everybody.'

'Oh, what a good idea! And I can bill him for all the hours I spend at the Record Office.'

'I've been meaning to ask. How long was your course in garden design at Capel Manor?'

'Five weeks.'

Then he did laugh, swinging round in the swivel chair and wheezing softly.

'I don't see what's funny. It was five weeks spread over a whole year. Nine thirty in the morning until five at night, but we could stay on and work until half past six. I stayed every time I was allowed to. We studied urban gardens, garden history right up to the present day, and big country gardens too, site surveying, contracting and drafting specifications. Then in the last week we learned all about getting started as a business, marketing, advertising, accounting, legal and tax. There was lots of work in the weeks between. I really did learn a lot. I thought I could just go away and become a successful garden designer, but Richard is the first person to employ me, and now I've made a mess of it. He has to marry me.'

He started to speak, but couldn't think of anything useful to say. If he had the money to lend her, he would do it in a flash. As it was, he did her books for nothing, simply because she seemed so sweet and gutsy. Linus had been a qualified accountant for just five years, and if it weren't for his girlfriend's job they would be little better off than Fran. But at least, he told himself, he and Betty were on a firm financial footing, living within their means and having great prospects. Fran was living on borrowed time.

She interrupted his thoughts. 'By the way, will you do me a terrific favour? Will you go to Enfield and pay off my debt? I can't get away and the man is saying some quite nasty things when he visits me.'

'This is to be done with some of Richard Dumas's money? How did I guess? Will you tell him on your wedding night that you only married him for his money, or will you wait a day or two?'

*   *   *

The board meeting had not been particularly pleasant. Nigel Falkland had laid out his pens and pencils in his usual fashion, and in his usual fashion had quickly shown just how bright he was.

Richard had done business with him in the past. But that had been in sunny Florida. Falkland had seemed to be in holiday mood. He was quick to understand what was going on, always one jump ahead of the opposition, and ready to take risks. He had seemed a totally different person from the one who sat in Richard's apartment. Today he was unpleasant to anyone whom he thought he could bully, which included both Seb and Liz.

As none of the cafés were performing well, there was a heated discussion about the best way to proceed. Richard and Jorge were sanguine. They were in favour of giving the restaurants time to settle down. The weather was cold. No-one went to the seaside in cold wet weather. Wait, they said, until the holiday season began. The returns of the Colchester and Chelmsford cafés were reasonable, which was because there was plenty of passing trade every day. In the holiday season, the other cafés would also benefit from passing trade.

Sebastian, never one to agree with the Americans about anything, thought that even the Miami Spices in Colchester and Chelmsford were under-performing. Something was wrong. He thought it was the menu. Brits didn't like Cuban food.

Jorge admitted that there might have to be changes. Spicier food was his recommendation, because the British liked their restaurant food hot. Hence the popularity of curry houses.

Nigel Falkland chose to see in this remark an insult to British taste. 'I'm sick of these unending jokes about British food and British taste. You can eat a great deal better in London than in New York.'

'Don't be so damned stupid,' said Richard, 'Jorge is not here to insult the British people. He has found that the spicy dishes go down well, that's all. Let's try to keep this discussion on an even keel.'

Closing the café in Woodbridge was discussed, as was the simple measure of laying off one employee at each establishment. Richard favoured a special promotion, and won the day by force of personality, although he did register Falkland's slight annoyance at being so comprehensively bounced into a decision he didn't favour.

Richard had no patience for discussion on this day. Just before the board meeting began, he had been handed a bill for the replacement of the entire roof: £100,000. On top of other recent expenses, this had soured his mood.

He walked Falkland to the door that led into the courtyard. Falkland had said a curt goodbye, and was walking towards the gateway, when he turned back just as Richard and Sebastian were about to go indoors.

'Good Lord! That's the market trader I had a run-in with this morning. She's a rude bitch and not to be trusted.'

Richard looked towards the gateway, but there was no-one coming except Fran. She smiled at him, but frowned fiercely when Falkland turned round. Richard went towards her.

'Hello, darling, have you brought me some more plants?' he said loudly, kissing her on the cheek.

He took one of the pots from her and turned back to smile broadly at Falkland.

'Fran, let me introduce you to another member of our board. Nigel Falkland. This is Fran Craig who is redesigning the grounds of Gosfield Hall.'

Falkland was turning pink with suppressed emotion. 'Miss Craig and I have met. Take my advice and count the spoons, Richard.'

Fran was extremely friendly towards Richard when they went out to dinner, yet he was aware of an inner turmoil that kept her from giving him her full attention. They returned to his flat where she permitted him to kiss her several times, but he sensed that she feared being persuaded into bed. As he had no wish to trick or force her into loving him, he kept his distance thereafter. He wanted no reluctant lover and anyway doubted that she could actually find him attractive.

He apologized for being fully engaged for the next two days, but suggested that they go up to London on the Sunday. When Fran said that she couldn't because her son was bringing his girlfriend home for lunch, he was sure of a deliberate snub. Why, he wondered, couldn't she have the boy and his girl over on the Saturday?

They parted cordially, but with some stiffness on both sides. He would have to proceed carefully with Fran. He had not decided where his future lay. He was missing the Florida sunshine, the old easy ways, the big straight roads and the television. Yet he wanted to be close to Zoe. It was wiser, therefore, to back off from any sort of entanglement with Fran before his heart became too engaged. What he needed was a spell of quiet reflection, a chance to stand back and see where he was going.

On Friday afternoon he received a passionate phone call from Boca Raton. One of his companies was experiencing difficulties. The finance director had gone missing. They were still trying to calculate how much money had gone missing with him. This was Richard's perfect excuse. He said he would return as soon as possible and asked Liz to book him a first-class ticket to Miami on Monday.

Chapter Seven

Fran was at the Essex Public Record Office from the moment it opened on Monday morning and did not leave until late afternoon, when hunger drove her in search of a café. As she was in Chelmsford, and since she was curious about the Miami Spice cafés, she went into the town centre and sought out the Chelmsford branch.

At three o'clock in the afternoon, the café was empty. The waiter agreed to serve her and nodded without comment when she pointed to *Leche Frita con Salsa de Pina*. Fried Milk with Pineapple Sauce.

The coffee was strong, and the fried milk turned out to be gelatine squares made with almond-flavoured milk, dipped in egg and fried, the whole covered with pineapple sauce. It was delicious.

Having satisfied her hunger, she ordered a second coffee and began to consider her next move. First, of all the great houses in Britain, Gosfield Hall had to be one which never had a formal garden. Yet Linus's suggestion had been a good one. She could have built on old garden themes, taken ideas, elaborated and modernized. But it was no use. Now she would have to think again, and her mind simply would not engage. She was afraid of being exposed as a fraud.

She had not slept well the previous night. Trevor's visit with his girlfriend had been a disaster. They had quarrelled while the girl had sat silent, her blue eyes huge, her mouth slack. Trevor had called Fran such terrible names that the girl (Fran couldn't remember her name) had threatened not to take him back to her digs.

As if all this were not bad enough, Fran and Richard had parted on a cool note. She had been terrified that Richard would no longer wish to know her after Nigel Falkland told him she was a market trader who gave short change. The strain had been almost unbearable because Richard never mentioned Falkland, so she didn't know if the man had said something damaging about her or not. She knew she would have to make the first move to get the friendship back on a relaxed basis. As soon as she got home, she would ring Gosfield Hall.

'May I have my bill, please,' she called, and the young man slouched over with the bill on a plate. Seven pounds! She thought that was a bit steep, but made no complaint. 'What do you think of the new owner?'

'We see Mr Race quite often, but the Americans never come round. Apparently Alan, the first manager, was invited to Gosfield Hall for coffee, but I've never even been acknowledged by those two.'

'The first manager? Do you mean he's quit already? Or did they fire him?'

'Got a better job paying more money. Down in London. A real manager. I'm just the dogsbody. I wait tables, check the till, order the food and take all the hassle for nine thousand a year.'

For some reason, it took all Fran's resolve to pick up the telephone and dial Gosfield Hall. She thought this was a sign that their relationship really had taken a serious turn for the worse. She must be a clever gold-digger and get him to be friendly again.

'Mr Dumas has returned to the States,' said Liz Morgan coolly when Fran got through to her on the phone.

'But why?'

'Well, you know,' said Liz with heavy sarcasm, 'that is where his main businesses lie.'

'The restaurants? Gosfield Hall? I'm supposed to be doing some work—'

'Yes, and you are supposed to be sending me your account. Mr Race can handle any queries you may have.'

Fran hooked a kitchen chair with one foot and sat down heavily. Why did everybody always run out on her? What was she to do now?

'Hello?' said Liz sharply. 'Are you there? Do you wish to leave a message for Mr Race?'

'You had better give me his home address. Mr Dumas's, I mean. I have some papers for him,' she said calmly.

'I don't know if he would wish me to—'

'You know perfectly well he would wish you to, Liz. Let me have that address.'

There was a short pause, then: 'He lives at The Villa Royale, 2234 Ocean Boulevard, Boca Raton, Palm Beach County, Florida. Post takes six days at least and—'

'That's all right,' said Fran quickly and hung up. It was a simple matter to get his phone number from International Directory Enquiries, but by the time the number came through she had changed her mind about calling him.

The implications were too terrible to think about. Richard had gone home; Fran had no hold over him, no means of making him forget about the ten thousand pounds or getting him to wait for payment. His secretary or Sebastian Race would be sure to press for repayment of the unused portion of the advance on his behalf.

She took a turn around the kitchen, having no idea of how to proceed. She should never have built her hopes around a foreigner. Such a man was always likely to decide he liked his own country best. She had no means of luring him back. A telephone call would certainly not do it. She might interrupt him in the midst of some crucial business. He would be annoyed and unwilling to listen to what she had to say. Or she might awaken him. That could be even worse.

She thought of the boasts she had made to Linus and Trevor. How they would laugh! She must come up with a daring plan. In the past, she had found that hard physical exercise helped her to think. Perhaps a little housework, even at this late hour, would sort out her mind.

The bedrooms were under an inch of dust. She hung up all her clothes and those that Trevor had thrown on his floor. She scrubbed the floors, although they didn't look better for such violent treatment. The sitting-room (in which they never sat) was next on her agenda. The old three-piece suite was beginning to smell of damp.

She opened the windows and vacuumed and dusted. The furniture was moved to new positions several times, yet ended up where it had started. By early evening she was exhausted, but she had still not decided what to do about Richard.

The nursery received her attention next. An hour in the open air, working by torchlight, left her feeling chilled, so she came indoors. She was light-headed, aware that she had eaten nothing except the fried milk since breakfast. Now too tired to cook anything, she raided the pantry and served herself a can of baked beans and three slices of bread and the last of the butter. The television failed to keep her awake. With great effort, she rose from the kitchen table at half past nine and went to bed.

Sleep was instantaneous. In the early hours of the morning she was awakened by the scrabbling of mice in the thatch. As was her custom, she reached up and banged her hand several times against the wall. Silence. And suddenly she was awake, refreshed and ready for action.

Downstairs she filled the kettle and reached for the jar of instant coffee. Nearly empty, as was the milk carton. She scraped the dregs of the coffee jar into a mug, poured in the hot water, put a splash in the jar to capture the last whiff of coffee which she added to her mug.

'I'm sick of it!' she cried. 'I can't stand being tired and poor all the time. I want to be rich!'

Striding up and down the kitchen and talking aloud to herself, she beat the air with her fists. She knew what she must do. She must throw up every-thing and travel to America, catch him before he had time to settle into his old life. She had to fling herself at him and hope to God that there weren't a hundred American women ready and capable of doing the same thing.

When daylight came she rang the airlines, amazed that her voice was so strong, checked on times and vowed to be ready to fly at eleven o'clock the next day.

Her next thought, inevitably, was what to wear. She had an old black bikini, but had not shaved her bikini line in years. Anyway, her stomach sagged too much, not to mention her boobs. So a new swimsuit was a necessity – probably the serious one-piece type for competitive swimmers. She could swim, had been pretty good in the fifth form. She had, of course, never made it to the sixth form.

Trousers were next. She had some in summer colours – to be more exact, she had one pair of white cotton trousers. She would take the clean pair of jeans and some tee shirts. As for something to wear in the evening, there was the black cotton with three-quarter sleeves. And she had a silky print two-piece with a solid coloured jacket. That would be just right in the cool of the evening. Could she get away with the rich green velvet with the scoop neck and short sleeves?

She drove to Colchester and raided M&S for panties, bras, half a dozen pairs of tights, shoes, black bootleg trousers and three cardigans.

Although she had done a great many favours for Doreen, she knew that she couldn't count on her for help in an emergency. Linus, her poor put-upon accountant, was the man to be trusted. She telephoned him and tried to explain her dilemma.

'Look, dear, I've got to go to America tomorrow . . . Yes, I know it's short notice, but Richard Dumas has gone back to the States . . . No, I don't think he will let me off the debt. I think he's run out on me – everything was going so well –

because he was told I'm a thief, and what million-aire wants to marry a thief? Yes, I know, but I never said he loved me. I said he *fancied* me. That's different. It's up to me to land him. I'm tired of mice in the thatch . . . What? No, I haven't gone off my head. I can't explain what I mean now, for God's sake!

'Anyway, I don't want to lose my stall, so I must pay the thirty-four pounds rent. Just in case I don't land Richard. Stop nagging at me, Linus. Can't you see I'm desperate? Just tell me. Will you get the money to them? I'll repay you when I get back . . . Of course from Richard's money. How else? I'm only going for a week . . . I can't depend on Trevor for anything. We quarrelled . . . Of course I told him the truth. I want to be upfront with him. That's honest, isn't it? Oh, Linus, please don't preach. I *do* know what I'm doing. I'm a rat. OK? I hate myself already, but I've made up my mind. I'll be a good wife to him. He'll have no grounds for complaint. I'll be so good, a proper wife wouldn't be able to compete. Wait and see. There's a key to my house under the flowerpot by the front door . . . What difference does it make? I've got nothing to steal . . . Squatters? You must be joking. I'll love you for ever for this. Bye!'

Linus sat for several seconds with the telephone in his hand as the disconnect signal played an ac-companiment to his bewildered thoughts. A woman for whom he had enormous affection, in whom he had no confidence whatsoever, was embarking on the greatest folly of her life, and he felt unable to stop her. All he could do was to pick up the key to her cottage before anyone else did so,

and pay her market rental out of the money he and
Betty regularly set aside for the mortgage. Betty
would kill him if she found out.

The plane ticket cost more money than Fran had
planned to pay, especially as she had to go club
class. Getting to the airport the next day was a
nightmare. She had just enough time to change
some of Richard's pounds into dollars before
rushing to the assembly point. Then the plane was
delayed for an hour.

When the flight finally took off, Fran discovered
that flying club class meant an agreeable amount of
pampering. Because it was free, she failed to notice
how much alcohol she was consuming. This at least
had the effect of giving her four hours' unaccus-
tomed sleep in the middle of the day. She woke,
feeling dreadful, in time to be served her lunch. The
food cleared her head, if it didn't make her feel any
better. But halfway through the little dessert she
suddenly thought that she had no idea what to say
to Richard when she phoned him.

*Hello, Richard, I've followed you to America because
I want to trap you into marriage. I know we parted
rather coolly, but you won't remember that. Just
remember that* . . . Her imagination deserted her.
She couldn't even think of something stupid to say
under such weird circumstances.

When the lunch tray had been removed, she
fetched her blanket and covered herself entirely, as
if trying to sleep in spite of the light. Cocooned and
hidden from the other passengers, she shivered
beyond control. For the first time, she began to
wonder if she actually was mad.

Miami airport hit her like a thunderbolt, all

noise, Spanish voices, heat and a sense that everyone else knew where to go and what to do. Nevertheless, she was efficiently decanted onto the baggage claim area. She finally retrieved her dented suitcase, and only then began to wonder what to do next.

She had not booked a hotel. She didn't intend to stay anywhere but with Richard, so there was nothing for it but to telephone him from the airport.

As she was later to learn, American pay telephones are beasts with minds of their own. The first two attempts brought her nothing. The third time she lost her money. She was running out of change and beginning to sweat despite the air-conditioning. The fourth call was evidently misrouted, for a disembodied robot woman's voice told her that before any help could be given, Fran must explain her financial position. Guilt and panic swept over her as she slammed the receiver back onto the cradle. A moment's calm consideration convinced her that even in America, the phone company didn't want to know where one stood financially before completing a call. With her last few coins, she dialled once more and froze when she heard Richard's voice.

'Hello,' he said again, sounding suspicious.

'Richard?'

'Is that you, Fran? How nice to hear your voice. What's the weather like over there?'

'I'm at Miami airport.'

A short pause, then: 'My God! Why? What?'

'Why did you run away from me? When we said goodbye the other night . . .'

'You've come all this way to see me?' He sounded amazed, but also rather pleased. 'You think I would run away from you without a word?'

She took a deep breath. 'I had to see you.'

'Oh, my dear.'

She heard the sigh of pleasure in his voice and knew she had him hooked. All she had to do now was reel him in. 'Can I come and stay with you, Richard?'

He thought that would be just wonderful. She should walk out the door of the airport, hail a cab and get the driver to bring her to Boca Raton. He would be waiting.

When she stepped out into a Miami afternoon, the heat hit her, sucking her breath away. She knew in an instant that she was wrongly dressed and that everything she had brought with her would be suffocatingly hot. It was five o'clock in the afternoon, but the sun blazed down on her, making her eyes water. Five hours earlier, her internal clock had already registered five o'clock GMT. She felt somewhat light-headed.

The struggle to stay alert began in earnest as she fought for a taxi, then endeavoured to make the non-English-speaking driver understand where she wanted to go. Later, he managed to communicate to her that he was Haitian. A nice man but a dangerous driver who turned right on a red light. In answer to her scream, he tried to explain that this was legal in America. She didn't believe him.

Conversation lagged until he thought to tell her that Miami was a dangerous place. She said she had heard as much, because Versace had been shot outside his home. She added in pidgin English, 'Bad, bad.' He knew of Versace, but assured her she was safe, because he had a gun. He waved it with his right hand, just to prove it.

Fran thought she was in no danger from gunmen, as the taxi never turned off six-lane motorways jammed with cars which were forever manoeuvring to be on the far right-hand lane so that they could turn onto the slip roads. Unlike British motorways, there were dozens of turn-offs.

The houses were boring white bungalows, scarcely differing one from the other, with chain-link fencing and little attempt to build a garden, but the public landscaping took her breath away. Palm trees underplanted with huge impatiens in hot pink, strange trees she had never seen before blooming gloriously, and some she had seen, although they were infinitely smaller when they struggled to survive in British living-rooms.

'The house plants grow out of doors!' she cried, then spent the next few minutes attempting to convey this thought to a man who had never seen rubber plants or Joseph's coat growing indoors.

Eventually they reached Ocean Boulevard, and Fran shook off her drowsiness to look about her. The taxi drew to a halt under the portico of a magnificent modern tower block, and Richard walked out from the shadows to pay the driver. Fran registered that the building faced a lake and that the sea was on the other side of it. Villa Royale appeared to have been built on a sand bar.

When they were alone, he turned to her and kissed her warmly. She kissed him back in triumph. She had gambled and won. For once everything was going right for her. She was tired, but felt as if all the worries she had ever suffered were lifted from her shoulders as easily as Richard was lifting her suitcase.

The cool marble hallway was a dark blur after the

glare of the sun. The ride in the lift was also some-thing of a blur as he kissed her again. When it came to a stop they walked out into Richard's own foyer, and from there into the entry and the glorious living-room. Curving white sofas, jewel-coloured cushions and rattan furniture couldn't compete with the ocean, seen through vast floor-to-ceiling windows, beyond an enormous terrace.

'Well,' he said, grinning at her. 'The master bedroom is over there to your right. The guest bedroom is beyond the kitchen to your left. Where are you going to sleep?'

Dazzled by the splendour, exhausted by the heat and the long journey, she yet had no difficulty in answering such a loaded question. She had come prepared for just this moment.

'Where do you sleep, darling?'

'In the master bedroom. It's got his and hers bathrooms.'

'Lead the way.'

He beamed at her, vulnerable in his desire. Fran began to hate herself just as Linus had said she would.

After she had showered, hung up her few clothes in what Richard called a walk-in closet and put on the polyester print two-piece, he showed her round his condo. She counted four toilets, a laundry area with automatic washing-machine and dryer, and a kitchen with black granite worktops, a small break-fast table and two chairs painted pale blue, and every piece of stainless steel equipment that a professional cook could wish for. Memories of her own kitchen brought tears to her eyes.

The fridge and freezer were both empty except for some orange juice and small bottles and tins of drinks mixers. The cupboards – he laughed as she opened them – contained an assortment of savoury snacks and several bottles of gin, bourbon and rum. Nothing else.

'How long have you lived here?' she asked as he prepared a ginger ale for her.

'A year or so.'

'Just since your wife died?'

'That's right. I came back to Boca the other day to put this condo up for sale. I put this project together, the whole building, but I'm ready to disinvest.'

'And I thought you had run out on me.'

'Why would you think that?'

She took her tall glass and walked into the living-room, where she sat down with her back to the sea. Even though the windows were treated in some way, the light dazzled her. 'I thought perhaps that Mr Falkland had told you I have a stall on Braintree market.'

'He did.'

'Is that all he said?'

'Just about.'

'Aren't you put off? I mean about me being a market trader and a thief, although I didn't short-change him. But I don't suppose you'll believe that a wealthy businessman like him would cheat a poor market trader . . . He was rude. You should hear the way some people speak to me.'

'Is it illegal?'

'Of course not. I'm . . . it's an honest trade.'

'Then why be ashamed of it? Let me tell you how I began my business career.'

During the following fifteen minutes he gave her a graphic account of his early struggles, beginning with the sudden departure of his father and continuing on to the day when his mother thought she would go to California. Fran said little except to encourage him. It was a story of triumph over adversity, a story of one man's relentless climb to the top, and she had to marvel that he seemed untouched by the traumas. He was gentle and sensitive. He had preserved his inner decent nature, which was a triumph in itself.

Then, looking at his watch, he stood up. 'Come on, I've got to feed you.'

They rode in his Cadillac for the short drive to Plaza Real, and Richard parked in the lot by Jacobson's department store.

'You Brits like to walk. Let's stroll down the promenade.'

Tired as she was, Fran was enchanted. The promenade consisted of two single-direction roads paved with brick-coloured setts, divided by fifty feet of formal gardens. Octagonal Moorish fountains alternated with grey-blue and cream octagonal pavilions, themselves adorned with bougainvillea. Huge banyan trees were under-planted with impatiens, while lines of palm trees were underplanted with *Ophiopogon*. Most of the central area was paved, but there were smaller geometric plots of perfect, brilliant green turf, and the beds held petunias and marigolds. Old-fashioned branched street lights were already glowing, as the short twilight gave way to darkness.

The most extraordinary thing, to Fran's eyes, were the two-storey buildings that lined the roads. They had been built to present a unified whole, with colonnades and very wide pavements to make shopping more comfortable in the Florida heat, and all the buildings were painted pink with white trim. Behind the shops were huge blocks of flats, also pink. Occasionally the colonnading stopped, creating an open space in which were more palm trees, and beneath them tables, chairs, and umbrellas. It was to one of these open-air restaurants that Richard guided her.

'We call it Florida pink down here. Not Suffolk pink.'

'It's glorious. Surely the rest of Florida doesn't look like this? In fact, I know it doesn't. I've ridden from the airport.'

'A genius named Addison Mizner dreamed up the style. He platted out Boca Raton in 1925 and died in 1933.'

'Platted?'

'Marked out the streets in a grid pattern. Some say he was more a stage designer because he wasn't a trained architect, but he had this dream of a style that's been called Spanish-Moorish-Romanesque-Gothic-Renaissance. Or the Palm Beach look, because he designed that first. The colour schemes you see around here are pure Mizner. Pink, the special red clay tiles, with turquoise and white trim – it takes supreme confidence to dare to put up a pink town. Of course, those of us who came later were just following in his footsteps. I'd love to have met him.'

'So you're a property developer.'

'Worse than being a market trader, eh?'

She had been served a margarita, and now chipped away absent-mindedly at the salty crust on the rim of her glass. 'Is that why you bought Gosfield Hall?'

'I advise the crab cakes and a salad. You won't

want anything too heavy at such a late hour. A late hour for you, that is.'

'Yes, fine.' She was waiting for an answer to her question.

'I never thought about developing Gosfield Hall. I was in a bit of a state about my daughter, Zoe, and I got Sebastian Race to buy a house for me an hour's drive from Cambridge. That's where she lives. I specified about a million. He bought Gosfield with my money. Only I was thinking of a million dollars, and he was thinking of a million pounds. Very funny, wouldn't you say? I'm never likely to be so stupid again. However, once Gosfield was mine, I had to decide what to do with it. I've since learned that before the Second World War a làdy named Ruth Lowe lived there with her son. They had twenty-two indoor servants and seven outdoor ones. But those days are gone. I can't live in the whole of Gosfield. I must find a decent use for it. It would make a nice hotel, don't you think? Suitably restored, of course.'

'The residents of Hall Drive wouldn't be pleased with all the traffic.'

'You don't have much time for property developers, do you? But don't you think some intelligent developer with the best interests of the people at heart could make some much-needed improvements to Halstead High Street? My God, the incline is one in ten! The trucks and artics can't get down it. There isn't enough parking for the stores, and there are too many empty buildings. They should tear down some of the buildings and build a well-disguised multi-storeyed car park. Something needs to be done.'

'A development like this one would use up half

of Halstead, Richard, and the through traffic would have to be rerouted somewhere. The town fought off a ring road which would use up more of the countryside. When a ring road is built, a town dies a little. America, so far as I can see, is built around cars. This beautiful shopping area is an island of sanity, designed for people to come out and walk on the pavements, but even here the car isn't banned. In Britain we've got to do it the other way round. Britain has got to stay designed for people.'

'The automobile is here to stay. You can't put back progress. It won't work.'

'But we haven't room for the sort of development you're talking about,' she said. 'By the way, have you seen Docklands in London?'

'Yes, and it could have been done better. Anyway, I'm talking about Halstead, not London.'

'They're going to build houses all over our countryside as it is.'

The crab cakes and salad were served. They ate in silence for a minute or two, then Richard put down his fork. Fran could tell he was annoyed. 'So property developers really are more despicable, greater objects of hatred than market traders.'

She should have stayed silent, but she couldn't resist making one more point. 'All this development in Florida is draining the Everglades. A great national treasure!'

'So they say. Don't think I don't appreciate England's problems. Let me tell you something amazing. Florida and England (not Britain) are about the same size, same square mileage. Florida has sixteen million people. It's increasing every day, so I don't know the exact figure. England, on the other hand, has a fairly steady population of thirty-five million, yet there is an enormous need for more housing in both places. Because of fragmented families and higher aspirations in England. Because of all the new residents in Florida. And it will be done by developers, whether anybody likes them or not. The trick is to find good developers, which is made more difficult in England by the fact that architects haven't had the opportunities to practise their skills in a country that values the past to the point of obsession. I mean, how much building experience can British architects get in their own country? In the States, we've been able to learn from our mistakes, because we've got so much room to expand, and because we aren't afraid to tear down mistakes and start again.'

'We've got to defend our countryside. They're grubbing out hedgerows and—'

'Yeah, that's another thing. I hear all this talk about oh, dear, isn't it terrible that the hedgerows are disappearing. But I don't hear anything positive, like a great scheme to plant new ones. They're only plants. They can be renewed. That's where the emphasis should be. All life is about decay and renewal. It's natural.'

Startled by his vehemence, she said, 'I didn't mean to offend you.'

He smiled. 'I'm not offended, honey. I won that round. Besides, I'm a good developer. When I was building in Boca Raton, I went along with what is appropriate in this town. I didn't put up mock Tudor or anything like that. In Gosfield, I'm taking advice every step of the way from Frank Toombs. Whatever it costs me – and using lime mortar and old bricks is damned expensive – I will do it right. Hey, you're falling asleep. Let's go home.'

'OK, but can we cross over and walk up the other side of the road? I haven't seen the shops on that side.'

'Sure.'

He dropped some money on the table and they crossed the beautiful central reservation to stroll up the colonnaded pavement towards the parked car. Fran was now experiencing an out-of-body sensation. She had been awake for almost twenty-four hours, except for the uncomfortable sleep on the plane. As she staggered with fatigue, Richard caught her in his arms. She looked up at him, a little drunk, very jet-lagged. He kissed her.

'Well,' said a harsh voice directly in front of them. 'If it isn't old Dickie Dumb-ass. You haven't wasted much time finding a floozy to console you, have you, old buddy?'

Fran would have moved away from Richard, stunned by the venom in the man's voice, but Richard held her tight to his side. 'Hello, Arnie. You're drunk as usual.'

Like most of the people out on this balmy night, Arnie was dressed casually, wearing stone chinos and a tee shirt tucked in. He was fat, half a head shorter than Richard, with receding grey hair, worn long at the back.

'Yeah, I could be drunk. Maybe even "as usual". Well I work hard. Why shouldn't I play hard? Eh? I'm normal. At least I didn't kill my wife.' Fran felt a convulsive reflex travel through Richard's body.

'The surprise is that she hasn't killed you before now,' said Richard, calmly. Fran wondered why he didn't hit the man. She also wondered what prompted such a vicious accusation.

'We're divorced.' Arnie was so drunk he seemed

to be playing out the stereotype comic drunk from an old movie.

'Are you still with Amticonco Elektroniks?'

'Yeah, and still Chief Executive Officer. How'd'ya like that?'

'Brilliant. Just brilliant. Will you excuse us? We're just off home.'

Richard walked her quickly away. Arnie shouted something after them, but she didn't catch it. Now fully awake, her chest ached from the effort of keeping up with Richard's long strides. They were soon inside the Cadillac, cushioned in silence. Richard said nothing to her until he had opened his own front door and switched on a few table lamps. She flopped down on the sofa, wondering where they could possibly go from here. He came to sit beside her, but they didn't touch.

'I have some explaining to do.'

'You don't have to—'

'No, I owe it to you. I've been running away from it for months. You think it's disgraceful being a market trader accused of short-changing somebody? That's nothing, I assure you.' He stood up. 'Do you want a cup of coffee?'

'No. Sit down and tell me everything if you feel it will make things better.'

He gave a short laugh, but he sat down again, leaning forward with his elbows on his knees, looking at the floor. 'Jenny and I fought like cat and dog in the later years. As I told you, her parents died. I didn't mention that Jenny, an only child, never recovered from the shock. The poor kid had never been given a chance to develop her independence. She was lost without them and kind of took it out on me.

'Zoe was well aware of the atmosphere in the house, although we stayed together for her sake. Then Jenny got sick. She was not a particularly brave woman and she didn't want to die. It was . . . hell. It took two years, and even at the end we couldn't manage to be civil. She hated me for being healthy, for living past forty-two. And for that, I don't blame her. No woman should have to go through what she went through. Poor Jenny.'

He put his hands over his head. Fran waited quietly, not daring to touch him, not daring to speak. She could imagine the pain they had all been through. The death of a youngish person was always hideous. Fran wondered how much Richard had loved Jenny, how much he missed her now.

He looked up, turned to her, forcing himself to meet her eyes. 'I was grief-stricken, of course, but Zoe was off her head. I still say she was off her head, a little crazy.'

'What did she do?'

'Well . . . I hate to have to tell you this. She . . . she went to Jorge and Maria and told them I had killed her mother. I mean, that I had been responsible. Of course, they told her not to be silly, offered her comfort. But she wasn't satisfied. God knows who else she spoke to . . . One night, just after we'd had something to eat – tuna salad, I can't forget – there was a knock on the door. I opened it. It was the police! They had a complaint that I had killed Jenny. I just said that was ridiculous, but Zoe came rushing up to the two policemen and said that I had killed her, she knew it.'

'Oh, my God! How can you bear to speak to her ever again?'

'You know the answer to that. She's my

daughter. She was hysterical. One of the policemen asked her how I had killed her mother. Zoe looked kind of blank. She was as white as a sheet, in fact. She said I hadn't loved her enough.'

'Did that satisfy them, Richard? Did they leave you alone after that?'

'Hell no. They said they had to investigate. They dug up her body! My God, there was no stone left unturned. Jenny's doctor was called to make a statement.'

'And Zoe?'

'We had one hell of a knock-down-and-drag-out fight. I said she was a spoiled brat, and I don't know what else. She said I deserved all the trouble I was having. I hadn't appreciated her mother. That sort of thing. Zoe and I had never, ever talked to each other that way. We were civilized people with good manners. It was . . . terrible, I can't find the right word. Then, God, she ran off to England with this Englishman. They were married in Cambridge. She wrote me a letter to say it was for the best, because then she couldn't testify against me. Cosmo shouldn't have taken advantage of an hysterical young woman. He shouldn't have. Oh, I think he's quite a nice guy. He provides Zoe with a stable element in her life, but . . . She ran away and broke my heart.'

Fran was stunned by the tragic futility of it all. So unnecessary. 'I suppose the word got out—'

He laughed harshly. 'It got out all right. That's how that creep, Arnie, knew where to hit me. Christ, I haven't been called Dickie Dumb-ass since I left school. I didn't even know he knew about it. I'm small potatoes in a town as big and wealthy as Boca Raton, but my father-in-law had been a major player at one time. I was news. The whole thing lasted about three weeks – a month since Jenny's death. I lost my wife, my daughter and my good name.'

'You poor man.'

'You must understand. Jenny spent the last two weeks of her life in hospital. Her pain was well-managed, and I didn't have any opportunity to poison her, I promise you. You do see why I feel that England may be the place for me. For a long time, I have not been happy here. And it has nothing to do with money, pink buildings or sunshine. A person is either happy inside himself or he isn't. I've made a new start in England. Zoe and I get along reasonably well, although . . . Cosmo is a good sort. And I have you.'

Pity for him caused her to lean over and kiss him on the cheek. His face was warm. She could feel his breath on her neck.

'At least we value you properly in England.'

He broke away, cheered by a happy thought. 'I'm not the only one with a nickname. We always called Arnie "Noem", because whenever a famous, important or rich person was mentioned, Arnie would say, "I know 'em."' He looked at his watch. 'It's a quarter to ten and all of a sudden I want to go to bed.'

'Oh, Richard!' She was close to tears and had no word of comfort for him, overwhelmed as she was by too many assorted emotions of her own. No wonder he had just let that drunk walk all over him! He had been too stunned to do otherwise. He had to have the most even disposition she had ever seen in a man.

She told him she would get ready immediately

and stood up from the settee before he could reach out to her. In the bathroom she contemplated whether or not it was worth the effort to cut out the Marks & Spencer label from her new black satin nightie, decided labels would be the last thing on his mind, and concentrated on worrying about her drooping tits. Could she find some excuse to beg that the lights be turned off? Not only had she no love for her forty-year-old body, she was also afraid of the light like a vampire fears the dawn. Afraid of discovery. Surely he would read the calculation and greed in her eyes if she tried to have sex with him when he could see her every expression. This poor battered man was being stalked for his money, but, she assured herself, she would make up to him for all that he had suffered.

The nightie was smooth against her skin. Twisting before the mirror, she was struck by the way satin could maximize the slightest figure fault. She brushed out her hair, patted the tears from her cheeks, took a deep breath and walked into the bedroom.

Pools of soft light poured from the scarlet shades of bedside lamps. The scarlet spread had been turned down. There was a single thin blanket over the sheets on the six-foot bed. Ten steps would take her to it, but she wasn't sure she could make them.

'Which side do you sleep on?' he asked. He was wearing blue boxer shorts, and she was surprised at his muscularity. He was hardly Stallone, but neither was he the soft-fleshed man his casual clothes seemed to cover.

'Next to the window. Do you mind?'

'Not at all. I always sleep on the other side.'

She slipped past him. Sat on the bed and turned

off the light on her side. He opened the scarlet and white curtains, then the sliding glass doors, crossed the room and switched off his own light. Hot, moist air floated through the open doorway. The ocean swooshed faintly, and after a second or two when her eyes adjusted to the dark, she could see moonlight playing on the water, distant lights blinking. She slid down on the bed, felt his hand on her shoulder. His touch paralysed her.

Oh God, I can't do this! Not tonight, I'm too tired. Too much has happened. I'm not ready!

But, as he gathered her to him, she found that she was ready. His warmth aroused long-forgotten needs. Thoughts of Sean, of the good times, the early days of their marriage flitted through her mind, until Richard's urgent presence sent such thoughts to oblivion. He was a good lover, but then what did she know? There had been no-one before or since Sean. Yet she could appreciate Richard's sensitivity, and thank God for it, knowing that not every man would be so sweetly attentive.

Later, when they were both settled to sleep, guilt and a surprising degree of resentment gripped her. Why couldn't he tell she was false? Why didn't he throw her out? She had cheated him of her inner being, the place where she kept her love. And he hadn't even noticed. She tried to hate him, but was too sleepy, began to drift, surfaced again when he got out of bed to go into the living-room, wondered why. Then sleep overtook her.

When she awoke, her watch said ten o'clock. He must have been up for ages! Quickly she showered and dressed. He was seated at the dining-room table, the space furthest from the bedroom. His office shared a wall with the bedroom, so she assumed she had driven him away by sleeping late.

He said he had gone out for Danish pastries and coffee, so that they could eat breakfast in the condo. He normally had breakfast at seven o'clock at Denny's. They would eat there the following morning. Then she could see what comprised the great American breakfast.

He was cheerful and loving. She was still tired, but only until he told her that he intended to take her shopping. He was sure, he said, that she didn't have clothes suitable for south Florida at Easter. She admitted it was far warmer than she had imagined.

They returned to the promenade so that she could patronize the exquisite, pricey shops whose windows she had admired the night before. She was intimidated by the assistants, by the gloss and assurance of the other customers, by the prices. In the second shop they entered, a woman addressed Richard by name, spoiling her pleasure entirely in the little mint green silk pants suit for five hundred dollars she intended to buy. The woman was beautiful, groomed to the last inch and dressed expensively. His sort of woman. She was also polite, warm, not seeming to mind about the terrible things he had stood accused of.

Refusing to be driven away from his old haunts, Richard agreed only to travel as far as the Royal Palm shopping centre, a pink pedestrian area with many shops selling the sort of classy tourist fare that had no place in Fran's life.

Finally they drove into Fort Lauderdale, to the cool, elegant Galleria shopping mall which had huge, impersonal shops where she could browse, happily anonymous.

After a salad lunch and a single glass of wine, they returned to the condo. Fran's new clothes filled the lift, and they had to prop open the door while they made three trips to the foyer with parcels. Fran was drunk with pleasure, scarcely able to remember what she had bought.

'Will you do me a favour?' asked Richard.

'Anything.'

'Put on the pink silk pant suit with the little fuchsia top and the thongy sandals.'

'What, now? At three o'clock?'

'We're expecting company at three thirty. A little business matter.'

She shrugged, happy to oblige, and went into the bedroom to hang up and put away what she calculated were five thousand dollars' worth of clothes.

When she returned to the living-room, dressed as Richard had requested, she understood why he had wanted her to look her best. Arnie was seated on the edge of a rattan chair, looking sober and worried.

'Come in, honey. I didn't bother to introduce you last night. Arnie, this is Mrs Fran Craig, divorced, garden designer, very good friend. Fran, meet Arnie Cley, chief executive officer of Amticonco Elektroniks, of which I am now the major shareholder.'

Arnie leapt to his feet. 'What? How?'

'I bought out Wilkinson and Tauber. I paid them top dollar for their shares, and they nearly wet themselves, so pleased were they to be getting out from under a failing company. They think I'm crazy, but you know that I'm not getting mad, I'm getting even. I've invested nine hundred thousand dollars in this chicken-shit collection of bad ideas and sloppy management, and I intend to get my money back.'

'You try to get rid of me and it'll cost you.'

'I've no intention of getting rid of you,' said Richard quietly. 'I intend to go through the books with a fine-tooth comb. What little I've seen so far does not please me. A few irregularities, Arnie, a little sloppy accounting. Never mind, we'll get it sorted out. You have until Friday. I'll meet you at the office at half past seven. OK? You know the way out.'

Arnie headed for the door, then stopped, sighed, and turned to Fran with a weak smile. 'I didn't know. I was drunk and, believe me, I'm sorry if you were offended. Please accept my apology for my crude words.'

Fran nodded, afraid to speak lest she annoy Richard by being either too friendly or too stand-offish. He had shown her another side of himself, the incredibly tough businessman, the man who did not forgive a transgression and was prepared to punish ferociously, the man who did not get mad. The man who would one day discover what a scheming bitch she had been. The man who would inevitably get even with her. She shivered, but she couldn't help admiring his strength. My God, she thought, he wasn't even breathing hard after the confrontation!

He smiled at her. 'You can change into something more comfortable now.' He rubbed his chin, looking a little sheepish. 'The Boca Raton Club is the smartest place in town, but I don't want to go there. You understand?'

'Yes, of course. I don't want to go there, either. No, heaven forbid. Oh, Richard, let's stay away from old acquaintances. Let's go somewhere more casual.'

'All right. Let me see . . . I've got it. Wear that little blue dress with the buttons down the front. You won't need pantihose, because nobody will be wearing them, but you may want to take a sweater with you. We'll leave at half past five. Can you amuse yourself until then? I've got a little paperwork to do.'

'That's all right. I'll go down to the pool and have a swim.'

She changed into her new swimsuit and matching wrap, put on her flip-flops and let herself out of the apartment. Richard mumbled goodbye, caught up in his business papers, not at all interested in her. She pondered his attention to her clothes. Was he a control freak or a smart marketer who wished to show her off to the best advantage, or was it that he didn't think she would know what to wear because she was just a market trader living above herself? The latter, she decided, and was happiest with this explanation.

No-one spoke to her when she reached the pool area, although there were several women stretched out in loungers. She swam a dozen lengths of the pool, then pulled herself up onto the edge where she sat dangling her legs in the water. She was sure that everyone knew she was Richard Dumas's bit on the side. Feeling acutely embarrassed, she got out of the water, realized she had forgotten to bring a towel and padded back to the lift.

As the lift doors opened, Richard was waiting for her. 'Apparently you forgot to take a towel.' He handed her a thick white one.

'How do you know? Could you see me?'

'No.' He laughed. 'There are rules here. I doubt if you had gotten into the lift before someone complained. The porter rang me.'

'This is the land of the free, isn't it? I can't believe people could be that petty.'

'There are rules. Everybody buys into them, choosing to have order and beauty rather than chaos. Seb Race can't understand why I don't mind the restrictions on a Grade I home, but what would happen if there weren't any restrictions in this world?'

'Yes,' she said, quietly, not choosing to argue the point. 'I mustn't disturb you. I want to sort out my clothes.'

In the bedroom she threw down the towel, peeled off her swimsuit and got into the shower. Bloody well spied on! What harm had she done to their precious lift, anyway? Nit-pickers! Nosy buggers! Ten minutes later she had cooled down. She had washed her hair, rubbing so hard that her head still tingled. She pulled on a new pair of turquoise trousers and one of her own tee shirts, and went, bare-footed, to the walk-in closet already sorted. She had put the new clothes in rainbow order, for they were all bright with the exception of a pretty black jersey dress cut very low in the back.

They looked like jewels, these trouser suits, tailored dresses and shorts outfits. Six pairs of shoes were no less bright. In a country where even desiccated old ladies wore sugar pink shorts or lemon yellow trousers, her wardrobe was unexceptional. But what was she to do with these clothes when she returned to England where the light was different and women just did not wear silk trousers to shop at Sainsbury's?

That night they went to The Cove in Deerfield Beach for a drink. Richard drove up to what seemed at first to be a wooden shack, left his keys in the car and the motor running as he helped her out. A young man handed him a ticket and they started to walk inside.

'Is he going to park your car? There were plenty of spaces. You could have done it yourself.'

'Not allowed. More of our restrictive rules.'

'You mean you let a bunch of kids tree you, just for a tip?'

'The boys work for a valet parking company. Jorge and I used to own one many years ago. The boys get paid and the charge is fixed – a couple of dollars. As The Cove gets crowded, they will be able to drive the cars a couple of blocks away and retrieve them when the customer comes out. It can be a lucrative business, because no party-giver worth his salt would fail to call in a valet parking company to park cars for his guests. But you need a couple of million dollars' worth of insurance. These kids park cars so fast and with such style that they sometimes do a lot of damage. If the car is a Porsche, the bill can be considerable. There's also the occasional theft.'

The Cove appeared to have been flung together with odd pieces of rough wood, but that was merely the intended impression. Seating was arranged on three sides which were open to the elements above dado height. The timber ceiling was hung with dozens of baskets containing every sort of philodendron imaginable. The clientele was of all ages, including small children and babies, the music was loud, the servers, both male and female, were wearing short shorts.

Every restaurant has an atmosphere of some sort. The Cove's was palpable. People had come to have a good time. They were prepared to talk above the blare of the music. They were well off and aware that they were enjoying the good life. Fran had already decided that she loved it, before the waitress directed them to a small table for two within sight of the Intracoastal waterway, a man-made canal six times the width of an English one, that went, Richard told her, all the way up the coast of America.

Richard ordered two whisky sours, and when the drinks were delivered the waitress gave them tokens for two more drinks, free. Fran gaped.

'Would you like something to eat? It's free over there. Come on, I'll show you how Americans can have a good time at a fraction of the cost of the Brits.'

Under infra-red lights people were helping themselves to taco shells and filling them with minced beef, lettuce and tomato and melted cheese. Or they might just prefer freshly made popcorn. 'Don't eat too much,' warned Richard. 'We're going across the street for dinner.'

The Captain's Table was also a single-storey building, also directly situated on the Intracoastal. A road bridge was close by and from time to time its central portion parted to allow high-masted boats to travel through. The scene was continually changing and Fran enjoyed watching it all. On the other hand, she had not enjoyed queuing to get a table. The restaurant did not take reservations during the season, and every restaurant was, apparently, so much in demand that queuing was inevitable.

She thought it would have been better to eat the casual fare at The Cove. They ate a flat fish she had never heard of, and she marvelled at the very small portion of courgettes that was their vegetable of the day.

'Are you going to take me to a Cuban restaurant sometime?' she asked over dessert.

'If you wish. I'm not particularly fond of Cuban food.'

'Then why did you open a string of Cuban restaurants in East Anglia?'

He shrugged. 'Food's food.'

'No, it isn't. Nothing defines people more than what and how they eat.'

'Look, honey. Maybe food isn't just food, but business is business. I've been a money-making machine since I was fifteen. I've dabbled in every sort of business going, and the principles are the same. You've got to understand money. You must understand the principles of management and marketing, especially marketing. In retailing, you must know that the choice of location is vital. You need passing trade. A proper level of investment is important, too. I've got it right with the Miami Spice cafés. I've got my finger on the pulse of the business.'

'But you never eat at one.'

He sighed, impatient with her comments. 'I don't need to. I know what I need to know.'

Some imp of mischief had taken hold of Fran's tongue. 'Who's the manager of the Chelmsford Miami Spice?'

Now he smiled broadly, enjoying the challenge. 'Alan Beeson, tall chappie with a hollow chest. Big grin. A live wire.'

'How much does he make?'

'Never try to catch me out on figures. He gets ten thousand a year, but a bonus for turnover.'

'Wrong!' she crowed, and wished she hadn't when he frowned. 'Alan has left for a better job in London, more pay, a real manager's job, not just a dogsbody. I'm quoting. The new chappie is sour-faced and sloppy, also resentful. He gets nine thousand. I don't know about the bonus.'

Richard had that cool look she had noted with apprehension on several occasions. 'Staff turnover is thirty-four per cent in the food business. Was it busy?'

'Not at three o'clock in the afternoon. Why didn't you open something like The Cove?'

'I might have if I had started from scratch. Hmm. I must give Sebastian Race a call. I'll do that tomorrow.'

Searching for a neutral subject, she leaned towards him. 'This is a very posh place. I just saw a man with a motorized Zimmer frame.'

'Sometimes they have wheels.'

'And gears!'

Now he smiled. 'That's a brake. You must admit old people have the good life down here. They come in their millions. The only thing is, they sometimes leave behind families hundreds of miles away. When they get too frail to look after themselves, they either have to go back where they came from or put themselves into sheltered homes, if they can afford it.'

'The heat and the sunshine must suit them very well, but they can't walk to amusements. They have to drive. I saw a couple of quite terrifying near accidents on our way over here. There's no public transport to speak of and taxis don't seem to be the answer. Like at any other time of life, it's OK if you're rich.'

'Yes. I grew up in Deerfield Beach. Not so well-to-do as Boca, of course. I know a fair amount about retirees. They're more interesting than Cuban restaurants.'

Chapter Eight

Linus drove over to Fran's house shortly after she flew off to Florida and was appalled. The house was reached down a short unmade drive. There was a front gate which led down an overgrown path to the front door, but there was no fencing on either side of the gate. An annexe of black weatherboarding snuggled next to the house, and both structures had the shaggy look that very old thatch achieves. The roofs needed rethatching, but Fran would never be able to afford it.

Most likely built in the last century as a farm-worker's cottage, it would not have had running water or an indoor toilet, much less gas or electricity. Probably there had been no work done on the structure in fifty years. The plaster was certainly in need of attention.

The two downstairs window-frames were rotten. The front door was made of planks and had been painted blue many years before. The trellis-work around the door sagged to one side, too tired to support the branches of some unknown variety of rose. He knew without entering that the steep stairs would be directly opposite the door, that the ceilings would be low, that the shallow room on the right was the kitchen and the one to the left was the sitting-room, which was sure to be damp. Upstairs there might now be a bathroom, but it would have been made at the expense of one of the bedrooms. He supposed there must still be two, since Trevor had been living here until recently.

He walked around to the back of the house to inspect the nursery. A young girl of about twelve was watering the containers in the polytunnel, looking thoroughly bored. When she saw him approach she froze in terror, and he was quick to assure her that he had simply come to check over the house.

'I'm Mrs Craig's accountant, and I've just come to pick up some papers. I have a key, so don't worry about me. I'll not come into the tunnel. You can carry on with what you're doing or go home until I've left. Whichever.'

'I'll go home.' She switched off the water and ran out the back of the tunnel. It was irritating to know he had caused such a reaction, but he couldn't really blame the child. She was behaving sensibly. He returned to the front door of the cottage and studied what would be the view from the kitchen window. There was not another house in sight, although he could see a barn through the trees on the other side of the road. No wonder Fran had been able to buy the property cheaply. No-one in his right mind would want to live out here.

He retrieved the key from under the flowerpot and, after a moment's hesitation, let himself into the kitchen. What he saw depressed him enormously. The poor thing quite rightly saw marrying a rich man as her only hope. The kitchen was scarcely more than ten by fifteen, and he thought he could feel the damp rising up through the soles of his shoes. A clothes rack displayed two pairs of jeans above the vandalized fireplace which now held a wood-burning stove where the original homely range should have been. Perhaps half a dozen children of some farm-worker would have played on the brick floor while the wife peeled vegetables for the family's humble stew. It would have been a romantic sight, and Victorian painters would have delighted in portraying it.

In the Nineties, however, the kitchen told a very different story, one of poverty and despair. Such kitchens couldn't accommodate automatic washing-machines or electric cookers without looking pathetic. And plastic make-shift desks had no place in this nineteenth-century rural scene. Fran's desk looked like a storm had hit it.

He was reminded that she had thrown out all her bills and receipts which she kept in supermarket carrier bags, and smiled as he thumbed through the papers on the desk. She said she had thrown them away when cleaning up. It couldn't have happened all that long ago, and he had seen half a dozen black bin-bags by the side of the driveway. Perhaps she had simply panicked, imagining it to be too late to retrieve the papers. It would certainly be in her character to do so. Setting down his briefcase, he left the desk covered in neat stacks of paper, which he had arranged according to subject and in date order, and went outdoors to untie the rubbish bags.

It didn't take him long to find the two carrier bags, one with receipts in it, the other with bills. Returning to the house, he started to deal with them before remembering that he had scared the girl away from her watering. It would be better if he were seen to drive away. That way, the girl would return to her task. He gathered up all the relevant papers and, locking the door behind him, went back to his car. Then he remembered he had left his briefcase in the house. Putting the key in the door, he pushed it open in time to frighten a young woman dressed only in a man's shirt as she came down the stairs. Barefooted and tousle-haired, she looked extremely young, but Linus presumed she was Trevor's latest.

'Jesus!' she cried, and Trevor called from upstairs. 'What'sa matter?'

The girl had run past Linus, through the kitchen to the barn extension. Trevor, in tee shirt and Y-fronts, came to the top of the stairs.

'What are you doing here? How come you've got a key to my mum's house?'

'She asked me to come over and see what I can do about her finances.'

Trevor scratched his stomach. 'Did she tell you she's set a trap for some Yank? She left me a note. Apparently she's gone out to Florida to catch him. Silly bitch.'

'Don't talk about her like that!'

'Ooh!' said Trevor mockingly, and disappeared. When he reappeared in the kitchen he was wearing the same tee shirt, but had pulled on a pair of jeans and trainers. He had even combed his hair.

'I'm finished with her. How would you like your mother to offer herself to the highest bidder?'

'I don't see it that way. She can't make it by going on the market one day a week. She hasn't got any help to enable her to grow enough for several days on the markets. Her garden-designing business hasn't taken off, and she's sunk too much of her money in this slum. What can she do?'

'Run off to the sun, obviously. You need a mummy, do you? Think you'd like mine? No, I reckon you just like older women. My mother, you must admit, is pretty sexy.' Trevor's aggressive tone made Linus grind his teeth.

'My mother died when I was ten, my dad passed away eighteen months ago. Betty's mum went to Australia with her second husband. So we are a bit short of mothers. We both think that if we had a spare mother lying around, we'd treat her better than you treat Fran. Have you no feelings at all?'

'Listen, Charlotte and I are going to man the stall on the Thursday before Easter. I'll split the takings with Mum half and half. That's fair, isn't it?'

Linus could do nothing but agree. The girl came into the kitchen, dressed in tee shirt and jeans. She had combed her hair and now offered to make him a cup of coffee, but he didn't fancy sitting down for a cosy chat with these two, so he left almost immediately.

It being Thursday, he then drove all the way to Braintree to speak to the market inspector. Had Fran enquired, she would have found that she was entitled to several weeks' holiday and, therefore, didn't owe any money to the council. Linus said she would be away for one week and that her son would man the stall the following Thursday.

If he had any paying clients Linus would never have spent so much time trying to sort out Fran's accounts, but what with business being slack to the point of non-existent, he worked for many hours trying to rationalize her actions. First of all he assumed that he would be able to find a way to account for her spending of Dumas's money, so he paid all her bills.

But when he trolled through the receipts he saw that there was no honest way to make Fran appear to be solvent. She truly owed Richard Dumas ten thousand pounds' worth of garden-design work.

The previous week Linus had gone to Enfield to pay off the thousand-pound loan to Fran's mysterious contact. The man turned out to be a villain, a heavyweight of six feet something who was not particularly pleased to be handed a cheque for a thousand pounds.

'And the rest,' he had said menacingly. 'The silly cow didn't think she could get away without paying interest, did she?'

'I was just told to bring a thousand pounds.'

'What are you, then? Her toy boy?' the giant had asked.

'Her accountant.'

'Well, ain't she something. Can't pay her bills, tries to short-change an old friend, but she can afford an accountant.'

'I do her books for nothing. Look, what interest does she owe?' Linus had no intention of getting on the wrong side of this man.

'Two hundred quid.' He held out his hand, into which Linus eventually put a cheque of his own.

For some reason, it hadn't occurred to Linus that Fran would have access to British newspapers. He was therefore surprised to receive a call from her on Saturday evening. She wanted to know, naturally enough, if everything was all right. She had read that the weather was going to be exceptionally good over Easter, and moaned that she would be missing a lot of pre-Easter business. He told her he had paid her bills and that Trevor was going to open the stall on the Thursday before Easter. He also told her she would not be penalized for failing to open her stall on the previous Thursday. He did not mention that he had paid two hundred pounds in interest on her loan. Betty would murder him if she found out, so he preferred to put the whole business at the back of his mind.

'How's it going, by the way? Have you fallen in love with him yet?' he asked when he had given her all his news.

'I can't. It's wonderful being here and he's bought me thousands of dollars' worth of clothes, but I can't, Linus. Do you understand? I'm doing a terrible thing and I hate myself. I can't love him. He's gone to his business for a few hours, and I'm here alone in this beautiful apartment by the sea. Yet I can't settle. I can't read a novel or watch the television or try on all the beautiful clothes. Oh, Linus . . .' He heard her sniff. 'We've decided not to come back to England straight away, because it's hard to get plane tickets just when all the snow birds are going home. We're going to drive down to Key West and stay over Easter. Richard has taken care of it all.'

'Well, that doesn't sound too bad. I wish I was somewhere warm.'

'He can be very vindictive when someone cheats him. He's going to kill me when he finds out I'm only chasing after him for his money.'

'My God, Fran,' said Linus in exasperation. 'He sounds like a very kind man. I think I could fall in love with him, myself, if I were in your circumstances.'

'You don't understand . . . There's the lift! Goodbye!'

Richard had also made a phone call to England. He had called Jorge at home and discussed Fran's information about the Chelmsford branch of Miami Spice. It turned out he really was out of touch with the business. The original manager, Alan, had soon left for a better post, and the new manager was receiving less money. The Chelmsford branch was, nevertheless, faring considerably better than the Aldeburgh and Woodbridge branches. Richard and Jorge discussed the possibility of closing them in order to concentrate on the more successful sites. They decided they should wait until the weather warmed up, if it ever did, and see how the holiday trade took to Cuban food.

He had also phoned Liz to see if there were any messages. Nothing, she had told him, except that the local branch of the Red Cross had written asking if they could have a fund-raising evening at the Hall. To this he readily agreed and asked Liz to make the arrangements with the Red Cross committee.

He let himself into the condo just as Fran was hanging up the phone. 'Hey, honey, how's everything back home?'

'I'm losing business because I can't catch the pre-Easter trade. I don't think my plants are very well looked after, but Trevor and his girl are going to the market next Thursday. He's going to share the takings with me, but we'd take more if I were there.'

'Write off the whole damn market and live off

the money you make designing gardens.'

'I can't do that! You're my only client.'

'Fran, we're friends. Remember?'

She smiled. 'I haven't forgotten. Anyone would be proud to be your friend.'

He kissed her, then went to sit down on the couch, patting the seat beside him. She looked every minute of her forty years at this moment, bowed down by a minor piece of bad news. He didn't know how to convince her that losing business on the market wasn't a tragedy.

'I've got a confession to make. I rang Jorge from the office. You were right, of course. Alan did leave the Chelmsford Miami Spice for a better job, and the new guy isn't getting as much. Not worth it. But that branch is doing pretty well. It's the ones in Aldeburgh and Woodbridge that are losing money hand over fist.'

'If you had ever been to those two places before the cafés were opened, you would have known that the residents wouldn't care for them.'

'I know,' he said. 'But I bought into the six restaurants because I wanted an excuse to come to England. Because of Zoe, you know. There have been mistakes. I brought Jorge along, and the Cuban thing sort of took off. It's not as if you Brits don't like foreign food. You do. But the sites called for one sort of eating-place. Jorge and I are used to a different sort, and things just got out of hand. However, believe me. I'm going to win through.'

'I don't doubt it. I'm the last person to criticize. But I do think that being a market trader teaches you a lot of things. I grow what I know will sell. And I know what will sell because I actually talk to the customers, hear their complaints and requests.'

'Yes, that's the most basic form of business. The next step is to think bigger, to remove yourself from the producing and the selling, and yet know what's wanted. Hey, I've got an idea. I'm going to show you I know about the food business in my own country. Don't bother to dress up tonight. This place is casual. It's called the Seafood Connection, and I've been told they sell fifteen hundred meals a day. Or is it fifteen hundred meals twice a day?'

The Seafood Connection was a large building in its own landscaped garden with ample parking for all its many customers. Fifteen or twenty of those customers were standing outside, clearly waiting for their chance to get indoors. Fran hated queuing to eat, but the half-hour passed fairly painlessly as they talked about business, plants, restaurants and – quietly – about the other customers, who were mostly what Richard called retirees.

Once inside, there was another wait during which they had cocktails. Two for the price of one, they were assured. Two whisky sours were delivered to Fran at the same time. She found the first one rather weak, but the second was no better. Hoping that a single measure of alcohol had been divided between the two drinks, she finished them off with a clear conscience.

The restaurant was vast, clean, well-designed and on several levels. The noise was considerable as pensioners and young families occupied large tables and laughed loudly with their friends. The first course, salad, was free, being part of the meal. The fish was fresh and well-cooked, the desserts just the sort of gooey finish to a meal that everyone seemed to love. The coffee was constantly replenished, but of the mild sort Americans preferred.

'Economies of scale,' said Richard. 'The right way to run a restaurant. They are well-organized, give good value and can afford to keep their prices at rock-bottom. That's what Jorge and I would have done in England, if we had started from scratch.'

'Like Terence Conran with his restaurants in London. I understand they're huge, but I prefer somewhere a little more intimate.'

'Conran's places are also pricey. What I'm talking about is providing good, cheap meals in pleasant surroundings for older people as well as for young families. They are, you might say, the future. The population is ageing. They need to be catered for, and they have money. Not like in our grandparents' day.'

'If you think that your cheap chains are better than our cheap chains, I won't argue because I don't know.'

'And cheaper,' he said. 'That's important. They're cheaper.'

Fran commented on the fact that all the staff seemed to be very young. Richard agreed. When their waiter came to deliver the bill, Richard said, 'Are you working here to help pay for college?'

The waiter grinned, although it was an effort. 'I already have a degree and my master's degree. I work here full time.'

'You see?' said Richard when the young man had moved away. 'You and I were right not to bother.'

'I've never thought of it that way. It's true, though. I don't mind not having been to university.'

'I lie.' He laughed. 'I would like to have had just

224

one year, if only to convince myself that going to college isn't necessary. I've always felt like a dumb cluck because I don't have any experience of college life. But I was forgetting. You have a degree in garden design.'

She shook her head. 'A five-week course spread over a year with a certificate at the end. I'll tell you what, though. I won the prize for the student who made the most progress during the year. I was terrified when I enrolled. Stood outside for ages before I got the courage to go in. My spelling was a disgrace. I could scarcely add two and two, but just being there and learning something made me more confident. When I got the prize for the most progress – not, you understand, for the highest grades – I was so moved I just broke down and cried in front of everyone. Trevor was terribly embarrassed. Anyway, what it taught me is that I could do more than I imagined. And I started buying books! Second-hand, but about gardening and the history of it. That was a breakthrough for me, especially as my mother thought I was wasting my money.'

'You're wonderful.'

'No, I'm not. You've never been a dumbo like me. And I'll bet you've never done anything dishonest in your life.'

'Probably I have, but if you mean have I been honest in business, well, there's never been a need for cheating. I always thought I wouldn't know how well I was doing if I cheated. It's been a bit of a game with me. How far could I go playing strictly by the rules.'

She sighed and began fiddling with her coffee-spoon. 'After I got my certificate, I thought I could fly. I really was ridiculously big-headed for a while. I had already sold my house and put the money in the building society. Trevor and I lived with my parents until Dad died. Then I bought my property outside Toppesfield. An acre of land and a cottage. It cost me just about every penny I had. I thought I would be inundated with customers clamouring for my services. But nobody answered my advertisements. Then I thought I had better get a market stall. I'd buy from a wholesaler until my own stock grew. I saw an ad in the papers, a man was selling the goodwill on his plant stall on Braintree market for six thousand. I bought it, and fortunately it included the trestle-tables and the rods and plastic to make the stall, because the council don't supply those things. Then I discovered that I had been conned. The council won't automatically give you a place just because someone has sold you his goodwill. And, anyway, I could have got a place just by applying. One pound seventy a foot for the frontage.'

'You paid six thousand for nothing? Oh, God, Fran. I'm sorry.'

'We'd had to pay to have a bathroom and septic tank put in. I was broke, had no money for plants, and the wholesaler didn't know me so he wouldn't give credit. Trevor said he'd take care of it. Came the first Thursday, I had a stall full of small shrubs and bedding plants. It was June the first.'

'Where did he get the plants?' asked Richard quietly.

'He stole them from roundabouts. I didn't know for sure at the time, and I didn't ask. That's the worst of it. I didn't ask, as if ignorance would make it better.' She looked up at him, waiting for the words of scorn. He only laughed affectionately.

'Maybe in your place, I would have done the same.'

'Oh, don't. I know you must despise me.' He said nothing, just sat looking at her. She couldn't read his expression. 'Oh, say something, Richard.'

'I was just thinking several things. First, Zoe never knew what you and I have experienced.'

'Neither did your wife.'

'True. She was brought up as the poor little rich girl, although her old man was very keen to have the money I brought into the business. Jenny never knew how close he was to folding before I came along. Of the two of us, you and me, I had the best of it. I started when I was young, and I didn't have a child to worry about.' He sighed, shook his head. 'The other thing I was thinking is how often people decide to go into business when they've just got enough money to enable them to open. You need money for running expenses. It might be a year or two before the business takes off. You have to have something to live on in the meantime. Why, we borrowed four hundred thousand from the bank for that very purpose.'

'You didn't use your own money?'

'No, it's not a good idea to have all your capital tied up. On top of that, we borrowed a million from a business angel. I had to put up the deeds to Gosfield Hall, and I'll lose it if we don't pay back the million within five years. He drove a hard bargain. We have to pay fifteen per cent interest in the meantime.'

'My God! Is it worth it?'

'The way I look at it, it's the company's borrowing, not mine. It may seem a funny thing to you, but a lot of big business is based on borrowing. Some businesses are very highly geared, meaning they have borrowed a lot of money but that's risky. Let's go. We want to get an early start tomorrow, but first I'm going to take you for a long drive along the coast.'

That night as she lay in bed, Fran remembered the conversation at dinner. She had told him about the theft hoping that he would be so disgusted with her that he broke off their relationship. It was not to be, for some reason. The fool had shown her sympathy and understanding, had not uttered one word of condemnation. But – and here was the danger – had he just pretended to be unmoved by her confession, or was he plotting to dump her? He was capable of it. She had seen him in action.

So here she was in an earthly paradise, lying on her side in a huge bed, facing the sea breeze as it played on her skin. She had been wined, dined and entertained, her every whim indulged and . . . His hand came to rest on her shoulder and she jerked in surprise. She hadn't noticed when the lights went off, nor when the bed took his weight.

'I'm sorry,' he said. 'You're tired.'

She turned on her back and reached up to his face. As always, her body responded to him even as her mind remained detached. Eventually even her worries fled in the face of such a practised, sensitive assault, and for half an hour she gave in to uncomplicated pleasure.

The mood lasted for several minutes after they had settled for sleep, then he spoke in the darkness. 'Are you asleep?'

'No. Are you?'

'I just wanted to say something. I've spent some pretty tortured nights since Jenny died. We could have done better together while we had the time. I think I came to hate her for bringing out the worst in me. But since that first moment I saw you get out of the taxi downstairs with your red face and your old suitcase, I've been undergoing some sort of healing process. I've . . . it sounds pompous. I've learned to forgive her for being Jenny. One day, with your help, I may begin to forgive myself for bringing out the worst in her.'

She sighed, not wanting to hear this painful confession. 'I guess there was unfinished business between you when she died. You would have got it right eventually.'

'How kind of you to say so. What about you and Sean? Have you forgiven him?'

'No,' she said without hesitation. 'I still want to kill him.'

Richard's response surprised her. 'Well,' he said sadly. 'I'll have to try to make you forget him. When . . . if . . . you come to love me, Sean won't matter.'

For some reason, it was important that he not get the wrong idea. She raised up on one elbow and strained to see his expression in the dark. 'Listen. Sean came round one day looking for Trevor. He's a cabinet-maker and very good. He said my kitchen was a disgrace and if I would give him a hundred pounds, he would give it a make-over. Then he rang up and asked for another two hundred and said he would be coming over the next Saturday bright and early. You asked me to come to the grand opening of the restaurants on the Friday, but I said no so that I could go home and take down all the shelves and move everything out. And do you know what the bastard did? He rang the next afternoon and said he was married. I didn't get the new kitchen and he didn't pay me back my three hundred. Now you see why I want to murder him.'

'You're still in contact with him? I didn't know that. Perhaps what angers you is that he got married.'

'No, I tell you. You sound like Trevor.'

'Do I?'

She flounced over to her side of the bed, threw herself down and covered her head with her pillow. She felt him turn over, slipped the pillow partially off her head so that she could breathe, and finally slept.

In the night the wind strengthened, making the curtains flap noisily. Richard got up and closed the sliding doors and pulled the curtains, stumbled back to bed in total darkness.

She heard him mutter a curse, but was still so angry that she couldn't even say, 'Sorry you stubbed your toe.'

Her dreams were troubled and confused. There was deep within her a strong desire to do something worthwhile for Richard, to use his ten thousand pounds to make something absolutely wonderful at Gosfield Hall. That way, she wouldn't have to think of herself as a common thief.

Dreaming was not the solution, however. She didn't know what it could be. Something about living in an earthly paradise. Something about Moorish fountains splashing sparkling water in the Florida heat. Something about creating a paradise garden for this man. But the thoughts were garbled and soon dissipated with the morning light and the rigours of packing.

The room on the ground floor of Gosfield Hall that Richard had taken for his own was very handsome, with a high ceiling and linenfold panelling on the walls. Liz Morgan had a desk at right angles to Richard's and loved working in such elegant surroundings. Richard had bought her a powerful computer and every other piece of equipment she said she wanted. He paid her well and expected two things in return: efficiency and loyalty.

Liz was reminded of this when Sebastian Race entered without knocking. In spite of herself she smiled brightly and sat up in her chair, the better to impress him with her large bust.

'Good morning, Seb.'

'Good morning, sweetie.' He glanced behind him, then leaned forward to kiss her on the lips. 'How are you today?'

'Oh, Seb, you do take chances. All's quiet here. I've had word from Richard. He's staying in Florida until after Easter. You'll never guess who's with him.'

He pretended to think, then, 'Golly, I guess it's got to be the market trader.'

She laughed. 'You're a good guesser. She followed him out there. Rang me up and was rather put out that he had left the country without getting her permission.'

'Silly bitch.'

'Then, the next thing we know, he's calling to say that they won't be back in England as soon as he had planned. They're going down to Key West. He wants to show her Florida, if you can believe that.'

He picked up a brass paper-clip in the shape of a woman's hand. 'Nice. A replica from Past Times?'

'Yes. I suppose you would say that I shouldn't buy from a company that markets nostalgic replicas, but I like it.'

'Liz, don't be so sensitive. After all, you won't find a genuine Victorian brass paper-clip in the shape of a hand, if that should happen to be what you want. I like it, too. It's more appropriate in this house than some modern, plastic one would be. By the Victorian era this house was past its heyday, I suppose. A member of the Courtauld family bought it and put in central heating and just generally refurbished it.'

'I know lots of people had a hand in making this house what it is. Did Courtauld put in the grand salon?'

'No, no, that was much earlier. The whole of the east wing was greatly changed by Sir Thomas Millington. He bought the house in 1691. He was First Physician to William and Mary and to Queen Anne. He built the grand salon which is a storey and a half tall. That means that there is a useless room above it. It's six feet high and has no windows. Very strange. You could spy on people in the grand salon, and listen to their conversations if they happened to be talking near the fireplace. I wish Richard would entertain in the grand salon. I should love to spy on him. Does he know about the secret chamber?'

'I'm afraid he does, dear. The Red Cross is going to have a do here. You could spy on them, I suppose. Richard's been over all the house with Frank Toombs and the surveyors. He was worried about hidden empty spaces and the danger of fire. You know, like at Windsor Castle.'

'Oh, pity.' Sebastian idly thumbed through the papers on Liz's desk. 'Meet me for a drink tonight? King's Head?'

'We ought not, Seb. I'm a married woman.'

He bent forward and kissed her again. She made no move to get away from him, and he smiled at her foolish scruples. 'We're not—'

The door suddenly opened, making Liz jump guiltily. Jorge came in. 'Oh, hello, Seb. I'm glad I caught you. The takings from Maldon seem to have slipped down rather strangely. I thought we might drive out there to see what's going on.'

'Good idea. The young man we put in charge there is pretty useless, but I can't seem to recruit anyone in the area. I suspect he just can't be bothered to serve anyone. Maldon has some good restaurants, you know. Lots of competition.'

The phone rang and they stopped talking to find out who was calling. Liz held out the phone. 'It's Maria for you, Jorge.'

Jorge took the phone. There followed a lot of rapid Spanish.

He handed the phone back to Liz. 'My daughter, Antonia, thinks she's pregnant. I'll kill him. So help me God, I will. I can't go to Maldon, obviously. I'll get a secretary to book a flight to Miami. Hold the fort, pal. Richard will be back after Easter. Everything closes down for Easter Monday, doesn't it?'

'Lots of things open for the summer season at Easter. Tourists are on the move. Of course, it all depends on the weather. However, you must go home and get your affairs sorted out. Liz is manning the office. I'll do the rest. Don't give it a second thought, Jorge.' Seb patted Jorge on the shoulder, then held the door open for him. He watched Jorge until he was out of sight, then closed the door carefully and returned to Liz's desk.

'Tee hee,' she drawled. 'Things are bad all over.'

'I'll go to Maldon and sort out, but I'll be back in time for drinks with you. Now, don't say no. We're not doing anything wrong.'

'OK, but not at the King's Head. People are getting to know us. How about the Fox in Bulmer?'

'Not a good idea. The owners are Spanish. Maria and Jorge eat there three nights a week, and they're good friends. How about the Bull at Blackmore End? It's not too far out of your way, and we don't know anyone in that direction.'

At half past six Liz was on her second gin and tonic, afraid to drink more because she was driving, and very disappointed that Seb had not turned up.

Liz and Harry had moved to north Essex in 1980 from Chingford. Harry's work had brought him north to work in Braintree, and they had bought a rather nice bungalow in a new development. When the youngest of their three children had reached secondary school, Liz took a job as a secretary. There was plenty of work, but Liz had been rusty. She was fired from her first job, and her confidence had never returned. Working for Richard was the best job by far that she had ever held, and she owed it all to Sebastian. They had seemed to click straight away. Seb had trained her in the work. Seb was there for her when she needed to ask a question. Richard was a good boss, if somewhat remote, and she felt an absurd desire to reach his standards. There was no question of confessing to Richard

Dumas that she didn't understand a task she had been set. Seb, on the other hand, was very approachable. Their little romance had come about quite naturally.

Somehow she had found herself agreeing to meet him after work at a hotel outside Colchester. Looked at one way, she supposed the assignation could be counted a dismal failure. She had got cold feet. He was in a hurry. They had quarrelled. Seb had been on the point of leaving, when Liz called him back. Her original reason, she had told herself, was the importance of staying on good terms with a man she was dependent upon at work. But there had been an element of danger, too. A touch of that well-known feeling, getting a little revenge on one's husband, because Harry had not always been faithful over the years.

So she had begun to undress, as had Seb, and he was on top of her before she had managed to get under the covers. There had followed three or four minutes of what she liked to think of as foreplay. It had not included any kisses, nor any loving words. In fact it was all over so quickly that Liz was still lying on the bed, her head whirling with regrets, when Seb emerged from the bathroom and said a hasty goodbye, promising never to speak of what had happened to anyone.

However, over the weeks, she had managed to think of this farcical coupling as a romantic interlude in what had been a pretty dull life. She bore him no ill will although, equally, she had no desire to repeat the encounter.

She was about to gather her things and go home when Seb walked through the door looking furious.

'It's lucky I spotted your car. I've been waiting

for you for half an hour at the Bull in Blackmore End.'

'Isn't this . . . ?'

'This is the Cock at Beazley End. My God, woman, but you're careless. Don't you ever read road signs? Fortunately, I guessed what you had done. What are you drinking?'

'A ginger ale. I daren't have any more alcohol. I just saw a pub and thought I had arrived. I'm awfully sorry, Seb. Have you been waiting long? Oh, dear, I'm such a fool.'

'Never mind. I'll just go and get myself something from the bar. Have I got a story for you!'

He returned with a ginger ale for her and a whisky and soda for himself. 'A few days ago – I've been meaning to tell you this for some time now – we had Nigel Falkland out for a board meeting. You remember. Well, old Nigel spies Fran Craig arriving to see Richard as usual, and he turns to us and warns us in a stage whisper that she's a bitch from Braintree market who short-changed him. Richard looks out and sees Fran arriving, knows exactly whom Falkland is talking about. He walks out, gives Fran a big kiss that surprises the hell out of her and then introduces her as his friend and garden designer. You should have seen Falkland's face!'

'They are both free agents, of course,' said Liz, attempting to be fair. 'If I tell you something, will you promise not to tell a soul?'

'Of course.'

'He's given her ten thousand pounds, ostensibly for gardening projects. But she hasn't done much for the money! He just wrote her out a cheque. He must know it's a very peculiar thing to do.'

Liz arranged the scarf around her shoulders. It was a cold spring day, but she had miscalculated and left home without a coat. Her tweed skirt was long to draw attention away from her fat ankles. Unfortunately, the toning woollen jacket was too small to close over her large bosom. The scarf, brightly patterned and made of fine wool, was intended to draw the eye from the ill-fitting garments.

For a long time, Seb made no response to Liz's news. She thought he might not even have heard what she said. But he had merely been thinking deeply.

'And now she is in Florida with him, earning the money. You know, Liz, I really do think that Fran Craig is going to be Richard's downfall.'

Liz looked at him with alarm. 'That's as may be. You aren't going to use her to hurt him, are you?'

'Of course not, my dear. Why would I want to bring Richard down, for heaven's sake? He's our financial wizard. He's the man who is going to lead the Miami Spice chain to riches on the stock market. Drink up. You must be on your way.'

When Liz had left the pub, Sebastian paid his bill and drove back to the Bull at Blackmore End. He liked their food, but, in the event, he had only a ham sandwich to accompany three whisky and sodas. He drank his coffee with a large brandy.

By the time he reached the car park he knew that he could not drive far, if at all. Then he allowed his subconscious to remind him that Helena lived but a few yards away, a fact he had tucked at the back of his mind for several hours.

Getting behind the wheel, he drove out of the car

park and down the road a hundred yards and brought the car to rest with extreme caution beside her picket fence. Lights were on inside. He could see his cousin sitting by the fire, could make out the blue flicker of the TV.

She saw him coming up her front path. 'Seb! Good God, you look the worse for wear. What possessed you to drink so much?'

'Pressures of work, I suppose. I didn't notice the stone floor before. Do all the rooms have stone floors?'

She led the way into the sitting-room and began to draw the chintz curtains. 'No, as you can see, there are floorboards in here. Stone in the kitchen, however. Very hard on the feet. You probably think I've overdone the chintzy look.'

'I think you've done it perfectly. You really are a perfect home-maker, Helena. Why have you not been snapped up?'

'Waiting for Mister Right,' she said with a touch of bitterness. 'What's the matter with you, Seb? What are you waiting for? The next drink? Richard to drop dead? The share money to arrive? Oh, I do get cross with you. I don't like heavy drinking. Look at yourself.' Wrinkling her nose, she straightened his tie, helped him off with his jacket. 'This needs cleaning. It smells.'

'No-one to look after me.' His head was spinning. He had to sit down, and did so with a thump. Helena went into the kitchen; he supposed she was going to make some coffee. God, it was good to be in this cottage, safe from the outside world, being looked after by the little home-maker! His head flopped back against the seat.

'Water!' he cried, sitting up. 'I thought you were

going to make me a nice cup of real coffee.'

She smiled as she set down the tray holding a jug and glass. 'Coffee irritates the stomach lining, and you've already done enough damage with all the alcohol. I'm just trying to ensure that you don't have a splitting headache in the morning. Drink up. You're dehydrated.'

Obediently, he poured a glass of water and drank it all. 'I saw one of my daughters today. I was in Chelmsford. We walked towards each other. I saw her from twenty or thirty feet away. She was with her husband. I said hello, but she looked right through me. As we passed, her husband turned and shrugged helplessly. He looked a nice chap.'

'It's very sad. Here, have another glass of water. But you have just got to put them out of your mind. When you're rich, they may take an interest. They'll probably think they have some right to it.'

'They do have, and if money will buy me back my daughters, I will consider it money well-spent.' He put his face in his hands. 'Oh, Helena, what am I going to do?'

'Pull yourself together and start making something of yourself. Can't you see that the work with the restaurants is worthwhile and that you are good at it? This is your chance, Seb. Stop scheming and get down to learning everything Richard has to teach you. I know it sounds corny, but tomorrow is the first day of the rest of your life.'

'Easy for you to say.'

She poured him yet another glass of water, her expression hard. 'Yes it is easy for me to say. I had to face up to what I have become. Now I am changing myself. In the autumn, I will be taking a course in hotel management. By the time our

239

money comes through I shall have a paper qualification. I will probably take a few jobs before we go public. I want to learn everything I can, so that when I have some real cash I can buy a small country hotel. I'll be very good at fixing it up, but I must learn the rest. I'm studying some books now.'

Seb was struck by the change in his cousin. No stupid jokes to hide her sense of inadequacy, no ducking away from unpleasant reality. She had truly got a grip on herself. He felt ashamed.

'Must be going. Can't drink any more.'

'You most certainly are not going to get behind the wheel of a car. I have a spare bedroom. No pyjamas, I'm afraid, but you will have your own little shower room. You must be up and away before nine. The daily comes then and I want her to have a clear run.'

She showed him to the small twin-bedded guest-room which was done out entirely in a blue printed fabric and matching wallpaper. The pattern on the walls carried on to the curtains. The carpet was cream and the beds had blue duvets. The bedside lamp had a coral pink shade, the only touch of colour, apart from the blue. It was a clever room, its awkward shape disguised by the pervasive pattern. 'Little home-maker,' he murmured indistinctly. Yes, she was clever, and yes, he should settle down to learning from Richard instead of plotting against him. But he did have a plot. It was obscured by alcohol at the moment. But he would remember in the morning. Then Richard had better watch out.

Chapter Nine

Fran awoke and saw that it was only half past six. Nevertheless she went into the kitchen and poured a cup of coffee from the pot that was already steaming in the coffee-maker. This was Florida, and the best time of day was early morning. Richard, looking impeccable in fawn shorts and an open-necked black shirt, came into the kitchen from his study area and kissed her lightly on the cheek.

'Oi!' she said. 'Not good enough.' She kissed him on the mouth and smiled up at him. There was no carefree smile in return, and her heart was chilled. She was not to be so easily forgiven for saying too much about Sean.

'Key West is really a very informal place,' he told her. 'It will be hot, the sun will shine, and you won't even need to put on a dress in the evening if you don't want to. You can stay in your shorts. So pack lightly as soon as you've had your coffee and we'll be off. We can eat breakfast on the way.'

They drove for half an hour before stopping to eat in a Denny's, one of the innumerable chains of restaurants and cafés that lined the roads. The coffee-mugs were thick and almost too heavy to lift.

The tabletops were Formica, the seats imitation leather and the waitresses genuine middle-aged Floridians.

'Hi, what can I do for you folks today? A short stack and two eggs and bacon? French toast?' She was already pouring coffee into hot mugs.

Richard tossed the plastic-covered menu aside. 'I'll have orange juice, scrambled eggs and bacon. And give me an extra order of bacon. I've been in England for the last few weeks, and they have lousy bacon. In fact, it doesn't look like bacon at all.'

The waitress made a sympathetic face. 'Like Canadian bacon, huh? I'll fix you up. What'll you have, honey?'

'Scrambled eggs and no bacon as I don't like American bacon and—'

'Are you English?' cried the waitress, showing more interest that she could possibly feel. 'Hey, don't you let him tease you. He gets sassy, I'll sort him out.'

'And sausage,' said Fran, in no mood for a meaningful conversation with a total stranger.

'Patty or links?'

'I beg your pardon?'

'Links,' said Richard. 'She'll have links.' He seemed as irritated as Fran was by the cheerfulness of the waitress. Couldn't these people see that occasionally a person wanted to be left alone in gloom? She and Richard had not spoken for the last half-hour.

Fran now smiled at him with all the warmth she could muster. 'You see, food is so basic.'

'We'd die without it, that's for sure.'

'Suppose I was going to open a restaurant in Florida. I serve English bacon, black pudding, mushy peas. The customers want American bacon, grits, milk gravy or French toast. They wouldn't come to my restaurant, would they? I just don't see how the Miamis are going to be a big success.'

He grinned. 'It's going to be all right because we've made a major cultural adjustment. We've added French fries to the menu. We soon learned that you can't have a restaurant that doesn't serve French fries. Besides, think of cream cheese and bagels.'

'Yes?'

'At first this was a dish that was eaten in New York, then in other places where New Yorkers went to live, then all over the country. Nowadays there are cafés that specialize in bagels with assorted toppings. And they're becoming popular in Britain. I've seen bagels on plenty of menus. In London, especially.'

'You're saying . . .' The waitress arrived with their breakfasts and the serious conversation had to stop while the relentless badinage continued until another couple sat down in the opposite booth, relieving them of the waitress's attention.

'I'm saying,' said Richard as he picked up a stiff piece of bacon with his fingers, 'that it is entirely possible that Cuban food will take off. But I'm not bothered one way or the other. Let me explain. If you and I started a restaurant, a mom and pop sort of thing, just the two of us working our tails off to drag in the customers, we would have to consider very carefully what to serve. Pleasing every customer would be of primary importance. But I'm not into that sort of thing. I'm not a caterer.'

'But—'

'I'm a business doctor. I've bought into a chain

of six grubby seaside cafés. I've opened two larger, better cafés in larger towns in better locations. Ideally, I should open a place in London, but our angel won't fund it. So here's what my plan is. I could sell the whole eight restaurants to a rival firm who will refurnish them and turn them into Chopsticks Incorporated or Trattorias Unlimited or whatever. I'd probably get at least three times what I paid for the shares. A trade sale would bring us a very handsome profit because they would want our sites and the customer base we've built up, or because they want to cut down on the opposition. Or, in five years' time we will float the business on the stock exchange. Wagamama, the Japanese noodle-bar chain, is heading for the stock exchange. They have hundred-cover sites in London and turn them over ten times a day! They're rumoured to turn over three million pounds a year. Yet you would say that the British are not lovers of Japanese noodles, wouldn't you?'

'British people eat that many noodles? I can't believe it.'

'You could say that Wagamama is our role model. That's the route we are theoretically following, but it takes time and I'm getting bored with Cuban cafés. I'd rather sell to a certain potential buyer I've been nursing along. In the meantime, we must be efficient. Minimal wastage, a tight control of the money. As for getting the customer to cross the threshold more than once, it's got to be value for money, which we achieve by buying in bulk, by cooking some of the food centrally and servicing the other cafés with it, by advertising and having good locations and an exciting atmosphere.'

'And you don't care a damn for the type or

quality of the food? Just the price?'

'There are enough people in Britain, as there are in America, who want acceptable food at very cheap prices. It's harder in Britain because they slap on a damned great tax of seventeen and a half per cent.'

'The food's not as cheap as it looks in Florida. Because when you go to pay, they suddenly charge five per cent more that's not mentioned on the menu.'

He laughed, eating the last piece of bacon. 'You're not happy with me.'

'I hate to see the Americanization of Britain. We're losing our identity, and it started with McDonald's.'

'Listen, Fran, when the founding fathers came to this country, they were Brits. They brought trial by jury, the language, an upper and lower house political system and God knows what else. Now we're just returning the compliment. It was inevitable. It's not our food that we're giving you. That's a by-product. We're giving you our business ways, our lifestyles. Mom doesn't want to spend every day in the kitchen. Eating out is time- and labour-saving, but it's also entertainment. And by God we're raising your standard of living. People can afford to eat out now. Mom is getting used to being waited on. If people hated what's happening to them, do you think a million Brits would come to Florida every year?'

'I guess not.'

'Let me tell you a story. It happened in England and Seb told me about it. It seems there was a very nice restaurant on the edge of a tourist site. It had a terrific reputation and was full every night. A high-class place. But they couldn't get any lunch-time trade. Cars just whizzed by and ate elsewhere. So they called in a consultant.'

'They have restaurant consultants in England?'

'Sure do. This guy took just forty-five minutes to figure out what was wrong. He told them to take the tablecloths off the tables. People could see in and thought it was too fancy to have lunch in.'

'And it worked?'

'Of course it worked. They changed their lunch-time image and improved their business. Eating is business. Not everybody wants a chateaubriand on a coulis of how's-your-father with truffles *au jus*. Sometimes they just want a ham sandwich. The ham doesn't even have to be fresh. Ham roll will do, providing the price reflects the quality and the customer feels at ease in the surroundings.'

'I shall never be able to relax in a restaurant again.'

'I'll tell you something else. Mom and Pop may not be too careful about hygiene. They may not have the cash to update their equipment. A chain will have the money. The managers will know all about the latest regulations on displaying cheese or whatever. The customer knows what he's getting.'

'You're saying that people can't just set up in business any more, that they can't compete. Where is there room for the little man? We're losing our grocers and fruiterers and fishmongers. It's sad.'

'It's progress. The food at the supermarket is fresher and cheaper.'

'Oh, Richard,' she said. 'I think I'm beginning to understand what's happening. Some of us don't want progress at any price.'

'You're in a minority. Anyway, the last time you bought food, where did you shop?'

'Sainsbury's,' she said sadly. 'Let's go.'

The long drive to Key West was completely different from anything she had ever done, yet was also boring. Natural Florida land was incredibly flat with scrubby plants she couldn't identify. The built-up areas were dominated by power lines and poles, and by huge illuminated signs next to the road, proclaiming the business lurking behind the parking-lot.

On the other hand, Fran noticed that every bank was built on its own land with its own parking facilities. And each one was an outstanding piece of architecture. There was never a sign of a high street or social centre in any town, but there was also no litter anywhere.

By the time they began island-hopping by driving over huge bridges from one Key to the next, she was ready for sleep. Yet she dare not close her eyes, feeling it was her duty to see to it that Richard was not similarly mesmerized. To fall asleep on these roads would surely be fatal, and she didn't want to drown.

The hotel was the finest on Key West. Fran revelled in the luxury, but it soon transpired that there was so little to do on the island that the favourite pastime of tourists and residents was to go down to the dock and watch the sun set. The mixture of hippies and visitors gave the event a special twist, but she didn't feel the need to do it twice.

The next day they went sightseeing. Hemingway's home was interesting, though not very large. The bar he frequented meant little to her. That left the sea and the hotel pool. Fran said that after lunch she would really like to swim in the hotel pool. Oceans worried her. They were big and powerful, and she had done all her swimming in pools.

Richard went off to do some business telephoning, and returned an hour and a half later to find her still lounging in the sun. His anger caught her quite by surprise.

'I told you not to sunbathe for more than fifteen minutes! What's the matter with you? You'll be lucky not to blister. You'll probably be sick all night. The sun in Florida is dangerous. Why is it that out-of-towners will never believe it?'

She was sure he was exaggerating, but that evening her body felt as if it were on fire, and she couldn't bear to wear her smart black dress because it covered her burning shoulders and fitted too snugly elsewhere. She also felt very ill, but dared not admit it. They sat on the veranda as evening approached, watching people come and go and listening to the conversation of the large party at the next table. They were all drinking fairly freely, celebrating something.

'OK, let's do it,' cried a young man in cut-off jeans. He grabbed the hand of the girl sitting next to him and they trotted off, barefooted, towards a pavilion in the grounds that was simply a roof on stilts. The rest of the party joined them more slowly. They arranged themselves as for a wedding, and Fran realized with a shock that this was indeed a genuine wedding. The Justice of the Peace was a trouser-wearing woman who quickly finished her part in the ceremony while three others took photographs.

They were back at their seats within five minutes, ready to order more drinks as the Justice of the Peace said goodbye.

On Richard's advice, Fran went to bed naked. There was nothing she could have worn that was bearable. She lay down gingerly, feeling extremely sorry for herself. She had never been sunburned before, and one heard such frightening stories about skin cancer.

Then there was Richard. She had had more sex since coming to Florida than in all the years following her divorce, and the novelty was beginning to wear off. Even the thought of a chance contact during the night brought goosebumps to her sensitive flesh.

Richard approached her with an aerosol. 'It's supposed to deaden the pain. I'll just spray it on gently. See what you think.'

The spray was cold but soothing. It was Richard's continued kindness that brought the tears to her eyes. She slept fitfully for an hour and a half. Then awareness of pain chased away blessed oblivion, and she was suddenly awake in a strange hotel in the middle of a subtropical night, feeling totally alone. Richard slept, didn't wake as she struggled to find a comfortable position.

And she thought once more about Boca Raton and Plaza Real, about the median, as Richard called it, the dividing area between two roads. There a tiled octagonal pool was part of a scheme that blended some of the oldest traditions in gardening with some of the newest materials.

Persian Paradise gardens. The garden of Eden. Had there been bougainvillea in the first Paradise gardens? There had certainly been fruit trees. And water. She concentrated on cooling water, on the soothing sound of fountains. She would build a Paradise garden for Richard. It would be her way of repaying his endless gestures of kindness. On this happy thought, she slept.

They were back at the condo by the Tuesday after Easter. Richard rose at half past six as usual, but this time he didn't go directly into the kitchen to make coffee. Before dressing, he padded into the living-room and telephoned Gosfield Hall.

Fran heard his shout of joy as she emerged from her bathroom. 'What's up?' she cried, rushing into the living-room.

'It's been seventy-five all weekend, which I gather is hot for England. Sunshine. Roads bumper-to-bumper to the seaside. Colchester and Chelmsford each did seven hundred covers on Saturday. Closed on Sunday. But the seaside Miamis were so full all day for four solid days that people were pushing and shoving to get in! Police were called in Clacton. Residents complained of the noise in Woodbridge and Aldeburgh! It's in the papers! We're a success.'

'How wonderful. It snowed at Easter last year. I'm so pleased, really I am. Now you really will be glad you came to England.'

He picked her up and gave her a warm, celebratory kiss. 'I'm glad I came to England, but that has nothing to do with the cafés. I just like to be right, that's all. And we clearly had an early breakthrough because of the weather. Now look, the plane leaves tomorrow afternoon. I've some business to do this morning, so you're on your own. There's a nice driver I use sometimes, Jethro. He will drive you, if you like. He'll stay with you wherever you want to go. To the Galleria in Fort Lauderdale, or Fashion Square or Town Center. You haven't seen Town Center. There are good shops and it's a nice mall.'

'No thanks. None of the above. If Jethro will drive slowly along some of the residential streets, I'd like to take some photos. Then could we meet at Plaza Real where we had dinner that first night? Will you be finished at one o'clock?'

'If I get going, I can be ready by twelve. Meet you there. Jethro will drive me to work, then pick you up. He'll come back for me after you reach Plaza Real. Deal? Good. I must get dressed.'

Richard didn't ask why Fran wanted to take pictures of modest houses on the nearby streets, but she was very excited about the project. She had remembered that what Brits thought of as house plants grew in Floridian front gardens, and she wanted a photographic record of it. In the course of twenty minutes she snapped Aechmea, Agave americana, Allamanda, bird's nest and asparagus ferns, Strelitzia, the bird-of-Paradise, Scindapsus and Monstera deliciosa, the Swiss cheese plant, growing to enormous heights. Almost every garden had a hibiscus shrub and bougainvillea, but the most astounding sight was a rubber plant so huge that two men with machetes had climbed up its branches to hack it back. She didn't recognize all the different palms, but photographed them so that she could learn their names later, and she finished off her photo session with pictures of handsome Chlorophytums, spider plants, growing in a modest border.

Plaza Real steamed in the spring heat, its glowing purple bougainvillea vivid against the beige and red brick of the paving. Everything about this long promenade reminded her of all she had read about Paradise gardens. Addison Mizner with his fondness for Moorish taste had inspired this formal parkway.

The concept of a garden of Paradise had begun with the Persians who sought to create their idea of perfection in the midst of hot, dry plains and vast open expanses without shade or comfort from the searing sun.

Thus the Persian garden of Paradise would be enclosed, a secret place with guarded entrances. There would be water, cascades and fountains, and rills, water that ran in narrow channels. Of course there would be shade from the unrelenting sun. Trees would be planted in avenues, their branches entwining overhead. And there would be fruit – apricots, figs, pomegranates. Roses were essential to the plan. There were sometimes raised pavilions from which the garden could be viewed. Plaza Real had its own pavilions, cool and inviting with their metal benches.

It was a version of this concept which Fran, rather quixotically, thought she could reproduce in the courtyard of Gosfield Hall, because the idea of the perfect garden, a Paradise, had grown and spread. Monasteries in Britain had built their own enclosed gardens with a pond, fruit trees and shade, places for quiet contemplation.

A Paradise garden, she felt, was an attitude of mind as much as anything. She could produce something uniquely Gosfield, while at the same time paying tribute to an ancient concept. There would be huge pots with fruit trees or roses growing in them. There would be places of shade as well as sunny corners. And there would be flowers, changing with the seasons. Bulbs would greet the spring, annuals the summer. Colours would be brilliant, in contrast with the ancient stone and brick. She knew very well that she would not be allowed to change much in the listed courtyard. It would be a matter of adding pots, but not of taking anything away. The vital question was: would Richard like it?

Richard was certainly ready for his lunch when he eventually joined her. The day's business had gone very well. He was happy. He was inclined to tease her about British weather. Seventy-five! Imagine that! Well, he felt he could not deprive himself of Florida sunshine for the entire year. Perhaps, in the autumn, they should return to Florida and look for a suitable property in Palm Beach. They could spend a month or two in Florida, just relaxing. Would Fran like that? She said yes, not knowing what else to say. It was too far in the future for her to think about it seriously. Easier just to say yes.

In fact, she was a little homesick. Florida was for lotus-eaters. There was really nothing to do, and the weather sapped her desire to move at all. Two months of luxurious inactivity? Frankly, she wasn't at all sure.

Richard managed his jet lag rather better on his second arrival in England. He went to bed and slept a few hours, then awoke to hear all that had happened since his departure. It seemed there was quite a lot. Jorge was his first visitor.

'Richard, under other circumstances I would feel like a heel leaving you and the business so soon,' said Jorge. 'But I can see that you are very happy and fully in control. The restaurants are going brilliantly. I will soon owe you that ten thousand dollars. But the fact is Maria is so homesick for the sunshine, the heat, the family and the familiar shops that we have to go home. Then our stupid daughter had to go and get herself pregnant. We're both devastated. I've come back only to sort out my affairs and to resign as a director and company secretary. I'm sure Seb will have no trouble finding another company secretary, but I wouldn't advise you to take any more directors. The three of you are enough. Falkland admires you, I can tell. Between you, you can keep Seb in check.'

'I will miss you, old friend,' said Richard. 'Somebody to guard my back. You know what I mean. The Race family are hardly a problem, but still . . . Anyway, I've never said how much I appreciate your coming to England with me. It was one hell of a sacrifice.'

Richard took his good friend out to dinner and the theatre in London and they parted on their usual casual but friendly terms. Maria's homesickness had become a trial to others. She could see nothing to admire in England, hated all shops, the winding roads, the lack of malls, the old houses. The weather earned her fiercest criticisms, but the truth was she missed her family, that network of relatives whose lives and festivals gave shape to her existence.

Her fierce attachment to his country intrigued Richard, for he felt no such agony of separation. He knew that south Florida was the place from which all right-thinking Cubans organized the fight against the Communist Castro. Therefore, Maria felt she had to be present to lend support to the struggle.

On the other hand, Richard was more or less content with the way America was run. He could leave the country without feeling for a moment that he was deserting it. And, besides, England held all that was really dear to him: Zoe and Fran. He was content. He was even learning to love the tortuous traffic up Halstead High Street, realizing that easy movement for the car meant a loss of something precious for the people. He felt great affection for the old plastered houses painted in rainbow colours, and marvelled at the number of staircases he walked up and down during the course of a day. His aching calves reminded him that he never ever mounted a set of stairs in Florida. Florida was a one-floor state except when it was high-rise, when escalators and elevators replaced stairs. No-one went up or down steps, except at the gym.

Sebastian Race was the only shadow on the horizon, and Richard tended to ignore his complaints.

'I see that interview you gave with the *Telegraph* has finally been printed. Nice picture of you, Richard. Very nice picture of Gosfield Hall. My God, don't you look the grand gentleman.'

'I'm not responsible for the photo, Seb. Don't let it get you down.'

'Get me down! Of course it doesn't get me down. I do think you might have mentioned that I purchased Gosfield Hall. I found it, and you weren't too keen at all. As for the business, there was no mention of the Race family. Anyone would think from this that you created the whole thing from scratch.'

Richard sighed. 'Look, pal. I told him that you bought Gosfield Hall. I told him I wasn't too keen. I told him lots of things that never got into the article. I didn't write it. The man had his own agenda. He wanted a story about an American who comes over here and buys a gigantic old house. He wanted to see the improvements, wanted to know if I got on with the environment officer, if I did what I was told. He wanted to hear me praise this house, which I was well able to do without any help from you. What he didn't want was to hear about a man named Sebastian Race. So, too bad. Bite the bullet and get on with your life.'

This had not been the best way to handle someone of Seb's insecurities, but Richard had no patience with the man. Seb was actually doing a fine job of looking after the Miami chain. He was probably surprising himself, finding that he had talent he didn't know he possessed. Richard should really have given him some praise, told him what he was doing right. But every time he thought of doing such a thing, Seb would come up with some petty whinge, and Richard's good intentions would fly out the window.

In response to her phone call, Trevor was waiting at the cottage when Fran arrived back from Florida. His grin was shaky, his hug perfunctory, but he soon warmed up when he saw that she was prepared to meet him more than halfway. He had made a lasagne, and Fran went rather over the top in offering her praise.

'Do you want to have a sleep?' he asked. 'I could

256

keep this until later. We could eat about three o'clock. I don't mind.'

'Yes, I've got to get unpacked. Did you notice all my bags? I don't know what I'm going to do with all these summer things. They're mostly unsuitable for England.'

'Sell them. Mum, maybe I was wrong. I think it would be a good idea to marry this bloke. I mean, you can't carry on as you are. You're not making it.'

She shook her head, suddenly saddened. 'We'll just have to make it. I know I said I was going to trap a rich man, but I didn't know Richard then. He's a really wonderful person and he doesn't deserve to be hurt. It was a terrible thing to do. I'm ashamed and I hate myself.'

'You'll probably learn to love him. Give him a chance.'

'No. I'm finished with that sort of thing, I tell you. I can't love anybody any more. I think I've got love burn-out. My emotions are in a mess. No-one could possibly love the person I am, and I couldn't love anyone. And, no, before you say it. I am not still in love with your father. Anyway, we're going to dinner at Richard's daughter's house tomorrow night. That will finish it. She'll take one look at common old me and she'll tell Daddy to find some rich widow. She sounds like a handful and I'm terrified of her. She's married to some Cambridge boffin. Dr Cosmo something.'

'Cosmo? My God, you're right, Mum. Nobody named Cosmo is going to think you're good enough for his rich American father-in-law. Oh, bad luck.' Trevor shook his head, still amused by the exotic name.

257

Fran took all her suitcases up to her bedroom, aware of the smell of damp, not as entertained as she had imagined she would be by the sight of exquisite summer clothes in bright colours lying on a sagging single bed. Tears clouded her eyes. The dream life was over. Outdoors, the plants were waiting to be watered or potted on. There was grubby work ahead. There would be few fine meals in nice restaurants in future and even less sitting around than before. She was behind with her work, and Richard's money was draining away. The day of reckoning could not be far off.

A few hours' sleep lightened her mood. She ate Trevor's lasagne with gusto as she gave him a spirited account of her first-ever true holiday abroad, although she and Sean and Trevor had gone to Spain for a week many years ago. 'And everybody is so rich! But I couldn't live there. Life is too easy. I swear I'd be bored to death in six months. Richard likes it here, would you believe. He has the most beautiful condominium in Boca Raton, but he's selling it. Might buy something in Palm Beach. He's a very tough businessman. You should have seen him going for this one man. My God, I was scared. When he finds out that I've spent ten thousand pounds of his money, I don't know what he'll do to me.' She put down her fork. 'I wish I had never got started on this. I'd rather be poor and not know what it's like to be rich.' Her eyes filled with tears as she reached for the scrunch of Kleenex she had tucked up her sleeve.

Trevor watched his mother with concern. In the space of a few seconds she had talked with enthusiasm about her holiday and the fun she had had with Richard Dumas and gone directly to despair about the relationship. He concluded that she was not very stable at the moment, but his need for confession was urgent.

'Mum . . .'

She looked at him with alarm, recognizing the doom-laden tone of voice. 'What is it? What's happened? Are you all right? Are you in trouble?'

'Not really. I've left college.'

'Oh, Trevor!'

'It was the wrong course and I'm not suited for an academic career. Can you see me sitting around all day indoors? It was wrong. I'm going to get a job. I'll take over the market stall in Braintree, maybe get another one. But I really think you should make an effort with this Richard. I've been talking to Linus. He rang me last night and we had a heart-to-heart. Honestly, you've got to do something.'

Now she ranted, leapt up from the table to pace the floor. She was angry, confused and frightened. 'If you don't go to college, how are you ever to break out of this pit we're in? Somebody in this family needs some education and training. You can't end up like your dad and me, living from hand to mouth. You've got to do something. Forget about our getting out of trouble by my marriage to Richard. I'm not going to take further advantage of the nicest man I've ever met.'

She went on for almost half an hour, but he stuck to his guns. He would not go back to university and a social studies career. He had hated it. He would eventually find something in life, really he would. He had broken up with his girlfriend, was ready to work hard for his mother. Couldn't she at least be glad of his help?

In fact, she was very grateful. It was going to be

hard to throw off memories of her luxurious life and get down to the rigours of running a small nursery. Trevor seemed more mature than when she went away. She had to accept his decision.

Fortunately, the May evening that Fran and Richard were to visit Zoe was a mild one. Fran put on a navy silk trouser suit and white blouse and felt almost up to the ordeal of meeting Richard's daughter. Until Zoe opened the front door.

Zoe's height, perfectly symmetrical features, beautifully cut black dress and confident demeanour drained Fran's own confidence. She counted herself lucky to be able to say hello without stammering.

The house was large and tastefully furnished, on generously built Edwardian lines. It needed only children and a small staff to make it the perfect home. Cosmo, on the other hand, was terrifying. Fran was sure she would never find anything to say to such an educated man. Fortunately, Zoe forestalled the need for small talk by leading the way to the living-room. There Fran had an excellent view of the garden.

'But how perfect!' she cried, genuinely impressed.

'It's a mess.' Cosmo handed Fran a glass of wine. 'We haven't known what to do with it and so we just concentrated on the house. It was in a poor condition.'

'But it's perfect for the period of this house. The bones are there. All it needs is a bit of refurbishment. The garden is typical of Lutyens and Jekyll.'

'Really?' asked Cosmo. 'I don't suppose they had a hand in anything so small.'

'No, I'm sure they didn't, but someone has taken the trouble to complement the house with an imitation of their style. You are very fortunate. To have all that hard landscaping put in now would be very expensive.'

Richard and Zoe had not heard of Lutyens and Jekyll, so Fran explained that Lutyens had been a young and talented architect when he met the older artist, Miss Gertrude Jekyll, who had turned to garden design when her eyesight became too poor for painting. Together they had designed several grand gardens. Cosmo was intrigued and insisted that they all go outside in the fading light to view the bare beds, the sagging trellis-work on the pillared pergola, and the pond choked with weeds.

Secure in the knowledge that the others knew virtually nothing about gardening, Lutyens or Jekyll, Fran delivered a little lecture on the style of these two who were active around the turn of the century. By the time they came indoors for dinner Richard was clearly very pleased with her, and Fran had regained a modicum of composure.

Zoe turned out to be an excellent cook. Fran praised the food and said that she had no talent for cooking, but then the conversation struck a dry spot. She had nothing in common with these two and had to let Richard bear the burden.

He seemed rather strained as well. Zoe appeared to have her own agenda. Richard had always been married to his work, never had time for her when she was growing up. She hoped he would ease up; although it would be too late to benefit the young Zoe, they might, just possibly, become friends now that she was married. To this onslaught, Richard had no answer.

Cosmo said, 'Put another record on, Zoe.' She sulked for a moment or two, then began to talk about Cambridge and what the town had to offer.

After dinner Fran insisted on helping Zoe with the dishes. Zoe seemed to be such an intriguing girl that Fran was determined to get to know her. She began by talking about Florida.

The men sat down in the deep chairs in the living-room and talked about Richard's restaurants, his house and new acquaintances, before Cosmo gave Richard a much abridged account of his own work. Then they were silent for a minute or two.

'Well, what do you think?' Richard had watched his daughter and son-in-law carefully all through dinner, but, despite his close attention, he could not gauge Cosmo's reaction to Fran. It was plain, however, that Zoe resented her.

'If you are referring to Fran, I think she is very beautiful. A nice woman, and knowledgeable about gardening.'

Richard took a deep breath, prepared to be offended. 'But you don't like her. Wrong accent, is that it?'

'Richard,' said Cosmo mildly. 'She is not my friend. The choice is yours, for heaven's sake. Don't bite my head off. I would just remind you that it is difficult to judge people when they come from different cultures. She's not the sort of woman you would be likely to know in Florida, after all. You wouldn't meet her . . . that is, what I'm trying to say is someone like Fran Craig wouldn't come into your social circle.'

'You've got her pegged, haven't you? Know just what she eats for breakfast and which newspaper she reads. I know she's poor. She makes no bones about it. You think she's not my type, not my class. The fact is, she's not Zoe's type, not Zoe's class or background. But Fran and I are alike. We come from just the same sort of background. Your father-in-law is a guy whose mother couldn't wait to put a continent between herself and her son. I'm the kid who has had to fend for himself since the age of sixteen. Fran understands that. Zoe couldn't possibly. Her views on Fran are—'

'Her views on Fran are not mine,' interrupted Cosmo. 'And they are much more personal. It hurts her to see that a woman, who is not her mother, can make you so much happier than her mother ever did. That takes some getting used to. Give her time. I take your point, however. You know better than anyone what you and Fran have in common. I really don't want to be put into the position of judging the woman my father-in-law loves. That said, I would add one thing. I believe you will have to give Fran some time, too. She does not strike me as a woman who is eager to jump into your life and take your name. Maybe she has devils to work out before she starts a new life.'

This was such an astute observation that Richard's respect for his son-in-law increased even as he felt furious with the man for speaking un-palatable truths. He sat in silence for several seconds before suggesting that they join the women in the kitchen. They found Zoe and Fran discussing the dress shops on the Plaza Real with great ani-mation and friendliness. Cosmo raised his eyebrows at Richard and smiled slightly. Richard was not consoled.

In the car on the way home, Richard posed his question. 'Well?'

'Darling, she's gorgeous. I've never met anyone so young with so much poise. She could be a model, really. And I loved the house. Do you know, we got on really well in the kitchen. It's a lovely kitchen, by the way. The chintz in the main bedroom is just gorgeous. Well, she doesn't know what to do with the garden and I said I will draw up a planting plan and Trevor will come over and do the work. Of course, I wouldn't charge them for my work, but she's going to pay Trevor five pounds an hour and he can really do with the money. Isn't that sweet? I wasn't so afraid of Cosmo by the end of the evening, but he is awfully brainy.'

'I don't know what to say to him. I'm just hoping that in time we'll find some mutual interests. Neither of us is interested in football, so there's no hope there. He does like old houses, though. That's a start.'

Zoe had given Fran a complete tour of the house, and she was full of all she had seen. She talked about the house and its furnishings for some time, until tiredness and the smooth hum of the car sent her to sleep.

'Come on, honey,' Richard said when he had parked the car at Gosfield Hall. 'Wake up. Let's get you inside. Is your bag in the van?'

Fran sat up and rubbed her face. 'I'm not staying, dear. I'm awake now. I'll be all right.'

'You don't want to stay with me tonight? Is this to be how we're going to go on in future? I thought after Florida . . .'

'Please, dear. Just let me get my affairs sorted out. Trevor has dropped out of university. I really was so cross with him, but he says he hated it. Not the academic type. I don't know what he's going to do with himself. I must—'

'Yes, I suppose you must. Trevor comes first. Cosmo warned me that you show no signs of wanting to jump into my life. Nicely put, don't you think? Sums up the situation perfectly.'

Fran bit her thumbnail. 'Cosmo said that? It's none of his business. Why do people always have to put their oar in? He doesn't know me or what I think. It's only natural that I should want to sort out my son's future, for heaven's sake. You wouldn't want me to abandon him. Now Cosmo has put ideas in your head.'

'I didn't need to have ideas put into my head, believe me,' said Richard. 'But don't worry, I'll not carry you off against your will. You will have to decide for yourself where we go from here.' He kissed her quickly on the cheek and told her to get in touch with him when she wasn't too busy.

His own affairs kept Richard on the move. The Red Cross party was keeping him busy. There were to be a hundred and twenty people for a buffet supper, and he wished to be sure that all of them would have somewhere to sit, even if their dinner had to be eaten off their knees. The food would be served in the grand salon. The guests could then drift into the hall, the library or upstairs into the ballroom. He had recently engaged the services of an interior decorator who had chosen the paint for those walls that Frank Toombs said could be redecorated. Woodfare Interiors had also bought some furniture for the public rooms. They still looked bare, but now they boasted thousands of pounds' worth of antiques.

For a man who prided himself on never joining

anything, Richard had signed up to a number of organizations in East Anglia. Safe in the knowledge that no-one knew of his humble past, he enjoyed the company of members of the East Anglia Institute of Directors where he could talk shop for hours.

He also discovered that the region had American connections of long standing. There was even an American Heritage trail for tourists. And there were thousands of Americans, mostly in the services, in Essex, Suffolk and Norfolk. He had soon agreed to host an evening for some of them.

The Miami chain was prospering. He missed being able to chew over the figures with Jorge, but there was no doubting the success of the project. Several days after the dinner at Zoe's, he decided to drive round to a few of the seaside cafés and see how they were doing first hand. He needed to get out of the house which always seemed to have some problem ticking over that required a decision.

When he reached Clacton, he found it transformed from the time of his first visit. The streets were crowded with holiday-makers, the sun was shining, and there were bright splashes of colourful flowers rigidly planted in public places. All the flower-beds displayed tulips – tulips with some little blue flower, tulips in contrasting colours, tulips in combination with flowers he had never seen before.

'Tulips!' Richard shouted to himself as he drove along the front. 'God-damned tulips! She couldn't even stick around long enough to give me some tulips!'

His anger had very little to do with tulips and nothing whatsoever to do with the ten thousand pounds he had paid Fran. But the absence of tulips and of a plan for his south lawn indicated to Richard that she was indifferent to him. She was neglecting him, couldn't even be bothered to turn up at Gosfield for a consultation about the garden. He felt he was losing her.

When he found a parking space, he pulled out his mobile phone and rang Fran. 'I don't know what the hell is going on with you,' he began without preamble. 'I gave you a commission to design a garden for me with tulips in it. Have you forgotten all about that? Can't you be bothered to fulfil your promises? What the hell is going on around here?'

Fran, caught completely by surprise, could find nothing to say for several seconds. She knew that Richard was probably not all that bothered about tulips or his ten thousand pounds, but, by demanding that she come up with something for Gosfield Hall, he was ensuring that the loss of the money would come to light. What if she were able to design a suitable garden for him? As soon as she attempted to buy what was needed to put the plan into action, the absence of cash would become evident. He would find her out and take his revenge.

'Calm down, Richard, please. I know what you're thinking, really I do. You think I don't care enough about you to design your garden. But it isn't like that, dear. We've only just got back from Florida . . . I had no time. I was going to . . . No, I'm not giving you the brush-off. That's not fair. I haven't been stringing you along. Richard, please. I'm going to hang up now. You must see sense, see that I . . . oh, Richard, goodbye.'

Fran put the phone on the cradle and sat down

heavily at her desk. 'Oh, my God, it's all over. Maybe he'll sue. I wonder if he can have me arrested. I must call Linus, but I'm too upset to talk sense right now. Oh, what am I going to do?'

'What was that all about?' asked Trevor. 'I could hear his voice all the way across the room. Was he that angry just because you haven't designed a garden for him? Why don't you just sit down and do it?'

'I haven't told you everything. You see, we were in awful trouble. The money was running out.'

'I remember very well. I guess it's been better lately. Don't tell me he —'

'He gave me ten thousand pounds to build a garden for him, but I could never think what to do. It's such a big place and I really haven't all that much experience in designing gardens. You don't know how big Gosfield Hall is.'

'He gave you ten thousand pounds, just like that?' asked Trevor quietly. 'He just said here you are, old girl, put that in your bank account and spend it as you please?'

'Not exactly. He suggested that he write a cheque for ten thousand and that I should put it into a separate account, keeping records of what I spend on Gosfield Hall. Well, I'll bet his interior design company is spending much more than ten thousand, but they can prove it. They'll have something to show for it. Anyway, I put the money into my own account and – we were starving, Trevor! – I had to pay my bills. Then I did buy some plants and containers and statues for the entrance hall. About a thousand pounds. I've spent nearly all the rest and Richard will soon know it.'

'How much is left?'

'It's almost gone. I had to buy my ticket to Florida. There were other expenses. I'm not sure, but I think there's a thousand left. Maybe more, maybe less.'

'Oh, Mum, what have you done? No wonder Linus spent so much time telling me you must marry this bloke. It's your only hope. Throw yourself on his mercy.'

She turned to face him bleakly. 'And see the look of contempt on his face? I honestly don't know if I could bear it. It's bad enough seeing how you're looking at me now. He'll kill me when he finds out. No, he'll do something chilling and cruel, which will be worse. Now can you understand why I can't marry him? I'm a thief and a gold-digger. I'm lower than the lowest and I haven't a clue how to dig myself out of trouble.'

'I feel like a fool. I never guessed.'

'If I could just come up with something to stave off the evil day. You never know. Something might come up. I could get together, say, seven thousand pounds and tell him that I couldn't think of what to do in the garden. Then I might be able to sort out my own feelings. I don't know if I want to go into a loveless marriage. But I've lost all my self-respect.'

Trevor snorted. 'I'll be getting five pounds an hour from his daughter. We'll save up seven thousand pounds in no time! Mum, he's mad at you now, this minute. You will have to come up with something to say to him in the next five minutes.'

She stood up, steadying herself against the edge of the desk. 'I know, I know. Oh, Trevor, how did I ever sink so low? Wait! I've an idea. I'll take him away. That's it. I can calm him down if I can just get him away.'

'On whose money? His or, er, his?'

For the first time, Fran smiled. 'His, of course. What choice do I have?'

The phone rang and Fran hesitated, thinking it must be Richard. To her surprise a woman's voice replied to her tentative hello.

'My name is Caroline Bassett-Vane. I have a small garden of half an acre in Earls Colne. We've just moved in and there is nothing at all in it. I understand you are a garden designer. I wonder if you would like to come over this afternoon to discuss what might be done.'

'Two o'clock? Just let me take down your address, Mrs Bassett-Vane. I'll be there.'

'You see?' she cried when she had hung up the phone. 'Everything's going to be all right. We're saved. My first commission. There will be money for you, too, darling. It's all going to work out.'

Trevor smiled wanly, still recovering from the shock of his mother's revelations. 'It is a start.'

'And I'm going to build a Paradise garden at Gosfield.'

'Whatever that is.'

Fran frowned at her son. 'I'll explain later. Listen, dear. I can't control what you do or say, but is it absolutely necessary to tell your father about this business?'

'Believe me, Mum, I don't want to tell a soul. I'm certainly not going to tell my father. Now, where are you going to take this bloke to charm him out of his mood?'

That afternoon when Richard returned to the Hall, his first question to Liz was about phone calls.

'Just one from your garden designer,' she said

coolly. 'It seems she has booked the two of you for a tour of the bulb fields in Holland. You leave from Stansted airport on Thursday morning, tour the fields the next day and come home the following one. She seemed rather upset when I told her you have a board meeting on the Thursday morning.'

Richard bit his lip. He had never missed a board meeting before coming to England. These days it was not always possible for him to attend board meetings in Florida, but that was acceptable because he was not the chief executive. Here, he would need a very good excuse to miss a meeting. But he had one. His private life was in crisis. He had behaved like an animal and was thoroughly ashamed of his outburst. He was also ashamed of his jealousy. The truth was, he was new to the mating game, had been away from such things for too many years. He didn't know how to go about winning the woman of his choice. But away on holiday in romantic Holland, looking at beautiful flowers, he thought he could repair the damage.

'I don't think they will need me for the board meeting. The chain is working so well, there aren't any problems. I'll speak to Seb. After all, in the next few weeks I will be totally tied up with the Red Cross and other things. Now get me Fran on the phone.'

Seb was stunned that Richard would miss a board meeting. 'But Nigel Falkland will be coming out here. He will expect to hear what you have to say. Is it something urgent? Must you travel back to America?'

Richard smiled. Liz would tell Seb the truth the minute his back was turned. 'Not to America, but

I do want to go to Holland with Fran Craig. I'll write my report and you can read it. We're a great success story, Seb. What we need to do now is plan on opening another Miami, this time in London. You ought to be looking for a suitable property. The thing is, Falkland must be convinced of the importance of doing this. You've got to swing it. I trust you. Show what you can do.'

'Oh, I will,' said Sebastian quietly. 'And I shall propose that we raise our prices. We've got the customers fighting to get in. We could increase our profits by charging more.'

'Not wise. We've captured the age group that eats out most frequently. The fifteen- to twenty-four-year-olds. They eat out where they've eaten before or where they have been advised to go by friends. They're price-sensitive. Tinkering with the prices could damage our trade. No, no. I can't agree to that.'

'Well,' said Seb. This had been his pet idea and he did not intend to abandon it. He'd see what Falkland had to say.

'Now then,' continued Richard. 'About taking him out to lunch. Give him a slap-up meal. How about driving over to Hintlesham Hall? That ought to impress him. You two won't miss me.'

'Right,' said Seb. He had yet to decide whether to inform Falkland in advance that his chief executive couldn't be bothered to attend a board meeting, or wait until Thursday. Of one thing he was certain, he would not be driving all the way to Hintlesham Hall for lunch with the business angel.

Chapter Ten

Mrs Bassett-Vane's house in Earls Colne was a red-brick, executive detached house like a dozen others on the winding road. It had five bedrooms, Fran was told, and half an acre of land. She calculated that the house, separate garage block and generous drive took up a substantial portion of it. The small turfed area at the front had been planted up, presumably by the builders, with three small conifers that hugged the wall beneath the window. Every garden on the estate had its own flowering cherry, but it would be years before the road lost its bald look.

Since the approach to the house was neat and the lawn was level, the back garden came as rather a shock to Fran. Nothing whatsoever had been done to it since the builders left. There was no patio on which to put so much as a table and chairs. No flower-beds had been dug around the perimeter of the plot, and even the fencing was chain-link, four feet high. However, the neighbours on the north side and the bottom of the garden were both busy putting up wooden panels which would force her clients to do the same. The ground was rough and weeds of every sort had taken charge. Fran could see an infestation of ground elder near the house which would undoubtedly resist all efforts to eradicate it. There was not a tree anywhere. The houses on both sides, and the back garden of the neighbour's house behind were clearly visible, and in an equally rough state.

'Well,' said Fran brightly. 'We certainly have a blank canvas to work with. Let's establish what sort of garden you like. I have a small album of gardens here. You tell me what sort you find most attractive.'

Mrs Bassett-Vane, wearing lime green boot-leg trousers and a clinging pale green silk shirt under a fuchsia jacket, grimaced as she took the album. She had short black hair set in a rigid helmet and was wearing all the contents of her make-up drawer, gold and red hoop earrings and a huge dress ring, all at two o'clock in the afternoon.

'Hmm. I don't want something terribly suburban. We're in the country now, after all. But, on the other hand, I despise cottage gardens. Anyway, this is a modern house and the garden should reflect that.' She turned the pages of the album slowly. 'Oh, my God! No! If you do this sort of work, I don't want to let you loose in my garden!'

Puzzled, Fran looked over her shoulder. 'Oh, that. Well, bright colours in the garden and coloured cement swirls in the patio seem to appeal to some people. I don't like it, myself, but if a client wants it, I'll do it.'

'Well, this client does not want it.' Mrs Bassett-Vane looked sideways at Fran, a knowing look that was not at all pleasant. 'Someone recommended you to my husband. A very grand house near

274

Halstead? You're a close friend of the owner, I believe.'

'Gosfield Hall. Mr Richard Dumas, an American. He seems pleased with my plans.'

'I dare say. And what will you charge for a plan of my garden?'

'Five hundred pounds. That's for working drawings and I won't charge you extra for a detailed planting plan or for this consultation. You can then do it yourself, hire somebody else or I will do it for you, bringing in a team of men, buying all supplies. My charges will be ten pounds hourly for myself and five pounds for the team, and the supplies will be at retail price.'

Mrs Bassett-Vane snapped the album shut. 'You may charge the owner of Gosfield Hall an exorbitant price, but I certainly won't pay so much.'

Her aggressive attitude unbalanced Fran, who had not expected any objection at all to her scale of fees. 'Mr Dumas is paying me thousands for my work, not a mere five hundred.'

'We all know Americans have more money than sense. Two hundred and fifty.'

'I couldn't do it for less than four hundred.'

'Three hundred.'

'No, I don't think I could justify the time it's going to take me if I get less than three fifty.'

'That's settled then. Three hundred and fifty pounds. Now, you'd better get your skates on. I want the garden completed by next Monday. I'm having a large party and—'

'Next Monday? But that's impossible! It will take several weeks. There's a lot of soil to be moved.'

'Ah ha!' said Mrs Bassett-Vane, as if she had

caught Fran out in a gigantic fraud. 'You people can't fool your customers any longer. I've seen it on television. Two men and a woman take a garden in terrible condition and do it up while one of the owners is away for two days. If they can do it in two days for a total of seven hundred and fifty pounds, so can anyone.'

Fran sighed. 'That's television, this is real life. They get paid by the TV companies for the design, and they don't charge the garden owners for the labour. Oh yes, and they bring in earth-movers sometimes. That's expensive.'

Mrs Bassett-Vane was not pleased. 'But what am I to do about next Monday? Oh dear. Now we'll have to keep the curtains closed. I hope the weather doesn't turn too hot.'

'I could probably get a nice drawing of the design to you by next Monday, although not the planting plan which will take longer. You could display it and tell your guests what you are going to do. That would be better than nothing, don't you think? So, shall we discuss what you want in the garden?'

'I suppose so. I just hope you're up to this. Surely even an American wouldn't let you loose on a country house if you have no idea.'

It seemed Mrs Bassett-Vane had several very grand, but not especially modern, notions for her garden. She wanted it on more than one level, with the back third reached by some shallow steps in a classical design. The middle third should contain a few mature trees and a formal water feature of some sort. She really thought she would like some balustrading around the proposed terrace. And how much, please, would that all come to?

'A thousand plus, at a guess,' said Fran, no

longer sure she wanted to deal with this woman. 'I'll have to price out all the hard landscaping more accurately. And don't tell me that they could do it more cheaply on television. I don't have access to fantastic bargains in railway sleepers or junk steel. Anyway, you want something formal and elegant, so I must buy from a good supplier. Now, if you will excuse me, I must take some measurements and photos. I'll be about an hour or an hour and a half.'

Fran's client went indoors while Fran got down to the measuring. The plot was about seventy feet by a hundred, large enough to put in a few striking features, if she could just think up something attractive. She indicated the direction of the sun on her rough sketch as well as the area which was in shade in the afternoon, noticing that as the back of the house faced due west, the new terrace would be sunny and hot in midsummer. Finally, she marked in the direction of the prevailing wind.

After about half an hour she was given a cup of coffee, but it took her another hour to complete her calculations. She went to the back door and knocked.

'I'm finished now. Shall I show you where, roughly, the steps and the terrace and water feature are going to be? By the way, have you any young children?'

'Our son is at Cambridge.'

'Safe enough around water, then.' Fran held out her plan. 'Here is the terrace of York stone, with raised beds giving it a cosy enclosed feeling. Rather better than balustrading, I think. Over here are two raised rectangles at right angles to each other. They are pools, one emptying into the other and they will be planted up. The raised beds around the terrace will contain plenty of colour in the foliage, as well as variety in the leaf shape. You won't need too many flowering plants, so they will be confined mostly to a selection of large pots over here on the left, close to where you will have your furniture – lounger and table and chairs. This is a sunny terrace, so you will want an awning or umbrellas.'

'That seems really nice!' exclaimed Mrs Bassett-Vane in some surprise.

Fran took a deep breath, revelling in the praise. The plan lacked that spark of originality that any good designer would have been able to come up with, but it was workmanlike. 'Now, you will reach the final third of your garden by way of semicircular steps that are a feature in themselves. Down the side of the garden which faces south I'm giving you a large mixed bed. As you can probably see from my sketch, you will have an oval lawn, set at an angle to the house.'

'I can't wait to see it all finished. Yes, yes, I do like the two pools.'

'I'll need fifteen per cent in advance.'

Mrs Bassett-Vane looked disgusted. 'Just get the plan here by Monday so that I can show my friends that we really are going to have something splendid.'

'You will owe me the rest of the three hundred and fifty pounds on delivery of the plan, Mrs Bassett-Vane. I can't proceed otherwise.'

'Of course.' Mrs Bassett-Vane didn't meet her eye, but led the way over the rough ground in her cork-soled mules. They went indoors where the furnishings were much as Fran would have expected. Fitted carpets softened their footfalls and went some way towards absorbing their voices.

Fran had to resist the temptation to whisper. The executive detached could hardly compare with Richard's country house. Yet this was what Fran had always dreamed of owning. She looked around, noticing the pale green carpeting, the white velvet three-piece suite, the numerous wall lights with large crystals suspended from them. The room spoke of comfort and friendly gatherings, of intimacy. Sighing with envy, she committed the living-room to memory.

Mrs Bassett-Vane handed Fran three ten-pound notes, then scrabbled through a handful of change to find, eventually, five pound coins. 'There, ten per cent. I'm sorry, I haven't any more money in the house. You'll just have to trust me.'

The next morning Trevor found his way to Zoe's Cambridge home and let out a low whistle when he saw the house. Set well back from the road, its front door was in deep shadow because of the arched brick entrance to the porch. The window surrounds were made of stone. Very posh. Very expensive.

He had set out full of confidence, but the sight of the house robbed him of the will to get out of the van. He had been told that it was in the Lutyens style which meant nothing to him. Now he could see that the red bricks and huge tiled roof lent a rather romantic air to the house. It made one think of vast log fires and uniformed maids bringing in the tea.

Just as he opened the back doors of the van, it occurred to him that this woman, Zoe, might one day be his stepsister. The thought took the strength from his arms. He had to take a couple of deep breaths to get a grip on his emotions before he could lift the lawnmower and a few tools onto the driveway. He didn't know what he felt about such a possibility. Curiosity, mostly. What would she be like? Probably snooty, probably already hated his mum, probably ready to patronize him. By the time he had rung the doorbell he was ready for a slanging-match if Zoe so much as uttered one unacceptable word.

The door opened. 'Hello, you must be Trevor. I've been so looking forward to getting this garden into some sort of order. Will you have a coffee before you start?'

She was blonde and beautiful. She was gracious. She was as tall as Trevor, and he had no idea what to say to her. He shook hands, grinned, wiped his shoes and followed her into the house.

'Wow!' he said when he saw the oak-panelled hallway. 'Wow!' again when he reached the drawing-room and saw the garden through the large windows. When they reached the kitchen, he had recovered enough to say, 'I guess this is a wow sort of house. Did my mother see this kitchen? I'll bet she broke down and cried.'

'She did seem to like it.'

'Your garden looks absolutely wonderful. There's lots of dead stuff. My mum says that you need new plants and they will require some looking after, so I hope you're interested in gardening. Your trees need seeing to. You'll have to phone a tree surgeon for that.'

'Cosmo likes gardening, so he can find a tree surgeon. As you can see, we've got a terrace across the back of the house,' said Zoe. 'The roof over it is held up by two pillars that match the ones at the bottom of the garden. It faces south and we want to make the most of it. I expect we'll be out there a lot, eating and entertaining. We were in a rented flat last summer. It was gross!'

Trevor took a few minutes to acquaint himself with the garden. The terrace at the back was narrow, about ten feet, but this led down three steps which were set off by short brick pillars. There followed a straight stone path with narrow beds on either side filled with weeds. Another set of short pillars flanked semicircular steps leading further down to a paved area and a rectangular pond, now empty. Finally, there were more steps up to the pergola which was entered halfway along its length, as it ran across the bottom of the garden. Laburnum, which had once covered the pergola, was struggling to give a patchy display. There were no clipped yews, which surprised him.

The garden was big enough to take the mature pink-candled chestnut, but several apple trees were in bad condition, and a pine tree threatened not only Zoe's garden, but also the neighbours'. It was nearly fifty feet tall and virtually dead. Trevor thought a strong wind would push it over. Elsewhere there was a weedy copper beech, which had probably been planted in the last year or two, and several cherry trees.

Cleaning up was the priority. It was almost impossible to see how much of the garden was intact as it stood. He worked steadily all morning, enjoying the work as he had never done when helping his mother. The terraces and steps were so well-designed and made that they were a lesson for any would-be landscaper, although occasionally he had to lift a stone that had been laid nearly a hundred years earlier and pack the ground with sand to level it.

Every breeze sent down a shower of cherry blossom, some of which stuck to the sweat on his forehead. He was in the act of wiping away the petals when Zoe called.

'Trevor! Do you like lasagne?'

He straightened. 'I love lasagne.'

'Well, come on in and get cleaned up. It's lunch-time.'

He left his tools and trotted inside, a happy man for the first time in several months. The downstairs cloakroom was larger than his bathroom at home and boasted much nicer fixtures. He washed carefully, using the nail-brush to clean his grubby nails, then ran his fingers through his hair in an attempt to neaten it.

'Where are we eating?' he called, when he had emerged into the hallway.

'In the kitchen.'

He found his way back to the large kitchen, noted the two-door American fridge, the Aga and an attractive dining area done out in blue and yellow. Walking over to the table, he counted the place settings. Three. His heart sank.

'Cosmo is joining us. He'll be home any minute,' Zoe said, setting a basket of foccacio on the table.

To look me over, thought Trevor, but he said nothing.

As if on cue, Cosmo opened the front door, called out to his wife and quickly joined them in the kitchen. He was tall, dignified, very good-looking and possessed of a manner bound to intimidate scruffy young men. Trevor, who had managed to relax with Zoe, could think of nothing to say beyond hello.

'Chianti with lasagne, I think,' said Cosmo,

putting a glass in front of Trevor. 'Will you have some?'

'Better not. That is, I do like red wine. However, I want to be able to work this afternoon.' Cosmo was smiling, holding the bottle ready to pour should Trevor manage to make up his mind. 'Well, all right. I'll have just one glass. Thank you.'

Cosmo sat down and looked solemnly at Trevor. 'What do you think of our garden?'

Trevor was tasting his wine. He put down the glass carefully so as not to spill any on the yellow cloth. 'It's a privilege to work in it. The lines, the hard landscaping, they're terrific. The pergola with brick pillars is particularly grand. It's the focal point. With some more plants as well as the trees and pond being seen to by specialists, your garden will be stunning.'

'Trevor says we must hire tree surgeons, honey. They're sick, I guess. Have some salad, Trevor. No, not such a small helping. Dig in.'

Cosmo served Trevor a huge portion of lasagne and pushed the dish of parmesan closer to him. 'It shall be done. Do you get great pleasure from working in gardens?'

'I do, yes. I've just completed a year at Essex University reading social studies, but I dropped out. I hated it. I have to be outside, in the open air. I don't care what the weather is. I mean, you obviously like being indoors with your nose in a book, but . . .'

Cosmo smiled. 'I'm quite often out of doors with my nose in a plant. I'm a plant geneticist.'

'Well, it's academic and I'm not cut out for it. I like to feel the soil. It's funny, Mum supported me through the last years of school by mowing lawns and looking after other people's gardens, but I never was interested. Now I've suddenly seen the light. This is what I want to do. This is the life.'

'You must get some training, however, some formal qualification. You should go to Writtle Horticultural College. It's near Chelmsford, not too far for you to commute. Get an NVQ.'

'Don't lecture him, Cosmo,' said Zoe, patting Trevor on the hand. 'What's an NVQ?'

'National Vocational Qualification. Or you might take a degree in horticulture or design. You're young. There's plenty of time. You've got a brain and a sensitivity to beauty. You should make the most of yourself.'

'Yes, I suppose so.'

'What is your mother's qualification? Does she have a degree in landscape design?'

'No.' Trevor looked down at his plate and shovelled lasagne into his mouth. 'Just the usual qualification.'

'Has she been doing this sort of thing for long?'

'She's been working in people's gardens for as long as I can remember, but she got her qualification from Capel Manor a couple of years ago.'

'Cosmo!' said Zoe sternly. 'That's enough questions.'

'What am I doing wrong?' asked Cosmo, the picture of innocence. He poured another glass of wine for Trevor and himself. 'I'm merely asking Trevor some questions about his mother. I'm doing it because you two don't seem to be addressing the situation that affects you both. Let's put our cards on the table. How will you feel if your mother marries Zoe's father?'

284

Trevor pushed back his chair and stood up. 'How the hell do I know? I don't know if she even wants to be Richard Dumas's wife. He hasn't asked her. That much I do know.'

Zoe wiped a tear from the corner of her eye very delicately with the edge of a folded handkerchief. 'I don't get on terribly well with my father. We're not close, you see. I just . . . I don't want—'

'Your father to marry a common sort like my mum.' Trevor sat down again. He was still hungry and the lasagne was delicious. First, however, he finished off his wine.

'No-one said she was common, Trevor,' said Cosmo coolly. 'She comes from exactly the sort of background that Richard does. This is important to him. He told me so.'

'He did? Well, there you are. It's none of our business, really. Zoe's and mine. I'm sure there will be a fortune for Zoe to inherit eventually. My mother could never be called a big spender.'

'Zoe does not need her father's money,' said Cosmo. 'It has been a source of some friction between us. But she needs to feel that he will continue to love her, that no-one will come between them, especially at this difficult time. Please believe me when I say I'm sure your mother is not a gold-digger.'

'She certainly is not.' Trevor wiped the sweat from his forehead, wondering if there was to be dessert or if he could now politely excuse himself and get back to work.

There was fruit salad and coffee. There was also Cosmo, relentlessly coming back to the subject of Fran and Richard Dumas. 'I suggest you keep this discussion on an adult plane as you explore the painful consequences. You two are acting like a pair of children.'

'We are a pair of children,' said Trevor, a little louder than he had intended. 'We're Richard and Fran's children. Except that Zoe's got two fathers, and she's married to one of them. Good grief, Cosmo. Let her ask her own questions.'

Cosmo, who could not be unsettled, calmly waved a hand in Zoe's direction before pouring Trevor yet another glass of Chianti.

She grinned mischievously at her husband. 'What plants should we put into this garden of ours?'

'Oh, Zoe, really. Take this opportunity to clear the air.' Cosmo looked at his watch. 'I must be going.'

When they heard the front door close, Trevor stood up. 'I must get back to the garden and work off the effects of all this wine. I didn't mean to drink so much. I don't want to talk about our parents. I don't want to think about them. I just want to do the best I can in your garden and get paid for it. I'll think about my future some other time, and about their wedding if it ever takes place. Why did you marry that man?'

'Cosmo? I love him! But he can be a pain in the ass sometimes. I've been so uptight about all this, I think he just wanted everything out in the open so that he won't hear any more about it at meal-times. I want to get along with my father. We were never close, because he was always out making money. Things are especially difficult at the moment, because I do want him to stay in England. And now he's interested in other matters. Not just your mother, but the house and his business. I just want . . . I don't know what I want, but I think I agree with you. They'll get married or they won't. There's nothing you and I can do about it. I want you to know, I liked Fran when I met her, even though I tried not to. And I like you.'

'And I like you,' murmured Trevor, embarrassed by all the soul-searching and eager to be gone.

All afternoon he worked with great ferocity, turning over soil, pulling out weeds, scrubbing and sweeping, while seething inwardly. How dare a complete stranger tell him what to do? Who did Cosmo think he was? If his mum married Richard Dumas, was Trevor going to have to knuckle under to Cosmo? Ridiculous!

The whole thing was absurd. No wonder his mother was having second thoughts about marrying Richard. Better just to go on as she was, getting as much as she could out of him, but not committing herself to him for ever. She knew that the two families were like oil and water, incapable of mixing.

Suddenly he had a vision of Sean Craig, in muddy jeans and wearing the silly expression that said he'd had a few too many. What would Cosmo and Zoe think if they ever met his dad?

At half past four, when Zoe paid him his money, she looked embarrassed, then said with considerable dignity that Cosmo had no right to lecture him as if he were Trevor's father. Please, could Trevor forgive and forget? She wanted to be friends and she wanted him to come again on Friday, as he had to go to the market the next day. She planned to make fish pie, and Cosmo was going out to lunch, so they would be alone.

For the first time all afternoon, Trevor laughed.

'Cosmo didn't sound like my father. Dad would say, "Hi, Trev, have a beer. You still hanging around that university, wasting your time?" No, Cosmo sounds more like my mum, but I'm not sure I want to do any more studying. Maybe it's not in my genes.'

Fran and Richard met at Stansted airport. She was eager to tell him about what they would see in Holland. He was full of admiration for the airport terminal. Brilliant architecture. He hadn't known how good British architects could be. The building had probably won a prize or two, hadn't it?

Fran didn't know. But she wanted to tell him that in Holland they would take a tour the following day to see the bulb fields and then go on to Keukenhof gardens. They were staying in The Hague which was the seat of the Dutch government, so it ought to be interesting.

Richard said something non-committal, but when they had checked in their luggage he insisted that they take a tour of the airport terminal so that he could point out its virtues.

So the pattern was set for the trip, thought Fran. He was not interested in bulbs. He was interested in buildings. So much the better. There were thousands of buildings in The Hague. She would keep him happy by taking him to see them.

That evening they walked past the formal dining-room of the hotel with its white tablecloths and ranks of cutlery in order to descend to the brasserie in the basement, because Fran had said she was not terribly hungry and couldn't face a three-course meal.

So far the trip could not be called a success.

Richard was enchanted with some of the buildings, but Fran was disappointed because the weather was very cold and windy, not even reaching twelve degrees. What would the bulb fields be like in such weather?

The instant they entered the brasserie, however, they both cheered up. Dark, like most such places, it had been furnished in a casual but busy style that seemed to welcome one and all and to create a relaxed atmosphere. A pianist was playing in one corner while a black American sang, apparently only when he felt the urge, coming in for a few bars, then sitting out the next minute or two. He had a hoarse voice that spoke of cigarettes and late nights, and the people standing at the bar seemed very appreciative of his blues style.

'It sort of reminds me of *Casablanca*,' she said.

Richard leaned close to shout in her ear. 'You can't tell me that food is the most important thing in this place. It's the atmosphere. We're going to have a good time tonight.'

'I agree. It's fun, but I can't put my finger on why that should be. Oh, Richard, I'm glad we came.'

Their dinner was not particularly well-cooked, but they continued to enjoy the evening until Richard spied a business-suited party of Englishmen.

'Hey! They're some of the guys from the East Anglian Institute of Directors. Come on, let's go over and speak to them.'

Fran didn't want to, but there seemed to be no way of getting out of it. Richard put his arm around her as soon as she stood up, guiding her towards the men with a firm hand, sensing her shyness.

Introductions were casual. Fran didn't catch any

of their names, but was reasonably sure Mr Bassett-Vane was not among them. She didn't even know if he was a member of the organization. However, if Richard had recommended her services, it must have been to a member of this society. He spoke of them often. They were his club mates and probably his soul mates. Business types to a man.

His pride in her was evident, and everyone was very kind. Nevertheless, she was glad to return to her dinner. Later the English contingent went upstairs to eat. The American continued to sing, and, at half past eleven, Richard and Fran went up to their suite in a very mellow mood.

The next day was not a triumph. Although it was dry, the wind blew strongly from the North Sea, straight across the flat, low land. The bulb fields were mostly just a sea of green, since machines had been over the land in recent days to cut off the spent blooms, so that the bulbs could store up nourishment for the following season. This was not too catastrophic for the visitors because their coach was warm, and they were not expected to walk among the topless plants, being merely required to look out of the window at the surprisingly sandy ground on which they were growing.

At Keukenhof, however, they were told that they had four hours to spend walking around the gardens. Eight million blooms shouted at them in brilliant blocks of colour. The heavily wooded gardens had wide, paved paths and wonderful vistas, if a little less hard landscaping than Fran would have expected in a British garden.

Richard, having no buildings to look at, was reminded of the cold. He huddled in his Barbour beneath his new flat cap and looked thoroughly miserable. Fran refrained with effort from reminding him that he was the one who had wanted tulips in his garden.

'These bulbs alone must have cost about two million pounds,' she said. 'I'll never see so many bulbs at one time again.'

'Yes,' he mused. 'But they're planted in blocks by different commercial growers. Each section has the grower's name on. Very good business, this place. And clever, too, because it's only open for eight weeks of the year. The guide said they get nearly a million visitors. I'd heard that the Dutch are great business people. Now I've seen it for myself.'

They arrived back at the hotel at five o'clock, both of them cold and tired, and each of them, for different reasons, feeling somewhat disgruntled. If this had not been the case, Fran would never have attempted to divert Richard by telling him about her first landscaping client.

'. . . And I asked five hundred pounds for the detailed working plan. And—'

'Is that over the odds?'

'No,' said Fran. 'I could have charged seventy-five or a hundred pounds just for the consultation. Then five hundred was fair for the garden design, then another two hundred for the detailed planting plan. Finally, if she had wanted me to construct the garden, I could have charged from thirty to sixty pounds an hour.'

'But you asked for just five hundred pounds, and she said she couldn't possibly pay that much.'

'Yes, and she offered me—'

'Let me guess. Two hundred and fifty. Half. And

you should have said, "Which half do you want me to do?" But I'm sure you didn't.'

'I told her that I couldn't possibly do it for less than four hundred.'

'Then you settled for three hundred and fifty. You're unhappy because you know the proper price was five hundred. She's unhappy, because she now knows you're cheap and she feels cheated. She thinks if only she had started the bargaining at two hundred, she could have had it for three hundred. You did say the client was Mrs Bassett-Vane, didn't you? I know her husband. You should have worn something terribly arty and demanded a thousand. Did you put in some outrageous feature, something that would really make their friends sit up and take notice?'

'I couldn't think of anything.'

'They can't boast to their friends that they're getting a garden design for three hundred and fifty pounds, but they would have paid a thousand and told everybody what a character you are. They could have shown their friends whatever way-out thing you had done, and raved that you were outrageously expensive, but worth it. You played your cards wrong.'

'But I thought as I'm new to this game, and haven't had any experience really, that I ought to charge reasonably until I've got a reputation. I'm sure you are right, but I can't do it.'

'If you can design gardens, then you're worth the money. If you don't have faith in yourself, how can you expect others to do so? Seriously, darling,' he said, 'you must project a more positive image. Don't present things as if you aren't sure yourself. Say, "Trust me. I have been in the business for

292

years and my plan will look marvellous." You will show up all the other gardens in the neighbourhood. People are looking for reassurance from the experts they hire. They want to be told that what is proposed is wonderful and in good taste. You've got to sell yourself and your vision. And once you've set a price, never come down. You must practise your approach.'

'You're right! I will be firm with her. She's horrible. What's the husband like?'

'If he's the one I think he is, he's a typical climber. Ambitious. He wears a gold bracelet. I bet he's got a five-figure overdraft. That type quite often has an expensive wife.'

'Richard, will you excuse me for a few minutes? I won't be long. Just stay in here.' Fran went into the sitting-room of their suite. He could hear her talking and came in to see what was happening. He found her standing in the middle of the floor.

'What's going on?'

'I'm practising. Go away.'

He laughed. 'I've got it. I'll be ready when you are.'

A few moments later she came into the bedroom. Richard was sitting in the only chair in the room with his knees together and his hands folded in his lap. He was grinning broadly. 'I'll pretend to be the client.'

'You are the client, Richard. This is just for you.' She started to sit down on the bed, but decided against it. Her little speech had to be delivered standing up. 'Many centuries ago in Persia, there grew an idea of what a garden fit for a king should be like. As Persia was a hot, dusty country made up largely of desert, they conceived a vision of Paradise based on what they lacked and craved. The old Persian word originally meant an enclosed park used by the king, but Paradise came to mean not only the Garden of Eden, but also the equivalent in Islam of heaven, as described in the Koran. The wonderful garden would be the Paradise which the righteous have been promised. I think it goes something like this: There shall flow in it rivers of pure water and rivers of milk forever fresh, rivers of delicious wine and rivers of clearest honey. They shall eat therein of every fruit. Something like that. I'm not quoting exactly.'

'The Bassett-Vanes won't like it.'

'But will you? A Paradise garden for Richard Dumas in the courtyard of Gosfield Hall, enclosed, with trees and tumbling water and four very small rivers. Trees will spread their shade around you and fruits will hang in clusters over you.'

'I don't know—'

'Trust me. I've given it a great deal of thought. You don't really like tulips. Flowers, as such, don't interest you. Don't try to deny it. I can tell. However, you do like the way they've done it on Plaza Real. That's a kind of Paradise garden, although not enclosed. So what I'm proposing is a variation on that theme. It will be a way of providing you with a retreat, while at the same time making the most of the courtyard at Gosfield.'

'I wanted the garden outside my windows done—'

'But I want to make the Paradise garden in the courtyard first.'

He stood up, taking her seriously now. 'Where would the rivers be?'

'Radiating arms from the pond, which should

294

have a better fountain nozzle and bigger pump. I'll probably use a bubbler. It makes a good sound. There must be fruit trees. Fig, peach, apple, pear, plum and cherry. And there should be some flowering climbers like rose and jasmine and honeysuckle. The paving around the walls is made of loose setts. I could take them up to plant. I'd put plants in huge pots, and there would be comfortable seats. It's a beautiful courtyard and it needs to be cleaned up and filled with plants. I suppose there could be some tulips around the pond basin.'

'If you want to do it, honey, I want to have it. I'll write you a cheque. How much will it cost?'

'Oh, Richard!' she cried. 'Haven't you given me enough? I can do it with some of the money you paid me.'

He liked the idea. He told her she was brilliant and that the Paradise garden would become famous. He praised her presentation as being perfect and predicted a glittering future for her. So positive was he that she almost believed him. But then she reminded herself that he was biased, a man in love. She wondered what it must be like to be able to give love so freely. Her own stony heart beat faster sometimes, but only when he told her she was wonderful. That wasn't love. Before he had finished praising her, the old guilty feelings were back to spoil the moment.

That night, when the lights went out, she slid across the bed to insinuate herself into his arms. They lay for some time without speaking. It was so easy in the dark. She could forget the past, forget Sean's jibes about her sexuality and give herself to Richard with a whole heart. Silently, she could love him. Yet she knew that tomorrow morning it would be different.

He found her mouth and kissed her, putting a stop to her introspection.

Much later he said, 'Fran, are you awake?'

She giggled. 'Yes, are you?'

'I just wanted to say that I don't understand you or what you feel. I mean, I don't have much experience with women. I knew Jenny for years and never understood her. I can't make Zoe out at all. You're so different from both of them. But I'll wait for ever if I must. I'll wait until you feel – or stop feeling – whatever it is. I want you to know I'm here for you.'

She didn't know how to respond and was silent for a moment. 'Darling, I've got to tell you about Sean.'

'And the famous kitchen?' asked Richard.

'I'll get to the kitchen eventually. When we got married, Sean thought I should go out to work. I didn't have any training, so I was a jobbing gardener. I didn't make much, but quite often it was all that came into the house for an entire week. Mowing lawns four or five days a week can be pretty tiring. That's mostly what people wanted. They liked to do the less tiring gardening themselves. The real problem was that Sean drinks. Nothing terrible, you know, just getting merry, then not feeling like going to work the next day. And because he only got paid on the days when he worked, he was always sneaking into the kitchen and taking the few pounds that I had saved up and kept in a biscuit tin. Once he took five pounds out of Mum's purse. Thank God I was able to replace it before she found out.

'Eventually I discovered that Sean was having an affair, so I divorced him. It was a big step and I was terribly afraid of being on my own, but we managed. A couple of years ago I went to the wedding of an old friend. Sean was there, drunk as usual. I saw him head towards the cloakroom and I followed him to say that I was moving out of the house which I was planning to sell, and moving in with Mum. I never got to say it. When I caught up with him, he was going through the pockets of the coats. Well, I told him just what I thought of him. I said I was ashamed that I had been married to a thief for all those years. I said a lot, let it all out.

'He didn't speak for a long time, then he snarled at me like a Rottweiler. "Listen," he said. "I lived with a frigid, selfish bitch for all those years. I only stuck it for Trevor, but you were glad to take him away from his dad in the end. I'm well rid of you. You've no call to feel superior to me, because you aren't." You probably think I'm a silly wimp to be so upset, but I was really devastated. I knew I had to do something to get back my self-respect. I decided to get a landscape design qualification at Capel Manor. I had been thinking about doing it for several years, but it was really Sean being so rude that pushed me into it.'

Richard had been lying on his back. Now he turned over and drew her into his arms. 'Fran,' he said, quietly. 'After all that, why did you want him to build a new kitchen for you? Why did you want him in your home for the time it would take to do the work? It must have been because you have some feeling for him. You know what he's like.'

'It's hard to say what I felt. I remember thinking that he was doing it to make up for the way he had treated me in the past. I would like to think I didn't waste so many years on a drunken, thieving slob. I would like to think that I'm a better person than the sort of woman who puts up with whatever her man does. I wanted him to do something right, just once. Then I would have been able to think that we parted because we couldn't get along, but that the father of my child was a decent sort.'

'Darling,' said Richard softy. 'I won't offer to have a new kitchen put into your home—'

'Oh, no!'

'Because I want you and Trevor to move into Gosfield Hall. God knows there's enough room.'

Fran moved away and sat up. 'I don't want to be kept.'

'Then—'

'Don't say it! I don't know what's going on in my head but I'm pretty mixed-up. I need some time. I'm all confused and it's driving me crazy. Is it so selfish to want to be plain old Fran Craig just for a while? To have some space to make a go of things, to prove myself?'

'No, it isn't. But I don't see how I'm stopping you from being Fran Craig. I'll do or not do anything you want. I just wish you would tell me what the hell it is, because the uncertainty is driving me a little nuts.'

'I don't know what I want from you or from myself.' She lay down again and turned to him. 'I'm not frigid, am I?'

He laughed. 'No. People accuse each other of frigidity when they want to cause pain. Can you sleep? Do you want me to turn on the light?'

'Oh, no. I'm all right. I mean, I feel better now

that I've told you about Sean. At least, I think I do. Go to sleep, darling.'

He gave a hollow laugh and turned over. 'I'll do that,' he muttered, and she knew she was tormenting him, but couldn't help it.

Liz Morgan had worn her one and only cashmere twin set to work the morning of the board meeting. It was a very soft shade of dusty pink and she thought it did something for her skin. Wearing cashmere certainly did something for her confidence. With her navy box-pleated skirt and the small pink and blue scarf held around her neck by a silver-plated toggle, she felt she had never looked more attractive. Richard was away. It was today or never. The office door opened, as it did each morning at nine o'clock.

'Oh, Sebastian, good morning. Quite a nice day, isn't it? It's cold, but at least the sun is shining. Shall we meet for a drink this evening? I'm sure I could find my way to Blackmore End this time.'

Seb frowned, then smiled briefly. 'I'm awfully sorry, dear. I won't be able to make it. I've a board meeting this morning, as you know. Then my cousins have asked to see me this evening. They always want a run-down of what went on at the board meeting. Another time.'

Liz studied him closely. Normally he wore a tweed jacket in need of a press and shapeless cord trousers, but on board-meeting days he always put on a navy pinstriped suit, also in need of a press. His maroon and blue tie, striped from left to right, looked vaguely as if it represented some organization. Liz did wish that the object of her disgracefully lustful thoughts was not so obviously a creep. It never ceased to amaze her that she wanted him so much. In some ways, her husband was a better man. But Seb was the one she wanted.

When he had gone, she shrugged her shoulders as if to shake off her desire and tried to concentrate on her typing. He was slipping away from her. She didn't know what she had done wrong, but suspected that the end of their affair had more to do with some unknown woman than with any failure on Liz's part. After all, had she not been willing in bed? And hadn't she been helpful to him at the office with titbits of information about Richard? She didn't know what she could do to get him back and she had a dreadful feeling that there would never be another man in her life, never another opportunity for excitement and intrigue.

Seb returned to his office and sat down behind his desk, trying to relax. Finding it impossible, he jumped up again and looked out of the window which faced south. At ground level, the view was not as spectacular as from Richard's windows. Whereas Richard could look down on the church, the lake and the golf course, Seb was more aware of the shrubs close at hand that obscured the greater view. A metaphor, perhaps, for their respective positions in life.

On the other hand, he should follow Helena's advice. Stop worrying about Richard. Concentrate on what he had already achieved. Plan for the future.

Of course, on this of all days, he was actively planning for the future. He had written out some notes for the board meeting. He had practised speaking them, trying out different inflections, and opting eventually for a tone of genuine regret. He would be forced to point out that Richard was not present at the board meeting for no better reason than that he wished to go away with his mistress. Then there would be a short account of Richard's profligate spending. Finally, but oh so regretfully, Seb would be positively forced to reveal that Richard was usually occupied with some other, mysterious, business and therefore seldom had time to confront the problems of the Miami chain. Nigel Falkland would be amazed when he heard, and surely grateful for the information about Richard, because information was power.

Seb looked at his watch. Nine o'clock. Another hour. He decided to fill the time by phoning every café and getting an update on how they were doing. Falkland would appreciate that.

'Richard Dumas is not here?' asked Falkland an hour later. 'He went to Holland with that market trader, instead of attending a board meeting? Remarkable.'

Seb shrugged, looking sad. 'I really don't know what . . . of course, he wrote his report for the meeting. I mean, Richard would never fail to do that. He said that since he had written a complete report, he wouldn't be needed.'

'Perhaps that's true. So there are only the two of us and the new company secretary. How is Gibson doing, by the way?'

'Very satisfactory, and pleasanter to work with than the Cuban. No complaints. Nice quiet chap. Well-qualified. Shall we join him? I've set everything up in my office. A very pleasant room. I don't believe you've seen it before.'

The new company secretary, Jonathan Gibson, was a stocky young man of twenty-seven. Seb had interviewed no less than twenty prospects, but Gibson had been his choice because of the young man's paper qualifications as well as his shy, uncertain manner. No problems from that quarter. No stabs in the back. Seb could handle Gibson.

He came into the room looking like a frightened rabbit and reddened when introduced to Falkland. Taking his place at the far end of the table and dumping a pile of papers in front of him, the young man watched with amazement as Falkland set out his paper and pens in a neat configuration. Seb smiled as Gibson now surreptitiously began to straighten his papers.

At the meeting Seb read out Richard's report in a lively voice, and said on putting down the paper, 'He has a succinct style, don't you think? Gets right to the heart of the matter. And we are doing very well. I took the trouble to ring each café this morning so that I could give you the latest data.'

Falkland nodded. He nodded again, several times, as Seb quietly said all that he had planned to say about Richard's shortcomings. Seb waited for a verbal response, something he could report back to his cousins.

'Hmm,' said Falkland. 'Where are we going for lunch today?'

Seb turned to the company secretary. 'I know you're terribly busy at the moment, Jonathan, so there's no need for you to come to lunch with us. I'll talk to you later.'

Falkland watched impassively as the blushing Jonathan Gibson gathered up his papers and said a stumbling farewell. The poor man had been looking forward to a good lunch and an opportunity to impress the chairman. He would have to wait his chance to shine. Today it would be Seb's turn.

When he had gone, Falkland raised his eyebrows and turned his head to one side in a gesture that was almost playful. 'I gather a treat is in store?'

'I hope so. Richard suggested that I take you to Hintlesham Hall, the place that used to be owned by the great chef Robert Carrier, but I thought you would want to see for yourself how well one of our flagship restaurants is doing. We're going to Colchester. You are going to be pleasantly surprised, I think.'

'Cuban food,' murmured Falkland. 'I'm sure I will be . . . surprised.'

It took half an hour to drive to Colchester from Gosfield Hall, then another quarter of an hour queuing to get into the multi-storey car park behind W and G department store. During all this time, Seb carefully pandered to his fellow director's ego.

'I wonder what your wife made of the Edwardian Japanese-type furniture you bought in Coggeshall? It was certainly in a poor condition.'

'She loved it,' said Falkland, allowing himself a little chuckle. 'A few years ago she took a course in upholstery and it has certainly paid off. She's a clever woman and surprisingly strong. She had those springs tied up and new coverings put on in no time. Honoria is a little older than I am, but we find that the ten-year gap suits us. She is the perfect wife for a man like myself. She understands her role in my success, you might say.'

'The suite fits in with the rest of your furnishings, then?'

'It could have done. I am interested in the Far

303

East, but I prefer genuine Eastern furniture and artifacts. I'm not interested in chinoiserie. So we sold it. You will remember I got the shop to drop the price a few hundred, and in the end I got it for seventeen hundred. Honoria did exceptionally well to reupholster the entire suite for three hundred. We presented it as early twentieth-century. Sounds better. And sold it to a dealer at auction for three thousand. By the time it reaches someone who wants to own it, the price will be closer to five thousand, I imagine. There's a good market for oriental-style pieces of quality. I'm always on the lookout for suitable furniture. We turned our investment round very quickly.'

'Indeed,' said Seb, fascinated by this insight into the mind of a financial whiz. 'Is old furniture your joint hobby?'

'Making money is our joint hobby. It can be very creative if you have that sort of mind. We have four homes. Hardly have the time to visit any of them, of course. But they are good investments. France, in particular, is a good idea. You should buy yourself a place in France. I can tell you which regions are most likely to prove profitable.'

'The food in France is marvellous.'

'While I love the French countryside, I find the food is too rich for me. I like simple food. We always eat at home when in France. It's necessary to take a few items with us, of course. Ovaltine. That sort of thing. The wine is cheaper in France, and I like the French wines in moderation. But I'm a man of simple tastes.'

'What do you think about the Euro, the single currency?' Seb was now delving into Falkland's mind. Any man who took Ovaltine to France had to be an interesting case for study.

'The Euro. Brilliant concept. Must come. Much easier for business.'

'We'll sort of lose our independence, though. All our reserves transferred to the Continent. End of Blighty, sort of thing.'

'Nonsense. We're all Europeans. Must think bigger, mix in, forget old boundaries. Much better for business.'

And this, mused Seb cynically, from a man who thought French food was too rich. And, he suddenly realized with a sinking heart, a man who would be unlikely to enjoy Cuban food.

The Colchester branch of Miami Spice was throbbing when the two men arrived at one o'clock. There was not a vacant table that Seb could see. Salsa music crashed against their ears as they stood in the doorway, spilling onto the pavement and causing passers-by to turn and stare.

'It's full,' shouted Falkland. 'Perhaps we had better go—'

'We've a table reserved for us, in a quiet corner. Ah, here comes Frank. Busy today, Frank.'

'Busy every day, Mr Race.' Frank, a handsome giant in his early twenties, had the air of a young man who wanted to go far and would not be too squeamish about stepping on the heads of colleagues. He was putting on the charm rather obviously, but Seb thought Falkland was just the sort to appreciate a little crawling. 'It's a young crowd,' Frank was saying, 'but of the best sort. No rough element. Welcome to the Colchester Miami, Mr Falkland. It's a pleasure to have you here. I'm afraid Mr Dumas has never eaten here, so we consider it a great honour to have you, sir. Come this way.'

'Good man,' shouted Seb in Falkland's ear.

'Well-trained,' said Nigel Falkland, more to himself than to Seb.

The menu was a mystery to the man who was funding the restaurant, but Seb had ordered in advance, and the food arrived swiftly.

'Tapas sort of thing,' shouted Seb. 'Deep-fried squid. It's the most popular dish on the menu.'

'Squid is a delicate dish,' said Falkland. 'But deep-fried?'

'Wonderful olives. Try the olives. The omelette is good.'

Falkland, Seb noticed, was wincing to the beat of the music. Never mind. Let him experience the atmosphere that attracted the young crowd. The drinks arrived in tall, ice-filled glasses. 'Cuba Libra,' said Seb. 'Means Free Cuba. Rum-based.'

Falkland took a sip. 'Very good. Strong. Should help to deaden the music, which is a great benefit.'

'I know. It's loud, but the young crowd are drawn to it. Look around. Not a soul over thirty-five. Except ourselves, of course. The place is jumping all day, I'm told. And on Saturdays they do seven hundred covers. Imagine it! People queue to get in. These places are gold-mines. Perhaps Richard is right. We could clean up if we were to open a place in London.'

Falkland was getting acquainted with the squid, pushing it around his plate as he tried to make up his mind about tasting it. 'Perhaps, but Birmingham is not far away. Then there's Cambridge. Tourists, students. Might go down

306

well. I'll have to think about it. I'll look at the figures.'

For the moment, Falkland was looking at the customers, noting that they were well-dressed business types, that they seemed to be eating enormous amounts of food, noticing also that the staff worked hard and with apparent efficiency. He took a deep breath and concentrated on his food, as if he wished to get it down as quickly as possible.

When their dessert was finished, Seb thought Falkland had been punished enough in the name of good business. Besides, it was now one forty-five and the crowd had reached uncomfortable dimensions. The waiting staff were sweating as they rushed between the tables carrying plates of exotic food. The level of conversation was such that the music was barely audible.

Seb leaned across the table. 'Shall we go somewhere else for coffee?'

Falkland, pathetically grateful for a swift release from purgatory, nodded enthusiastically.

Chapter Eleven

After work, Sebastian drove to Helena's cottage in Blackmore End. The countryside was looking particularly beautiful, he thought. The acid yellow of the oil-seed rape flowers was beginning to fade. Just a few fields were still in their full, nose-irritating glory. The flax from which linseed oil would be extracted was coming into bloom, however, casting a haze of blue over acre after acre. Hawthorns, both pink and white, and rowans with their flat white heads gave the countryside a different look from that which had prevailed just a few weeks earlier. Then, yellow daffodils and garish red tulips, harsh forsythia, flowering cherries in shades of pink, and the yellow-green leaves of the early trees were almost too much for the eye to digest.

Seb loved north Essex. Each time he slid behind the wheel of his car and travelled the narrow winding lanes, his heart swelled with pleasure. He even loved it on foggy mornings when driving was hazardous due to the deer which would suddenly appear in the road, or the geese that waited to waddle across to the sound of a motor-car engine. North Essex was far hillier than most of East

Anglia. Houses crowded the gentle valleys, their plasterwork painted in a delicate palette of pastels, or sprinkled the modest hills with old red brick and sagging, tiled roofs, their black-stained wooden barns close by.

Could Richard Dumas appreciate the fragile beauty of north Essex? Seb thought not. Richard was a money-making machine, a product of the New World, a philistine who had come to sit like a cuckoo in Gosfield Hall. Seb was mixing his metaphors somewhat, but he regaled himself with the thought that Richard would not recognize a metaphor if it ran him down.

In this mood, he drew up to the white picket fence that marked Helena's property. The front door was just fifteen feet from the road, but Helena was crowding the small space between with carnations and clumps of hollyhocks, loosestrife and lupins, love-in-a-mist and marigolds. She was creating a cottage garden, bless her!

Affection for this distant cousin suddenly engulfed him. What a splendid woman she was. She had a tendency to be facetious when nervous, but she was good-hearted. The perfect little home-maker.

When she opened the door to him he cried, 'Helena, you are a marvel! What a clever designer you are. Your garden is going to be delightful.'

She flushed with pleasure. 'It needs a lot more work and it will look much better next year, but I have high hopes for it. Come in. Have you had a large meal with Mr Falkland? Can you manage my *coq au vin?* I do hope so. Here, let's take your coat. You look very tired. I've made some Pimm's. You'll have a glass, won't you?'

He could almost have wept with joy at such warm cosseting. Why had he not realized what a little gem she was?

'I'll be delighted to have a Pimm's, and I did not have a large lunch. I took Falkland to the Colchester Miami. You should have seen him picking at his food. Do you know, the fool takes his own Ovaltine to France. Imagine it.'

'Perhaps he has a delicate stomach.'

'So he says. I've got his number, though. I can read him like a book. He's a desiccated calculating machine, never happier than when turning a few pounds, outsmarting his neighbour. He'd sell his grandmother for tuppence. He's the worst sort of xenophobe, a man without a finer feeling. And he didn't like it when he discovered that Richard had gone to Holland with the market trader.'

'Really? What did he say?'

'Well, he didn't say much, but I shafted Richard today. I made him look like a fool, a man too lazy to do his job. Falkland played his cards close to his chest, but I could tell he was taking it all in. I was very subtle; Richard will be lucky if Falkland ever speaks to him again, much less lends him any more money.'

'Don't be too hard on Richard.' She handed him a glass of Pimm's with a large sprig of fresh mint in it. 'Let's remember that he's a very clever man who saw the potential for the cafés. He arranged all the loans and put up the deeds to Gosfield and found Mr Falkland. That's doing something, although I know, dear, that you have your nose to the grindstone doing the actual work. But we couldn't have done it without him. He's the provider of our feast.'

'Falkland is the provider of our feast, and don't you forget it.'

She frowned, determined to make her point. 'I'm not forgetting that it was Richard who found Falkland, and that he lent the money because he had faith in Richard. He didn't really know the Race family, even if he had met your father.'

'Don't worry about the business, my dear. I'll attend to Richard. I know what I'm doing. You just carry on as you are. You are a great little home-maker. I was just saying so to myself as I drove here. A great little home-maker.'

She flushed slightly. 'A great little spinster home-maker. Or mistress. That's all I'm good for.'

He put his glass on the coaster. 'Oh, don't be sad. I didn't mean to upset you. Come here. Let me give you a cuddle. Make it better.'

She was in his arms like a flash. He found himself doing rather more than giving her a cuddle. Without really thinking where his actions could lead, he kissed her on her pretty little mouth. Her response, totally unexpected, set his blood racing. He wanted her passionately, more than he could remember ever having wanted anyone. Yet there was more to his longing than mere physical attraction. She was a woman who gave him great comfort, something he had sorely missed since leaving his parents' home many years ago. Thoughts of *coq au vin* and freshly ironed shirts, of a comfortable home and loving partner waiting for him at the end of the day, all tumbled about in his head and were probably responsible for his next words.

'Helena, we were meant for each other. We're a team and—'

'Oh, Seb! I love you. I do.' Helena clung to him. She was so much shorter than he was that she couldn't do much more than gaze up at him adoringly. 'Ever since that day we met at the solicitor's. You are such a clever man, yet there's no-one to make things easier for you so that you can get on with your important work. I could do that. Will you stay? Will you come and join me in my little cottage? I'd look after you. You wouldn't regret it.'

'I know I wouldn't regret it. I'm not saying I want to start a family, mind you. I'm too old for that sort of thing.'

'One step at a time,' she replied, and kissed him again before slipping from his arms. 'Let's eat. I've got a bottle of champagne in the fridge. We'll celebrate. Oh, I do love you. I think this is the happiest day of my life.'

When eventually they sat down to the *coq au vin*, it was everything Seb had imagined it would be – so tender that the succulent meat fell off the bone. Looking at her happy face as she served his wine, it occurred to him that her determination was every bit as strong as his own, if not stronger. Nature was on her side, what was more. Thoughts of wet nappies and broken nights flitted through his mind, quickly drowned by lust. He would put her off, tell her it was too soon, wait out her biological clock.

Fran and Richard arrived at Gosfield Hall shortly after lunch. Fran was to stay the night as the Red Cross function was the following evening.

Capricious as ever, the weather had suddenly turned unseasonably hot, both in Holland and England. In response to her frantic phone call from

Schipol airport, Trevor had delivered several of Fran's gowns and shoes to Gosfield. Tonight she would be able to wear the acid yellow dress with the sequinned bodice and matching shoes from Florida that she had thought would probably lie mouldering in her wardrobe for ever.

Getting dressed was the easy part, she found. Coming downstairs to greet over a hundred strangers was another matter. She wouldn't let Richard go down on his own, but clung to his arm as they descended the stairs.

Several members of the Red Cross committee were already present. Some looked anxious, hoping that everything would go off well. Others seemed very tired, and no wonder, since the entrance hall had been transformed by dozens of floral decorations, all provided by committee members. Even the statues had been given laurel wreaths.

Richard was quickly among the guests, addressing people by name, making some jocular comment, introducing Fran with a few words about her designing skills, before moving towards the door where gorgeously dressed women and dinner-suited men were crunching their way over the gravel.

As the guests approached, it occurred to Fran that these were the very sort of people she had always regarded with awe. Their accents, their education, their self-assurance all served to remind her of her extremely humble past. Fran Craig, mower of lawns, market trader, thief. She reached into her dainty evening bag and pulled out a scrap of tissue to wipe the sweat from her forehead. It seemed as if the guests were approaching to catch her out, to uncover her deceit, unmask her

313

as a fraud. Tears filled her eyes. She could no longer focus on them and she felt slightly sick.

'I can't do this,' she murmured. 'You're very good at it, but I can't think of anything to say.'

He squeezed her hand. 'Believe it or not I hated doing this in Florida, but I enjoy it here.'

'That's because you don't think of Brits as real people. You can't go wrong, can't make any terrible gaffes because it's all make-believe.'

He didn't laugh. 'You may be right. Gosfield Hall has given me a new hobby, one I'm really suited to. I love buildings. I never realized how much I love them until I came to live in this house. I am really indebted to Seb. I should have asked him to come tonight, but I didn't think of it. However, I have invited a bunch of Americans from the airfields to an evening here next month. If I think of it, I'll invite Seb to that. Hello, Aurelia! How are you? May I introduce my fiancée, Fran Craig? Fran is a garden designer. She's about to transform this courtyard into—'

Aurelia gave a little gasp. 'You're not going to destroy all that's been here since—'

'Certainly not,' said Fran in a slightly quavering voice. 'English Heritage wouldn't let me. I'm aware of my cultural responsibilities.'

'The committee members are inside,' said Richard hastily. 'Do go on in and get yourself a drink.'

Fran peered at the dozen or more people now heading towards the entrance and swayed against Richard in panic. 'I've had enough of this. I can't make it. I'll see you later.'

Richard took her by the arm. 'I need you here. Stay and work through it. Not everybody is going to say something you don't like.'

'You don't understand.'

'I do, but I'm not going to let you run. Stand and fight.' There was the hint of steel in his voice, reminding her that he could be extremely determined. She looked at the ever-increasing wave of elegant guests. Certainly, they frightened her, but not as much as Richard did in his present mood. She stayed and, like arachnophobes who must surround themselves with spiders in order to be cured of their fear, she found it easier to greet the last guest than the first. By the time the final arrival had crossed the threshold, she had even forgiven Richard for introducing her as his fiancée. So much more acceptable than 'girlfriend'.

As the last guest passed into the grand salon, Richard gave her a little squeeze. 'You look like a delicious lemon drop and you were wonderful with the guests. It wasn't so bad, was it?'

'No, surprisingly enough, it wasn't bad. I almost enjoyed it. But, Richard, must we now go inside and speak to them all again?'

He laughed. 'Of course. You're wearing the most glamorous dress of all. Don't you want to show it off?'

When Trevor had delivered clothes for his mother on the Saturday he had handed them to a secretary at a side door, before dashing off to be with his mates in Braintree. He had not taken a careful look around, having just the impression of Gosfield Hall being a very large building. Fran had told him in her phone call from Schipol that she intended to make a Paradise garden in the courtyard. He had no idea what a Paradise garden was, but had obeyed her command to turn up ready for work on Monday morning.

The courtyard was entered through a red-brick Tudor arch, broad and slightly pointed, and flanked by two huge lamps on plinths. A pair of enormous wooden doors were standing open, their weight so great that they ran on rollers over metal strips set into the ground. There was a smaller door, man-sized, cut into the larger one on the right, but he guessed that they were never closed, for what would be the point?

Trevor stood before the trickling fountain in its large basin and stared at the enclosing walls, mesmerized. There were more windows than he could count, all with stone surrounds and small leaded panes. The double doors to the house were nail-studded, guarded by two more large standard lamps on plinths. This wall was given added interest by the sculpted heads of solemn men on tall white stone plinths, placed between the windows.

He studied the pond which would be the source, he was convinced, of innumerable problems. She had said something about small rivers. What on earth could she mean? The fountain itself was insignificant; it rested on four large clam shells set in a circle and could not give much of a display in its present form. Around the basin was a flower-bed of about eighteen inches, and beyond this a mower's width of grass.

There was a stone sett walkway next to the walls all the way around. Inside this were two corner segments of lawn, north and south, which didn't match in size or shape, giving the courtyard a slightly messy feeling.

The beauty of the house was largely lost on him,

but he was obsessed by its size. It was a staggering thought that one man owned this vast place and lived here alone. This man wanted to marry his mother, to bring her here and wall her up in isolated splendour. It could mean that he and his mother need never want for any material thing for the rest of their lives. Yet he couldn't see himself in such a situation. Would his dad drop in occasionally? And what of Trevor's mates? He couldn't imagine them coming over for a cosy chat. Perhaps Richard Dumas would buy him a house of his own. Then Trevor would lose all sense of himself and his own worth. It was a nightmare.

He shook his head as he walked over to the south wall and pegged down his measuring-tape to take the dimensions of the courtyard, as he had been told to do. When his mother had first talked of this mysterious man, she had emphasized his personal qualities. She had gradually accustomed her son to the idea of a very rich American who was infatuated with her. But the house changed everything. Now that he had seen it, now that he was measuring its courtyard, the whole idea of being dependent on such a wealthy person became repugnant.

The tape wasn't long enough to reach from one side to the other. He made a mark in the gravel, went back to retrieve the end of his tape, brought the end to the mark he had made. It was not on. He would say so as soon as he could get his mother alone. She could not marry a man rich enough to own Gosfield Hall. She must forget the whole thing, come down to earth. It wasn't that he didn't want her to find happiness with another man. He did. He needed to know that she would never be lonely when he left home, that she would be looked after and not have to work all hours. She was getting on and couldn't always expect to work as hard as she was presently doing. But she needn't rush into anything. Ten years. That would be soon enough. Trevor could be happy thinking of her marrying again in ten years' time. But not to some excessively wealthy foreigner. Not to Richard Dumas, not to the owner of this stately home.

He retrieved the end of his tape and placed it on the second mark in the gravel, and in this way finally reached the north wall. Ninety-seven feet! Was she mad? Had she really thought that the two of them could afford to build a Paradise garden in the ninety-seven-foot courtyard of Gosfield Hall? They hadn't enough money left to renew the gravel on the drive!

It was at this moment of his absolute despair that one of the double doors opened and his mother emerged into the brilliant sunlight of a perfect May day, followed closely by a bald-headed bloke in jeans and tee shirt. Trevor thought Richard Dumas had probably gone bald on top and decided to shave it all off. It looked cool; the man had a large, well-shaped head. He was tall and had the perfectly even features that Trevor had admired on Zoe. He also had an aura. Perhaps it was the sunlight, but Trevor had the distinct impression that this man glowed with wealth and power. He was smiling, but Trevor thought he could detect the ruthlessness beneath the smile that his mother seemed to fear.

As he walked to meet them, the sweat prickling his armpits, he felt a sudden overwhelming pity for his father. What chances had Sean ever had in life? Not like this man who had most likely been born with a silver spoon in his mouth. Richard Dumas was probably a genius, while Sean Craig had left school without a single O level. Fran was dazzled, would never see the good qualities of Sean now. And this grieved him, for Trevor harboured the hopeless desire to reunite his parents. Even Sean's marriage had not dimmed that dream. Richard Dumas had.

And this privileged *home-wrecker* had just put a proprietorial hand on his mother's shoulder! They were a couple, ranged against him, shutting him out. This man had shared a bed with his mother the previous night, and Trevor quivered with loathing.

'Hello, Trevor. How nice to meet you at last. I understand you're going to help your mother to build the Paradise garden. It seems a big task to me.'

Trevor shook the hand of the man he now hated, forced a smile, mumbled hello and looked to his mother in panic.

'Have you had breakfast?' she asked.

'Yeah.'

'Ready to start taking some measurements?'

'Yeah. I mean, I've already measured across. It's ninety-seven feet.'

'Right. I'll help you measure the other way.'

Trevor didn't take his eyes from his mother's face, yet he was acutely aware of Richard standing beside her.

'I understand,' said Richard quietly, 'that Zoe is very pleased with what you've done so far in her garden.'

'Yeah.' This was not good enough. Trevor knew he had to make some effort at intelligent conversation or risk a bollocking from his mum. 'She's a great girl. We got on just great. Cosmo's a bit . . . I'm not criticizing. I just think—'

'He's interfering? Bossy?' offered Richard with a smile. 'That's what I thought, but Zoe seems to like it.'

'Exactly.' He managed an answering smile, beginning to relax a little.

Richard removed sunglasses from his pocket and put them on. 'Shall I tell her that you won't be able to come to her for a few weeks, while you're building the Paradise garden?'

Trevor slapped his forehead in dismay. 'I forgot! I can't let her down like that, Mum. What am I going to do?'

'Go to Zoe's, of course. I just need you today to strip the turf. There is a gardener here, after all. We'll do the rest together.'

'That's settled then.' Richard took a step backwards. 'Fran, I'm going to be busy all day. I must spend some time with Seb. Dinner tonight?'

'OK. I'll see you at seven. Nothing fancy. I'll be tired.'

Richard waved goodbye to Trevor, saying that he would phone Zoe and tell her to expect him the next day.

Trevor said, 'Yeah.'

Fran watched Richard enter the house, then turned to her son. 'Where's your manners, for God's sake? I was mortified.'

'You were mortified!' he hissed back at her. 'That was the man who's screwing my mum. We don't need money that bad. Tell him to go to hell. You don't have to get into bed with someone you hate. You're selling yourself.'

'I'm not selling myself and I don't hate him.'

'You're screwing someone you don't love. I wouldn't mind if—'

'What an interesting lecture, Trevor. Have you given it often to your father? Or am I the only one? If that side of things was awful, I wouldn't do it. Now, calm down. I can understand that you're upset. The thing is, you've got to come to terms with the fact that just as you are an adult and can do what you please, so I am a woman with no ties. I had to let you make your own decisions the first time you fell for some big-bosomed girl. Now you've got to tell yourself it's none of your business who I sleep with.'

'You asked for my help—'

'That was to help me square the ten thousand. I could go to jail for what I've done. It's important that I produce a good garden here, so that he'll never know what I did with his money.'

His lower lip came forward, the way it used to do when he was five. 'This is just an affair? You won't get really involved with him or think about living in this prison of a house? Promise me, Mum. It wouldn't work.'

She looked around and sighed before answering. 'I know that. It's absolutely ridiculous. I thought so when I woke up this morning. Absurd.' She sighed. 'Now then, let's get on with this measuring. Let's do east–west.'

'About the money, Mum. How much is left? I mean, enough?'

'Yes. No. I don't think so. Oh, God, why did I come up with such an expensive plan? I've paid off all my debts. Well, I had to. This way, I only owe Richard. The phone won't be cut off. My credit card is paid up, so we can carry on getting petrol.

And I've paid off that friend of your father's. He was getting nasty. I've got a couple of thousand, I guess. Maybe less. Linus knows. But don't you see, if I can just do this, I'll be straight.'

'What, exactly, are you going to do here? I make that seventy-seven feet the other way. It's not a square.'

Fran stood up and began reeling in the tape. 'We must measure the pond basin. I'll be adding small rills to the fountain in four directions and—'

'You must be mad! That'll cost a fortune. You don't know much about water features and I don't know anything at all.' Trevor grabbed handfuls of his hair, pretending to pull them out. 'Ye gods, Mum. Was Richard bald when you met him, or did it drop out when he started going out with you?'

'He'd go hairless if he knew what I'd done with his money. Listen, I've got to have the rills. They represent water, milk, honey and wine. So they're necessary. Now, what I want from you today is to strip off all the turf. This courtyard does not need turf. We'll put in plants instead. I'll have huge pots to hold roses and jasmine, possibly fruit trees as well—'

'Huge, expensive pots.'

'I know a supplier,' she said airily, but she looked worried. 'I'll need to find someone willing to sell me a few rather mature trees. It's got to look like something. This pond basin is thirteen feet, by the way. Did you realize it was that large?'

'Yes,' he sighed. 'I realized. Even though you've got me for nothing and you won't be charging for your own time, you haven't got enough money, Mum. What's going to happen to us?'

'I don't know. We'll just have to keep trying. I'll

leave you here for a little while. I've got to take my plan over to Mrs Bassett-Vane. I won't be long.'

The crunch of gravel alerted them to the arrival of Jim Hornby, the gardener. 'What are you two doing?' He had a hoe in his hand and wore a battered hat against the sunshine.

'Oh, Jim, I was just going to look for you. We're fixing up the courtyard. Nothing too drastic. I was hoping you'd help me for a few days. This is my son, Trevor. He'll strip the turf—'

'Strip the turf? You're going to strip the turf? All of it? What for?'

Trevor picked up his spade and leaned against it, amused at his mother's attempts to convince Jim that she wasn't going to damage the grounds of his beloved Gosfield Hall. She took him by the arm and led him round the courtyard. Trevor couldn't hear what they were saying, but when they had made the circuit and returned to the strip of lawn surrounding the fountain, Jim was smiling.

'That's going to be beautiful,' he said warmly to Trevor. 'Just what this place needed. Nobody ever cared around here, until Mr Dumas came. But you'll have a bit of trouble with the fountain and little rivers, I think.'

'Yes,' murmured Fran. 'That had occurred to me, but I'll face it when the time comes. I must be off.' She looked at her watch. 'It's half past eight.'

It was almost nine o'clock when she reached her cottage, and the phone was ringing as she put the key into the lock. Dashing inside, she managed to reach it in time. 'Hello?'

'Is this Fran Craig, the garden designer?'

'Yes, it is! How may I help you?'

'This is Mrs Bassett-Vane. I've been trying to

323

reach you for days. I've just called to say that my husband has decided not to go ahead with remodelling the back garden. So I won't be requiring the plan. He says he doesn't want you to be out of pocket, so you may keep the thirty-five pounds advance. Is that understood?'

Fran sighed. 'Yes, it is, Mrs Bassett-Vane. Thank you for calling.'

She hung up the phone and took a turn round the kitchen. She should have known that this client was going to be difficult. Richard had warned her. Nevertheless, this was another failure to add to all the others.

She needed a cup of coffee, so she switched on the kettle and went to look at the mail Trevor had placed, unopened, on her desk. Bills. Of course she could pay them with Richard's money. In fact, she had no choice. The trick would be to find a supplier of very large terracotta pots at a ridiculously low price, and mature trees on the same basis. Then she could charge Richard retail prices and . . . She covered her face with her hands for several seconds, but she didn't cry. Her situation was too serious for tears. Why had it not occurred to her that Trevor would be shocked once he actually met Richard? Why, for that matter, had she made such an unbelievable mess of her life?

She made coffee in her favourite mug and sat down at the kitchen table to glance through the previous day's newspaper. She didn't order a paper regularly as it was an expense she couldn't justify, but Trevor occasionally brought home a copy of the *Daily Mail*. Flipping the pages idly, she came to an article about a schoolteacher who had taken the money he had collected for a school holiday and used it to pay his mortgage. He had been sentenced to nine months. She began to shiver. Even several sips of scalding coffee could not warm her.

She would have to sell the house. That was the answer. She knew that councils did not look on people kindly if they made themselves homeless, but surely she wouldn't be forced to sleep on the street.

But what was she thinking of? What would she say to Richard? 'I've sold my house and I'm now homeless but I don't want to move in with you. You see, I stole some of your money and . . .' No, she couldn't do that. Every idea she came up with was worse than the one before. It was like being in quicksand. The more you wriggled, the worse it got.

With great effort, she stood up and went to her desk where she had a list of suppliers. Sam answered his phone eventually and, when asked for his best price on terracotta pots, said he would do what he could for her.

Her next call was to the tree nursery where she found that she could buy almost all the mature trees she would need at an average of fifty pounds apiece. A thousand pounds. Probably another thousand or two for the pots. Then there were the fountain and its rills.

She acknowledged, in a moment of complete honesty, that she had not the skill to renovate the fountain and build the rills. Fenton's Water Nurseries could do it beautifully. She knew Mr Fenton quite well, but he was pricey.

Finally, she telephoned Linus. 'I'm coming over,' she said when he answered the phone. 'I have to see you.'

As usual, Linus made her a cup of coffee when she arrived, took her into his office and listened attentively and without interrupting as Fran explained her difficulties. 'And so I've come to a decision. You remember I had borrowed some money from an acquaintance in Enfield—'

'You're not doing that again! You had a terrible time paying it off and he was not a nice person. I met him, remember, when I took some of the Dumas money over to settle your account.'

'You're such a good friend, Linus. I shall be indebted to you for your kindness and your patience for the rest of my life. I don't intend to borrow money from those people again. Look, dear, I saw this ad. Five thousand pounds over sixty months to be paid back at one hundred and eleven pounds a month. I could do that. I could get out of my difficulties with Richard. I'll get known for my work once the courtyard is finished, because Richard entertains a lot of people and he tells everyone about me. My business is bound to take off soon.'

'One hundred and eleven pounds, you say?'

'One hundred and eleven pounds, ninety pence.'

He wrote rapidly on a piece of paper and pushed it towards her. 'One hundred and eleven pounds, ninety pence for sixty months works out at six thousand seven hundred and fourteen pounds. That's what you would pay in total. One thousand seven hundred and fourteen pounds interest for the privilege of borrowing five thousand. Think what you'd be taking on, Fran.'

'Try to understand how I feel. I could go to Richard and tell him that I had spent his money. You and I both know that he would probably say it didn't matter. Although he might take a very different attitude. Anyway, it matters to me. In the last few weeks I have done two things so terrible I can't live with myself. I spent another person's money that was supposed to go elsewhere. And I set out to get into the bed of a rich man I didn't care about. Can't you see what that makes me? Why, I always felt a little superior to Sean because of his stealing. But I'm worse. I can't live with it, with the knowledge. What have I sunk to?' She took a turn around the room, wringing her hands. 'I know it's going to be a terrible burden, paying the money back to the loan company. Perhaps that's my punishment. I can't help it. For God's sake, Linus. Help me to get this loan.'

He shrugged. 'I'll need the deeds to your house.'

Although it was sunny and warm out of doors, the house was too cool for Richard's comfort. He found a sweatshirt before going downstairs to Sebastian's office. 'Hey, Seb, how's things? Did it go all right with our friend Nigel? Sorry I couldn't be here, but I think my report said it all. Did you eat at Hintlesham Hall?'

'No, I took him to the Colchester Miami. I think he was quite impressed with the place. It was packed.'

'I'm glad you showed him what we can do. But he's beginning to hold us back. I thought he had more vision.'

'Surely you don't think Falkland is damaging the business? That's absurd.'

'Have you ever heard of Allyson Svenson?'

'No.'

'How about the Seattle Coffee Company?'

327

'I've had a coffee in one of their cafés, I believe.'

'OK. Allyson Svenson is an American who came to this country to marry an Englishman. A year or two after she arrived, she started the Seattle Coffee Company with a hundred thousand pounds of capital and, I suppose, the benefit of having a husband who is a banker. The first café opened in 1995. The next year the banker left his job to become the chief executive. Soon they had fifty outlets. Fifty, Seb, five-o. Then they sold the company to Starbucks Coffee Company, an American firm, for eighty million. That's dollars, not pounds. But not bad, eh? In two years? We need to get going. We need to open more outlets. We're lagging behind. We're sitting on a gold-mine here and we're not capitalizing on it.'

'What you mean is, the British are too slow, not like that dynamic American woman.'

'You said it. I didn't,' said Richard, always happy for an opportunity to tease Seb.

Sebastian sucked the end of his pencil for a moment. 'Why don't you phone Nigel Falkland and tell him about Allyson Svenson?'

'Good idea. Can I say you're behind me on this?'

'I'm sure you don't need my support, Richard.'

Richard went back to his own office and asked Liz to put in a call to Falkland. 'Nigel, hello. Sorry to have missed the board meeting! Everything all right?'

'Oh, yes,' came the smooth voice on the other end of the line. 'I was most impressed.'

'Have you,' asked Richard, 'ever heard of the Seattle Coffee Company? Allyson Svenson came to London to marry an Englishman, opened the

Seattle Coffee Company about four years ago and—'

'I think you'll find her husband is also from Seattle, not Britain. Started with a hundred thousand pounds capital. Fifty outlets. Sold to Starbucks Coffee Company. She will spearhead the expansion into Europe. Clever woman. I think I know where you're heading. You want to open more outlets. Probably a good idea within reason. What does our Seb think?'

Caught by surprise, Richard said, 'I don't think it's his department, really. But yes, I'm sure he's with us on this.'

'Hmm. You're right. It doesn't matter. I'll speak to him sometime. Put him straight. By the way, I think there is no need to trouble ourselves with board meetings in June and July. You're busy, I know, and I'm going to be abroad some of the time. Suppose you go ahead and rent five to ten outlets around the country. Wherever you think we would succeed. Cambridge? Oxford? Other university towns? Send me the details and I will study the plans. If I'm happy, I'll make more money available. London may have to wait. All right?'

'Great. I'll put Sebastian onto it straight away.'

Richard sat at his desk doodling for a minute or two. He felt dissatisfied. Back home, he would have spent hours chewing over the business with other executives. They would have discussed the future from every angle, laughed a good deal, tossed around figures, put forward their ideas for new sites.

But he was not in Florida now. Falkland was a man who played his cards close to his chest. So far as Richard could tell, he had no small talk. Richard found it impossible to get a real conversation going with the man about the business or any other subject. He had the greatest respect for Falkland's intellect, but somehow he robbed business of the fun and excitement. Damned pedant! Putting him right about Allyson Svenson.

On the other hand, Sebastian was a reasonably intelligent man with a variety of interests. He had shown his ability to manage the chain and was important to its success. Richard should discuss the new moves with Seb. Yet the man had a gigantic chip on his shoulder. Richard knew that he would very quickly lose patience. They would start snapping at each other. Richard would begin to wonder about Seb's motives. Seb would become sarcastic. The truth was, the two men were on different wavelengths. They could not be in the same room without descending into playground antics, squaring up to each other, attempting to out-stare, pushing out their chests. It was absurd, but at least, Richard told himself, he could see the absurdity. Seb had no sense of perspective.

He shrugged. At half past one he would ring Jorge in Florida. His old friend would be happy to talk about the Miami chain and would make some pertinent suggestions, while at the same time satisfying Richard's need to clarify his own ideas.

Pleased with this thought, he told Liz he was going up to his apartment, and escaped to look at the architect's drawings of Gosfield's interior. For the next two hours he was lost in problems of plumbing and wiring, creaking floorboards and damp patches.

*   *   *

Three weeks later, Nigel Falkland rose from his desk, a spartan affair from old Japan. The office was entirely furnished with antique Japanese pieces which Falkland bought from a British firm. As the furniture came from an earlier time, it was not particularly well-suited to modern business. No Japanese businessman would furnish his office in this way, but that was just the point. He had nothing in common with modern Japanese. They didn't interest him. It was their history, or part of it, that held him in thrall.

Prints were carefully arranged on the grey silk walls. He went up to each one in turn, as was his custom when he wished to sort something out in his mind. There were twenty-four reproductions of erotic scenes from the Edo period. Drawn without perspective, they didn't seem vulgar at all. They were Art. Acceptable. More than acceptable, they announced to every visitor that Nigel was a bit of a lad, sophisticated and daring. He liked the image they projected. Visitors always commented on them.

The twenty-four reproductions on the opposite wall seldom drew a single remark. They were all of samurai engaging in various forms of martial arts. Nigel would have hated anyone to imagine that he was some sort of martial arts aficionado. He never sought to imitate these men, although he knew exactly how one method of fighting differed from another, and what were the names and characteristics of all the arcane weapons once wielded by these mysterious warriors.

He certainly wasn't ashamed of his interest in samurai. He simply wished to keep this important fact to himself. Not even his wife knew about the book – *Secrets of the Samurai* with its chilling line drawings – which he frequently withdrew from his desk to study in private. Samurai had taken the inflicting and enduring of pain to a high art, and it was this which intrigued Nigel Falkland. The restrained, bloodless drawings indicated with frightening accuracy the wounds to flesh which were the samurai's stock-in-trade.

A samurai, if he was to live beyond his twenties, had to be alert at all times, ready to fend off an attacker, ready to inflict an injury so telling that the opponent would not rise to fight again. So Nigel Falkland regarded business. A continuing battle in which no prisoners were taken. It was disappointing that so few business opponents seemed aware of their place on the battlefield. They bumbled along, hoping for the best, looking confused and pathetic when they were outsmarted.

He withdrew the book from its hiding-place and turned to a favourite picture – a samurai standing with sword upraised, preparing to test the new blade in the time-honoured way. Before him a prisoner was staked to the ground face upwards. The sword would slice downwards, right through . . .

The phone rang and his secretary told him a Miss Race wanted to speak to him. Was he available?

He contemplated saying no, then changed his mind. He was in no doubt that the caller was Karen Race, who fancied herself as a hard-nosed business-woman. He would take the time to speak to her because she amused him.

'Nigel?' came the self-important voice. 'I hope I am not intruding too much on your busy day. No-one knows better than I how irritating it can be to have one's thoughts interrupted. How are you? Silly question. I'm sure you don't need idle chit-chat.'

'Nice to hear your voice, Karen. How can I help you?'

'I'm worried. It's difficult to express myself properly on the phone.'

'What is the area of your concern?'

'Richard Dumas. The American. Not that I have any prejudice . . . Seb, my cousin, Sebastian, thinks . . . but I don't listen to everything those two . . . He's different, isn't he? Richard. His methods may be . . . he's so taken with that garden designer . . . I never gossip, but . . .'

Nigel put his hand over the mouthpiece so that she could not hear the wheezy attempt at suppressing his laughter. What a silly little woman she was!

'My dear Karen, we must meet to discuss this. Are you free tomorrow?'

'Well, I'm always busy, as you can imagine, but I could make some excuse to get up to town. What time?'

'We'll combine our meeting with lunch so that you won't be spending any more time than necessary away from your work. Do you know St Christopher's Place? It's a pedestrian lane of great charm close to Selfridges.'

'Yes, I believe I have walked down it. Very quaint.'

'Have you ever eaten Japanese food?'

'Why no! I don't know if I'd like—'

'You'll love the food and you can't miss the restaurant. Masako. It's the only Japanese one on

333

St Christopher's Place. Shall we say half past twelve? I'm really looking forward to it.'

Falkland made quite sure that he arrived early at the restaurant the next day. He chose a table close to the window and sat down on the red velvet banquette with a sigh of pure pleasure. His waitress, graceful in her colourful kimono, quickly approached with the menu, and Nigel, with matching speed, ordered a meal for two, running through the menu with considerable confidence. From the corner of his eye he saw Karen hesitantly approaching the door, and quickly ordered two quarter-bottles of sake before it was necessary to rise to greet her.

She was wearing a suit of that unfortunate shade of green from which school uniforms were so often made. Perhaps she had worn a blazer of a different colour at school, and so had not developed an aversion to bottle-green. Or perhaps she was the sort whose greatest success had been in school, and was dressing as she had dressed then. He'd met a few in his time, men and women who were always harking back to the good old days.

'Karen, how nice you look! Green suits you. And you've come alone. We have never had a chance to get to know one another.'

Flattered, she murmured that she was delighted to be here. But her darting eyes and the distracted way she allowed herself to be seated suggested that she was uncertain about what she was about to eat. He decided to put her mind at rest.

'I've ordered lunch. Now you are not to worry. We'll not be eating live fish today. Nor monkey's brains.'

'Do they really—'

'Of course, you must try the raw fish. That's quite different.'

The waitress arrived with hot wet flannels, and Nigel instructed his guest what to do. She was thrown off balance, very ill at ease in a new situation, as he knew perfectly well she would be.

Members of the Race family gave him infinite pleasure. He liked to think of himself as a student of human nature, and the Races had enough little quirks to keep him interested for hours. Their mistrust of Richard Dumas amused him immensely. He had considerable respect for Richard, knew the quality of the man's business mind, and trod warily when dealing with him. But the Races, with their inflated ideas of their own importance, couldn't see the American's strengths.

The waitress returned with two hot bottles of sake. Nigel said, 'It's about the strength of sherry, but warm. I think you'll like it.'

She did. Commenting on the small size of the sake cups, she drank the first one down in a couple of ladylike sips. He refilled her cup and watched her drink the second one with equal speed.

Nigel liked Japanese food for several reasons. Its delicate flavours and small portions, beautifully presented, always stimulated his appetite. The absence of sauces and the quick simplicity of the cooking could not be matched by any other cuisine.

But there was a further reason why he liked Japanese food. There was a ritual connected with eating it. One needed chopsticks, for one thing. One needed to learn how to use them correctly. Then there was the pouring of the sake, which diners did for each other, never for themselves.

The rice bowl was to be held in the tips of the fingers, never clutched. The initiated had a subtle advantage over the uninitiated at a Japanese meal. And this was the purpose of his invitation to Karen. He needed information, and what better way to get it than from a young country bumpkin who didn't like looking foolish?

Very small bowls were placed before them. 'What is it?' asked Karen. 'Must I eat this with chopsticks?'

'Yes, you must. It's an appetizer. I must confess I don't know what it is. Perhaps sea urchin. Dig in. Don't be shy. Bring the bowl up to your mouth if – ah, you made it! Have some more sake.'

The raw fish course met with Karen's approval, although she was embarrassed by her inability to eat it neatly. 'There are a number of things I want to discuss. First, the competence of Richard Dumas. I really want your gut reaction to the man and his ability. Then, this enormous debt we have. It worries me, I can tell you.'

The plate was removed and the waitress brought covered bowls. 'Miso soup,' he said. 'Very delicate.' With a deft twist, he removed the lid from his bowl and set it on the table.

Karen watched, then attempted the same movement. However, the hot soup seemed to have a strange effect on the light bowl and its cover. The lid resisted her first efforts to remove it, and there was no handle. She pushed. No luck. She pushed again. This time the lid came off, the bowl skittered across the table, spilling hot broth as it went. Most of the liquid landed on the table, but a goodly portion landed in Karen's lap, and it was very hot. She squealed in pain, flapping her arms as she scooted across the banquette. A wet patch the size of a dinner plate darkened the bottle-green skirt.

'Not to worry,' said Nigel. 'The waitress will soon have the table cleaned up. The ladies' room is through the restaurant and down those steps at the far end.'

She left, whimpering, and was full of apologies on her return. He told her not to worry, that she wouldn't require a spoon as the soup was drunk directly from the bowl. And, as it was no longer very hot, she could drink it straight away. He thought the fishy, salty taste would meet with her approval. Quickly finishing her soup, Karen gave him an uncertain smile and said that she was really enjoying her first Japanese meal. The skirt wouldn't stain, she was almost sure of it.

Their main course was tempura, prawns and pieces of vegetable dipped in a light batter and deep-fried, which Karen managed to eat with enthusiasm, helped along by the contents of another quarter-bottle of sake for each of them. Nigel had ordered it while Karen was downstairs.

'Tell me what you know about Richard Dumas,' he said.

'Well, I can tell you one thing, though I shouldn't. He thinks you're a stick-in-the-mud. He actually thinks you're preventing the chain from expanding. He thinks we're sitting on a gold-mine and that you are holding us back. Can you believe such a thing?'

Nigel's eyebrows shot up. No, he couldn't believe it. 'Why did he make such a preposterous remark?'

'Something to do with a coffee company. I didn't get it quite straight, as I heard it third-hand from my sister. She and Seb are . . . I shouldn't mention it. They are living together in Helena's house. I do hope that this time . . . He thinks we should be spending millions on expanding! Well, I said to Helena, who told Seb, I don't want to get hopelessly in debt. Goodness, it frightens me enough as it is.'

'So that's why you wanted to talk to me.' He smiled at his guest, who was attempting to shovel sticky rice into her mouth with a pair of chopsticks. 'Yes, these Americans can be very impatient.'

'He's going around renting properties all over the place. In the last two weeks he's taken up leases on five new properties in Cambridge, Oxford, Birmingham, Brighton and Eastbourne. Sebastian is very worried. Can you believe the man is doing something so reckless? Did you know about this?'

'Perhaps there's something about it in my paperwork,' he murmured.

Had Sebastian Race not told her that Falkland approved these new rentals? Or had Richard Dumas not told Sebastian? The two men were like chalk and cheese, couldn't say good morning to one another without squaring up. Nigel had seen it often in business. Two men, each talented in his way, could make a mess of an entire project because of personal enmity.

Karen picked up her little sake bottle and shook it. 'Not that Richard spends all his time on the business, as he should be doing. That garden-design friend of his has built what she calls a Paradise garden in the courtyard. Seb says she often spends the night.'

'That would be a distraction.'

'It certainly would! Always entertaining. Seb and

Helena are going to some bash Richard's giving for Americans. They don't want to go, but think it might be a good idea to keep an eye on Richard.'

'Very wise.' Nigel signalled to the waitress and ordered two glasses of plum wine. 'Dumas seems very fond of that house.'

'Dotes on it. Seb says he spends more time fiddling around on the house, inviting people to parties, talking with the man from English Heritage and this Frank Toombs from Braintree Council. What can they have to talk about? Seb is so afraid that he'll be allowed to do something dreadful to our national heritage, just because he's so stinking rich.'

'That would be a pity. I do appreciate your coming all this way to warn me.'

'And all the articles in the newspapers. That really annoys Seb. Writing Richard up as some kind of landed gentleman. Why, it was Seb who actually purchased Gosfield Hall. It makes me sick to think of some American coming over here—'

'Happens all too frequently. What do you think of the plum wine?'

'I really shouldn't drink any more. I'm feeling a trifle . . . it's delicious, isn't it? Oh, Nigel, this has been such fun. I don't get away very often. Nose to the grindstone. Well, my sister is so lazy . . . if Seb marries her, that'll be a load off my mind . . . but not, of course, if we all end up in the bankruptcy court. Oh, God, Nigel, you won't let that happen will you?'

'Don't worry about it, my dear.' He signalled for the waitress, then looked at his watch. 'Good heavens! Is that the time? Can I give you a lift to Liverpool Street? It's on my way.'

339

'Yes, thank you. I do appreciate your taking the time to put my mind at rest.' She stood up, swaying a bit, and looked down at her skirt. 'I'm sure it won't stain. It's my best suit. I think dark green suits me and looks right for business, don't you? Oh, Nigel, you have been so kind.'

'Delighted to have been of help, he said.

Chapter Twelve

The day after Trevor stripped the turf from the courtyard, Fran and Jim set to work. Although she had explained her plan carefully, even showing him the drawings, Jim was surprised by the size of the terracotta pots. They were delivered at half past nine, and Fran examined each one very carefully. They had been hideously expensive, and she had no intention of taking delivery of a cracked one.

Together they moved the pots into place and stood back to admire them. 'This courtyard's bigger than you think,' said Jim. 'Those pots are huge, but they don't look too big once they're up against the walls.'

'I know. I must get some fairly mature trees to put in them. Jim, let's try lifting a few of the setts in the path next to the walls. I think we could dig out the soil and plant some climbers. Not ivy or Virginia creeper, nothing to damage the brickwork. I don't think English Heritage would be too pleased if we did that, but a few nails and some wire for climbing roses won't hurt anything. Won't it look lovely in a couple of years' time!'

The John Innes potting compost for the pots arrived that afternoon. There was so much of it that

Jim had it delivered beyond the old well, saying that he would happily barrow it round rather than have compost all over the gravel drive.

Where indicated on Fran's hasty sketch, Jim lifted setts and began digging out some of the old clay soil and replacing it with a rich mixture of the clay and well-rotted manure. Because of the way the sun fell in the courtyard, it was not possible to have a great many roses on every wall. Fran chose the pink semi-double Morning Jewel for a slightly shady spot, and the magnificent old white Kiftsgate which she placed on the north wall. Yellow Maigold, carmine Zepherine Drouhin and white Seagull all earned a place, but the container-grown plants looked ridiculously small against the old Tudor bricks.

Gardeners had to think in terms of what their plants would look like in a few years. However, Fran had a feeling that this was not understood by Richard. He was a man who expected results quickly and would probably be surprised that nothing was in bloom the day after it was planted.

On the Monday of the following week Mr Fenton, the pond supplier, came out to give a quote. He arrived a minute or two before Richard, who had come outside to see how Fran and Jim were getting on.

'No problem,' said Mr Fenton. 'It's easy enough to do as you ask, but I do think you should consider putting a really nice feature in the middle of that basin. I mean, you've got four clam shells there. Wasn't it Aphrodite who rose up out of the water? There's a painting by Botticelli and we've done a few on that theme.'

'But that would cost thousands!' cried Fran. 'I

mean I couldn't afford it within my budget.'

'I'm sure the work on the fountain would be well beyond the money I've put into your fund, Fran. Mr Fenton, calculate your costs. Include a good statue and send me your quote as soon as possible.'

'It shouldn't be brand-new,' added Fran. 'It should be old with moss and lichen on it.'

Fenton rubbed his chin. 'An antique statue, you mean. That's what a place of this quality needs, but I warn you it's pricey.'

'Nevertheless,' said Richard. 'Give me something that is suitable for this fine old house.'

Richard then said he was going to be away for a few days with Sebastian Race. He would telephone her that evening from his hotel. He didn't know exactly where he would be, so she couldn't phone him. Fran said she had no plans to go out, and indeed she didn't. Her whole attention was on the courtyard garden.

She went home shortly after Richard and Sebastian drove away, leaving Mr Fenton and Jim to discuss the pond. She had been struck by Mr Fenton's words and was amazed at her own audacity in building anything in the courtyard. How had she thought she could produce a design worthy of Gosfield Hall for a few thousand pounds? She should have purchased genuine stone containers for the trees, but they were beyond her resources. At least the fountain would be properly built by Mr Fenton, and paid for directly by Richard.

Going out of doors, she examined the many rows of box edging that she had been growing on. Bushy, nine-inch-tall box plants retailed for about three pounds. She would need hundreds, preferably larger than the ones in her nursery. Nevertheless, she would plant what she had and charge Richard two pounds each. All of the turfed segments that Trevor had stripped would be edged and divided with box. Inside she would plant— what? She couldn't decide.

Box should be clipped, which meant the courtyard would be rather formal. Herbs would be a logical choice. But she didn't like the messy look of herbs set out in sections of clipped edging. Besides, she had no herbs.

No, she would do what she had wanted to do all along, fill the shapes with clipped plants. Each segment would be divided into three. She would plant purple sage in one. Then variegated euonymus in another and grey santolina in the third. Once they had grown to fill the space, they could be kept trimmed to give a very pleasing effect. As for the trees in each segment, grey-leaved weeping pear trees were very attractive. They could be clipped into a ball. But the santolina was also grey. The two wouldn't give a good contrast.

Fran found the tissue she had thrust up the sleeve of her sweatshirt and wiped her forehead. She was getting overheated. She should calm down. But this was so important! Her entire future happiness depended on it. She sighed, admitting that she was in danger of total panic. Two deep breaths and a stern word to herself followed. She would not think any more about the courtyard until tomorrow. She needed a break from it. Looking at her watch, she gasped in surprise. It was half past four, and she had forgotten to eat lunch.

'Who are you talking to?' asked Trevor, coming outside to join her.

'Myself. I don't know what to do. Trevor, I shouldn't have attempted to do anything at Gosfield Hall. It's too grand. It deserves the very best, lots of money spent on it.'

'What you're doing is all right. Except that the fountain is going to cause trouble. I think you should have forgotten about the rills. Very complicated.'

'Oh, that will be all right. Mr Fenton is going to do it. And he's going to buy a stone figure for the fountain, and Richard will pay his bill.'

'Then what are you worrying about? It's all settled. I worked seven hours at Zoe's today.' He pulled a roll of notes from his pocket. 'Thirty-five pounds. There you are.'

Fran took the money. 'Here's a tenner for yourself. Are you going out tonight?'

'Yeah. With Freddie. He's calling for me. Are you going to be home?'

'Yes. Richard is away. I'm going to watch the telly, if there's anything on. Or I might read the Jilly Cooper I bought at the airport. I don't know. Maybe I'll open that bottle of Chardonnay and get drunk. Have fun, darling. Don't worry about me. I'm going to relax!'

Trevor did not return home from his night out with friends until half past one. He said a noisy goodbye to Freddie and the others, then slammed the car door shut. Fran, sitting slumped over her desk, didn't waken.

'Hey, Mum! What are you doing down here? Why aren't you in bed?'

She struggled to wake up, shook her head and looked at her son with heavy eyes. 'I just couldn't make up my mind what to do about planting the corner segments.'

'You were going to have a cherry tree in each one.'

'Yes, but—'

'Plant cherry trees and put in some summer bedding until you make up your mind what to do permanently.'

She blinked at him in admiration. 'You know, you're going to make a good landscape gardener. You're able to think on your feet. That's what I'll do. Play for time until I can get my head together.'

'You're taking this business too seriously. You're driving yourself crazy.'

Fran knew that this was true, but didn't see how she could take a more laid-back attitude. It was important to get the thing done, to put an end to her worry about Richard's money.

Nevertheless, thanks to Trevor's common sense and calm manner, she awoke the next morning feeling quite confident. The mood lasted until she discovered what she should have realized the night before: it was too late to buy decent bedding plants. Those which had not been sold in the last few weeks were flagging in their trays. She packed the van with her own box edging plants and drove to the wholesaler where she bought another hundred.

Mr Fenton greeted her warmly when she arrived at Gosfield Hall that afternoon. He was well on his way with the fountain and its four new rills. These extended no more than six feet, so as not to interfere with the driveway. The water in them would be no more than twelve inches deep and eighteen inches across. Pipes fixed close to the surface would spray small jets into the rills from either side. A terracotta pot was called for at the end of each rill. She made a note to buy some.

The figure of Aphrodite lay on the ground, its bubble wrap cut open to expose lichen-covered grey stone. Fran guessed that Mr Fenton already had the statue when he mentioned it to Richard. He had found a happy way of getting rid of old stock. She admired his business acumen, as she admired the statue which was just right for the fountain.

With Jim, she set about planting the box edging, and soon discovered that many more plants would be needed. Jim realized also that there would be a fair amount of clipping to be done.

'Are you going to redesign the south garden?' he asked. 'Because a big formal scheme will be an awful lot of work for one man. What with everything else.'

'I can't even think about that now, Jim. So relax. Let's just see if we can get the courtyard looking beautiful. I hope His Nibs likes it.'

Richard and Sebastian set off for Cambridge to meet two commercial property companies. Seb drove and kept up a running commentary about the stupidity of every driver on the road. Every other minute he would suddenly say, 'All right, madam, I know you're crazy. Just try to keep your old banger on the road.' Or, 'Listen, you young thug, I know your type. Given to road rage, I'll bet, but I can handle your sort.'

To take his mind off his companion's irritating driving habits, Richard concentrated on Fran, bringing to mind the short conversation with her and her son. Trevor had come as a welcome surprise. The boy was not the young roughneck he had half expected. It was true that Zoe had spoken approvingly of him, but then Richard's view of people seldom agreed with hers.

He thought he detected disapproval in Trevor's manner towards him. Maybe he should do something for the boy. But what? He had seen the old jalopy Trevor drove. Perhaps a small second-hand car. For a moment or two he gave way to a daydream in which Trevor was extremely grateful for the gift and urged his mother to marry Richard.

Sebastian spoke, dragging him from his reverie. 'I beg your pardon?'

'I said I've booked the first estate agent before lunch and the second after lunch. We have only seven properties to view altogether. I know which one I prefer, but I'll say nothing.' He gave a blast on the car horn. 'Let me pass, you old bat!'

'We'll want to stand outside each one and see what the passing traffic is like. There's to be nothing down a side street. We must be at the heart of things.'

'Where the students go,' agreed Sebastian.

They passed the old site of Addenbrooke's hospital, noting that this area was just too far out for good business, and chatted on in a quite friendly manner until it was necessary to queue up to get into the multi-storey car park. Richard made the mistake of saying that Americans would not put up with such inconvenience, which led Sebastian to retort that Americans would soon lose the use of their legs altogether due to their fondness for the motor car. As a result of this exchange, they were scarcely speaking by the time they reached the office of the estate agent.

Strangely, considering their antipathy, they were as one in choosing a site in Lion Yard shopping centre. This was the closest Richard had seen to a mall, and the foot traffic was considerable. He thought it a perfect site.

They swiftly concluded their business and headed for Birmingham where they were equally successful. Liz had booked them rooms at the Copthorne Hotel right in the heart of the city, but this displeased Sebastian who had wanted to go out of town to a country hotel. He didn't like the modern black-glass block which Richard thought superb. Sebastian refused to eat in the restaurant, but personally booked a table for them at the Sir Edward Elgar restaurant which was much more to his taste. Rather than get the car out of the car park, they hailed a taxi.

Richard had to admit that the restaurant was very attractive. Seated in Edwardian splendour, he read the menu and thought that a week's profits of the company would be spent on the meal. However, the food was good and they both drank more than intended, thus mellowing towards each other a little.

Sebastian cupped his brandy glass in his hand and swirled the contents around. 'I've got a fellow to run the Birmingham operation. He's been an air-traffic controller, but he wants a complete change. Good fellow. Very bright. I can train him to do the job. He's got what it takes.'

Richard sighed deeply. 'Seb, let me give you a piece of advice. Never hire a turkey to climb a tree when you can get a monkey to do it without training.'

'Ah, the voice of experience.'

'And success.'

'Next you'll tell me how much money you've made over the years down to the last penny.'

'If I knew that,' drawled Richard, determined to be offensive, 'I wouldn't be very rich, would I?'

Sebastian drank his brandy in one long gulp. 'I'm going to bed.' He stood up and swiftly left the elegant room.

Seeing the departure of his companion, the waiter was quick to present Richard with the bill. He was in no mood to pay with a credit card and wait for the receipt, so he read through the charges, then dropped a hundred and thirty-five pounds onto the table. 'I can eat this well in Florida for half that amount,' he muttered, but the waiter didn't hear him.

Outside, he realized that Seb had already taken a taxi. He was forced to wait five long minutes for another and was extremely angry by the time he reached the hotel.

The four days and three nights that the two men spent together, while very successful from a business point of view, were extremely trying to both. In Manchester they found a very large site at a surprisingly cheap rent. Although it was in the area where students lived, Richard was suspicious that there wouldn't be enough money in the pockets of the passing trade to pay their prices. He insisted that they rent a very expensive large property close to the Arndale Centre. This infuriated Seb, who scarcely spoke on the four-hour journey home.

As they reached Sible Hedingham, just a few miles from Gosfield Hall, Richard suddenly said, 'I tried to get you on the phone the other night, but

I was told the line had been disconnected.'

'I've moved.'

'Oh, yeah? In with whom?'

'How did . . . ? It's none of your business, but I've moved in with Helena.'

'It is my business if I want to get hold of you. Give me her address and telephone number.'

Sebastian hesitated for a moment. 'Look, I've no objection to your knowing where I am, but life would be simpler if you didn't tell Liz.'

'Ain't life complicated?' laughed Richard. 'I don't want floods of tears around the office, so I won't tell her. But she's a good old stick. You've been pretty mean to her.'

'Again,' said Seb, 'let me remind you that's my business. Am I to understand that you won't let me hire my air-traffic controller?'

'Do what you like. It will be on your head if he talks the customers down to their seats, instead of showing them the way with a smile and a menu.'

'Very funny,' said Seb.

At last Seb turned down Hall Drive and crept over the traffic inhibitors to the old Tudor gateway. He pulled the latch that freed the boot lid.

Richard retrieved his suitcase and waved goodbye, feeling reasonably satisfied with the work they had done. The truth was, he had missed Gosfield Hall with all its problems. Cuban restaurants, though profitable, bored him.

It was six o'clock in the evening. He had repeatedly failed to get Fran on the mobile phone, and he was lonely for a little pleasant company. Walking through the courtyard, he was impressed by the progress so far, and delighted when Fran opened the door. She was dressed in a very attractive green pants suit, smiling broadly, although he thought she looked a little nervous.

'Hi, babe, how're you doing?' He waved a hand and trotted towards her.

The day before Richard was due to return to Gosfield Hall, Fran received a telephone call from Lester Manners, the TV producer. 'Fran! You're never home. I've been trying to call you for days. Can we meet?'

Hoping for some filming money, Fran was eager to see Lester again. 'I can be at your house in twenty minutes.'

'It's more like half an hour to Maldon. Please arrive in one piece.'

Lester's home looked just as it had the last time she visited. The pink paint was still in need of renewal. The chained Labrador was still too amiable to raise a fuss, but the old Vauxhall had been towed away. She had not entered the house on her first visit, which was just as well. She thought she would not have gone on with the filming if she had.

Lester seemed to think that the entire house was one large office. Boxes of papers and videotapes lined the hall so that it was difficult to reach the sitting-room. Here, papers cluttered every surface, including the cushions of the settee.

'Sit down.'

'Where?' she asked, and, with a sigh, Lester cleared the settee of all papers and dumped them in the hearth of a beautiful old fireplace. 'I've made coffee. Clarice! Bring the coffee!'

Clarice, twenty-something, tall and blonde, entered with two cups on a tray. She didn't speak as she set the tray on a table and departed.

'What have you been up to, Lester? Is business prospering?'

'Better than I expected, I have to say, but I haven't got much to sell. I've done the best I could with the small amount of air time I was able to get out of what we did, but that wasn't much. Harry's difficult. You know Harry. But I've sold the show in Canada, so I've got hopes for lots of other countries.'

'Why should the Canadians buy our show?' asked Fran, taking a sip of the very strong coffee. 'Haven't they got shows of their own that talk about Canadian gardens?'

'Listen, let me tell you how it is. We screen Canadian garden shows over here on satellite and cable. We screen all sorts of programmes during the day. Why, the other day I watched a couple of Americans showing viewers how to wire a wood-framed house in the States. We don't even have the same power! They've got 110 volts and we've got 220. Yet somebody bought it and somebody screened it. I'm not saying it was badly produced, just irrelevant.'

'They shouldn't buy all this junk.'

Lester smiled patronizingly. 'There's a little thing called digital television which the world will soon have. Never mind about the technology. What it means is that there will be a lot more channels, but virtually no more programmes to fill the air time. They'll be editing and re-editing the same old shows, compilations, that sort of thing. The world will be screaming out for what we can give them.'

'I want more money this time, Lester. I need it.'

'Love, I'm going to make you rich. I've got Jack

353

who is a good sound-man and I've hired an editor. I'm not going to try to do it myself.'

'I think you're very wise. I'm going to join the union. I want union rates.'

He shook his head sadly. 'You don't understand. I can put this thing out only if you and Harry and I don't take a fee. It'll cost ten thousand just to pay the others – editor, sound-man, secretarial, duplicates, mailing shots, travel – although Clarice will do the secretarial for nothing, because she's my girl.'

'But why should I forego a fee? I've got to live, too. I don't get it.'

'We're two and a half thousand short of the ten. I want you to invest. You'll make much more in the end. Be a producer. It could lead to the big time. What you want is to get exposure. Then the big deals will come along. I wouldn't be surprised if you didn't find yourself one day on *Gardener's World*. Not Harry. He won't make it, but he's helpful to me now. He's a character. But you! You've got what it takes.'

'And you want me to invest two and a half thousand pounds? My accountant would kill me.'

'A pen-pusher. You've got to take chances to make big money. That's what business is all about. Come on, Fran, let's make money.'

She stood up, a-quiver with excitement which she was trying to hide. 'I'll have to think about it. I've got to talk it over with my accountant and also a business friend.' She didn't mention Trevor, but he would certainly be consulted.

'He could do worse than invest in our business. Tell him you're going to be a star.'

Fran smiled. 'You know how we met? At Radio

Essex. He had seen me on television, thought I was a big star.'

'You will be a big star. Hold onto that dream. This is the deal of a lifetime for you.'

'Isn't there something called repeat fees? Shouldn't I be getting more money for my time in the last series?'

Lester was gently propelling her to the door. 'No, because you didn't have that sort of agreement last time. I gave you a one-off payment. Next time, of course—'

'Next time I won't get paid at all, or so you said.'

'But you'll be a shareholder. Bigger payments, and they'll keep coming in. I've got to be going, love. You think about it and get in touch with me in the next few days. Remember, if I don't hear from you, I'll find somebody else.'

Fran drove straight home, and later couldn't remember how she got there. Linus, when she spoke to him on the phone, was not at all enthusiastic. In fact, he was nearly hysterical in his pleading. She must not spend two and a half thousand pounds on a dicey project. She didn't have the money. No, she must not think of the five thousand she had just borrowed as her own money. It wasn't.

'But I'll be making big money and I can pay off the loan easily. After all, I've sixty months to pay it off.'

'You've got to pay one hundred and eleven pounds sixty times over. Think of it that way. Look, I've got a good idea. Talk it all over with Richard Dumas. Tell him about the deal and ask his advice. Then stick to it. Will you do that?'

Fran said she would, which was why she was

waiting for him in a state of high excitement when he came home from his trip with Sebastian Race.

'Was your trip successful?' she asked, in reply to Richard's greeting. He looked rather tired.

'How wonderful to see you, Fran. I'm worn-out and it's my own fault. I cannot keep a civil tongue in my head when I'm around that creep. Four days in his company is more than flesh and blood can stand. And he has very fancy tastes in food, I can tell you. No hamburgers and fries for our Sebastian. I've eaten enough rich sauces and weird meat and fish to last me a lifetime. Let's go down to the Bird in Hand and have a steak.'

'That would be fine. You've walked right past all the new work in the courtyard. What do you think?'

'I haven't had a good look. Walk me around and tell me all about it.'

They toured the courtyard arm in arm. All the hundreds of box plants set out in neat rows six inches apart looked pathetically inadequate. They had not grown enough to touch each other and they were far too low to clip. There were no other plants in the courtyard except for the trees and climbers; none of which were particularly attractive, having only recently arrived in their new homes. The fountain and rills, on the other hand, looked very impressive. The fountain had been turned on, the statue placed in position. Jets of water splashed into the rills most attractively.

Geoff Stone, the caretaker, had unearthed four six-foot-long wooden benches which had been rubbed down and stained a dark brown. These were in position next to the walls, one on each side.

Richard watched the splashing water for a

minute or two. 'In Florida, on the West Coast, there's a show called the Waltzing Waters. It's a load of piping that sends up water in different patterns to music. It's beautiful, coloured lights and everything.'

Fran took this to mean that he thought his own fountain was a pretty poor show. 'You wouldn't want something that flashy in your own home.'

'Of course not. I just mentioned it. I spoke to Liz every day while we were away. Old Fenton didn't waste any time sending in his bill. I'll get no change from five thousand. I don't know how you're managing.' He looked around. 'But I suppose your stuff isn't so expensive.'

'No. Do you see the four benches? A Paradise garden is meant to be a place of contemplation. You can come out here and be perfectly quiet and peaceful.'

This amused him. 'I never have time to sit around, I assure you. Especially not now when I've got a few irons in the fire. No, no. It's very pretty, but I won't be meditating here. Come on. I want to wash up and change, so I can have my steak.'

They spent two pleasant hours eating a hearty dinner. The pub was crowded and there were many people they knew who came to their table to speak to them. Richard had little interest in explaining what his trip had been about and how it had gone, but he returned to the subject of Sebastian Race more than once. 'That guy makes the hairs on my arms stand up every time he comes near. Doesn't he have that effect on you? He's moved in with his cousin, Helena, by the way. You haven't met her.'

'I hardly know Sebastian. I thought he fancied your secretary. Weren't they—'

357

'Dumped her. Doesn't want her to know he's moved in with Helena, which makes things rather awkward.'

Fran thought Richard's mood was not promising, and that she would be wise to leave discussion of Lester's proposal until the next day. However, when they returned home and Richard had sprawled in front of the television, she couldn't resist telling him her exciting news.

He was not impressed. 'Don't do it, Fran. You don't need to get involved in anything like that. I'll always look after you, you know that.'

She gritted her teeth. 'Thank you very much. However, if I were to get involved in a business venture of this sort, what kind of questions would I ask?'

'Ah, now if you're talking business in general, I always enjoy that. Let's see. A television production company. First of all, you'd want to know their track record. What have they produced before? Then you'd want to know how much money others are putting in. What were the viewing figures for the last series? Have they got a contract to produce the next series? What would your share of the company be? You'd want a breakdown of the expenses and expected profit. You'd want to know what your share of the profits would be. I don't know anything about TV production, but every discipline has its own rules. You'd have to know something about television companies and how they work. My God, there must be thousands of people eager to make programmes, and not enough time for them all to be shown. Television is big money. Big money invested and big money made. Stay away from it, Fran. You're no businesswoman.'

'But you take chances all the time, invest in different things.'

'Calculated risks based on years of experience.'

'You had to start somewhere and you made it. Wasn't that a risk?'

'I was lucky. I really didn't know what I was doing. Our Miami chain has borrowed a million pounds at fifteen per cent. A million pounds! That's a calculated risk if ever there was one, but we know what we're doing and we won't get burned. You stay away from hole-in-the-corner projects. You can't trust these little guys not to run off with your money. Take my advice.'

'Fifteen per cent? Isn't that rather high? I mean wouldn't you expect to pay twelve per cent? Something like that?'

'We couldn't borrow the money at a lower rate and we couldn't expand without it. It's done in big business all the time.'

She thought this was extremely interesting, but told him she would take his advice about Lester. That night, she had trouble getting to sleep. It was all so exciting. Trevor's reaction the previous night had not been encouraging, but she didn't care now. Armed with Richard's expert advice, she could hold her own with Lester. She rehearsed the meeting, going over exactly how she would play it.

She would ask him each question Richard had raised. She would wait for a clear answer. She would demand a contract in writing. And only then would she hand over the money which Linus had said was now deposited in the building society. She would take a risk and make a lot of money. Everything was going to work out beautifully.

As for the ten thousand, she had done all that was

necessary for Richard. He didn't seem to be thrilled with the courtyard, but that wasn't the point. With the exception of a few plants, she was finished. No-one could accuse her of theft, which was her main concern.

Then there was Trevor. She really was grateful for his help these days and had to admit that she was glad he had dropped out of university. The money he earned at the market each Thursday was a great help. His work for Zoe was at an end, but those few pounds had kept them in food. She would make money on her investment in TV and from this would come dozens of landscaping contracts. Richard wouldn't look down on her then. She would show him that she was competent, and honest.

The next day Fran rang Lester to say that she wished to discuss the deal with him. They quickly agreed that they would meet that afternoon at his home.

Fran arrived armed with her piercing questions, but the meeting did not go quite as she had anticipated. Harry, wearing dirty trousers and a blue vest, sprawled on Lester's old settee. Meanwhile Lester paced the floor, clearly in a foul mood, leaving Fran to settle herself as best she could on a straight chair.

'First of all, I want to know about the viewing figures of the last series,' she said.

Lester shrugged. 'How the hell do I know? Two old ladies in an old folk's home. What difference does that make to us?'

'Well then, have you got any promises from the satellite channel to buy our next series?'

'No, I haven't. We've got to do it on spec. They're not going to get into some fancy deal with us. We're at the rock-bottom, cheap end of the market, just trying to get a toehold in the industry. Your ideas are altogether too grand, old girl.'

'Now look here, Lester. I want to be businesslike about this, and I have some further questions. If I'm not happy with the answers, I'm not going to invest.'

'It's only two thousand five hundred pounds, for God's sake. Most production companies need tens of thousands to put out a series. But this next series of ours should make your reputation. That's what you've got to bear in mind. Didn't you say this friend of yours thought you were a big TV star? I'm telling you, Fran, this is the reality of our time. Everybody admires someone who's been on television. You see it all the time. Some nobody appears in a fly-on-the-wall documentary and makes an absolute idiot of themselves. Next thing, they're stars. Everybody wants to know them. Everybody loves them and wants to give them work. If we can get this series of films off the ground you'll be up and away, into the big time, and so will I.'

She glared, trying to hide her excitement. She knew it was true about being on television. 'What are your proposed expenses?'

'Ten thousand.'

'What profit do you expect to make?'

'We won't know that until we see how many channels we can sell the series to and how many times they repeat it.'

This seemed perfectly logical to Fran. She

wondered why Richard thought the question was important. 'What's my share? And who's putting money in besides me?'

'Your share is one quarter,' said Harry suddenly. 'And damned lucky to get it. I didn't want to cut you in at all. I've got a quarter share and Lester's got half.'

'Well,' said Fran. 'I've asked my questions and you've been kind enough to answer them honestly. I guess I'll do it. Whom do I make the cheque out to?'

'Manners Productions. I didn't want a fancy name like some production companies have. Just Manners Productions.'

'And I'm now a partner. Or am I a director?'

Lester stopped wandering around the room. 'You're now a shareholder. You're not a partner and I'm the only director. You're just a shareholder.'

'You'll draw up the necessary papers?'

Harry heaved himself up from the settee and leaned over her in a menacing way. 'Look here, Madam Gardener, I trust Lester, so I don't see that you have any cause to go demanding papers. Whatever the hell that means.'

'I just want to be businesslike,' she said softly. 'It's important. I must have a receipt or something to show I've given you all this money. I've got to have a contract soon, as well. What would my business friend think?'

'I'll give you a receipt now and then get something legal drawn up. Lawyers cost money, you know. And these chaps who are going to do the editing and sound belong to a strong union. I've got to pay them a lot.'

362

'Why not offer them shares?' asked Harry.

'I tried that,' said Lester. 'No dice.'

Fran pushed her cheque-book and pen into the depths of her handbag with shaking hands. Reason had no part in her thinking. She had stars in her eyes, could see herself as a famous TV personality. She knew it would happen. Every week millions of people had the same illogical dream of sudden wealth. Those people knew that the chances of winning on the lottery were incredibly small, yet almost each week one or more people did win the big prize, and thousands won smaller amounts of money. So they weren't fools to hope, were they? And Fran felt the odds in favour of Lester's project were far greater than on the lottery. She felt special. She felt lucky. It would all be OK.

They spent the next two hours quarrelling about what was to go into the programmes. In fact they argued for half an hour about how many programmes they would be able to make. Fran was reminded of her days at primary school when she and her friends would argue through the whole of break about which game of make-believe they would play, never getting around to playing anything.

Eventually some progress was made, and the next day Fran met the entire crew at the home of Clarice's parents where filming was to take place. Unlike Harry's scrapyard style of horticulture, the Flemings kept a beautifully neat garden with a large greenhouse that overflowed with handsome plants. They lived in the village of Clare, in a sprawling old house. Fran was forced to revise her negative opinion of Clarice when she saw the girl with her parents. The Flemings were all tall and good-looking and

363

extremely charming. Surprisingly, the elder
Flemings seemed to be quite fond of Lester.

He led her into the greenhouse and positioned
her behind a trestle-table which had been set up to
look like staging. Wearing tight jeans and a pink
shirt unbuttoned to her cleavage, Fran gave a lesson
in sowing different kinds of seeds, then talked for
about five minutes about how to pot on small plants
into larger flowerpots. Finally, using the plants in
the greenhouse, as well as some she had brought
from home, she ran a short clinic on greenfly,
whitefly and mildew in the greenhouse.

The day was overcast but bright, which seemed
to please Lester, so after beer and sandwiches at a
local pub they returned to the garden to take some
outdoor shots.

'This is a really beautiful shrub border,' said
Lester. 'What I want you to do, Fran, is to walk
along its length and talk about the shrubs. The
camera will follow you as you go. Just start at this
end and finish up down there.'

Fran surveyed the shrub border which was
beautifully maintained and planted with a few
rarities she didn't recognize. She could hardly
criticize such perfect management or suggest
additions.

'Let me tell you a story from Capel Manor.' At
these words, everyone immediately took on a
look of extreme boredom and discontent. 'It's
important!'

'Make it short,' said Lester. 'We're paying Jack
by the hour.'

'Frances Perry did some TV at Capel Manor.
She walked down the north border which is planted
beside a high brick wall, talking about each plant as

364

she walked. She didn't hesitate or fluff a line and everything she said was relevant and interesting. When she finished, the crew applauded.'

'What's your point?'

'Frances Perry was a great broadcaster and was terribly experienced. If it's so difficult that the crew actually applauded, how do you expect me to be able to do it?'

'We should get this Frances Perry,' said Harry. 'I told you Fran wasn't up to this.'

Fran glared. 'She has been dead for some years.'

Lester ran his fingers through his hair. 'Look, Fran, let's just try it. Remember that time is money. Stand here to start and look at the camera occasionally. And keep smiling. Everybody smiles on television. Smile. Keep those teeth showing. This is supposed to be the greatest fun you've ever had. Get on with it.'

Now in a panic, she looked at the border and knew that she couldn't think of anything to say about the shrubs, and, worse, that she didn't know the names of half of them. Two attempts failed utterly. She could no longer get out three sentences in a row without stumbling over the words or drying up completely.

Clarice's mother was sent for. She agreed to walk down the border with Fran, making comments and asking advice. First, however, she wished to have her hair done. Mrs Fleming was adamant that she could not possibly appear on TV unless her hair looked clean and properly set. Protestations from Lester that she looked absolutely marvellous cut no ice.

Clarice ran indoors and returned a few minutes later to say that the hairdresser in the village could take her mother immediately, and would be finished in half an hour.

Lester paced around the garden, mumbling to himself. Harry suggested that while Fran got her thoughts together and Clarice's mother went to the hairdresser's, he would tour the garden making his own comments to camera. Lester leapt at the suggestion, coming over to him to shake his hand and offer extravagant encouragement.

Meanwhile Fran rummaged in her bag and found some paper and a pen. She sat down on the patio, out of the way of the camera, and began making notes of what she would say about the border, but her concentration was spoiled by Harry's remarks which came to her clearly.

'This is the kind of poncey garden I can't abide. It's not natural. It's too neat, no rough grass, no uneven edges, no provision for wildlife, no attempt at recycling anything. And they probably use chemicals. Typical suburban garden by typical uptight suburban residents. I'd make this sort of thing illegal if I could.'

When he had finished criticizing everything he saw and the camera was no longer following him around, Fran went over to him and told him exactly what she thought about his rude remarks, reminding him that Clarice and her father were present and had heard every one of his hurtful statements. Harry replied in kind and the argument became quite abusive. No-one intervened, but later Lester told them that the entire quarrel had been filmed, and bits of it would be used in the programmes.

By the time Mrs Fleming had returned from the hairdresser and put on a suitably casual outfit and

Clarice had quickly put some make-up on her mother, it was late afternoon. The sun had come out from behind the high clouds and was casting long shadows across the garden. Lester decided that there was nothing more they could do. They all agreed to come again the next day.

Fran was very happy to be reunited with Lester's young sound-man, Jack. 'Well, Fran,' he said when they had a moment to themselves. 'Back in harness. You were very good in the greenhouse this morning. I think Lester got about six minutes of top quality film, although I expect he'll put in twelve minutes. That's Lester.'

'Does he know anything about being a cameraman? I thought he would hire someone.'

Jack pulled a few twigs from his hair and grinned. 'He used to be a cameraman for BBC outside broadcasts, he got drunk once too often and they fired him. That's not to say he isn't good behind the camera. He is. And he's teetotal these days. The problem is he's running this project on an absolute shoestring. I'll grant that this time he's hired someone to edit the film. That will make a difference. And he's sleeping with Clarice, so she'll do all the secretarial work for nothing. That helps. I just hope you've got yourself fixed up properly. Union rates. Repeat fees, that sort of thing.'

'Oh, no. I'm a shareholder now, so my money will come from the profits.'

Jack raised his eyebrows and shrugged. 'It's your affair. I'm not in the charity business, so I'm going to make sure I get paid.'

They returned to the Fleming garden the following afternoon. By this time Fran had done her homework, and was able to chat about the

367

shrubs with Mrs Fleming in a quite natural way. They repeated the exercise twice more, then Lester said that it would have to do. He thought he had three minutes, and had filmed ten minutes with Harry in his own greenhouse earlier that morning.

Fran was beginning to realize that even the basic sort of programmes that Lester had in mind took time and money. They always had to photograph out of doors and were, therefore, in need of gardens they could use as backgrounds. Mr and Mrs Fleming volunteered some of their friends, all of whom were pleased to have their gardens filmed.

It was Fran's task to suggest something interesting to talk about in each one, and she found herself stretched. It would have been a relief to discuss the work with Richard, but she had already decided that she would tell him nothing. For the same reason, she couldn't offer the courtyard of Gosfield Hall as a filming site. Better not to mention the project at all, since Richard had told her not to get involved.

When Lester one day said in despair that he needed a brand-new garden, one in which nothing had been done, she suggested they try the Bassett-Vanes.

'Perhaps we could actually do some work there. The garden is a complete wilderness. In return for letting us film, we might actually fix up a part of it,' said Fran. 'What do you think?'

Lester was delighted. He obtained the telephone number from Fran and later rang her to say that they would be in Mrs Bassett-Vane's garden the next morning at half past nine. Would she meet them there?

Fran arrived a little late and heard voices from the back garden. Walking down the path at the side of the house, she saw Mrs Bassett-Vane in a cerise trouser suit, and the film crowd looking customarily scruffy. She hardly noticed the people, however, as her eye took in the Bassett-Vane terrace.

'You've stolen my ideas!' she cried, and everyone turned to look at her. 'That terrace is exactly like my drawing. The two raised pools and everything.'

'You!' screamed Mrs Bassett-Vane almost simultaneously. 'If I had known you were involved, I'd not have—'

Lester almost embraced Mrs Bassett-Vane in an attempt to calm her down, putting an arm around her shoulders and walking her firmly some distance away from Fran as he endeavoured to charm her. 'I see you two ladies have met. Well, well, so this excellent design is by our resident expert. You look like perfect TV material to me, Mrs B. Why don't you tell us to camera how you discussed your ideas with Fran and how she drew up a sketch for you?'

'I won't—' began Fran.

'Not to her,' said Mrs Bassett-Vane. 'I'll talk to Gypsy Harry. And you did promise you would do some work here.'

Lester ignored Fran's mutterings, agreed with Mrs B. and they began walking around the garden to map out what she would say to Harry.

'I've had enough of this,' said Fran to Jack. 'I'm going. Lester can do the rest without me. I understand he intends to be here for several days, and I'm damned if I'm going to work in that cow's garden for nothing, after she cheated me out of my fee.'

'Go home and cool off,' he suggested. 'I'll get Lester to call you tomorrow.'

Fran's evenings were spent listening to Richard's stories about his search for a suitable site in London to open a large Miami Spice restaurant. Richard wanted to take the site just off Leicester Square which would seat four hundred. Sebastian was frightened to commit so much money, since they were already planning to open several other Miami Spices around the country. In his conversations with Fran, Richard spoke casually about hundreds of thousands of pounds, of risk-taking and borrowing requirements.

Meanwhile Lester was becoming increasingly irritable as he spoke of pounds lost and the impossibility of getting a loan. Fran began to worry about her investment.

Richard's party for seventy-five Americans resident in East Anglia fell on a particularly warm evening. The fountain was working perfectly and looked as if it had been in place for a hundred years at least. Fran had managed to secure enough brilliant geraniums to fill the bare earth. The effect was not at all garish because of the great size of the courtyard. Americans coming through the gateway invariably commented on it all, which caused Richard to beam at her.

As the latest group approached, Richard leaned over to kiss her on the cheek. 'Cheer up, honey, you're a success. You've been awfully preoccupied lately, as if you're somewhere else. I'm hoping to get you back tonight.'

'I'm all right. Just tired.'

'I've noticed that. You work too hard.'

She turned to face him angrily. 'And next you're going to suggest that I become your concubine and never have to work again.'

'Fran, for God's sake!' He turned to the approaching guests. 'Hello! Welcome to Gosfield Hall. This is my fiancée, Fran Craig.'

Fran smiled at the Americans. Inwardly she felt totally miserable. She couldn't speak to Richard without snapping at him, and she didn't know why he aroused this reaction. In bed, they had the perfect relationship, but had ceased to exchange confidences in the dark for fear of spoiling what pleasure they took in their intimate times together.

And she was coming to realize that Richard, gallingly, had been right about Manners Productions. Lester was falling apart and would never be able to bring the series to a happy conclusion. He had bitten off more than he could chew.

'Oh, here come Seb and Helena Race,' whispered Richard. 'Try to be nice to her. She drives me up the wall, but you may be able to handle her.'

Fran knew Sebastian slightly and didn't like him, so she concentrated on the little woman at his side, neatly dressed in a long turquoise gown. Helena Race looked up at Seb adoringly from time to time as they crossed the courtyard. The perfect consort. How happy Seb must be to have this clinging vine! And how happy Richard would be if only Fran could be as submissive!

The second of Richard's grand parties went with a swing. Everyone was very friendly towards her and she found herself relaxing in a way that had been impossible at the Red Cross party. Richard was everywhere, speaking to everyone briefly before moving on, invariably leaving smiling faces behind him. He was, she acknowledged, the perfect party host.

She was standing in a corner, sipping a glass of champagne, when a voice spoke directly in her ear. 'You're getting quite accustomed to being the *grande dame* of Gosfield Hall, aren't you?' asked Seb. Fran jumped. She hadn't known he was anywhere near her. He smirked. 'Oh, dear, did I catch you out in a little forbidden dream?'

She shrugged, struggling for composure. 'I wasn't having any forbidden dreams. This is really too big for me. I was thinking about my business actually.'

Seb opened his mouth to reply, but Helena, who was never more than a few paces away, came over to slip her arm in his. 'It's a lovely party, Fran. The Americans are all gaping. Some of them are quite awestruck, I think.'

'It is an awesome place, don't you think?'

'I suppose,' agreed Helena, making a little moue, 'but then I'm not mad about gloomy old places. You two must rattle around like peas in a pod at weekends.'

Filming continued for three weeks, and by the time Lester thought he had enough tape everyone was tired and irritable. Lester was scarcely able to speak civilly to anyone, so that Fran had to screw up her courage to ask him about the contract which would acknowledge her investment of two and a half thousand pounds. She had recently told Linus about it. His reaction had been positively explosive. She dared not tell Richard what she had done until she had something to show for it.

'For God's sake, Fran!' said Lester at the wrap party. 'Don't you think I'm human? I've worked all the hours there are to get this series in the can. Clarice is sending out tapes to the channels. We're doing our best, but I just haven't had time to get on with it. Can't you trust me just a little?'

Committed as she was, she had no choice but to trust him and didn't mention the money again.

Two weeks passed, during which Fran returned to her old life of tending her little nursery and packing up plants in the van for Trevor to take to the market. On the second Thursday she accompanied him to Braintree and found that she actually enjoyed the passing crowds, the badinage and, above all, the company of Trevor who seemed to be maturing and turning into a son any woman could be proud of. He had several lawn-cutting commissions which paid for his entertainment. They were managing to keep their heads above water.

The following day she awoke knowing that she couldn't bear to wait any longer to hear how Manners Productions was progressing. She telephoned Lester at half past nine and counted twenty-nine rings before she hung up. Each hour after that she tried again, but without success.

At half past three she jumped into the van and drove to Maldon, pushing the motor to its limits. Lester's house was deserted. The dog was nowhere to be seen, and about the property there was a forsaken silence. She approached the house, put her hands to the glass of the sitting-room window and peered in. The room was totally empty. No furniture. No curtains. No sign of life. Just pale patches of wallpaper where pictures had hung for decades. He'd skipped!

Unable to accept this simple fact, she drove directly to Gypsy Harry's scrapyard where she found the gardening guru shifting parts of an old car. 'You mean he's gone?' asked Harry. 'That bastard! Skipped! I'll flatten him if I ever see him again. He's got a couple thousand quid of mine. Bastard! I'll hunt him down. I'll—'

Fran made a helpless little gesture of sympathy and backed away. She didn't need to witness Harry's fury. She was furious enough for two.

Besides, she had one last hope. She would visit Clarice's parents in Clare. It was a long drive, but it might result in getting her money back. Harry could fend for himself. She drove dangerously fast but didn't care. She had to find out if her money was gone for good. She pushed the old van to its limits and arrived in Clare, sixty miles from Maldon, a little over an hour and a half later.

The handsome house looked ominously still. No activity, no car on the driveway, no elderly gardener pottering in the shade, every window tightly shut.

Nevertheless, she left her van in the drive and rang the doorbell for five full minutes. Perhaps they were just having a nap, or maybe they were out to dinner. If so, she must wait to speak to them.

'Yoohoo!' called a female voice from the next garden. Fran located a smartly dressed woman in her fifties peering through the shrubbery that divided the two properties. 'They've gone away.'

'For how long?'

The neighbour looked worried. 'You're from the

TV, aren't you? A friend of their daughter's boyfriend?'

'I'm trying to find him.'

'They'll be away for a month or so. There's been trouble. I don't know what sort. I don't like to pry, of course, but I couldn't help hearing, well, raised voices.'

'Thanks,' said Fran, heading towards the van. 'I don't suppose there's any hope now.'

The neighbour frowned. 'Are you all right? You don't look very well. Would you like to come indoors for a moment?'

Fran waved the woman to silence. 'No, I'm fine. Must be off, must find Lester.'

Chapter Thirteen

Fran's first thought was to reach Richard, to throw herself into his arms and receive the sympathy and understanding she craved. She had to make him understand what a disaster the loss of two and a half thousand pounds was for her, without actually telling him why it was a disaster.

The engine began to sputter. 'My God!' she cried, 'I can't break down here!'

She managed to steer the van into a lay-by and put on the brake. The petrol gauge registered empty. She looked around vaguely, hoping to see a phone box, then suddenly began to cry. Putting her head on the steering-wheel, she gave way to great, uncontrollable sobs.

After a while, there was a tap on the window. She raised her head to see the large but reassuring features of the driver of an articulated lorry which had pulled in behind her. Her tear-ravaged face clearly shocked him.

'Are you all right?'

'It's all my own fault,' she said, opening the door. Fresh air revived her a little. 'I've nobody to blame but myself, and now I've run out of petrol. They were right and I was wrong. I've got to pay off more debts and I don't see how I'm going to do it.'

The driver's face registered his sense of helplessness in the face of so much feminine anguish. 'You should carry a jerrycan.'

'Jerrycan?'

'Spare diesel. This van runs on diesel, doesn't it? You should carry a spare gallon.'

'But I have a spare can and I forgot all about it.' She scooted out of the van, dashing her tears away with the heel of her hand. 'It's all right. I do have a can at the back, but I don't know if it's full.'

The rear doors were opened, the full can withdrawn and emptied into the tank. 'How far are you going?' asked the driver.

'Gosfield, near Halstead.'

'You'll have to get more diesel. Look, if you're short, I could—' He reached into a shirt pocket and pulled out a five-pound note which he extended to her at arm's length.

'Oh, you are so kind! But it's all right. I have enough. It's just, I was conned out of two and a half thousand! I'm so sorry, please don't mind me.' She searched for a tissue. 'I don't want to cry again, but you're so kind after what that man did to me.'

He took a few paces back as he pocketed the note. 'Well, if you're sure you're all right—'

She nodded, blowing her nose, then got into the van and drove away with surprising smoothness. Half a mile down the road she turned into a petrol station, and the lorry-driver sounded his heavy horn as he passed.

Entering the courtyard of Gosfield Hall much too fast, she brought the van to a screeching halt before the double doors, sending gravel shooting in all directions. Since the door was unlocked she let herself in, calling Richard's name as she ran down the hallway toward his office.

The ornate mahogany door opened and Liz stood gaping at her, only to be pushed aside by Richard. 'What is it? Is it Trevor? My God! Are you hurt? You look terrible.'

'No. I must talk to you.' She looked around. The house was enormous, but she couldn't think of anywhere on the ground floor where they could be guaranteed privacy.

'The library,' he said, and took her by the arm. 'Wait until we are alone. There are a dozen people working here with the company, and about the same number of builders. I'm sure you don't want to tell them all about your troubles.'

He led her into the room and, when he closed the door, she turned to him and was gathered into his arms at once. He held her fiercely and kissed her hair, murmuring some nonsense about everything being all right now that they were together. Being close and feeling his warmth and strength was wonderful, but she had to move away from him in order to find the courage to tell her story.

Two red leather settees flanked the huge fireplace, facing each other with an oak coffee-table between. She sat down on one and indicated that she wanted him to sit on the other. Safely seated with the low table between them, she could start at the beginning.

'When I asked you about investing in Manners Productions, you advised against it. I know now that you were right. I invested two and a half thousand pounds and was to be a shareholder owning twenty-five per cent. Lester was to have half and Gypsy Harry a quarter, like me. We filmed and filmed and I got no money for appearing in the series, because I was a shareholder. One day, to get some outside shots of a garden in the making, we went to the home of Mrs Bassett-Vane. Richard, it's half finished. My design! The two rectangular pools at different levels and everything. The bloody woman has used my design for her garden and cheated me out of my money. She got somebody else to do it.'

'I'd let that go. I expect people do that quite frequently with garden designs. I'm more interested in the producer who can make a series of gardening programmes for ten thousand pounds.'

She took a deep breath and turned away from him, mumbling, 'Lester has skipped.'

He rose to his feet. 'Skipped town, do you mean? Run off with your money? And you probably have no paperwork to back up your claim on him.'

'I have a receipt.'

'Good grief, Fran, how could you imagine that a serious TV producer could make an entire series for ten thousand pounds? The man was a con artist. Did you ask the questions I told you to ask? Did you find out anything at all about other TV production companies and how they operate?'

'Digital television,' she muttered, keeping her head down.

'Digital television? That's his explanation? Lots more channels and—'

'And no plans to make more programmes. There will be a lot of repeats. But our stuff was to be cheap, and Lester reckoned he could sell the series all over the world.'

'These people always sound plausible. Fran, I beg of you, stay out of business. You don't understand it and you're bound to be taken for a ride. Stick to your garden designing. If you want, I'll handle your business affairs. Leave it to me. And if this scam has left you short, I'll give you—'

She jumped to her feet, relieved to have found an excuse for shouting. 'Don't be so patronizing. I'm a human being with feelings. I don't want—'

'I am well aware of your human qualities. But God only knows what you want. I just want to take care of you. It's clearly not safe to let you out on your own. What's going to happen to you? And why do you always push me away when we talk during the day, then in bed it's—'

The library door opened and Trevor came into the room. 'Mum, thank heavens I've caught up with you. Freddie gave me a lift. He's a brick. I used his mobile to ring here and Richard's secretary said you were here, so we drove straight over. We were just outside the Green Man anyway and . . .' He paused to gasp a breath. 'I'll have to take the van. My car's a write-off. I ran into a ditch trying to avoid a cyclist. It wasn't my fault, I swear it. The breakdown man said the car would cost more to fix than we paid for it. I'm sorry, but I couldn't hit the guy . . .' He looked from Fran's tear-ravaged face to Richard's grim one. 'I'm sorry. I guess I'm interrupting something.'

'I'm glad you've come,' said Richard. 'I presume you knew of your mother's investment in Manners Productions.'

'Yeah.'

'Then why didn't you talk her out of it?'

Trevor stuck his fists into his jeans. 'She's a grown woman. I told her it was a mistake and so did her accountant, but she wanted to do it. Why, what's happened?'

'Lester has skipped town, Trevor,' said Fran. 'I went to his house this morning and it's empty.'

Trevor looked horrified and seemed incapable of saying anything.

Richard approached him. 'Trevor, there is a spare BMW here. It belonged to my friend Jorge Arnez, but he's gone back to Florida. I'll get your name on the insurance as a designated driver and—'

Fran hastened to his side and put a restraining hand on his arm. 'Don't you dare, Richard! You think you can buy anything and anybody. Well, you can't.'

He blinked. 'When I bought Jenny a BMW she said thank you.'

'Jenny could afford to buy her own.'

'Yes,' said Richard, missing the point. 'But she still said thank you and she didn't accuse me of trying to buy favours. I don't understand you at all.'

Trevor gently moved his mother away from Richard. 'Thank you for the offer of the car. I would be very grateful. I'll do my best to take good care of it.'

Fran glared at him. 'You couldn't afford to keep it in petrol.'

'I won't,' said her son angrily, 'if I can't get to work.'

'You'd drive the BMW to a lawn-mowing job? Keep the mower in the boot, will you?'

Trevor ground his teeth. 'Then you drive it and I'll have the van. I think you've gone off your head. I really do. Nothing pleases you. You've lost all that money and now Linus will—'

'I wish I was dead!'

Richard, now looking very haggard, took her in his arms and held her despite her half-hearted attempts to escape. 'This is ridiculous. I could give you the money you've lost and never notice. All I want to do is make you happy, Fran, always assuming it's possible for you to be happy. I love you.' He looked at Trevor and smiled slightly. 'I even quite like your son. Let's get real here. We are three adults. We can surely work out something sensible.'

'I'm going home,' said Fran, wriggling free. 'Home to the little hovel that is all my own work. I know I'm stupid and ignorant and not safe to be let out—'

'I didn't really mean that—'

'And every other thing you can think of to say to me, but I must find myself . . . or something.' She ran clawed fingers through her hair. 'I know what I mean, but I can't put it into words. I'll have to talk to Linus, God help me. He'll go ballistic. Leave me alone, both of you.'

'Drive carefully,' said Richard. 'You're in a terrible state. Please concentrate.' He turned to Trevor. 'Come on. We'll get this car business sorted out.'

Linus was no more sympathetic than Richard and Trevor had been. At first he was horrified and worried about her loan. Then, when he was told that Richard had offered to pay her the two and a half thousand, he was puzzled that such a generous man had been snubbed.

'There are too many men in my life,' said Fran. 'None of you understand. Don't you see that I'm useless, and that Richard's generosity just makes it all worse? Whatever I do to make a go of things I just get deeper in debt through my own foolishness.'

'Where's your common sense, Fran? Stand back from all this and try to get a little perspective. You are not the first person to be taken for a ride by a con artist and you won't be the last. Others have lived through it.'

She finished the coffee he had prepared for her and helped herself to another cup. 'It would be all right if I loved him, but I don't.'

'Then why do you sleep with him?'

She gasped, outraged. 'That's none of your business.'

'No, it isn't, so don't give me the answer. Give yourself one. I know you well enough to believe that you wouldn't, couldn't have an affair with a man you didn't care for. But you're stuck, aren't you? You can't love Richard until you learn to love yourself.'

'If one more person bores me with psychobabble, I'll scream. I'm going home to think. I don't know what will happen now. Maybe I'll advertise more. On local TV, perhaps. That might help. If my clients don't cheat me out of what is rightly mine, I may succeed in making a living.'

She had been home only a few minutes when Trevor drove up in the gleaming black BMW. 'Well, Richard's managed to buy my son,' she muttered angrily, and went outside to watch him park it out of sight of the road.

'Don't want it stolen,' he said. 'That would be embarrassing.'

'Never mind. Richard would just buy you another one.' She cocked her head. 'Phone's ringing. I'll get it.'

She had not heard from Doreen for some weeks and didn't want to talk now, but she put on a cheerful voice. 'How are you, dear? Children all right? Well, a runny nose is pretty standard for young kids. I shouldn't worry.'

Fran waved Trevor to a seat at the kitchen table, but he brought a chair for her before sitting down.

'Money?' Fran said suddenly. 'I'm sorry, Doreen, but I no longer give out my money willy-nilly like I used to do. I'm getting some sense. Well, you should have thought of that earlier. I'm sorry, but you're going to have to find some other banker . . . I've had it . . . I am not crying. I never cry and have no intention of starting now. It's just that I work hard for what I've got and I'm not going to give it away.'

'Just going to have it taken away by a con artist,' muttered Trevor. She aimed a half-hearted kick at him but missed by three feet.

Eventually Doreen realized that the telephone call was costing her money, and that there would be nothing forthcoming from Fran. The two women said goodbye to each other and Fran hung up the phone, turning to glare at her son.

'Well done,' he said. 'You've learned to say no to family and friends. Soon you may be able to say no to slippery strangers.'

'I'm tired,' she said. 'I'm going to lie down.'

He frowned. 'You never lie down during the day.

Besides, it's half past five. What are we going to do for dinner?'

'Why don't you get into your brand-new motor and pick up a take-away from somewhere?'

'We could both get into my new motor and drive to Thai Light in Halstead.'

'No, I don't feel like going out.'

This worried him, but he didn't know what to say. He hurried out to his beloved BMW and drove off at speed to get something to eat. She was probably just hungry. He'd get some food inside her and she would return to being the mother he had always known and depended upon. Meanwhile, her strange mood frightened him. He was determined not to be gone long.

Richard couldn't remember what he had been doing when Fran arrived. He returned to his office and picked up each piece of paper on his desk, but the words refused to make sense. Aware that Liz was watching him as she shuffled her own papers, he bent his head and began making little stacks. Liz had been a very good secretary when she first joined him, but was now something of a liability. He knew his own work was suffering because of his worries about Fran, but he thought Liz's would-be romance with Seb was not sufficient reason for her to abandon her job. A plain woman, she had glowed with confidence when she joined him, and it had given her a certain attractiveness. Now she skulked around the office and was forever apologizing for some lapse or other. Why did she waste her time on someone who didn't want her? She had a husband, after all.

The phone on Liz's desk rang. 'It's Zoe,' she said. He picked up his extension.

'Hello, Zoe, how are you?' The paper uppermost on his desk caught his eye, one Liz had not drawn to his attention. It was a copy of a letter from Seb to Nigel Falkland, dated two days previously, stating his objections to the Leicester Square site. What the devil was the man doing writing to Nigel?

'Hi, Dad. Can you come to dinner tomorrow night? You can bring Fran if you like.'

'Oh, I don't think . . .' Was Seb trying to play some game here? He'd soon find out he couldn't go behind Richard's back.

'Oh, Dad, you never come over. You're always too busy to have any time for me. It's just like it always was.'

'Zoe, please. Look, I'll come. I don't think I'll ask Fran. She's rather tired just now. Some work she's been doing.'

'Well, don't put yourself out.'

He ground his teeth. 'Do you want me to come or not?'

'What I want is to be able to ring you up and have you say, just once, how much you'd like to come over to see me.'

'I do want to see you, but it hasn't been a very good day, Zoe. Now, shall I come tomorrow night or not?'

'Yes, please. We're going away for a month in ten days' time. I thought we might have a nice cosy chat. For once.'

'Away for a month? Did Cosmo lose his job? Oh, yeah. I keep forgetting about academic holidays. Are you going to the States?'

'No, travelling around Europe. Anyway, we'll

see you at half past seven tomorrow night.'

Richard put the phone back on the cradle and stood up. 'It's turning out to be a very bad day, Liz. I think I'll go up to my apartment and do a little thinking. Do you know where Seb has been all day?'

'In Manchester.'

'Yeah,' he said, grimly. 'Lucky for him.'

Upstairs, he turned his thoughts to his latest project. England being such a small place (or so he thought) it was necessary to squeeze as much housing into existing cities as possible. The idea, as with Docklands, was to demolish what was no longer needed in a particular part of London and to build again on the site. A brownfield site, it was called, to distinguish it from virgin soil in the countryside where nothing had been built before. A greenfield site, in other words.

There were difficulties connected with these brownfield sites. Buying up the land, for instance, chasing down the owners, getting them to sell. Planning permission for what one proposed was another problem. The neighbours sometimes objected vehemently. And London wasn't like New York where everything was constantly being renewed. Londoners grew attached to their old buildings and didn't want them torn down. As if all these problems were not enough, there was always the unknown – what pollutants were already in the soil. The subject was a new one for him, for in south Florida there was enough land to allow all buildings to be on greenfield sites, and for most of them to sprawl in single-storey units.

All things considered, it was more trouble and more expensive to build on brownfield sites. And this was just the reason why Richard was intrigued.

There were people within the Institute of Directors who were involved in planning this work. He had made some interesting contacts, thought there might be something in it for him. It was problem-solving of a sort that gave him welcome relief from the emotional problems of the women in his life. Thinking about brownfield sites was as close as he ever came to relaxing or enjoying a hobby.

The next morning Fran felt no better. She had no idea how she was going to make the next payment on the loan or what was going to happen between herself and Richard. That being so, she sought some activity to take her mind off her troubles and went out of doors to water her plants. It had not rained for eight days and no rain was forecast. East Anglia might be in for another period of drought, always bad news for nurseries. The least she could do was to keep her stock in prime condition and make plans for the coming year.

She had sharp hearing, and the phone's insistent ring had her running eagerly towards the house, although she could hardly expect good news.

'Hello,' she gasped, grabbing the handpiece on the fourteenth ring. 'Fran Craig, garden designer.'

'Miss Craig?'

'Yes.'

'The Miss Craig who is a gardening designer?'

'Yes.' The speaker had such a heavy accent that Fran suspected a hoax caller. 'Is that you, Trevor? Sean? If it is, I'm not amused.'

'Excuse me? This is a bad line, I think. I wish to speak to Miss Craig who is a gardening designer. Please put me through.'

'Speaking.' Perhaps he was genuine after all.

'I would like to come to Essex to visit you, Miss Craig, as I would like to commission you to build a garden for a gentleman in Milan.'

'Milan, Italy?' Some joker. 'Oh, I'm frightfully busy and could not possibly leave the country for less than ten thousand pounds.'

He didn't answer immediately. 'That is your fee?'

'Yeah.' Now she was not so sure. He might have a real Italian accent. A genuine caller?

'It is to design an English-style garden for a new house on the shores of Lake Como.'

'How big is this garden?' If it was a joke, the man was keeping it up for a long time.

'A hectare.'

'Right.' She had no idea how big a hectare was, except that it was larger than an acre. 'Is the ground flat?'

'But, no. You are not familiar with Lake Como?' Now he seemed to be having second thoughts. 'It is on a steep site and will need to be terraced. However, this gentleman, who is very wealthy, wants an English garden for his summer home, you understand?'

'I understand. I'd have to have my fare paid to Como and somewhere to live.'

There was a slight pause. She thought she might have gone too far. 'We could discuss these matters when I see you. I may come to your home?'

'Oh, no! That is, you are in London?'

'I am.'

'Then may I suggest you take a train from Liverpool Street station and get off at Braintree. Anyone will direct you to the public library. It's new and it's round. You can't miss it. I'll

389

meet you by the door. When will you come?'

'This afternoon at four o'clock. My name is Agnelli. Marcus Agnelli. I am the lawyer of Signor Andreas Manotti whom you know.'

'I do?'

'Yes, you met him at the home of Mr Dumas at a party for the Red Cross. Mr Dumas recommended you to Signora Manotti.'

'Oh, yes, of course.' She vaguely remembered a handsome Italian. His wife, in a very low-cut white beaded gown, was indelibly printed on her memory.

'And you will bring your certificate of qualification when we meet?'

Fran took a deep breath. 'You want to see proof that I have had training, is that it?'

'You will not be offended. You come highly recommended, but I must guard my client's interests, you understand.'

Hanging up the phone a few minutes later, Fran was convinced that once Mr Agnelli had seen her qualification, he would refuse to go ahead with the commission. However, at four o'clock that afternoon, seated by Historical Fiction in Braintree library, Fran received the second ten-thousand-pound commission of her career and a cheque for five thousand pounds. Mr Agnelli had looked her over and found her suitable. Also, he was very impressed that she had been recommended by Mr Richard Dumas of Gosfield Hall, yet another debt she owed to Richard.

'You could live in the guest wing,' said Agnelli. 'I will send you an airline ticket to Milan. Can you complete the work in three weeks?'

'So soon?'

'Signora Manotti is a lady of instant . . . er . . . ideas. She does not like to wait for things. And, I have to tell you, she might change her mind.'

'Oh, don't you worry. I can go as soon as you wish. The Manottis will pay for labour, plants, hard landscaping?'

'Money is not important to my client, Miss Craig. Quality is important. And, of course, you must be finished and away in three weeks.'

'OK, yes, all right.'

'You will deal with me at all times. I shall meet you at Milan airport. Is that understood? You will not let me down?'

'Of course not.'

He handed her a folder which he said contained a rough drawing of the site and some photos. She would have two days to prepare for her journey. He wished to see her on Monday next at Milan airport. They shook hands and Mr Agnelli departed.

Fran, saying that she wished to consult some books in the library, didn't leave with him. As soon as he was out of sight, she raced to the section containing Italian dictionaries, but they wouldn't let her borrow one.

First of all, she would telephone Linus. The five thousand pounds Agnelli had given her must be carefully guarded, must be put beyond her reach. And Trevor's, of course.

She had a strange feeling, a lightness that she had never experienced before. Improbable as it was, a rich Italian whose face she could not clearly recall actually wanted her to design an English garden for him. He believed she could do it, believed in her. The heady feeling was the sudden resurgence of her own confidence, the certainty that she would not disappoint him.

She found her passport, searched out the suitcase from the attic, began to plan what clothes she would take with her. All her jeans and tee shirts, of course. But there were the evenings and weekends. She would take a few of the beautiful dresses and trouser suits Richard had bought for her in Florida, the very ones she had thought she would never have occasion to wear.

It was a miracle, her going to the home of classical gardening to put her own English mark on the landscape.

The finest Italian gardens were built between the fifteenth and the seventeenth centuries, and were the direct descendants of ancient Roman gardens. In an Italian garden the vegetation always complemented but never dominated magnificent staircases leading upwards, perhaps to an exedra, a semi-circular expanse of turf with a hedge forming a curved boundary, where statues of divinities were placed. There were arcades and pergolas and artificial grottos. There were also fountains and terraces and arcades. What was, these days, referred to as hard landscaping was the foundation of the Italian garden. The planting scheme was chosen so as to heighten the drama but never to dominate the architecture.

The great age of French gardening followed the Italian period. The French built larger gardens and extended the vistas. They also built on the flat, which gave their gardens a totally different feel from Italian ones.

It was in a reaction to the strict formality of the French garden that the English garden came into being. In the English scheme, the vegetation must appear to be natural. The visitor must be able to fool himself into thinking that the garden had just happened. Thoughts of earth-movers, groves of carefully arranged trees and dozens of gardeners tending swathes of plants from all over the world had to be banished from the mind. Capability Brown's greatest triumphs looked like nature perfected, though he might have moved a village and dug a huge lake to create his effects.

Studying the photos, Fran knew she couldn't take up much space with England's great invention, the rolling green lawn. Also, as the plot (all of two and a half acres) rose steeply, she would have to do some terracing.

Nevertheless, she would give them the romantic garden they craved. She would give them sprawling old-fashioned roses and yellow Alchemilla mollis encroaching on the paths, garish herbaceous borders and luscious unclipped shrubs dripping with blossom. There would be laburnums and wisteria, nodding peonies and armies of lupins. Mr Manotti would gasp with delight.

Linus arrived the next day to see the messenger appear with Fran's plane ticket. Trevor came soon after, and they all went out for a celebratory lunch at the Red Onion. Fran drank so much she wondered if she would be able to think clearly during the afternoon, for it was essential that she give some thought to her design. She needed to pack her drawing paper, tape-measure, coloured pencils and half a dozen reference books.

'It's such a big garden!' she cried, 'but I can fill it ten times over with my ideas and plants. You know, Richard wouldn't understand what we're celebrating. He deals in high finance and he always knows everything, so he wouldn't see all this as a miracle. He's perfect.'

'Is that what you think?' asked Linus. 'That he has no feelings because he's perfect? The man I met seemed to be a very real person with real feelings. I also think he deserves someone who understands him better, somebody who appreciates his good qualities, who's there for him when he needs her.'

Fran was startled, but didn't let Linus rile her. 'He doesn't need me. He really doesn't know what it is to fail. I understand him well enough.' She sighed. 'I made a dead set at him for his money, which was a terrible thing to do. The sort of cheating thing—' She glanced at Trevor, and didn't finish the thought – that it was the sort of thing Sean would do. But Sean, she had to admit, had not looked for a rich woman to marry. He had, for once, been more honest than Fran. 'I no longer need the money. I'm all square. I've accounted for Richard's ten thousand and I'm on my way to a successful career. I've put all the bad times behind me. He doesn't need me and I don't need him.'

Her companions were silent, and she was aware that they did not approve of her callous attitude, but there was steel in her heart now. She was Fran Craig, garden designer, on top of the world.

The next day she drove over to Gosfield Hall in the BMW, because Trevor wanted the van. She felt a bit uncomfortable in it, not only because Trevor had told her she wasn't insured to drive it, but because the huge, silent car was another reminder of Richard's wealth and power. She had never driven a car so large, nor an automatic with power steering. The journey was hair-raising, but she made it safely.

'I'm losing you,' Richard said, when she told him she was going to Italy for three weeks.

'I just want these days to myself, to sort out my own thoughts. I don't want you to fly over for the weekends. Three weeks won't hurt us, Richard. Do try to understand. You've never appreciated my work.'

'That's not true!'

'Yes, it is. You never go out to look at your court-yard. You don't love it.'

'I have no time!'

'Goodbye, Richard. We'll talk when I get back.' She kissed his cheek, but he wouldn't let her go until he had pressed his lips to hers, reminding her in the best way he knew that she felt for him an almost overpowering desire. The kiss was long, but Fran eventually broke away, breathing heavily, her eyes filled with tears. 'I'll come home safe and sound. The real Fran, the real me without any—'

'Hang-ups? That'll be the day. Just remember while you are away that I love you, whoever you are.'

She left the library laughing, as he had intended, but she had been shaken by the look of pain in his eyes. There was no time to think about other people's suffering at the moment, however. She was too full of her own recent suffering and present triumph. It had been a long time coming and victory was sweet.

The following morning was frantic. Despite her best intentions, she was running late. The postman arrived as she was about to close the cottage door behind her. She shuffled through the envelopes and left behind every one she thought contained a bill. The rest she stuffed into her handbag to read on the plane. Trevor drove her to Stansted airport, and she was the last to board. There, cramped into a seat by the window, she fastened her seat-belt and held her large handbag on her lap. The seats were so narrow it was only with elbows tucked well into her sides that she managed to open the bag and extract her mail.

The first letter was bulky. Legal documents spilled out when she slit open the envelope, but she set them aside in order to read the letter which was from Lester Manners. He said he had sold his house to fund the production of the series, that he would make sure Fran was paid for performing, that he hoped she would understand why he could give her nothing immediately, but promised to see that she was well rewarded eventually for her faith in his project. Several TV channels were showing interest in the series, he said. Manners Productions would go on to bigger and better things, but he would never forget her initial belief in him, in spite of everything. And please would she sign the enclosed papers, keep one copy for herself and return the other set to him?

The plane raced down the runway, loud, bumpy and frightening. The front wheels left the tarmac and the huge weight fought gravity for supremacy. It was frightening, thrilling and dangerous, and when it reached cruising height Fran felt she had just relived all the sensations that Lester's letter had evoked.

Investing in business was frightening, dangerous and terribly thrilling. She was part of a real business venture and she could see how this might be addictive. She had taken a chance, backed her own judgement with borrowed money, and had been right to do so, even though she might never see her two and a half thousand again. She wasn't a helpless fool after all. If only Richard could be beside her at this glorious moment!

When she laughed out loud, her neighbour jumped and gave her a worried look. She promised not to startle him again. 'Good news,' she explained. 'Doesn't come my way too often.'

With the exception of Harriet and Geoff Stone, Gosfield Hall was empty by half past five. Seb always took work home, but he never stayed a moment later than five thirty these days. Helena was probably making a few demands on him.

The builders, having arrived early, left at half past four, so that gradually the house was returned to Richard. The old brick walls, warmed all day by the sun, gave off their heat at this time of the afternoon. The courtyard could be exceptionally warm. Almost warm enough to take the chill from Richard's bones.

He followed the sun, sat down on the mellow teak of the old wooden bench in the south-west corner and looked around him. Everywhere there were memories of Fran. She had wanted him to sit in this courtyard, to appreciate her work. Yet his memories of it being built were of a woman pushed to her limits, worried, tired and irritable.

He was hardly the picture of contentment at the moment. That morning he had received two letters, one from each of the sisters. Karen's had been blunt to the point of rudeness. She had not wanted him to rush 'willy-nilly' into opening a huge 'white elephant' off Leicester Square. He should proceed with some caution. This was Britain, after all. What did he know of the ways of this country?

The second letter, from Helena, said much the same thing, but in Helena's customary pathetic way. Nevertheless he detected Seb's hand and he was furious. Firing off two almost identical letters, he told the women in plain English that he was running the Miami Spice chain, and that although he hated the name which had been thrust upon him, he was running it to great effect. The chain was thriving. The chain would make them all quite rich in a short space of time. Why must they listen to Seb's moans, when all Seb had to do was to speak directly to Richard?

Satisfied with these efforts, he had ordered Liz to type them up immediately and post them during her lunch-hour.

As five o'clock approached, however, he began to regret his haste. They weren't hardened businessmen whom he might shout at with a clear conscience. He therefore asked Liz if she had posted the letters. She had.

'Well, ring up that florist in Halstead and send them each a bunch of flowers. About twenty pounds each. Say something like . . . er, No Hard Feelings. That'll do the trick.'

She gave him a stony look, pursing her lips in disapproval, but she made the call.

'They will arrive sometime tomorrow,' she said as she hung up. 'I always think it's better not to say rude things in the first place. Then you don't have to apologize.'

That led him to remember when he had gone to

dinner with Zoe and Cosmo a few days earlier. His beautiful daughter had been extremely irritable. She had, as usual, been on at him about working all the time. He had countered that she led a totally idle and useless life. Cosmo had intervened to say that Zoe was very active with several charities. Zoe had then said that at least Cosmo kept his work in perspective, which had led her loving husband to remind her that he took his work extremely seriously. It had been farcical from start to finish, as family quarrels often were. But no-one had been laughing that night.

Richard watched the water splashing into the basin for several minutes. Fran's accusation that he didn't love her Paradise garden was not entirely true. He had to admit that he had no great feeling for plants, for flowers. Tulips, once he saw them *en masse*, left him cold. But the shape of this courtyard, the combination of water, trees, bright flowers and plants climbing the walls was extremely pleasing. He could respond to the design if not to any individual plant, and his response was to feel at peace. His eyes closed and he nodded off, to be awakened with a jerk when his head fell sideways. Time to think about dinner. And suddenly he stood up. Trevor! He would ring the boy and ask him out to dinner.

'I'll call for you, Trev,' he said when the young man had agreed to be his guest for the evening. 'It's about time I saw where you two live. And, by the way. Put some clothes on. I'm taking you to Le Talbooth.'

With the aid of a map, and confident that he would eventually come to the end of the winding narrow lane, Richard finally arrived at the Craig home. Fran's cottage took him by surprise. He had not realized how poor she was. In fact he had forgotten that anyone in the late twentieth century could live so basically, so close to mere subsistence. It was a humbling sight.

He glanced into the kitchen, aware that Trevor was watching him closely. 'Your father was going to install a new kitchen, wasn't he?'

'My dad is not very dependable. Great fun. Really. But Mum couldn't always see the funny side. And over the business about the kitchen she just blew her top. Women are funny about kitchens.'

'Yes, they are. Come on, my friend, let's eat.'

Trevor had put on a jacket and tie, combed his hair and shaved off the beard he had been growing along the edge of his jaw. He looked handsome and uncomplicated. Richard put an arm around the boy's shoulders. 'I'm sure glad you could come out tonight. I was beginning to talk to myself in that great house.'

'Must be spooky at night.'

'It's weird, I'll say that. It's like living in a huge condo when yours is the only one occupied. And no ocean. I grew up within ten minutes' walk of the sea. Saw it every day. But I'm no fan of your seaside resorts. I prefer being inland here.'

'Will you go back?' asked Trevor as they sped along in the Mercedes.

'I'm going to buy someplace in Palm Beach to spend a few winter months. But I couldn't go back to living in Florida.' He glanced at his young companion. 'I've got too much emotion invested over here.'

After that they talked on general subjects and were well into their main course and the red wine

400

before Richard said, 'So what are you going to do with your life? Training? More education? Into business with your mother? I sound like Cosmo, don't I?'

'No, I don't feel that you're pressurizing me. Cosmo can be pompous, you know.'

'I had noticed,' said Richard. 'I only ask because I'm interested. I'm not your dad. You'll have to decide for yourself what you're going to do. But if you need funds—'

'You're very generous, Richard.' Trevor looked away, overcome. He knew his mother had hurt this man badly, yet Richard's generosity was undented. 'You'd pay my way through a training course even if Mum dumped you, wouldn't you?'

'God forbid, but yes. I like you, as I've said before. Besides, it's nice to be able to talk to someone of Zoe's generation and not get my head bitten off.'

'She says you never had time for her. I told her she's lucky to have you.'

'I guess I was always chasing the almighty dollar. I've tried to tell her that it's different now, but she says it's too late.'

'She's spoiled rotten. Thinks the world revolves around her.'

'Did you tell her that, too?'

'You bet. Besides, Cosmo keeps telling her that she's too hard on you.' Trevor accepted the dessert menu from the waiter but the words failed to make sense because his head was filled with so many conflicting, painful thoughts that he couldn't concentrate on which of the complicated dishes might appeal to him. Rather than raise the subject of his mother, he asked what he thought would be a neutral question, though still interesting. 'Would you mind if you lost it all?'

Richard laughed. 'Hell yes! There's two things here. Let me try to explain. My dad went off when I was a kid and we never saw him again. Mom was a waitress, and women in her position were not always treated properly. Sometimes the boss cheated her and sometimes customers treated her like dirt. And I couldn't do a thing about it. We were poorer than most of the kids I knew, and I didn't do well in school, I have to tell you. They used to call me Dickie Dumb-ass. I was at the bottom of the heap socially and not too much higher academically.

'Nowadays no-one calls me Dickie Dumb-ass. Well, somebody tried it recently, but he regretted it. I've got money and that buys me a certain position. I like that. It's better than being poor and at the bottom, looked down on by everybody. God, sometimes I have a nightmare that I've lost it all and I'm back to being that kid. I wake up in a sweat. Yes, I'd mind if I was suddenly poor.'

'I can see why, but must you work so hard now? You've made it.'

'I said there were two things. The other is business itself. It gets you like an addiction. Look, everybody in this country seems to be obsessed with soccer. It's like that. In a soccer game, you put twenty-two men in a field, half of them going one way and half the other. Twenty-two men, and any one of them can do something brilliant and any one of them can do something stupid. The coach can scheme all he wants to. The press can write all they want to. Fans can discuss the games, the teams, the managers till they're blue in the face. But one man, when you least expect it, can destroy everything. Or make it. The match always throws up surprises. The outcome can be a total upset. People can argue the rights and wrongs afterwards for hours.

'But that's nothing, compared to business. There, you might have a few thousand members on your team, and you can't be sure how loyal, clever, stupid or hard-working any of them are. You can send them here or there, wonder if you've done the right thing. You can scheme and make your plans, and still someone will come forward and put the ball between the goalkeeper's legs, so to speak. It's the most exciting thing in the world, endlessly interesting. New projects. New products. New challenges.

'I never got to do higher mathematics in school, but you can't catch me out on money. I'm good and I know it. Figures sing to me. I can take a few sheets of paper, glance down them and tell you pretty well how good the management of the company is, where it's headed and how well it will succeed. I can also smell it when the figures have been massaged. I'm Pelé. I've never made an own goal. I'm the man they all have to beat and I love it.'

'You make it sound really interesting.'

'Better than keeping goldfish. So, what are you going to do with your life?'

Trevor grinned. 'I'd like to go to Mum's old school, Capel Manor, and take an NVQ in garden design. Run my own business one day.'

'Capel Manor is near to your dad, isn't it? Why not go to the horticultural college close to Chelmsford?'

'It's not about being close to Dad. He's married

to this young woman and . . . It's to do with getting away from home. I think it's about time, don't you?'

Richard agreed that it was, and they discussed Trevor's future for the next quarter of an hour while Richard drank his brandy. At half past eleven he excused himself and went off to the men's room.

They had moved into the lounge for coffee, and Trevor now looked around at the fashionable crowd occupying the other easy chairs, and sighed with contentment. This was the life. Lounging back on the settee, he thought he could get used to having money very easily. But he'd work for it. Oh, yes. Nothing handed to him on a plate. Richard would be proud of him.

Then sadness settled on him as it did so often, just when he thought he was having a really good time. His dream of getting his parents back together again had been shattered several weeks ago. He had gone past that point. He saw his father knuckling under to a woman only four years older than Trevor, saw him happily curtail his drinking, saw him going to work every day. Sean did this for a bleached blonde nag, although he had never been willing to do it for Fran. His mother had never nagged. Perhaps she should have. They should both have tried harder.

He also saw his mother in an emotional turmoil, leading a perfectly decent man a terrible song and dance. Why couldn't she sort out herself and her feelings? Sometimes he felt as if he were the adult and his parents were the adolescents, going through the courting business when it should have been his turn. Sometimes he felt very old.

Richard came back to the table. 'I've paid the

bill. Come on. I'd better get you home, kid. I don't want to rob you of your sleep.'

Trevor leapt to his feet, happy to follow, basking in the great man's good humour. His mother was so wrong about Richard Dumas. He was a pussy-cat who surely couldn't get mad at anybody if he wanted to.

Richard occupied himself as best he could over the next few days, and would have surprised Trevor with a spurt of anger two days after their dinner. Nigel Falkland telephoned to say that Richard must not under any circumstances sign the lease for the property off Leicester Square until Nigel had had the opportunity to assess the site.

Richard lost his cool and told Nigel in plain English that he was running the Miami Spice chain and that no amount of whining from Sebastian Race and the sisters was going to change the way he operated.

Nigel replied very stiffly that he was never at any time influenced by the thoughts of the Race family, singly or collectively. Before Richard could reply, he hung up.

Richard sat fuming with the dead phone in his hands for several seconds. There had been no opportunity to tell Falkland that his warning came too late. Richard had already signed the lease. He had also drawn up plans for the interior. Furthermore, he had been nursing along a possible buyer for the chain.

He had no heart for the catering business, already bored by the ease with which he had got it up and running. However, his home continued to enthral him. He invited two representatives of a housing association and Frank Toombs to join him for dinner at the George in Colchester. He told them about the dry rot he had treated at great expense, about how every drainpipe was in good condition, every piece of lead, every slate in place. The discussions were going extremely well, and they were about to retire to the lounge for coffee when Seb walked in with Helena and Karen.

Richard directed his guests to go into the front of the hotel and find comfortable seats, then walked over to the table Seb and the Race sisters had just occupied.

They did not seem pleased to see him. Karen was wearing one of her severe suits, this one a deep green. Helena, however, had abandoned suits for a pretty little patterned dress with tiny sleeves. It was sheer and clung to her in a most attractive way. Seb's influence, he thought. Helena was a woman waiting to be handed her opinions and style of life by someone with more confidence than she could muster.

'Not eating at the Miami?' he asked through gritted teeth.

'You'll be happy to know it's full,' said Seb. 'Not that we intended to eat there, but I did check. When you leave the George, I think you'll be aware of the music from our little establishment, if the police haven't made them turn it down.'

'Look, Seb. Let's stop playing games, OK? I think it was really shitty of you to write to Nigel Falkland about the Leicester Square site. And to get the girls to write to me. If you've got something to say, say it to me.'

'I think you'll find that Seb can write to whomever he pleases,' said Karen sharply. 'And I

406

happen to know that dear Nigel is very happy to hear from him.' Both Seb and Richard glared at her with disbelief, until she lost her bravado and looked down at her menu. Helena's cheeks were flaming as she busied herself with the destruction of her paper napkin.

'All right,' said Seb. 'I'll say it to you right here and now. I think you're trying to drag us into too much debt. I believe I had a perfect right to say it to Nigel, to warn him. You can write anything you like to him, putting your point of view. I wouldn't seek to stop you. But remember this. We don't want your dangerous, gambling ways. This is Britain. We proceed with a little more caution here.'

'That's your opinion and I respect it. You'll never make a great businessman, Seb. You think small.' Richard turned on his heel and went to join his guests, but it took him several minutes to put the confrontation behind him. Damn the Races!

Then, smiling, he turned his attention to the conversation of his guests which was about Gosfield Hall and its many rooms.

Sometimes when she first got up in the morning, Fran felt too tired to face the day. She was always up by six and rarely went to bed before midnight. The excitement of the challenge always carried her through, however. This was her great adventure.

Time had dragged on the plane, giving her ample opportunity to get cold feet. Therefore her first words to the lawyer were, 'Mr Agnelli, what is the Italian for JCB? How am I going to get workmen? Who's going to get across to them what I want?'

'I confess I do not know what is a JCB, but I have employed a foreman for you. He speaks English and he will put into operation the plans which you will draw up.'

She had made a dozen quick sketches with ideas for parts of the garden, but she learned, to her profound disappointment, that the Manottis were not given to looking at plans. They wished to be surprised. And pleased, of course.

When they reached the Manotti house, she realized that Agnelli's air of wealth and position was as nothing to that of his client. And Signor Manotti had a wife whose glamorous exterior was matched by a diamond-hard personality. On the first day, both were in the house awaiting the launch which brought Agnelli and Fran from the Como side of the lake. Signora Manotti lounged on the white banquette in her new summer home wearing fuchsia silk trousers, a wide acid-green belt and a yellow silk camisole top, looking so gorgeous that Fran could scarcely concentrate. The woman, who was about Fran's age, frequently ran long, painted nails through her thick shoulder-length black hair. And with each movement of the bejewelled arm, Fran gaped, mesmerized.

They were seriously rich, and it was their intention to amuse themselves with an instant English garden. Speaking in English in the same effortless way that they did everything, they said they had no clear picture of what comprised an English garden, but they knew that roses must come into it somewhere. Fran, they said, must surprise and delight them.

At the moment, most of the property was scarred with raw earth which had been left by the bulldozers. Nevertheless, in three weeks, they wished to be able to walk the paths of their new garden. They were sure Fran would manage this in good time. Mr Dumas had been most impressed by her work.

The house itself was single-storey, situated about fifty feet up from the shores of the lake where an ancient stone wall and landing-stage indicated that some previous dwelling had been torn down to make way for the new structure. The house was in two parts, the smaller one connected by a covered way to the main building. Fran had been assigned a stunning room with a terracotta floor and *en suite* bathroom in the part of the house reserved for guests. The Tuscan red outside walls and red-tiled roof sat easily in the landscape, and there were numerous pine trees which Fran was determined to incorporate into her plan. Close to the shore there were also pencil-slim conifers that soared well above the house. Fran had never seen anything like them. They didn't form an avenue. They were too tall to have been clipped into their exotic shape, so she decided that they were simply natural phenomena, to be treasured. Later she was to discover that they were called Mediterranean cypresses, *Cupressus sempervirens*.

When her interview with the Manottis was over, and she had been given her vague instructions, the golden couple returned to their motor boat and sped across the lake to the small town of Como. Since they took Signor Agnelli with them, Fran was left alone with the staff to think about what she had so blithely undertaken.

She made many sketches, walked the grounds, took endless measurements, and the next day began a serious sightseeing expedition. She needed to discover what Italian gardens were like, in order to give the Manottis something totally different.

On Lakes Como and Maggiore she found gardens of staggering beauty which married regular arrangements of old statues and terracotta pots with a determined mastery of all greenery. Everything that could be clipped or trained was made subservient to the overall design. She saw ivy trained over many years into festoons along a low stone wall, small-leaved *Ficus pumila* grown neatly up an avenue of trees so that it formed a solid shield of green to a height of six feet. She was astounded to see aspidistras in a mass planting as shade-loving ground cover. Paths zigzagged up the lower slopes from the water's edge. Palm trees, banana and canna lilies gave splashes of colour, as did formal beds of geraniums, impatiens and marigolds. The effect was, not surprisingly, typically Mediterranean. There were no shrub roses. It followed that Fran must give the Manottis a rose garden and hidden surprises, a playful garden.

Soon she was on excellent terms with the foreman, Joseph, who made all things possible. He was no more than thirty years old, handsome, brawny and efficient. He had a great sense of humour, and he could probably have built the garden without Fran's involvement.

She also liked the bulldozer operator and was eager to take his advice about what was possible. An army of workers with a millennium of experience behind them were able to see what she hoped to achieve almost before the words left her mouth. Water cascading down a set of steps? They knew all about such things. Many gardens in Rome featured water in a way that the English had not dreamed of. They could do it. An iron willow tree that spurted water at unwary visitors? Now that was original! Fran didn't tell them that such a feature had been at Chatsworth for hundreds of years. She preferred to let them think she was capable of something new and different. They assured her they could construct something just as playful.

Within days, working plans for a pergola had been drawn up and the men were busy constructing it. The winding paths that led to the top of the property were cut the very first day. Paving-setts were being laid. Piping and electrics for the cascade and the surprise fountain were under way.

She ordered four hundred roses, modern shrubs as well as the large-flowered and patio ones, in every colour that roses could manage. Since they had to be container-grown at this time of the year, the air freight was enormous. Signor Agnelli encouraged her to let her imagination run riot, and to spend whatever was necessary. She could demand whatever she wished. Money and the talent of the Italian workforce flowed like honey, so she ordered a very English brick and stone gothic folly, showing the men a picture from one of her books – and it was done.

Each night she fell into bed, exhausted and exhilarated by her power. She could do anything!

In Florida, Richard had given little thought to the rain. It came in sheets, flooded every hollow, stood on the lawns, then drained into the sand minutes later when the clouds moved away. The rain brought no relief from the heat, so that water on one's clothes and skin evaporated within minutes.

Getting caught in the Florida rain could be quite amusing.

Not so in England. With the clouds came, as often as not, a chill wind. The sky blackened. Gloom settled. Short, fierce showers were rarer than in Florida. Often the rain, slight but spoiling, came to stay for the day, or the week. Such a depression was upon the country at the moment. After breakfast Richard put on his favourite yellow sweater and his most comfortable moccasins and went downstairs towards his office.

Walking silently along the corridor, he saw a most ludicrous sight – Liz, hiding herself from view in order to spy on Seb. She was outside Seb's office, the door of which, he assumed, was open. Richard's view of her was of little more than a huge projecting bosom and one large flat-shoed foot. The rest was hidden.

Irritated for reasons he couldn't explain, he approached her and took her by the arm. She flinched at his touch and gasped in surprise, but allowed him to lead her silently back to the office they shared.

Before they could reach that sanctuary, Seb suddenly left his own office and walked briskly to the company notice-board to pin up a piece of paper. He didn't seem to see them, so intent was he on his mundane task.

'For God's sake, Liz,' Richard said when the door had been shut. 'Don't let yourself down this way. He's living with Helena Race and—'

'But she's his cousin!' Her face crumpled. Tears started to her eyes and her skin flushed in ugly patches. Richard looked away, ashamed of what

412

he had done to her, but determined to make his point.

'Distant cousin. It's all perfectly legal. It's also, I suspect, permanent. Seb told me the other day that they hope to buy a country hotel with their share of the Miami Spice sale. Don't let him see you pine for him. Have some pride and get this son of a bitch out of your system. He's not worth it, I assure you.'

'You must think me—'

'I don't think anything. I just don't want to see you hurt any more. Now then, let's put the whole thing out of our minds.'

As if that were possible! He wished he had not seen her lurking, wished he had not approached her. He wished, in fact, that he had not got up that morning. If only the day could start again! Too late for that, however. He must make the best of a wretched piece of work. He would take her out to lunch, make it up to her for the humiliation he had caused.

Events moved another way, however. He received a call from a fellow member of the East Anglian Institute of Directors and was soon excitedly agreeing to meet for lunch. Liz was left to flounder in her misery.

Liz's embarrassment soon turned to resentment. When Richard told her that he was going out to lunch with a friend and would not return that day, she nodded mutely, but grumbled under her breath when he was gone. He hadn't told her how to reach him in an emergency, hadn't given her even a hint of whom he was meeting. He didn't trust her, that was the truth of it.

When, some half an hour later, Sebastian Race entered the office, she was able to put aside her painful discovery of the truth about his affair with Helena Race, while nurturing a resentment about Richard's discovery of herself eavesdropping.

'Richard has told me that you and Helena Race are living together.'

'Yes, we are. I hope you'll understand that there was no future for us, my dear.'

She assumed as dignified an air as possible, seated behind her desk. 'And you hope to buy a country hotel.'

'We would like to. After Miami Spice is sold, of course. We won't have the capital until then.'

'I wish you well, of course.'

He smiled with relief. 'Does Richard give you a hard time?'

'He's so secretive.'

Seb raised his eyebrows, but said nothing.

'He's gone off today and I've no idea who with or for how long. I can't reach him if he's needed.'

'Typical. He hasn't got his mind on the Miami Spice chain, that's for sure.'

'You're so right,' muttered Liz. 'He seldom dictates anything to me about the chain, although there's an endless stream of letters on other subjects.'

Seb was curious, but events were moving too fast. He must do what he came to do and be off. There was so much to plan and so many secrets to be kept, at least for the moment. Therefore, without commenting on what she had told him, he withdrew a sealed letter from his inside jacket pocket and handed it to Liz.

'Give this to Richard when he comes back.'

Liz took the letter and pushed it into her central desk drawer. 'I'll probably be gone before he returns.'

Seb smiled. 'Then leave it on his desk.'

She agreed to do so. However, at five o'clock, when she had still not had word from Richard, she packed up her papers. Having spent the entire day nursing her various grievances, she forgot about the letter. As usual, she locked her desk and was driving off in her car as the Gosfield Hall clock struck a quarter past.

Chapter Fourteen

It was half past nine in the evening when the phone rang. Trevor flicked the mute button of the TV and reached for the receiver. He had been hoping to hear from his mother, but it was Sean Craig on the other end of the line.

'Word comes to me that your mother is in Italy!'

'Yeah,' said Trevor. 'Big commission. She got ten thousand pounds just for the design and supervising the work.'

'Well, well, no wonder you don't want to come home to see your old dad. Living the good life, are you?'

'It isn't that. You haven't invited me. I don't know how your bride might feel.'

'Stop being cheeky. Get your tail over here for the weekend. You could at least do that. Some of your old mates have been asking after you. And it might occur to you to see your Gran now and then.'

It was Thursday evening and Trevor had made great plans for the weekend. However, he realized he did want to see his father very much. He said he would leave home first thing in the morning. He didn't mention that he would be driving a BMW, as he was planning to spring that little surprise later.

He rang off and set about cancelling his other plans.

The following morning at half past six he watered all the plants, checked that everything was in order and drove off at eight thirty, not planning to be back in Essex until Monday afternoon.

Richard's head was full of schemes about brownfield sites. He had spent a wonderful day with half a dozen developers and builders in East Anglia. The problem of where to build had kept them all talking for hours. With England no larger than Florida, but with thirty-five million people within its borders, finding suitable sites to build on was difficult. However, one of the men had found two such places for consideration, and they all planned to form a consortium to exploit them.

He kept this side of his life a secret from Liz, since he knew she would tell Seb all about it. So it was not until ten o'clock that he came downstairs to his office. He scarcely had time to say hello to Liz before Seb burst in.

'Come on. In my office. Nigel's here.' Seb hurried out again without explanation.

'Oh, God!' sighed Richard. 'He's on about that Leicester Square site. Dragging Nigel into it. Well, it's too late. I've signed the lease.'

'I wouldn't know,' said Liz primly. 'By the way, there's a letter for you.' She handed him the envelope and, being just in his shirtsleeves, he folded it and stuffed it into his back trouser pocket.

They were all present when he entered Seb's office. Seb was wearing his favourite tweed jacket and fawn trousers. Karen had put on her most severe black suit. Even Helena looked serious in a black linen dress with a multi-stranded pearl necklace. As for Nigel, his pinstripe made no concession to country living.

Overnight, the rain had disappeared. East Anglia was once again basking in brilliant sunlight and high temperatures. Nigel's forehead was greased with a film of sweat and he looked strangely excited.

Feeling at a definite disadvantage, Richard patted his shirt pocket. 'No pens. Back in a minute.' He started to leave, planning to get his jacket, but Nigel stopped him.

'I have a number of pens, Richard,' he said. 'Let's get going.'

Sensing something very serious in the wind, Richard took his seat.

Nigel cleared his throat. 'As you know, we have gathered to discuss your performance as managing director—'

'*As I know?*'

'In the letter,' said Seb. 'Don't pretend you haven't received it.'

'The letter, yes, but I haven't had time to read it.'

'That,' said Nigel with a spurt of anger, 'is the sort of thing that has irritated me for weeks. You can't be bothered to do the work required of you. We will pause while you read the letter.'

'And I put a notice on the notice-board yesterday,' said Seb. 'That's all the law requires. You should have checked the notice-board, but oh, no, you were out and your secretary didn't even know where you were.'

Richard withdrew the letter from his back pocket and tore it open. Nigel, he saw, had called an Extraordinary General Meeting. On the agenda was a single item:

To express the displeasure of this Board at the conduct

of the Managing Director in ignoring the wishes of the Shareholders in the Leicester Square deal, and also to issue a formal warning that the wishes of this Board must not be ignored in future.

'Are you trying to tell me that I can't even open a prime site without Karen and Seb giving their permission?' asked Richard when he had read the agenda.

'You left out me,' said Nigel, rearranging his pens.

'But you, of all people, know what a great deal it is! You must have checked it out by now. Nigel, think! Twenty sites. The London one our flagship. I've got a buyer lined up. A trade sale. No need to wait and float on the Stock Exchange. That's dicey. This is money in the bank. Give me six months and I'll make you a million or two. Everybody will make money.'

'I have inspected the site,' murmured Nigel. 'You had already signed the lease without first consulting me. If you act in this high-handed manner again, you will be dismissed by the shareholders. We can vote you off by a simple majority.'

Now Richard smiled. 'I have fifty-two per cent of the shares and . . .' But as he spoke, he remembered that he no longer had a controlling interest. He had given up some shares to Nigel, leaving him with just forty-nine per cent.

'There you are!' crowed Nigel. 'You haven't got your mind on the business. You don't even remember how many shares you have. Forty-nine per cent, Richard. You are the managing director of Miami Spice cafés, but you can't damned well—that is, you can't be bothered to attend to the business. Meanwhile, you busy yourself in other areas.'

419

'Wait a minute. I'm not some schoolboy to be ticked off by the teacher. We spoke on the phone. I had your verbal approval. Hey, what's going on here? Am I being set up?'

Nigel Falkland met his eyes calmly and stared back, a slight smile playing on his lips. 'A man who goes off with his mistress when he should be at a board meeting cannot be said to have the best interests of the company at heart. I have a very large sum of money invested in the Miami Spice chain which gives me a perfect right to question the competence and dedication of the managing director. Don't you agree?'

Richard, now realizing that he had a fight on his hands, deliberately slowed his breathing, taking his time before answering in a soft voice. 'Indeed you have, Nigel. I can't conceive why it was necessary to call an extraordinary general meeting just to ask me how the company is progressing. Do you want to see the figures, the accounts? I can have them before you within five minutes. The company is very healthy. The Leicester Square site will greatly improve our profitability and make us an even better candidate for a trade sale, as I'm sure you know. Seb can't see it, but that's beside the point.' He turned to Helena. 'Helena, my dear. I understand you want to buy a country hotel. But time is passing, isn't it? Wouldn't you rather have the money for your hotel in six months' time than wait for years?'

'Don't try to bully her!' cried Karen. 'I notice you didn't try to appeal to me. I'm too clever for you. I see right through you.'

'Let's get to the point,' said Seb. 'I propose that Richard Dumas, the managing director, be severely reprimanded for his failure to carry out his duties properly.'

'I second the motion,' said Karen.

'One moment,' said Nigel. 'We are voting to express the displeasure of this Board at the conduct of the managing director in ignoring the wishes of the shareholders in the Leicester Square deal, and also to issue a formal warning that the wishes of this Board must not be ignored in future. You have a right to appeal, Richard. Is there anything you wish to say?'

'Yeah. Why don't you just fire me?'

'Ah,' said Nigel softly. 'We wish we could, but by legislation we can't fire you without due warning. And you can appeal.'

'Don't bother. I'm not going to be reprimanded by a bunch of clowns. I resign.'

Nigel Falkland was in a state of high excitement, loving the moment, curious to see how Richard would respond to his imminent execution. What was he supposed to do, play Sidney Carton? *It is a far, far better thing that I do . . .*

'You don't have a contract,' said Nigel softly. 'Which was rather careless of you. In fact, you seem to have been rather careless in setting up this company. A sign of gross incompetence, I would have said.'

A tremor went through Richard. Now he knew what it was all about. He spent a moment of mental thrashing about as he fought the hook imbedded in his flesh, but he knew he was caught, a gasping fish tossed on the shore, awaiting the gaff.

He was aware of an expectant hush as his enemies relished his pain. He knew that the humiliation of his ignominious departure was reddening his face and probably his entire head, for he could feel the heat of blood pounding in his temples. Thoughts of a legal battle were quickly dismissed. He could attempt to sue for unfair dismissal, but it would be a dirty, damaging affair. For a few seconds more he struggled with the problem, searching for a way to turn the tables, then admitted defeat. There was no way out.

Richard Dumas, forty-four years old, self-made millionaire several times over, had just been brought to earth by a very clever businessman and three clowns. He had not seen it coming, and for that he deserved defeat. A goal had been scored, and the ball had gone right between his legs, just the way he had so smugly described it to Trevor. Metaphors tumbled about in his head, but really there was no comparison to anything else. Business was more like war than football or fishing. But mostly, there was nothing like it. He loved the fighting and manoeuvring. He loved the challenges, but this time he had lost. And Nigel was the ultimate warrior. He had to admire the man now that he understood his own dismissal in the scheme of things.

'Let me understand this,' he said softly. 'I've been pushed into resigning as managing director, although I still have a considerable investment in the project. Meanwhile, huge loans have been secured with my property in Florida and the deeds to Gosfield Hall. And I am expected to stand on the sidelines and let your puppet run the Miami Spice chain into the ground?' He waved a shaking hand in Seb's direction.

'My puppet has done very well so far. However, there is a way—' began Nigel.

422

Richard cut him short. 'I suppose you want to buy my shares, Seb.'

Sebastian jumped. 'I haven't got that kind of money!'

'Helena? Karen?' They shook their heads.

Richard turned slowly to Nigel. This, the disposal of Richard's shares, had been the object of the plan. Nigel's plan, not Seb's. Even before he spoke, Richard knew that Nigel would offer to buy the shares, and according to the agreements they signed, he need offer Richard only what had been paid for them, although they were now worth much more. As an inducement, Nigel would probably offer to return Richard's deeds to the Florida property and to Gosfield Hall immediately.

Within the next minute and a half, that was exactly what Nigel Falkland did. And Richard accepted, glad to be able to leave the room with something salvaged.

He stood up and nodded formally to everyone. 'I presume you will remove your business from my home within the next seven working days. My incompetence took several forms, I'm afraid. We never signed a lease, you know. I just allowed Miami Spice to trade here for a peppercorn rent.'

'It's all in hand, Richard,' said Nigel, and Seb looked at his chairman in surprise. 'We will be moving the business to the City, close to my own office. I have rented premises for Sebastian and the rest of the staff.'

'No!' cried Seb and Helena in unison.

Richard managed a grimace, a faint mirthless smile. 'In that case, everything is settled.'

Leaving Sebastian to contemplate a daily journey of about an hour and a half from Blackmore End to

Liverpool Street, Richard left the room. He was surprised he was able to walk away with such apparent calm. He thought he must be on autopilot.

Back in his office he told Liz what had happened, saying he would give her a good letter of recommendation, or she could probably follow Sebastian Race to the City.

Liz wept and complained that she couldn't possibly travel to London each day. She had a husband to look after. Richard raised his eyebrows at the mention of her husband, but said only that he would personally give her five thousand pounds as compensation. She was startled and extremely grateful for his generosity, and cheered up immediately. He felt he had gone some way to atoning for his cruel exposure of her passion.

For the next hour he kept busy by clearing out his papers, handing over to Seb's office all documents connected to Miami Spice. How he hated the name! He had even allowed the Races to name the damned chain. What a fool he was! And all the while he went over in his mind what had happened, wondering what he could have done to prevent such an inglorious departure, knowing that the seeds of his destruction were sown before he ever thought of bringing Nigel Falkland on board.

The knowledge that he had been comprehensively out-manoeuvred and deserved what he had got in no way lessened his pain. The trouble was, he had set up the company at a time when he had not been thinking clearly. Then he had discovered that he wasn't really interested in the chain, would have preferred a different business activity in England. Finally, and most seriously, he had hated and underestimated Sebastian Race. Oh, yes, he deserved to go, but oh how his pride was suffering!

He also imagined himself telling his friends at the Institute of Directors how he had been removed, telling Zoe and Cosmo, telling Trevor, telling Fran. He had no trouble in imagining their embarrassment on his behalf. Perhaps they would say the obvious – live by business, die by business. But not Fran. Her response would be very different.

He winced as he remembered the scene in the library when she had told him about her investment in Manners Productions. Surely she wouldn't be as contemptuous of him as he had been of her! In any case, he dreaded telling the world about his failure. He would put it off as long as possible. Zoe and Fran were away. There was no need to tell Jorge and Maria. The bad news could wait until he had learnt to tell it with a jaunty nonchalance.

Not surprisingly, none of the shareholders invited him out to lunch. He returned to his apartment, rang for Mrs Stone and asked that some ham sandwiches be sent up to him.

A telephone call to the housing charity secured the deal he had been working on secretly for several weeks. He had possession of the deeds and could sell Gosfield Hall immediately. He told them no more than was absolutely necessary, simply that he had severed his connection with the Miami chain and would be moving on to other projects.

The afternoon dragged on. He needed to talk about what had happened to him, and so telephoned Jorge after all. He was immediately glad he did, for he received sympathy and understanding. And a sense of perspective. This was no big deal. He hadn't lost all his money. He was still a millionaire several times over. Everything else he had touched continued to thrive.

'Every businessman,' said Jorge, 'sooner or later suffers a setback.'

'Yes,' Richard said.

He wondered if every businessman suffered the same terrifying loss of confidence, the same unnerving loss of identity. For years Richard had seen himself as an impregnable businessman. Now he knew he wasn't. Some mighty adjustment was going to have to take place before he could look at himself in the mirror without flinching.

As the hours stretched before him, he wondered how to occupy himself. The plans of Gosfield Hall failed to hold his attention. Brownfield sites had temporarily lost their fascination.

Getting into the Mercedes, he drove to Fran's cottage in search of Trevor. The house was deserted. He peered into windows, inspected Fran's stock of plants, noticing that they were all well-watered. He wanted to see the boy, yet why should Trevor hang around over the weekend? The kid had probably gone off with friends. Richard sighed, returned to his car and drove into Sudbury, where he knew no-one, and ate an anonymous dinner in a town-centre pub.

The light was fading by the time he returned to Gosfield Hall. The courtyard was heavily in shade, but he could still see the shrubs and trees that Fran had planted. The bench was sun-warmed and he sat down to listen to the rooks squabbling in the nearby trees, and to hear the soothing sound of splashing water.

Gradually, the sense of calmness and peace in the Paradise garden began to seep into his bones. He relaxed. Muscles that had been held taut all day let go and his headache eased. He thought he would go back to Florida for a few days. Sort out a few things. Speak to Arnie. Not to apologize for having humiliated him, just to see how he had survived. Observe the man, take notes, as it were. For Arnie, by all accounts, had stopped drinking. He had certainly turned the business around. They spoke often on the phone, always amicably. There was life after disaster. Richard was going to learn how to live it.

It was his habit on a Saturday morning to come downstairs, collect the mail, sort it and put it on the proper desks. It was unnecessary, of course. The mail could wait, unopened, until Monday morning. Yet the habit was ingrained.

He rose early, but had not finished shaving when the phone rang. It was the *Financial Times*. What statement would he like to make about his sudden departure from Miami Spice? Caught completely by surprise, he gave a few stumbling replies, roundly cursing Seb as he did so. Had it been necessary to rub his nose in his failure?

He had no sooner hung up than the *Daily Mail* called. In the next hour and a half every newspaper with any interest in financial matters had spoken to him. And all the locals, the *East Anglian Daily Times*, the *Halstead Gazette* and the *Neighbourhood News* wanted a quote. He knew whom to thank for this unwanted local publicity.

His anger helped him through the day as fellow IOD members rang with commiserations. He was invited out for Sunday lunch and accepted readily. To hell with the Races and to hell with the most

427

cunning businessman with whom he had ever crossed swords. Nigel Falkland deserved his victory. He was a shark who had earned the right to be feared.

Returning home from his luncheon date, he was in time to take a call from France. Zoe was in tears. She had read the *Sunday Telegraph*, seen the small item about his being forced out of Miami Spice, couldn't believe it. He played down the disgrace, told her he had learned to appreciate that business really was not the most important thing in the world. He hoped she was having a wonderful holiday.

Zoe fretted that he was alone. Should they travel back to England to give him comfort? Cosmo came on the line, wanting him to move in with them in Cambridge until Richard had sorted himself out.

For the first time since he had been removed from office, his eyes filled with tears. He had lost a worthless post, but it seemed he had gained a daughter in exchange. He was no longer entitled to see himself as the greatest businessman around. Instead he could pass himself off as a loving father who was also loved. They spoke for half an hour and, later, Richard thought he would remember every word for the rest of his life.

The mail never did get sorted over the weekend. On Monday morning he came downstairs with a light heart and greeted Liz pleasantly. She glowered and mumbled a greeting. His desk, he saw, was covered with newspaper clippings, spread out enticingly beside a small stack of his unopened mail.

'Seb brought them,' said Liz. 'He thought you might like to know what the papers are saying about you.'

'He did all this for me?' he asked, 'and you didn't open my mail? That is right and proper. We're separate organizations now.'

Working methodically, he carefully opened each letter, read it and placed it on one of two small piles, either to be answered or thrown away. Only when this was done did he pick up the first clipping.

'Bald American tycoon gets the red card!' screamed the *Sun*.

'Richard Dumas, fabulously wealthy American, has been wondering what went wrong after having been forced to resign by the shareholders of the Miami Spice chain of Cuban restaurants. The bald businessman may be regretting his ten-million-pound purchase of Gosfield Hall as the company moves out,' said *The Times*.

All the others had the same sort of story, putting the blame for his departure on his playboy lifestyle, and mentioning his bald head, as if the lack of hair indicated his talent, state of mind and working capacity. The supposed value of Gosfield Hall went sky-high. He wished it were possible to get the sort of price for the house that the papers thought it was worth.

Nowhere did the journalists make it clear that he had not lost all his money. There was, however, great play made of the fact that he had been obliged to sell his shares for what they had been worth at the company's inception. 'He had to sell to save his home,' was the way most of them saw it.

There was a knock on the door and Seb came in

immediately. Richard turned to Liz. 'Could you find something to do in another office for the next few minutes?'

She jumped up from her desk and fled, obviously afraid of witnessing the confrontation between the two men.

Seb flopped into the chair in front of Richard's desk with a nervous smirk. 'All's fair in love and war, Richard.'

'Yeah. I take it you were the joker who set the papers on me. Well done. Must have given you a lot of pleasure.'

'Oh, dear, are you upset? I thought you enjoyed posing in front of your palatial home. You like publicity, don't you?'

'Sure,' said Richard. 'I'll be getting a little more soon. I've sold Gosfield Hall to a charitable trust. They fix up places like Gosfield and rent apartments to retirees. Made a million pounds profit.'

Seb looked so put out that Richard was glad he had exaggerated. Still, a quarter of a million pounds profit, the true figure, was pretty good going in little over six months.

'You can't have made so much,' cried Seb. 'You've only done a few repairs. How can it be worth so much more than you – than I – paid for it?'

'It's lived-in now. I've drawn up detailed plans of how the conversion could take place. I've applied for planning permission. I've got English Heritage on my side. I've saved this house from complete collapse, replaced a hundred panes of broken glass, treated miles of dry rot, put in a central-heating system and two hundred radiators. I've restored painted ceilings and put in chandeliers. I'm a good guy where this house is concerned. I have not failed to do my duty. I've done nothing the authorities dislike and I've consulted them every step of the way. No bucking their wishes. I didn't set out to change the face of the house-preservation business. I went along with it. I deserve my little profit.'

'Congratulations.'

Richard rummaged in his pile of mail to extract a thick, embossed invitation card that had just arrived in the post. He tossed it towards Seb. 'How about that? An invitation to have drinks with your Prime Minister. A bunch of us developers have been invited down because we've donated our services to finding solutions to brownfield sites. I'm not the playboy you chose to paint to the media, Seb.'

'I'm glad that my getting rid of you didn't—'

'You? You didn't get rid of me, you pompous idiot. Falkland did. It was his plan all along. In your place I would have begged, borrowed or stolen the money to buy my shares. Don't you see that he has bought, for a hundred and ninety-six thousand pounds, shares that are already worth double and may eventually be worth millions? He's got you three right where he wants you. He can outvote you on everything. You're three little pawns in his game. You'll get moderately rich when he says so and not before. You and Helena want to buy a country hotel? Well, fella, you can always sell him your shares for a pittance. Those are the rules. Meanwhile, you'll trot down to London on the train each day, because he says so.'

'I only wanted him to cut you down to size.'

'Not cut me out? Why, you're a bigger asshole

than I thought. You wanted me humbled. So why did you all push me out?'

'Well, Nigel thought it was in the best interests of the company to reprimand you. How did I know you'd resign?'

'Best interests of the company, my eye! In the best interests of Nigel Falkland. My God, but he's a smooth operator. It would never occur to me to chop someone that way. I'm not that greedy, but I should have seen that he is.'

'I wouldn't have been so opposed to you,' muttered Seb, 'if you hadn't seemed to despise me.'

'Forget it. We can't stand each other. Wrong chemistry right from the beginning. And don't pretend you didn't hate me from the start. I've seen this sort of thing in business when two men don't gel, and it's always bad news. I just didn't see the danger for myself. Anyway, I wanted to be free of Miami Spice. I think I only just realized how much I love buildings. I guess I owe you a debt of gratitude. Forty-four years old and I've just discovered what really turns me on.'

'Well, you had a funny way of showing your gratitude. Meanwhile, I've got to start commuting as of next Monday. Helena's pregnant and—'

'You're starting a family at this time?'

'Well, I wanted to wait, but—'

'Helena outsmarted you. Story of your life, Seb. You don't lead your life. You don't plan it out. Things just happen to you. You're a permanent victim. You know, old buddy, you've got a fair amount of talent. I could always see that. But I think pomposity is in the Race blood. Hey, let's hope the baby doesn't turn out to take after its Aunt Karen, instead of its mother. There's a funny thought.'

Seb rose from the chair and headed for the door. 'So happy to have given you so much amusement.'

He turned with his hand on the knob and smiled viciously. 'But Helena's a sweet little woman who's going to make me happy for the rest of my life. Not like you. Fran Craig is who really turns you on, but maybe it's fortunate for the sake of your sanity that she ran out on you. And you so rich, too. My God, she really must hate your guts to pass up all that money. I might not have been able to get rid of you if she didn't have you by the balls. But I expect when news gets out that you've been dumped, other gold-diggers will come out of the woodwork.' Quickly closing the door behind him, he left Richard fuming.

That afternoon Richard packed a small case and left Gosfield Hall for a hotel near Heathrow, having booked a seat on Concorde for the next day.

The weather would be getting cooler in England, but Italy was still luxuriating in warm, sunny days. As usual, Fran was up early, but this day was special. The lawyer, Signor Agnelli, was coming to pay her and to take her to the airport. For the first time, her clients would see what she had achieved in their garden. Since it was a special occasion, she put on a dress that was one of Richard's favourites, a turquoise short-sleeved shift. Looking at herself in the mirror, she half turned first to the left, then the right, and suddenly smiled. She looked great. A little plumper than she had been three weeks ago, thanks to all the wonderful food, but a lot less drawn and haggard.

'I'm an all-right person,' she told her image happily. 'Not a thief. Not a fool. A career woman who can hold her head up in any company. I'm the new me!'

All twenty members of the construction team were present for the big occasion, and Joseph was in great form, making everyone laugh. They were in freshly washed work clothes and every man had shaved, a fairly unusual occurrence. They looked as excited as she felt, and she went to each one to thank him for his help.

The launch hove into view. Fran went to the small landing-stage to await its leisurely arrival, and long before the boatman tied up she could see that Signor Agnelli was alone.

'Where are the Manottis? Aren't they coming?'

'A party in Rio de Janeiro. They lead busy lives, you know. I have come to inspect. You must satisfy me, my dear.' He glanced ahead as they started up the path. 'And I can see that you have succeeded magnificently. It is good that the Manottis do not see the garden now. When they do arrive, everything will have grown just a little.'

'All of us had been hoping to see the Manottis. They are the clients. It's their home.'

He turned and smiled sympathetically. 'I know. We must make the best of it. You know, you have worked a miracle.'

'An expensive miracle.'

She took him along the gently meandering path, pointing out the many small trees which had been planted in clumps. She had gone for autumn colour, she explained, although some of the trees also bloomed in the spring. They would look particularly attractive then because thousands of bulbs had been underplanted.

She had levelled a quarter of an acre at the

highest point of the property, and here she had planted a semi-formal rose garden. She pointed out the aggressive roses that had been positioned to climb through tall Mediterranean cypresses. She had planted mostly modern, repeat-flowering roses, because she could not be sure when the Manottis would turn up during the summer months. There must be something for them to see, although she had arranged one seasonal surprise – a valley of lupins.

Azaleas and rhododendrons would also give a brilliant display in the acid soil of Lake Como. They would show off their gaudy colours over several weeks.

He nodded enthusiastically at everything he saw. They walked on the broad path side by side, but when they approached the gargoyle's head which would spout water, she hung back. Signor Agnelli received the full blast of several ounces of water.

'An amusing trick!' he said through gritted teeth as he brushed water from his exquisite suit. 'You would have played this trick on Signora Manotti?'

'Perhaps not. I would probably have got you wet to amuse her.'

This made Signor Agnelli laugh out loud. When they had completed the circular walk he sent to the launch for the dozen bottles of wine he had brought. They all toasted the garden from plastic cups and spoke of the difficulties and triumphs of the past three weeks.

'But perhaps the pleasure is spoiled for you,' said Agnelli, 'because your clients did not come.'

'Not at all.' She was surprised by her own reaction. 'I am a professional and I know I have done well. We've all shared in the building of this garden, and we are pleased that you like it. That's important. The clients don't have to love it or appreciate its finer qualities. It's enough that they gave me the money to carry out my vision.'

'Bravo! But you're crying!'

She wiped her eyes. 'It suddenly occurred to me that I have learned so much in the last three weeks. Now I'm homesick. I want to go home to . . . to my loved ones.'

Trevor did not return to the cottage until Monday afternoon, and since he seldom bought a newspaper it was not until he had opened his stall in Braintree on Thursday morning that he heard about Richard Dumas. Later, after he had closed down his stall, which was doing poor business, he managed to find a newspaper from the previous Monday.

Reading the account of Richard's downfall, Trevor felt as if one of the pillars of his life had been knocked away. Richard, the invincible, had been fired? He couldn't comprehend it.

Taking his van, he drove the seven miles to Gosfield Hall, still telling himself that there must be some mistake. The Hall was silent, however. There were no cars, except for Richard's Mercedes. Even this proved to be a cruel deception, for when Mrs Stone eventually opened the door she told him that everyone had moved away and Mr Dumas was in America. She didn't know when he would be back. She had been told that the house was sold.

Trevor returned to the van and drove, somehow, to his home. His mother was due back on Saturday. How would he tell her that Richard had lost everything?

*   *   *

Richard arrived back at Gosfield Hall on Friday evening and went straight to bed. Fran should be coming home any day. He wanted to be fresh and rested, because he would need to have his wits about him when he told her what had happened. It would be important to explain the situation carefully. She must not think less of him, as he thought less of himself. Her good opinion was very important.

The following day he rang Trevor but, getting no answer, he knew he was going to have to be patient. A blitz on his personal possessions revealed that he had acquired quite a lot during his few months in England. And where would he live in future? Cambridge, without Fran? Or somewhere else with her by his side? He couldn't think about it rationally. Seb's parting shots had unsettled him.

While it was true that he had been preoccupied with Fran during recent months, he would not lay the blame for his dismissal at her door. She had caused him pain, but pain was a sign of life. He welcomed it, because there had been a time after Jenny died when he was incapable of feeling joy or sorrow, when the prospect of the next sunrise held nothing for him.

So he clung to his suffering as a sign of returning normality. And every now and again when he thought about it, a ripple of excitement shook him. He had been invited to Number Ten, yet his own country had never seemed in need of him. His new country wanted his experience and perspective. It was all very satisfying.

As evening drew near, he made himself a stiff drink and wandered out to the courtyard. He'd miss it. Over on the north wall he had watched a few rosebuds open, and on the west wall honeysuckle was thriving. He bent to snap off a spent geranium bloom as he had seen Jim do it, and came away with the entire small plant in his hand. He put down his glass and replanted it as best he could. Better leave the gardening to Fran.

His favourite seat was still bathed in sunshine. He sat down gratefully. Fran was not a gold-digger. Far from it. In fact she had resisted his every offer of money or gifts, had really hated him for thinking that she would take anything.

And then it hit him. Jenny had been unhappy her entire life. And every time she had complained her father had given her some present, trying to buy satisfaction and fulfilment while never letting her travel away from him, either physically or mentally.

When she married Richard she was soon unhappy again, although Zoe's arrival gave her some pleasure and purpose in life. Later, when she was no longer young, she had refused to allow Zoe to attend an out-of-state university. Zoe had eventually rebelled against the smothering love by running away, but in doing so she had tied herself to a man who was every bit as protective of her as her misguided parents had been. Richard hoped she would not regret her marriage in later life. She needed to taste freedom.

Following the death of her parents, Jenny had begun to whine all the time. And how had Richard tried to help her? By buying her presents.

'Oh, Jenny, I'm sorry!' he said. 'Why couldn't I have understood that you needed to do something to make you feel worthwhile?'

Fran was made of sterner stuff. She had some

438

secret agenda that he had not understood. She knew she needed to succeed. She could not be bought.

Trevor met Fran at Stansted airport, relieved to see her home again. These three weeks had enabled him to sort out a few things, but he was nevertheless delighted to have his mother back to look after him.

She talked all the way home. 'You'll never guess what happened! Lester Manners wrote to me and sent me a contract. He didn't skip after all. He just sold his house to fund the series. Can you imagine having that much confidence in yourself?'

'A person could lose everything in business,' said Trevor.

'Oh, I know, but it's been glorious being involved in a business venture. I understand Richard a little better now. It's a great feeling. And I'm now a proper garden designer. Oh, Trevor, I want you to travel in Italy, see the gardens. It's a wonderful place. You'll love it. A few more commissions and I'll be able to afford to send you.'

'I've decided to go to Capel Manor, get an NVQ. I start next month, already signed up.'

'Oh, darling, that's wonderful! Have you told Richard? Or your dad?'

'Dad thinks I'm wasting my time. Wants me to come into partnership with him. I understand what's in his mind, but I could never hammer a nail in straight. Richard didn't say much. He's a nice guy, really. He took me to Le Talbooth. Can you imagine?'

'How generous of him. But I don't suppose he thinks about how much these places cost.

Wait until you see the clothes I bought you.'

'Oh, Mum, are you sure I'm going to like your taste?'

'Of course you are. And I bought Richard a proper leather wallet. He just has one of those tiny American billfolds. Now he'll have a proper wallet.'

'He'll hate it.'

'He won't!' she laughed. 'He'll love it.'

When they reached the cottage he carried her bags inside, put the kettle on and made her a cup of tea, while she spoke non-stop about her pleasure at being home. She had missed Richard more than she could have imagined and wanted to see him as soon as possible.

'Mum, there's news I have to give you first. Here, I've made you a cup of tea. Sit down. Richard has run into some bad luck—'

'Is he hurt? Dead? Oh, Trevor!'

'Nothing like that.' He handed her the newspaper with the article about Richard in it. 'I think this explains it. I tried to see him, but he had flown home to America.'

She read it through, then flung it onto the table. 'Oh, my God! Do you know what such a terrible humiliation will do to him? He's a proud man. I suppose it was that Sebastian Race who was responsible. I must go to him, tell him it doesn't matter.'

'But he's sold Gosfield, gone to Florida!'

She reached for the keys of the BMW. 'Nonsense. He knew I was due home this weekend. He'll be there waiting for me. I know him! He only resigned last Friday. Do you think he could change his whole life in such a short time?'

'Let me take you. You aren't insured to drive that car.'

'No, thank you, dear. I want to see him alone. I think he will want it that way, too. As I don't intend to have an accident, it doesn't matter.'

'You're not used to driving anything quite that powerful.'

'Oh, Trevor, I love him. It's the most wonderful thing. I know I love him. I'm not used to being in love, but that doesn't mean I'm going to run into anything. Don't you understand? He was always so self-sufficient and smart. Everything he touched turned to gold. Now he needs *me*!' She waved and drove off in a manner that gave Trevor grave doubts about her competence behind the wheel.

'He's always needed you, Mum,' he said, but she was already barrelling down the road.

Fran found the smooth performance of the car very thrilling. It would have to be sold, of course. They wouldn't be able to afford anything this grand. Richard could get a little second-hand runaround and she would continue to drive the van.

She banged her fist against the steering-wheel in a sudden fury. How could that weasel, Seb Race, have treated her dear Richard so badly? How had he managed to outsmart the most brilliant man in the world?

'I love him,' she said out loud. 'I love him and I thought I would never be able to love anyone again. I love him and I'm not afraid to have strong emotions. I won't fall apart if I trust him, because he won't let me down. Even Lester didn't let me down in the end. I'm a grown-up person who can look anybody in the eye. I'm Fran Craig, garden designer, and he needs me. But God knows, I need him, too. And I'm not afraid any more to ask for help. Later, when we've got on our feet again, I'll send money to Mum and Doreen. They're just weak women and they'll always need help. Not like me. I'm strong and I've proved it. Oh, Richard, I do hope you like the new me.'

She drove down Hall Drive rather faster than was advisable, and the traffic inhibitors sent her bouncing painfully against the roof. She had not made up her mind where to park, but seeing that the great doors leading into the courtyard were open, she swung the wheel violently, having decided that she wanted to drive right up to the front door.

Richard was lost in thought and didn't hear a car approaching. It was the crash that woke him from his reverie. He jumped up and ran to see what had happened, finding the BMW wedged against the gateway, its offside fender badly crumpled.

Fran was just disentangling herself from the seat-belt. 'Oh, you poor darling. I've come as soon as I found out. Listen, dear, I know I've crashed the car and I'm not insured, but maybe we can say you did it and collect anyway. Besides, it's just the wing.'

'Fran! Are you hurt?'

She flung her arms around him and kissed him passionately as he tried to get to the car in order to turn off the engine. 'You know, Richard, it is rather more powerful than I'm used to, but I think the bricks suffered more than the car.'

As she spoke, she covered his face with kisses. He gave up attempting to see to the BMW.

'My God, woman. I nearly lost you. Can't you drive more carefully? What's the matter with you? I swear I'll have to get you a chauffeur.'

'There'll be no money for things like that, darling, but it doesn't matter. You must get used to it. But don't despair. It's not so bad being poor. You can move in with us. The cottage is a bit run-down, but we'll build up my business. Perhaps it would be a good idea if you did handle the money side, after all. And it would give you something to do. Oh, dearest, do you mind awfully about losing your money?'

'Fran . . .' His voice was unsteady. For the second time in a week, he was overwhelmed by the warmth of a woman he loved. Ah, the rewards of failure. He should have tried it earlier. 'You are offering to take me in, even though I'm broke?'

'Of course. Now, listen. I got a total of ten thousand pounds for this Italian business. You can have what's left to get started again, if that will help. Don't you know I love you? Richard, remember when I said I needed to find myself? Well, I've found myself in Italy, and I'm a pretty all-right person. I like me, and I hope you will, too. So there. We can start again together.'

He hugged her fiercely and began to laugh. 'I can't remember when I've ever had a better offer. I am deeply touched, honey, but I think it only fair to tell you that I lost my job, not my money. I've made a quarter of a million on the sale of Gosfield Hall. I'm still rich, so do you still love me?'

She blinked. 'Not poor? You've still got bags of money?'

'Bags.'

'Oh, darling, I love you even more, although you don't need me after all.'

'Money's got nothing to do with it, you idiot,' he laughed. 'I need you today and every day for the

443

rest of my life. Only we will have to find somewhere to live that's a little smaller.'

'Somewhere old,' she agreed, kissing him again. 'I couldn't bear one of those new, shiny houses.'

'Will you marry me if I promise you dry rot and falling slates?'

He caught her up in a breathtaking embrace, and she didn't say anything more.

Mark Twain had said that a jackass who travels round the world is still a jackass. Richard felt that travel had changed him into the happiest jackass the world had ever known.

THE END

CAPEL BELLS
by Joan Hessayon

Charlotte Blair had worked hard all her life. Raised amongsy the porters and street sellers of Covent Garden, she had achieved unusual success for a woman in 1911 – her own flower shop. It was unfashionable, in a poor part of London, and made only a small profit, but Charlotte had a secret ambition, to become one of the great floral decorators of the period, transforming the ballrooms and grand houses of the aristocracy.

When she was bidden to Capel Manor for her first floral assignment she fell in love with the house, but cruelly – fate snatched the commission away from her before she had even begun. It was several weeks later that she learned Capel Manor could be rented and, borrowing every penny she could, she moved her business to the beautiful old house, believing that this would give her an entry into the greatest families of the neighbourhood.

Beset with every problem, cheating gardeners, the crooked plans of her old friends in Covent Garden, and the return of Matthew Warrender, the owner of Capel Manor, Charlotte fought to realize her ambition to become the most famous floral decorator of her time.

0 552 14220 4

THE HELMINGHAM ROSE
by Joan Hessayon

Joyce d'Avranche had always been the poor and ignored member of the d'Avranche family of Helmingham Hall. Her childhood had been one of hardship, and over her dead mother hung the disgrace of an old scandal. Then, when the legitimate heir went missing on an Amazon exploration, Joyce was brought to Helmingham and told she could well be the new owner of the beautiful old house and garden.

Almost at once she fell in love with it and wanted, more than anything, to possess it. But her background had not prepared her for the running of a huge estate. Everything she did was wrong and her only friend was Rose, wife of the head gardener. Rose, too, had sorrows to bear. Barren, in spite of her longing for a child, she sublimated her sadness in the gardens of Helmingham, concentrating all her energy on the breeding of a new rose – the Helmingham Rose.

As the two young women watched the gradual unfurling of the perfect flower, so their own lives moved towards maturity and unexpected happiness.

Joan Hessayon continues her magnificent sequence, begun in *Capel Bells*, of combining a house and garden which actually exist, with the breeding of a new flower to create a fascinating and evocative novel.

0 552 14535 1

THE CREW
by Margaret Mayhew

There were seven in the crew – seven very young and very inexperienced airmen who, nearly every night, flew their heavily-laden Lancaster bomber into the exploding skies over enemy Germany.

On almost their first flight Piers, the navigator, managed to get them lost and Van, the pilot, nearly crashed the plane on landing. Charlie, the rear gunner, who was only seventeen but who had lied about his age, spent his time reading poetry and trying not to spew his guts out on every flight. They were from mixed backgrounds and nationalities but somehow, heroically, they welded together into a courageous fighting unit, helping each other and desperately hoping they would survive their thirty bombing flights.

And on the ground were the women who waited. Section Officer Catherine Herbert, in love with Van but already committed to another man. And Peggy, the little waitress who found herself being ardently wooed by the aristocratic Piers. And Charlie's young and pretty mother, living right on the edge of the airfield, praying every night that her son would come back.

The heroic and incredible story of seven brave men, and the women who loved them.

0 552 14492 4

A SELECTED LIST OF FINE NOVELS
AVAILABLE FROM CORGI BOOKS

THE PRICES SHOWN BELOW WERE CORRECT AT THE TIME OF GOING TO PRESS.
HOWEVER TRANSWORLD PUBLISHERS RESERVE THE RIGHT TO SHOW NEW
RETAIL PRICES ON COVERS WHICH MAY DIFFER FROM THOSE PREVIOUSLY
ADVERTISED IN THE TEXT OR ELSEWHERE.

14058 9	MIST OVER THE MERSEY	*Lyn Andrews*	£5.99
14060 0	MERSEY BLUES	*Lyn Andrews*	£5.99
14516 5	SOPHIE'S SCANDAL	*Virginia Blackburn*	£5.99
10277 6	EMILY	*Jilly Cooper*	£4.99
10576 7	HARRIET	*Jilly Cooper*	£4.99
14095 3	ARIAN	*Iris Gower*	£4.99
14447 9	FIREBIRD	*Iris Gower*	£5.99
14537 8	APPLE BLOSSOM TIME	*Kathryn Haig*	£5.99
14385 5	THE BELLS OF SCOTLAND ROAD		
		Ruth Hamilton	£5.99
14566 1	THE DREAM SELLERS	*Ruth Hamilton*	£5.99
14553 X	THE BRASS DOLPHIN	*Caroline Harvey*	£5.99
14686 2	CITY OF GEMS	*Caroline Harvey*	£5.99
14220 4	CAPEL BELLS	*Joan Hessayon*	£4.99
14535 1	THE HELMINGHAM ROSE	*Joan Hessayon*	£5.99
14333 2	SOME OLD LOVER'S GHOST	*Judith Lennox*	£5.99
14599 8	FOOTPRINTS ON THE SAND	*Judith Lennox*	£5.99
13910 6	BLUEBIRDS	*Margaret Mayhew*	£5.99
14492 4	THE CREW	*Margaret Mayhew*	£5.99
14498 3	MORE INNOCENT TIMES	*Imogen Parker*	£5.99
14499 1	THESE FOOLISH THINGS	*Imogen Parker*	£5.99
10375 6	CSARDAS	*Diane Pearson*	£5.99
14400 2	THE MOUNTAIN	*Elvi Rhodes*	£4.99
14577 7	PORTRAIT OF CHLOE	*Elvi Rhodes*	£5.99
14549 1	CHOICES	*Susan Sallis*	£4.99
14636 6	COME RAIN OR SHINE	*Susan Sallis*	£5.99
14606 4	FIRE OVER LONDON	*Mary Jane Staples*	£5.99
14657 9	CHURCHILL'S PEOPLE	*Mary Jane Staples*	£5.99
14502 5	THE LONG ROAD HOME	*Danielle Steel*	£5.99
14476 2	CHILDREN OF THE TIDE	*Valerie Wood*	
14640 4	THE ROMANY GIRL	*Valerie Wood*	

Transworld titles are available by post from:

Book Service By Post, PO Box 29, Douglas, Isle of Man, IM99 1BQ

Credit cards accepted. Please telephone 01624 675137
fax 01624 670923, Internet http://www.bookpost.co.uk
or e-mail: bookshop@enterprise.net for details

Free postage and packing in the UK. Overseas customers: allow £1 per
book (paperbacks) and £3 per book (hardbacks)